THE
FOUR MARKS
MURDERS

Twenty grizzly tales from a sleepy corner
of Hampshire between the years 400 and 2020

CHRIS HEAL

Published by Chattaway and Spottiswood
Milverton Taunton Somerset

fourmarksmurders@candspublishing.org.uk
fmmurders2020@outlook.com

This is a work of historical fact and part-fiction. The names and characters of the
principal characters, businesses, events and incidents are, as far as possible, based
on research which is in the public domain.
The author is a real person and is a principal character. Other principal and non-
principal characters, still living, have been contacted for permission to include
their names.
Established historical events and well-known characters and organisations
are used as background to the stories. Opinions about these events, characters
and organisations, unless specifically attributed, are invented by the author for
furtherance of the work. Quotes attributed to living non-principal characters are
assembled verbatim from their published, attributed or by-lined sources. These
quotes have been placed in contexts which are fictional and not those in which the
quotes were originally made. Every effort has been made to maintain the spirit and
intention of the original context.

A catalogue record for this book is available from
the British Library

5 4 3 2 1

ISBN 978-1-9161944-2-7

Maps by Paul Hewitt, www.battlefield-design.co.uk

Design by Vivian@Bookscribe

Printed and bound by Sarsen Press, Winchester

THE
FOUR MARKS
MURDERS

MURDER MAP

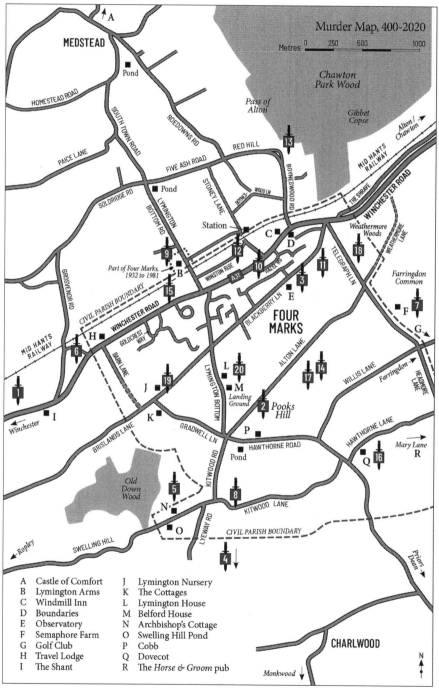

Murder Map, 400–2020

MEDSTEAD

Chawton Park Wood

Pass of Alton

Gibbet Copse

HOMESTEAD ROAD

SOUTH TOWN ROAD

ROEDOWNS RD

PAICE LANE

RED HILL

Alton / Chawton

FIVE ASH ROAD

SOLDRIDGE RD

BOTTOM RD

LYMINGTON

STONEY LANE

BENTLEY

WOOD LN

MID HANTS RAILWAY

Pond

Pond

Station

THE SHRAVE

WINCHESTER ROAD

Weathermore Woods

WEATHERMORE LANE

13

9

12

10

3

11

18

C

D

B

E

Part of Four Marks, 1932 to 1981

CIVIL PARISH BOUNDARY

WINSTON RISE

A31

HAZEL RD

BOYNESWOOD RD

TELEGRAPH LN

Farringdon Common

15

GROSVENOR RD

WINCHESTER ROAD

BLACKBERRY LN

FOUR MARKS

F

7

G

MID HANTS RAILWAY

H

GOLDCREST WAY

BARN LANE

ALTON LANE

WILLIS LANE

Farringdon

HEADMORE LANE

6

19

J

LYMINGTON BOTTOM

L

20

14

17

1

I

K

M

Landing Ground

2

Pooks Hill

HAWTHORNE LANE

Mary Lane

R

Winchester

Q

16

BRISLANDS LANE

GRADWELL LN

KITWOOD RD

P

HAWTHORNE ROAD

Old Down Wood

5

N

LYEWAY RD

Pond

8

KITWOOD LANE

CIVIL PARISH BOUNDARY

O

Prors Dean

Ropley

SWELLING HILL

CHARLWOOD

4

Monkwood

N

A	Castle of Comfort	J	Lymington Nursery
B	Lymington Arms	K	The Cottages
C	Windmill Inn	L	Lymington House
D	Boundaries	M	Belford House
E	Observatory	N	Archbishop's Cottage
F	Semaphore Farm	O	Swelling Hill Pond
G	Golf Club	P	Cobb
H	Travel Lodge	Q	Dovecot
I	The Shant	R	The *Horse & Groom* pub

The numbers on the daggers refer to the chapter numbers.

For my mother
Regina Lilian Elizabeth Heal,
who died in unhappy circumstances, aged ninety-eight,
a resident of Belford House, Four Marks.
Regina always enjoyed a 'good murder',
especially if it was true and scary and happened next door.
Sadly, she read only three chapters.
'Good boy. More like that, please.'

WITH THANKS

Godfrey Andrews, Alresford Heritage

Dr Keith Brown, archivist, the Watercress Line

Debbie Burt, Office for National Statistics

Nick Clarke, Microsoft protagonist

Confidential contact, Hampshire Constabulary

Charlie Fletcher, article procurer

Holly Fletcher, population recordist & chart production

Suzanne Foster, archivist, Winchester College

Anthony Frankland, Lymington House

Dr Mike Frost, British Astronomical Association

Kate & Richard Hesk, Observatory

Diane Heal, critic

Murray Heal, gore consultant

Sam Heal, outreach

Michael Huggan, photographer

Professor Nick Lomb, Centre for Astrophysics,
University of Southern Queensland

Peter Matthews

Sophie McLean, Curtis Museum, Alton

Jeremy Mitchel, Edward Thomas Fellowship

Martin Mobberley, amateur astronomer and author

Mike Overy, medstead.org webmaster

Norman Read, butcher and farmer

Dr Alan Rosevear, road and transport historian

Mike Sanders, Video4Business

Julia Sandison, Hampshire Field Club and Archaeological Society

'Sophie', findmypast

Jacqui Squire, americano confidante

Geraldine Thom, internet bloodhound

Jim Trenchard, technical adviser

Richard Ward, Parliamentary Archives, Westminster

Dr Richard Whaley, North East Hants Historical & Archaeological Society

Charlotte Whitely, British Land

CONTENTS

We sholde be lowe
And loveliche of speche,
And apparaille us noght over proudly,
For pilgrymes are we alle

The Vision and Creed of Piers Plowman
William Langland, 1370–1390

LETTER FROM THE AUTHOR

This book is about a large number of deliberate or untimely deaths in what was thought to be one of the quiet backwaters of the county of Hampshire. I could have called it *Four Marks: The Murder Capital of Southern England.*

I have written it because my mother asked me to. She was ninety-eight and lived in a local residential home. Regina was upset that my previous books were 'too difficult', 'too long' or didn't have enough 'action'. The command was, 'Write something that I'll enjoy and don't put in too many adjectives.'

We discussed what the book could be about and my mother decided that she would like a collection of 'good murders' for her hundredth birthday present. It was an idea I had been investigating for some time. My mother read and passed three chapters before she died earlier this year, a side casualty of Covid-19. I suspect she would not have been so happy with some of the later chapters that have plenty of gore or ask difficult social questions.

So, you will understand that *The Four Marks Murders* is dedicated to her.

There are twenty chapters; each is complete in itself. They recount over sixty violent deaths, many judicial hangings and, in passing, four self-murders, altogether a shocking total.

The first killings uncovered occurred in 407, then 1248, 1644, 1798, three in the 1820s and 30s, two in the 1860s, three around World War I, three just after World War II, two at the turn of the century and three within the last few years. You can read them in any order.

I was first told about a Four Marks murder, the 'Battle of the Shant' (Ch. 1), in difficult circumstances when I was near the Mountains of Mourne in County Down in 1968. Until then, I did not know that Four Marks existed. Today, in one of those coincidences, I have lived here for thirty-five years.

I came across two other chapters by chance. I found a burglar in my study and, having long despaired of police interest, I decided to take matters into my own hands (Ch. 17). Another time, I stumbled across some archaeological remains near Old Down Wood, which suggested dark deeds (Ch. 5).

Two more chapters came straight out of the history books, there for anyone to read. The first concerned robbery and murder at the top of Chawton Park Wood; a lot of local people were hanged for that (Ch. 13). The second examined a major smuggling ring that was run by the gentry in Ropley in the nineteenth century (Ch. 4).

Some among you may quickly point out that Chawton Park Wood and Ropley are not in Four Marks. That's true. But, then, Four Marks wasn't formed until 1932 and the first murder happened well over a thousand years ago when the area was little more than unattractive, uninhabited gorse and scrub. In truth, I have strayed very little. For my money, the wood is so close, and the event so important, that the story demanded inclusion. Sixty-four per cent of today's Four Marks is made up of old Ropley parish lands. There were certainly smugglers and their hideaways this side of the new administrative border.

Five more chapters came from straightforward research (Chs. 7, 9, 11, 15, 20). I wasn't looking directly for the murder I found, but I had heard rumours and I discovered proofs, or near-proofs, when I searched the documents.

The other ten murders, I came across in, perhaps, an offhand sort of way. I asked friends, acquaintances, especially in the *Castle of Comfort* in Medstead, if anyone knew of any stories. Over several years, word spread and suggestions started to arrive. I don't hold a magic magnet for attracting this sort of information but you will understand that once you start asking, once you start looking, then people start talking. Odd facts jump out from unrelated pages and take new meanings. People brood for a month or two then make contact. Collecting murders is like rolling a snowball.

When was the last time you asked a relative stranger in a pub if they knew of any good local deaths? That led within a week to a phone call one evening asking if I was 'the chap what wanted to know about local murders'.

There were a lot of send-ups, of course, but I investigated and found plenty that could well be true. Within each chapter, I have explained as much as I can about how the stories came to me, naming my sources as much as I have been given freedom to do so. I have shared my research and then told the story.

Can I absolutely vouch for each of the ten? Just about. The tenth chapter about drug use among local teenagers is my biggest worry. What I can promise is that the facts check out and that college students have read and agreed the background.

My mother was bursting with pleasure when she rang to tell me that one her friends in her residential home was an eyewitness, or her mother was, to a nasty ending (Ch. 3).

At the end of the day, you come down to someone's written records or someone's memory of what they saw or heard. You are welcome to check my work as best you can.

I've added a timeline, maps and photographs where I thought they would be useful. At the end of each chapter, there are a limited number of explanatory footnotes and some suggestions for further reading if you find the tale is of particular interest.

You will understand that some stories need direct speech to bring them alive. In several cases, this is dialogue invented by me. In the same vein, some people's names have been changed; a few place-names have been nudged a little to the left or right. I would like to protect the innocent. I also have to be wary because a few of the murderers are still living today. There are bodies unfound.

I can also tell you that there are at least another seven stories that I could have included: the enclosure riot of 1785, a supposed accident at Medstead railway station in 1865, the water butts murder of around 1900, the conscientious objector driven by taunts to hang himself in the old mill behind the *Windmill Inn* by its 'rough and ready clientele' during World War I, the chimney death at the *Lymington Arms* from before 1920, the arsenic murders of the 1940s and, of course, the poisoned umbrella assassination of Bulgarian writer Georgi Markov. I felt twenty was enough. I have let the chapters fall where they may.

Some of you may be surprised, even upset, that there is a recurring criticism of the lack of local police activity, particularly in the more recent stories. I regret this, but then I am acting as a conduit for some of this feeling. I am not alone in thinking that police forces across the country have lost their way, officered at the highest level by politicians who have broken their contract with the population at large. I understand that funds are limited, especially given international and technology-based illegality, and with new social crimes arriving every day. However, it cannot be right that burglary, sexual assaults, street loutishness and violence and knife use, leading to a general fear of attack and insult, are now commonplace in country communities. Emphasis often seems to rest on 'thought crime' and using speeding for revenue collection. If people cannot rely on police support, then some will think about organising their own protection and, sometimes, the police encourage this. If matters get out of hand through a growing lack of trust, then police leadership will have to shoulder some of the blame.

At the end of the book, I have added a personal *Conclusion*, much of which is new research. It is lengthy. This chapter is for those people who want to know more about the development of Four Marks. Using a new study, I have examined the population development of the village from the 1830s, before it was a village, to the present day. I use graphs based on data from deconstructed census returns and the ever-helpful Office for National Statistics (ONS). This work also explores employment patterns and the places of origin of the people who now admit to being from Four Marks.

Several myths are exploded on the way. I have also taken a look at the village from a different perspective, thrown away the civic boundaries, and explained how Four Marks from prehistoric times was always a great funnel for travel because of its high ridge shared with Medstead. I seek to show the many routes across the ridge and how the ridge itself became a spur to habitation and employment.

The Conclusion explores whether Four Marks has seen an unnatural concentration of murders because of these defining factors, the far-flung roots of its population, its lack of an historic centre and its high geographic position between the sources of the rivers Alre and Wey. There are some interesting revelations.

My thanks to all of the experts who have reviewed my work. Errors, of course, remain my responsibility. If you do spot any or you have comments to make or additional information to share, please let me know on fmmurders2020@outlook.com.

I hope that you enjoy finding out about the many fascinating people who made Four Marks their home and, of course, those, too many, who died too soon.

Chris Heal
Four Marks
September 2020

MAPS, CHARTS AND TABLE

ILLUSTRATIONS

Confirming copyright for photographs, where it exists, can be a difficult matter. Where some claim or indication of ownership has been found, contact has been made and approval for use in this book agreed. However, many photographs more than fifty years old give no indication of ownership. Rather than deprive readers of a worthwhile illustration, these photographs have been assumed to be out of copyright. If anyone feels that any illustration used in this book falls within their copyright ownership, which they can prove, and they wish to assert that copyright, please contact the publisher on fmmurders2020@outlook.com so that honour can be satisfied.

1 BATTLE OF THE SHANT

Racism and the coming of the railway

THE SHANT, NEAR ROPLEY SOKE
1863   BODY COUNT: 6

I thought it was hail spattering against my side of the vehicle. I twisted in my cramped seat and just caught my rifle as it slid from between my knees. The soldier opposite grinned, wagged a finger and started to lecture me, 'Your rifle is your best ...'

'Incoming,' shouted the platoon sergeant, all calm like they are supposed to be. The Browning machine gun in the small turret above our heads let out several short bursts. Large men around me stood and tried to poke their SLRs through the armoured car's side ports. It was comic. Saracens are much less than eight feet wide, a self-loading rifle almost half that. You need to practise this manoeuvre as these six raw infantrymen were finding out the hard way. If anyone got over-excited, an internal ricochet could end someone's career.

'Sit down, you bloody idiots,' yelled the sergeant over the din. 'Wait for orders.'

Our six-wheeled personnel carrier, a 'sixer' to its men, a 'pig' to the IRA, was a long-term stalwart of the roads of Northern Ireland. It was 1968 and our Saracen was on lone patrol. We had travelled for an hour with two other vehicles on this fine summer morning in June, dodging around builders' vans and farm and school traffic on our way from Belfast to Newcastle at the foot of the Mountains of Mourne. There we split for a little bit of flag-waving in the country. The men with me were all new arrivals. It was a first tour for a detachment of the 2nd Battalion, Queen's Regiment, one of those sorry amalgamations that brought together once proud units. When we met for the first time that morning, I realised most of the men were from Kent. Their accents were a little hard to follow.

Our vehicle commander was arguing with the driver while at the same time trying to get a decision from the senior officer, an inexperienced Rupert with the beginnings of a moustache. He looked somewhat out of his depth. A couple of the young infantrymen went pale as short bursts of machine gun fire ran along the vehicle.

'Can't see 'em, Sarge,' offered our gunner as he reached for a new ammunition belt. 'Shall I fire anyway?'

'Steady, lads, steady. Wait for the lieutenant.'

Several heavy calibre rifle bullets hit the vehicle and flecks of hardened paint flew off the inside wall stinging bare skin. One young lad was caught near an eye, which bled heavily.

'Radio's gone,' shouted the driver. 'They must have got the bloody aerial.'

'There's nothing on my walkie talkie,' added someone. 'Must be the bloody mountains.'

That was when the road bomb detonated blowing the axles off two wheels, reducing us to a crawl. Inside, the sound of the impact was deafening. Bodies and equipment flew all ways, the vehicle tilted alarmingly and the boy with the wound started crying.

'Farmhouse just ahead, Sarge,' called the driver.

'So, what?' muttered the lieutenant.

'Well, sir, it's got a telephone.'

'Right. Get as close as you can to the front door.'

It was then I realised that in the jumble I was nearest to the back exit. I would be first out and the others would wait to see if I made it. If I got to the front door and it was locked, I would be a sitting duck.

'You three to firing positions,' ordered the sergeant. 'Give covering fire now, and, you with the Browning, brief pulls only. First man out. Now. Go.'

This was no time to argue. I kicked open the garden gate, trampled some primulas and prayed the green door was unlocked. There was a little pixie with a fishing rod and red hat on the doorstep. As I reached for the handle, the door opened and a buxom woman in her fifties with a big smile wished me, 'Top of the morning.' I fell sideways and brought my SLR up at the ready, remembering my training.

Steady your breathing. Control your heartbeat. Bring your pulse down. Check for targets. Evaluate threats. Communicate.

All firing stopped. There were chirps from blue tits and a warning rattle from a wren in a blue-flowered lavender bush. It was a lovely morning.

'Will you all be coming in now, do you think? Shall I put the kettle on?'

'All clear, Sarge,' I yelled.

'Right, lads, off you go. Two at a time. Remember your weapons. No pushing.'

And, so, there we all were, a few men on guard at the windows, the rest sitting in easy chairs drinking hot, sweet tea, dipping chocolate digestive biscuits, served by the farmer's wife, 'Call me Betty', and her breathtaking daughter, Mary, I think she was called.

'Don't worry, boys,' said Mrs O'Connor. 'They've had their fun. They won't be shooting up my house or I'll tell their mothers.'

It was then that the lieutenant made his first decision. 'I'll just go and use the telephone, if I may, to call Thiepval Barracks, at Lisburn, you know.'

Mrs O'Connor ushered him away and as he got through, I could hear his public school authority returning.

'So you're the brave one, my big lad,' she offered me a few minutes later. 'You fair flew out of your banjaxed motor. And, then, all up and keeping dick in one movement. I think you've done this before, a little bit more than that eejit on the phone?'

'Just instinct, Mother,' I replied.

'Where are you from?' she asked.

'I live near Andover.' She looked quizzical. 'In Hampshire,' I added.

'Hampshire, issit?' Her look wandered back over the years. 'Hampshire. That place means a lot to our family. Places called Ropley and Medstead. Do you know 'em?'

'Don't think so, unless … is that where they're closing a little branch railway? It's a big county.'

Mrs O'Connor became quite agitated. 'That's it, the railway,' she all but shouted, causing a couple of the men to look up in worry from their tea.

The lieutenant came in from the kitchen. 'Listen up, lads,' he said. I've always hated that expression. 'The cavalry will be here in force with a breakdown truck in about two hours. Sergeant, set up a watch. The rest of you make yourselves comfortable.'

The sergeant almost rolled his eyes, leaving the watch where he had positioned it ten minutes ago. 'Yessir,' he barked. 'You all heard the officer.'

'Tell me your story, Mother,' I suggested. 'We've got a little time.'

She began a well-practised tale, clearly passed down over the years around the family table and in the pub. It had taken place over one hundred years before and the inherited memory was still bitter. She went to the fire mantle and returned with a cracked photograph of an old man in a blackening, silvered frame.

'This was my great-granfer, Liam,' she said, letting her guard down in her anguish. 'He was there. I never knew him, but I heard that he always hated the English since then.'

Mrs O'Connor told me about the 'Battle of the Shant'. Over the years, I have learned additional background to her story which I have added piece by piece. I hope it helps you fill in the picture.

Liam Ryan was the youngest of twelve cousins who left Dundalk for Dublin and travelled to Britain on the ferry to Holyhead to seek work. Ireland had been ravaged by epidemic typhus during the great famine of the 1840s, which had halved their families. It was the autumn of 1863. Traditional work for Irish navvies on the canals had dried up as they began to fall out of heavy use. The new steam railways came so quickly that the bargee way of life was lost in a generation. The cousins hoped that the explosion in railway construction would find them employment and enough money to send home for food.

Over two months, the men worked their way south from Holyhead, walking from small job to job, often living off the land, scratching lice and dodging landowners and town bailiffs without finding anything regular. One of their number, Seamus, woke on a cold morning to find himself with a fever and covered in a rash. In his weakened condition, the typhus killed him within days. They buried him in a wood in Shropshire for no churchyard would accept a ravaged body.

The men arrived in Alton late in the year and applied for positions at the office of Smith & Knight, the sub-contractors who were building a rail route from the town to connect with the Southampton line near Winchester. Smith & Knight had just finished the Metropolitan Railway with its gas-lit wooden carriages hauled by steam locomotives, the world's first passenger-carrying underground railway; it connected central London's financial heart to what were to become the Middlesex suburbs. The contractors started work in Hampshire immediately and quickly moved much of their plant and workforce. The men would have found the local chalk rather different from London clay.

This new Mid-Hants railway was a large and rapid undertaking: about seventeen miles had to be completed on a three-year, fixed-price contract, including all stations, and to a mainline standard. The authorised capital from shares and mortgage was £200,000. The complexity of the heavy earthworks and bridges along the line meant that work was managed at eight points, the first at the Butts near the *French Horn*. These were complex, distanced operations only connecting near the end of the project. The defining problem was the ridge at Windmill Hill planned to be sliced through by a deep cutting, but even then it needed to climb a gradient of 1:60, which was more than the directors thought comfortable. A half-mile tunnel around the northern side of Chawton Park, which would reduce the gradient to 1:75, was considered, but the additional cost of £25,000 to the shareholders, always tight on money, put paid to that idea.[1]

Going Over The Alps: A train from Medstead and Four Marks entering the Chawton End Cutting, the highest point on the Watercress Line at over 600 feet. © *Colin Smith, cc-by-sa/2.0*

The company was locally promoted by landowners and businessmen who expected the railway to benefit their interests. The chairman was Edward Knight of Chawton, a nephew of Jane Austen. Ironically, it was the railways that were currently enhancing Austen's reputation by selling inexpensive editions of her novels to Britain's working classes at their new commuting stations. At just pennies a copy, these reprints were some of the earliest mass-market paperbacks.[2]

Knight's company's prospectus remarked that 'the prosperity of towns and villages which are deprived of railway access is retarded and the cost of the necessities of life greatly increased'.[3] Certainly this would be true of Knight's own business, and particularly that of William Ivey, another promoter of the new line and proprietor of the Prospect Hall estate in Medstead, who sought and eventually got a private siding serving his brickworks and other businesses. For the lower classes, however, the two intervening stations before Alresford, at Medstead and Ropley, were up to two miles from their village centres.

The Irish navvies were told to take a chit and walk south along the turnpike until they crossed the ridge and, after another mile or so, they would find on their left at Ropley Soke a collection of black and white buildings called the Shant where they would be given short-term lodging and appointed to a ganger.

Fox hounds at *The Shant* in 1938. Built probably early in 1863, the building closed as a pub about 1985, when it was called the *Watercress Inn*. Some say it was also called the *Nips Inn*. I think I may have been about the last customer. I asked for a pint and was given two half bottles of beer, two half-shants, if you like. It was home for a local labourer and his family in 1881; a pub retailer, George Kneller ten years later; beer retailer Harry Smith in 1920; and, much later, an Indian restaurant called *The Star*, a kitchen fitting company and, last time I drove by, a private house. Edward Knight, the chairman of the railway company, was also a leading light in the Hampshire Hunt. The Hunt's kennels at Ropley were served by the railway which provided an exclusive overbridge east of Medstead at an annual rent of £5. The bridge is still there, but not in use. A writer in *The Field* wasn't impressed: '[The railway] will be a great nuisance for fox hunting as it bisects the best part of the country.' *Lost Pubs Project*

The owners shunned wasting time, moving large numbers of men at the beginning of each day's work. Several large groups were semi-permanently stationed along the line for up to two years. With insufficient or inappropriate local accommodation, a series of shanty towns sprang up at these focal points, particularly on the ridge and at Ropley Soke.

Gangers were also keen to keep their men near the job in the evening and not walking miles to the nearest pub. There were several inns along the turnpike route from Alton to Alresford, often providing turnpike services: first, in Four Marks, the *Windmill Inn* and *Lymington Arms* (which was beside a railway bridge), then in North Street, Ropley, the *Chequers* and *Anchor* Inns, and in Bishop's Sutton, the *Ship Inn*.

The 'beer' gap was at Ropley Soke where considerable earth movement was needed to form the embankment. Hence the Shant was built, probably at the contractor's or owner's expense, to provide the encampment with refreshment, limited accommodation and a truck shop. The Shant is often assumed to be a short form of 'shanty' because of the supposed fall-down condition of the newly-erected structure.[4] Well, the *Shant* still stands in 2020 which suggests a degree of permanence. Shant is also slang for a pint, usually of beer, which might be a more appropriate name source in this case.[5]

In April 1861, perhaps two years before the *Shant* arrived, Ropley Soke, a short distance south, had seventeen homes housing sixty-one people, all from local families, a mix of agricultural labourers and the elderly.[6] It was the last group of houses on the turnpike before Alton, almost seven miles north. All that existed in Four Marks was the *Windmill Inn* and two nearby homes for a farmer and a bricklayer. Dotted off the road were isolated farms, one of which at Lymington Bottom housed the *Lymington Arms*. The effect of the navvies' arrival after February 1863, and the construction of the Shant, on the inhabitants of Ropley Soke can barely be imagined.

A parliamentary report commented on shanty towns that grew near railways,

> *... its suddenness, and its temporary location at particular localities, often spots before thinly populated, have created or developed evils, the taint of which seems not unlikely to survive their original cause ... They are crowded into unwholesome dwellings, while scarcely any provision is made for their comfort or decency of living ... They are hard worked; they are exposed to great risk of life and limb; they are too often hardly treated; and many inducements are presented to them to be thoughtless, thriftless, and improvident.[7]*

Lieutenant Peter Lecount, one of Robert Stephenson's assistant engineers, had first-hand knowledge of the horror of handling these men,

> *These banditti, known in some parts of England by the name of 'Navvies' or 'Navigators', are generally the terror of the surrounding country; they are as completely a class by themselves as the Gipsies. Possessed of all the daring recklessness of the Smuggler, without any of his redeeming qualities, their ferocious behaviour can only be equalled by the brutality of their language. It may truly be said that their hand is against every man ...*[8]

To make the embankment at Ropley Soke each navvy had to lift nearly twenty tons of earth and rock every day, mostly taken from the ridge cutting. The spoil was dumped into trucks, which horses dragged along to where it was packed into the embankment's gaps. The men who slogged on the steep slope from Medstead to Ropley returned at day's end to their rough shacks and to the Shant. Inside, near the door, stood three tapped barrels of beer from competing Alton breweries, the keys of which were chained to a strong leather girdle around the waist of the presiding crone. One historian claimed that, across the country, £1,000 was spent on drink for every mile of railway built.[9] There were rough benches and tables of green wood where food was eaten and cards played.

The *Shant* was built with four inter-connected halls of simple construction, fitted up with shared bunks from floor to roof like the between-decks of immigrant ships. 'Nestling between the navvies were dogs and litters of puppies, mostly bullhounds and lurchers, which the men used for fighting or poaching.'[10] Haggard women cooked over a large, open fire, made beds, swept occasionally, mended clothes and provided personal services at the drop of a coin. Even with the *Shant*, and accommodation found in the few nearby villages, there was still far from enough room. Dozens of wooden huts sprang up, tar-coated and, perhaps, whitewashed, the larger ones housing whole families and their lodgers. Others were piles of turf reaching six feet high. Trade followed the navvies: brewers' drays, hucksters, packmen, cheap-jacks, milkmen, shoemakers, tailors and likeness-takers.

In the midst of all the filth, lice and mayhem, the great scam, the truck system, was worked on the men. New arrivals began their employment with no money and were paid at the end of the month, a deliberately long time. Until then, they had to live on credit. At the end of each day, the navvy could ask his ganger for a 'sub', a subsistence allowance. The 'sub' was a ticket that could only be exchanged at the truck shop at the Shant or in pubs that were part of the embezzlement. Goods were generally bad, the butter rank, bacon poor, beer watered and bread mouldy. Prices were high and short weight given. After the ganger took his cut, usually a ten per cent commission across the board. Men complained that a sovereign was worth no more fifteen shillings.[11]

The truck shop at the Shant was also called a 'tommy shop'. By the end of a month of hard grind and tommy rot, navvies were often left with only a few shillings.[12] The greenest were skimmed the most. In the case of the eleven Ryan men, this meant no money to send home to their starving families. The easy-going Irish Catholics were dismayed; the belligerent Presbyterian co-workers disdainful. When it came to a fight with foreigners, every ordinary English navvy would side with the man from Hampshire who ran the local truck.

There is no record of what occurred; no crime sheet with the authorities in Alton; no local stories. Only, perhaps, Mrs O'Connor still knew. She told me that tension in the Shant simmered over several days. There were frequent fights. A contrived accident on an embankment left one Ryan with a broken leg from a chalk fall. Work had been stopped temporarily, much to the annoyance of the site engineer because, as one team dug to remove a mound opposite the shacks, they came across a small, stone Saxon coffin. An enthusiastic team of scientists came up from the Hartley Institution, newly-formed at Southampton, and requested more digging which found nothing. The coffin was moved to St Peter's, Ropley's parish church.

On the third night after pay day, with no money left and forced back into the truck system, an argument started between the Ryans and the tommy shop manager, an employee of one of the local businessmen who had promoted the railway. An hour later, at a pre-arranged signal, the unarmed Ryans were set about with shovels, scythes, pitchforks and pickaxes. Everyone was in drink. It was a frenzy of hatred and boredom based on racism. After a few minutes, six Irishmen lay dead and dying. The remainder, including Liam Ryan, took to their heels. It was almost a year before two of the men made it home, the last few of their family dying of wounds and disease in English hedgerows.

Faced with the consequences of what they had done, outright riot and murder, it was no surprise that the killers' first thought was to hide the crime from a merciless justice. Executions were still held in public and transportation ships left regularly for Australia. Two navvies had been hanged beside the railway line during the construction of the Edinburgh and Glasgow Railway for killing a ganger.

The bodies were taken that night to the deep hole left by the coffin's excavations. Chalk was piled on top and the level raised to the track bed, the communal grave unmarked.

'I can tell you their names,' said Mrs O'Connor. She repeated the litany from her heart. 'Séamus, Pádraig and Sean Ryan, Liam's brothers, and his cousins, Sean and Caoimhín McGrath and Colim Walsh.

'We always meant to go there, to that *Shant*, to make remembrance and to say a prayer in that heathen place and maybe do some mischief to that railway.'

At that moment, there was a cheer from the soldiers at the window. Two Saracens drew up corralling a big-load carrier for our wreck. I never found time to say 'goodbye'. We were on our way back to the barracks where I left the platoon and got about my other work.

There was an unexpected postscript many years' later. I was doing a job in Oman and staying at a plush new hotel outside Muscat, the Chedi, I think, all marble, palms and swimming pools. I ordered a cold beer at an outside bar, watching a sprinkler at work on a crisp lawn, looked up and recognised Sarge. He had put on weight, but still looked fit enough to hold a weapon. We didn't share why we were there, but reminisced about our brief incident.

'You know,' he said, 'that our Rupert got a mention in despatches for his calmness and leadership under fire. No surprise there considering who his father was. Anyway, a sniper from Unity Flats got him in the shoulder two years later.'

We raised our glasses.

'You spent a lot of time talking to that woman,' he remembered.

'Listening rather than talking,' I grunted.

'Well, the theory, afterwards, was that the whole thing was a set up,' he explained. 'The gunfire drove us towards a remotely controlled IED designed so that we had to stop outside the farmhouse.

'That woman, your mate, was a notorious IRA sympathiser; her husband was a local commander. She hated the English from the bottom of her heart. Her job was to get close to one of the squaddies and try to squeeze intel out of them while we were all waiting to be rescued.

'Now, then, buy me another and tell me what secrets you gave away.'

ENDNOTES

[1] Hardingham, *Mid-Hants Railway*.

[2] Barcas, *Lost Books of Jane Austen*.

[3] Brown, 'Origins'.

[4] Hill, David, *Out of His Sphere*, '… this old wreck of a shant …'; Akers, Alan, *The Havilfar Cycle*, '… that cramph of a shant …'; Cordell, Alexander, *Tunnel Tigers*, '… that apology for a shant.'

[5] Bentley, Richard, *Greenbeard*, '… will take out enough for a shant and some fun …'; Moorcock, Michael, *Whispering Swarm*, '… ordered him a shant of dark porter …'; James, Christopher, *Sherlock Holmes and the Adventure of the Ruby Elephants*, '… sub me a shant of bivvy …'.

[6] 1861 census.

[7] *House of Commons*, 'Report from Select Committee on Railway Labourers', 1846 (530) XIII.

[8] Coleman, *Railway Navvies*.

[9] Williams, *Our Iron Roads*.

[10] Coleman, *Railway Navvies*.

[11] Coleman, *Railway Navvies*.

[12] Several Georgian pennies have been found near the railway line in this area by metal detectorists. Other finds include a collection of eating forks and the metal remains of digging tools.

Reading list:

Allen, Matt, *The Mid Hants Railway, The Watercress Line* (Halsgrove, Wellington 2007)

Bancroft, Peter, compiled, *Railways Around Alton, An illustrated bibliography* (Nebulous Books, Alton 1995)

Barchas, Janine, *The Lost Books of Jane Austen* (John, Hopkins University Press, Baltimore, USA 2019)

Brown, Keith, 'The Origins of Medstead Station', in *South Western Circular, Journal of the South Western Cycle*, April 2012; 'A Brief History of the Mid-Hants Line to 1973', unpublished chapter on the origins of the Mid-Hants Railway.

Coleman, Terry, *The Railway Navvies, A History of the Men who made the Railways* (Pelican, London 1969)

Hardingham, Roger, *The Mid-Hants Railway from Construction to Closure* (Runpast, Cheltenham 1995)

Williams, Frederick S., *Our Iron Roads, Their History, Construction and Administration* (1883; Alpha 2019)

2 THE ELF AND THE ARCHBISHOP
The village's only mass murder

POOKS HILL, ALTON LANE
1960   BODY COUNT: UP TO 13

If blue plaques on the walls of building were the measure of national success or notoriety where would the youthful Four Marks stand among its peers, not yet the age of its oldest resident?

Pride of place must go to a borrowed son who was born in a thatched cottage opposite the village pond in 1766. The rough and ready building, no windows or stairs to the loft bedrooms, was said to be the oldest in Ropley, but today, just, it would have been in Four Marks.

Archbishop William Howley's cottage by Four Marks pond. © *Alresford Heritage*

Our lad's mother was from West Meon peasant stock and could neither read nor write. Surprisingly, then, the father was William Howley, vicar of Ropley, whose office included the church at Bishop's Sutton. William Howley, junior, began his education at Winchester College and, in 1783, went to New College, Oxford. He became chaplain to the Marquess of Abercorn and, in 1809, was appointed Regius Professor of Divinity at Oxford University where a pupil was William II of Holland. At Lambeth Palace, he was consecrated Bishop of London.

Fifteen years later, and for the next twenty years, he was Archbishop of Canterbury. He presided over the coronation of William IV and Queen Adelaide in 1831. Accompanied by others, Howley went to Kensington Palace early one morning in June 1837 to tell Princess Victoria that she was now Queen of the world's greatest empire.

Queen Victoria receives the news of her accession to the throne. Archbishop Howley is on the right. *Painting by Henry Tanworth Wells from* The Letters of Queen Victoria, *Arthur Christopher Benson, Viscount Esher (1907)*

Archbishop Howley had his detractors, but none of us is wholly bad or good who start our lives under Old Down Wood. Howley stood for some things that would today be questioned: his heart-felt opposition to the Great Reform Act led to his carriage being attacked in the streets of Canterbury; he was an old-High Churchman who held Catholic beliefs, but was consistently anti-Roman, and, at the same time Master of the Royal York Lodge of freemasons in Bristol. Howley spent over £60,000 renovating Lambeth Palace. He died in 1848 and his blood lives on through aristocrats of the Beaumont family.

What lives of the famous and infamous lay hidden even for a short time behind other walls in Four Marks?

The occupants of one bungalow in Alton Lane may not approach the eminence of the Archbishop of Canterbury, but the building must lay claim, through its residents, to the largest number of potential blue plaques in the village: a record-breaking lady aviator, an educational mathematician of renown and world-record book sales, a tea planter, a leader of the fight against the IRA, a village doctor, and Four Marks' only known mass murderer – so far. Another plaque might note that four published authors 'lived here'.

Pooks Hill at the bottom of the lane near the primary school at Five Ways takes its name from Rudyard Kipling's book, *Puck of Pook's Hill*, a series of magical and fantasy short stories set in different periods of English history. The stories are told to two young children by an elf, Puck, or by people plucked by him from history. Puck is a development of the character in Shakespeare's play, *A Midsummer Night's Dream.*[1]

The white bungalow, slightly shabby but with a delightful garden, is set a little back from the road behind a short, half-moon driveway and five-barred gates. I was invited to examine the house deeds and mortgages by a helpful owner. With a genuflection to William Howley, the Ecclesiastical Commissioners for England lay claim to all mines and minerals under the property below 200 feet and allow no

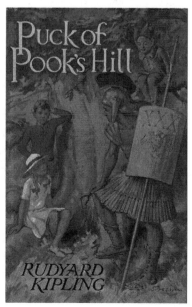

Parnesius, a centurion of the Seventh Cohort of the Thirteenth Legion, the Ulpa Victrix, discusses catapults with Una while Pucks looks on from his branch on a beech stub in the Far Wood.

building to be constructed or used for the sale of intoxicating liquor, for a school, institution or lunatic asylum, inebriates, consumptives or persons of unsound mind, or for a shop, trade or factory. One hopes that today's Lords of the Manor of Bishop's Sutton would be more sympathetic to the less fortunate. One also wonders if these restrictions are continued up and down the road, how many properties could claim not to undertake some sort of trade?

Pooks Hill was once part of the Herbert Park Estate, bought from next-door *Jock's Lodge* in about 1912. There was a lot of early selling and reselling until builders Walter and Minnie Hards of South Croydon and Medstead got to work and sold on in 1924.

The first main occupier was Clement Vavasor Durell, therefore the first recipient of a virtual blue plaque. Durell was born in 1882, the fifth son of a rector. After service as a lieutenant in the Royal Garrison Artillery during the Great War in which he was mentioned in despatches, he became housemaster of Chernocke House at Winchester College. It was not a position to suit his talents for he had grown into a shy person, reportedly brow-beaten by his elder brothers in childhood. He was poor at personal relationships.[2]

Durell found a substantial second career and income in writing the best-known textbooks on mathematics, over twenty different titles, some of which have been reprinted in this century. His publisher claimed that 'there can be few secondary schools in the English-speaking world in which some at least of Mr Durell's books are not now employed in the teaching of mathematics'. Many elder Four Marks' citizens today may not recognise the surname, but they may recall, some with dread of the subject, one of *The Teaching of Elementary Algebra*, *General Arithmetic* or *Elementary Geometry*.

Durell's writing career was so successful that when he retired to East Preston, Sussex, accompanied by a housekeeper, gardener and large dogs, to play golf, he was also able to spend his winters in Madeira and, then, South Africa where he died in 1968. He left over £200,000.

I like to imagine Durell ending a quiet weekend in Four Marks by catching a train from the local station, sitting in the first class carriage and checking the proofs of his latest mathematical blockbuster, while chugging down the hill to his schoolboys in Winchester, unknowingly passing over the bodies of six dead Irish navvies buried in the first chapter of this book.

Pooks Hill was sold for £650 in 1932 to the Honourable Mrs Mildred Mary Bruce, a British racing motorist and aviator who was the first woman to fly around the world solo over land.[3] Here is a worthy second blue plaque. Bruce used to land her wooden, single-seat aerobatic biplane, the only *Miles Satyr* ever built, in the field opposite Pooks Hill. She was visited at home, at least once, by Amy Johnson, the first woman to fly solo to Australia, and others who all landed in the same field.

Mary Bruce's Miles Satyr in a Four Marks field with, possibly, John Pugh, aerobatic ace. In the background is Alton Lane and, right, her home in the white bungalow, Pooks Hill. Bruce damaged the plane in 1936 when, trying to land in a small field near Stafford for a bet, she flew into telephone wires (for which the telephone company charged her £80). Bruce was unhurt.

Mildred Petre was born at Coptfield Hall in Essex in 1895, the daughter of an English landowner, a descendant of Sir William Petre, and an American actress of little repute, Jennie Williams. Petre was fined many times for driving under age or speeding around London, including three days running at Bow Street Magistrates Court. She had an illegitimate son by a wealthy landowner and married, in 1926, the Honourable Victor Austin Bruce, son of Henry Bruce, 2nd Baron Aberdare, who won the 1926 Monte Carlo Rally.[4]

On a whim, Mildred Bruce started the 1927 Monte Carlo from John O'Groats. After travelling 1,700 miles in seventy-two hours without sleeping, she finished sixth overall and won the *Coupe des Dames*. She held several motoring endurance records including planting the Union Jack about 250 miles north of the Arctic Circle, a feat that remained unbroken until this century. She drove a Bentley 4½ Litre for twenty-four hours to capture the world record for single-handed driving, averaging over eighty-nine miles per hour.

In 1929, she switched to powerboats making a record-breaking return crossing from Dover to Calais and, later that year, broke the twenty-four hour distance record by travelling 694 nautical miles on a course around a lightship and a yacht moored in the Solent.

Taking up flying and getting her qualifications in one week, Bruce set off for Tokyo. An oil leak forced her down on the shore of the Persian Gulf where she was sheltered for two days by Baluchi tribesmen. Torrential rain brought another unplanned landing in a jungle clearing beside the Mekong River where she contracted malaria. Next year, she flew across America to reach her mother's birthplace in Indiana. Two crashes later, and returning to Europe on the *Île de France*, she flew to Lympne Airport where she was given an aerial escort by Amy Johnson.

Mary Bruce, right, with Amy Johnson at Croydon in 1931 after Mary's world-record round-the-world flight.

In the months before Bruce moved with her husband to Four Marks, she made three failed attempts over the Solent to break the world in-flight-refuelled endurance record by staying in the air non-stop for four weeks, all foiled by technical problems. She was then invited to join a flying circus for which she bought the *Miles Satyr* through her company, Luxury Air Tours. She also bought a *Fairey Fox* bomber from a scrapyard for £2 10s, plus £10 for an engine, modified it at Hanworth Aerodrome, and took her commercial pilot's licence so that she could carry fare-paying passengers. She crashed both the Fox and the Satyr a few months after leaving Four Marks.

For the story of the rest of her life, her autobiography, *Nine Lives Plus*, is recommended. She became a successful businesswoman. In 1974, aged seventy-eight, Bruce test drove a Ford Capri Ghia at 110 miles per hour around Thruxton circuit. Three years later, she looped the loop in a twin seat de Havilland Chipmunk.

Bruce died, aged ninety, and was cremated in London. Amy Johnson, her friend, died in 1941, aged thirty-eight, after bailing out over the Thames Estuary. It was claimed by some that she had been shot down by friendly fire. Succumbing to a freezing sea, she was likely sucked into the propellers of a naval rescue ship. The tragedy was hushed up and became a conspiracy theorists' delight.

Bruce doubled her money on Pooks Hill when she sold to Dr Robert Oliver White, an Irish physician and surgeon from Kerry and Dublin. Aged fifty-six, he had served as a senior medical officer in Nigeria and the Gold Coast during the Great War and, later, had been in practice at West Ealing. It is White who brings us indirectly to the mass murderer.

White lived at Pooks Hill for twenty-seven years until 1960. Through the main door, the first room on the right was a waiting room, the second, the surgery, both now bedrooms. The current owner claims guests sleeping in these rooms sometimes report, unprompted, nightmares where they imagine they are trapped in some long-term suffering.

White picked up a small number of local patients and used a pony and trap when home visits were necessary. Part of the old stable still remains. His wife, Jane, also from Ireland, died in 1952, aged seventy-three. That same month, July, White, aged seventy-four, remarried another Jane from Alton on his doorstep. Jane Luff was twenty-one, over fifty years his junior.

White's practice fell away. He was left with a few dozen committed elderly patients whom he had treated for much of their adult life. Six months before his end, family employed a live-in locum, hoping against all the evidence that White might return to work. He never did and died in 1960 at a nursing home in Ashtead, Surrey. He left almost £4,000. White, as a village doctor, might have brought Pooks Hill its third virtual plaque.

The locum moved on and Pooks Hill was bequeathed to White's son, Robert and daughter, Nora, the latter taking ownership of the property by agreement. There was no word of the widowed Jane, who died aged fifty-nine in Basingstoke. Nora lived at *Pooks Hill* with her husband, William Chambers Hollingsworth Hudson, and their children.

Hudson, uncle of Jeremy 'Paddy' Ashdown MP, one-time leader of the

Liberal Party, is a candidate for the fourth plaque. His book, *Myself When Young*, a memoir, concentrated on his almost forty years as a tea planter in Assam, latterly accompanied by Nora, and on his war service in the Western Desert at the time of generals Erwin Rommel, Claude Auchinleck and Bernard Montgomery. Montgomery, incidentally spent his last years nearby at Isington Mill in a hamlet off the A31 four miles from Alton. He is buried in an unremarkable grave at the back of Holy Cross churchyard in Binsted, which is worth a visit to pay grateful respects.

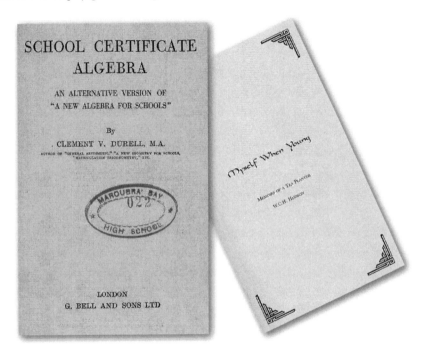

Two of the many books written at Pooks Hill: Durrel's *Algebra*, 1958, and Hudson's autobiography, 2001.

Hudson was hit by a bomb from a Stuka dive-bomber while hiding behind sandbags during an air raid, lost part of an elbow and was left with a large splinter like a knitting needle sticking out of his forehead. After months on sick leave, he married Nora at Ropley parish church. In 1966, she died of cancer and a brain tumour, peaceful at the end, at the Lord Mayor Treloar Hospital in Alton. Bill Hudson kept the property although he mostly lived in Kenya running his firm's tea business. He sold Pooks Hill in 1972 and died in 1998.

The Archdales, Audley and Brigid, occupied Pooks Hill around 1980, both with entries in *The Peerage*, a website listing the British nobility. Living in the newly-built annex were Brigid's parents. Her father, Major General Denis Grattan Moore, of the Royal Inniskilling Fusiliers, was once of Mountfield Lodge, Omagh, a substantial pile developed from a hunting lodge. He was a Deputy Lieutenant and Companion of the Order of the Bath (CB).

Moore was tangentially involved in the 'Hackett Affair' when General Sir John Hackett, the General Officer Commanding Northern Ireland in the early 1960s, was warned to cease all contact with the IRA Provisionals in Dublin after sending William Whitelaw, the Northern Ireland Secretary, notes of his unofficial telephone conversations with their leader, David O'Connell. Whitelaw warned Hackett that his unofficial contacts with the Provisionals made him open to a charge of treason.[5]

Hackett tried to persuade O'Connell that bomb attacks on the British mainland such as those against the Old Bailey and Scotland Yard were counter-productive. He also hoped that secret negotiations could be opened through him. Reporting a phone call in 1973, Hackett told Whitelaw that he had upbraided O'Connell because 'my friend Major General Moore had that very morning received a letter bomb, one of four delivered to retired soldiers and policemen in County Tyrone'. No one was hurt.

'I reminded O'Connell that General Moore had his house burned down in 1957 and he and I had agreed that this was probably enough and the Moores should now be left alone.'

Perhaps this old and senior soldier is worthy of Pooks Hill's fifth plaque?

The family of Audley Archdale, one-time partner in *Les Grands Coteaux*, wine merchants, deserves a passing mention. Archdale's grandfather, Lieutenant Colonel Theodore Archdale of the Royal Artillery fought in the Boer War where he was mentioned in despatches and won the DSO. He died in 1918, aged forty-five, a month before the armistice, when RMS *Leinster*, the Dún Laoghaire to Holyhead mailboat, was torpedoed by U-boat UB-123, the only ship it sank during the war. It was the greatest Irish Sea maritime tragedy with at least 560 people lost.[6] Archdale's grandmother, Helen Russel, was a militant suffragette standing alongside Emmeline Pankhurst; she worked throughout her life in London, Geneva and Kent for women's rights. Russel was the first editor of *Time and Tide*, 'Wait for No Man', a feminist political and literary weekly review. Archdale's great-grandfather, Nicholas Archdale was Deputy

Lieutenant of County Longford and High Sheriff of County Fermanagh. He died, aged fifty-six, 'in the hunting field'. Other family members were MPs; one refused a peerage rather than support Irish Union.

About twenty years ago, I was enjoying an after work beer in the *Castle of Comfort* in Medstead with a local doctor who was contemplating, like so many of his colleagues, retiring a couple of years early through despair at the management of the NHS. Over the course of our ramblings, I told him of my collection of Four Marks murders. He went quiet for a while.

'There is a story I heard about Pooks Hill,' he said, 'which has always bothered me.' He took a deep pull of Young's. 'I can tell you about it because the colleague who told me about it, Bill, another doctor, died a few months ago. Massive heart attack. Just dropped dead in his surgery in Southampton.'

'Let me get another round,' I offered.

By the time I got back with the beer and some crisps and scratchings, Jim, let's call him Jim, had got his thoughts ordered. This is what he told me:

After he graduated, Bill spent a number of years working in Africa. He caught a bad case of malaria and came home to Hampshire to recuperate. Recovered, his first position was as a general practitioner in Winchester. It was 1962. He was asked by his practice leader, in confidence, to conduct a quiet investigation into a spike in the number of local deaths of elderly people around Alton. The leader had received a phone call from the British Medical Association (BMA) in London who wanted some associated rumours checked before any contact was made with the police. A number of criticisms had been made by letter. Two relatives were asking simple questions.

Bill's enquiries led him first to the death records for the last few years. Two points quickly came to the fore. There was a spike and it was in Four Marks. Normally, this small community of some 1,500 people might see fifteen deaths a year, about one per cent, with perhaps half of them among the over-sixty-fives. In four months in the middle of 1960, there were eighteen deaths alone within the resident elderly population. Jim checked the actual death certificates. There was nothing unusual in individual causes of death; all were from a variety of common events naturally associated with long-term illnesses or old age.

There was one recurring factor, however: the illegible scrawl of the doctor's signature on thirteen of the documents. By identifying those other doctors practising in Four Marks before and after the spike, and eliminating deaths in nearby voluntary and state hospitals, Jim noticed the complete absence of Dr White's signature.

And, so, he came to discover the existence of the locum. Nowhere could Bill discover this person's name. White's records were lost. Nothing was known among the other doctors of that time. There was no information to be found at Winchester. The locum was a shadowy figure. No one could recall meeting him. Enquiries with the district nurses and local undertakers brought nothing except, occasionally, the slight scent of something suspected.

Bill reported back to his practice leader and both of them wrote to the BMA. And they waited. And waited.

Their chases were met with holding replies. Almost two years later, the formal response arrived: there was insufficient evidence of malpractice. Numbers of deaths were high, but not statistically abnormal. Through local maladministration, the name of the locum, if he even existed, was not known. Exhumations were possible in only three cases and this would be expensive and also distressing for the relatives, if they could be found. Deaths by natural causes would be the almost inevitable findings, if indeed there were any findings.

'I suppose one shouldn't be surprised,' said Jim, his story over. 'The BMA's *raison d'être* was always, is always, about protecting its members and that means looking after reputations. One bad apple threatens the barrel. Why stir up old bruises when there are more important things to be spending time on?

'But it always stuck with Jim. He thought hard, but could find no more to do. Time went by and now he's dead himself.'

'Do you have any proof that any of this actually happened,' I asked?

'Got the scent, have you,' he smiled? 'Well, I do, actually. A few months before he died, Jim sent me his files. You can have them, but you can't do anything with them until I'm gone.'

I found the documents utterly convincing. I still do.

Jim retired early and died two years later of cirrhosis of the liver. I attended his funeral with several hundred others on one of those cold, rainy days in February that seem built for purpose. Jim was well loved.

The BMA investigative branch agreed to a meeting when I told them what I had, but I got nowhere. I was met by two men in their fifties in dark suits with blue ties. Their false smiles soon turned to fixed and disapproving scowls. They even tried to confiscate the papers I produced and only backed off when I said the originals were with a solicitor. I was warned against 'causing trouble' and the personal consequences of slander and libel.

I believe that the sixth blue plaque outside Pooks Hill, the main one, has an obvious candidate. My difficulty is that I don't know his name or his date of birth. I do know that he lived there in 1960. I also know the reason for his notoriety:

'Murdered up to thirteen elderly Four Marks' residents.'

ENDNOTES

[1] This is not Kipling's only local influence. Treloar Hospital, then *The Princess Louise Hospital*, was built by public subscription and the *Daily Mail* in 1901 for sick and wounded soldiers returning from the Boer War. It was commonly known as *The Absent-Minded Beggars Hospital* after a Kipling poem of the same name. It was more than a nickname as that was how it was recorded in the 1901 census, empty apart from two night watchmen. Kipling also has a role in Chapter 4: 'Smugglers and the Vicar', in this book.

[2] Michael Price, *ODNB*.

[3] Bruce, *Nine Lives Plus*. Wilson, *Queen of Speed*.

[4] Mark Pottle, *ODNB*.

[5] Peter Day, *Daily Telegraph*, 1/1/2004.

[6] Philip Lecane, *Torpedoed!*, *The RMS Leinster Disaster*.

Reading list:

Bruce, The Hon. Mrs Victor, *Nine Lives Plus, Record-breaking on Land, Sea, and in the Air* (Pelham, London 1977)

Durell, C V, *School Certificate Algebra (Bell, London 1958)*

Hudson, *W C H, Myself When Young, Memoirs of a Tea Planter (No publisher 2001)*

Kipling, Rudyard, *Puck of Pook's Hill* (1906; Macmillan, Basingstoke 1975); *Rewards and Fairies* (1910; Penguin, London 1987).

Wilson, Nancy R, *Queen of Speed, The Racy Life of Mary Petre Bruce* (ELSP, Bradford on Avon 2017)

3 PATHWAYS TO HEAVEN
Pilgrims at the Observatory

FOUR MARKS
1919   BODY COUNT: 1

It is unnatural in a large field to have only one shaft of
wheat and in the infinite universe only one living world.
Metrodorus of Chios, 400–350 BC[1]

Do you believe in little green men from another planet?

'Of course, not.'

How about some sort of primitive life on Mars now that water has been found by NASA?[2]

'Might do.'

What about intelligent life somewhere in the cosmos?

'Possible. Lots of places to look.'

Well, what do you think of some all-knowing, guiding presence in the heavens?

'That's not something I want to talk about in public.'

So, no God-like figure, then?

'I thought this was a book about murders in Four Marks?'

❅ ❅ ❅ ❅

In 1174, Henry II, the Duke of Normandy, and his entourage passed along what is now Blackberry Lane.[3] The passage of a king over the Four Marks ridge to descend through the Pass of Alton to the River Wey was not unusual.[4] This circumstance was unique. The royal party landed in July at Southampton from Barfleur and called at Winchester, where his queen, Eleanor of Aquitaine, began a long imprisonment for backing the wrong side in the dynastic struggles. Henry continued to Canterbury, the capital of Kent, where he walked the last yards barefoot and was lashed gently 300 times by the monks as penance at the tomb of a murdered archbishop.[5]

Had some fearless and impertinent watcher asked questions about the existence of the saviour, the king and his men would have declared their belief in a Christian deity and raised their eyes to heaven in deference. Henry's motives for his public pilgrimage may have had the more earthly objective of buffing his God-given authority to rule that had been severely tarnished by the murder in the cathedral. Over the next 300 years, thousands of penitents, rich and poor, would travel through the Four Marks waste in expiation of their sins, a few barefoot or on their knees, or wearing sackcloth and ashes, declaring an absolute belief and submission to the Almighty.

❀ ❀ ❀ ❀

In 1912, also probably in July, a small party of well-dressed men, chief among them James H. Worthington, collected by horse and buggy from the railway station at Medstead, halted mid-way along Blackberry Lane. Worthington was precocious, 'filthy rich' and the epitome of a new-style of aggressive amateur astronomer; a 'product of peace, prosperity and optimism, with an enormous social confidence in what the unfettered private individual could achieve when working with a group of like-minded friends'.[6]

Worthington was in Four Marks to close a deal to buy just over five acres of land on which he intended to build with great speed an impressive observatory.

As the eldest son of a prosperous Manchester clothing manufacturer, he might have brushed off the spiritual questions, but he would have dealt with those about Mars with a religious fervour. Three years before, he confirmed that he had seen on Mars 'canals and oases so distinctly and steadily without intermission for an hour and a half that no doubt was left'.[7]

Perhaps no little green men, but certainly canal builders.

Worthington was in Four Marks to provide the answers that would sweep the doubters before him. 'What quest could be more innately romantic than harnessing the inventive ingenuity of the age to fathom the "length, breadth, depth and profundity" of the Universe, expressed as the adventure of the private individual who was answerable to his thoughts to no earthly power greater than himself?'[8]

By chance, two men of letters were in Four Marks at this time and left descriptions.

Edward Thomas, out of sorts with his world, and with Four Marks, rode a bicycle in 1913 from London to the Quantock Hills in Somerset. He was only a year from meeting his 'Wild Girl' at the 'Pub with No Name' in Priors Dean that sparked the journey that led him to become one of England's greatest poets.[9]

On the second day of his ride, the Saturday before Easter, Thomas wrote, 'The road ascended, parallel to the railway, in a straight, narrow groove, and was bridged on both sides for some distance, up to and past the highest point, by hedgeless copses of oak and beech, hazel, thorn and ivy. An old chalk pit among the trees had been used for depositing pots and pans, but otherwise the copses might never have been entered except by the chiff-chaff that sang there, and seemed to own them. Once out in the open at Four Marks, I had spread around me a high but not hilly desolation of gray grass, corrugated iron bungalows and chicken-runs. I glided as fast as possible away from this towards the Winchester Downs.[10]

Hilaire Belloc, a prolific French-British writer of the early twentieth century, was on a more determined mission, in 1910, to find the lost route of the Pilgrims' Way.[11] He argued that ancient paths followed the rivers from either side of a divide and left them only when they had all but disappeared and the best straight route was found up and over an uninhabited saddle. This law took early travellers from the south to the source of the Alre at Bishop's Sutton, near to Ropley. From the north, the road followed the Wey passed Farnham and found the river's source in Flood Meadows at Alton.

This was an old British track, predating the pilgrims, on which caravans of merchants brought tin ingots from Cornwall to be shipped to the great port of *Rutupiae*, near Sandwich in Kent, and on to the Mediterranean.[12]

The pilgrims sought a route for their holy trampings from the shrine of the apostle Saint James the Great in the cathedral of Santiago de Compostela in Galicia in north-west Spain to Winchester and the tomb of St Swithun and on to St Thomas Becket's tomb in Canterbury. This ancient motorway left Winchester through the now lost North Gate and the street of the Jewish moneylenders. The 'Old Road' was not paved and mostly unbanked. Over the years, when modern roads took other directions, the Pilgrims' Way fell into disuse, or was dug by a plough, and was lost. The road never turned a sharp corner unless forced by an outcrop, cultivation, a river bend or the need to find a ford.[13] As the road from Winchester to Alton became the main artery between the South and the Straits of Dover, Four Marks, high on its hill, was the apex of the preferred straight-line route to connect the sources of the rivers Alre and Wey.

Hilaire Belloc laid out his detective work, which uncovered the old pilgrim road from the *Anchor* public house in Ropley. It led him by a series of relics in the landscape to the foot of Brislands Lane.

We were on one of those abandoned grassy roads, which are found here and there in all parts of England; it ran clear away before us for a couple of miles. It was very broad, twenty yards perhaps. The hedges stood either side guarding land that had been no man's land since public protection first secured the rude communications of the country … Long fallen into disuse, it had escaped the marauding landlords during three centuries of encroachment. They had not even narrowed it. So much of its common character remained: it was treeless, wide and the most of it neglected; never metalled during all the one hundred and fifty years which have transformed the English highways. It was the most desolate, as it was the most convincing, fragment of the Old Road we had set out to find.

It had an abominable surface; we had to pick our way from one dry place to another over the enormous ruts which recent carts had made. For generations the land had been

Blackberry Lane, 1910.

untenanted, but there is a place where, in the last few years, an extraordinary little town of bungalows and wooden cottages had arisen on either side of the lane.

Not satisfied with the map, we asked of a man who was carrying milk what local name was given to this venerable street. He told us that the part in which we were walking was called Blackberry Lane, but that it had various names at different parts [like Furze Bush Lane].[14]

At the very summit this way we joined a modern, well-made lane called Farringdon Lane [now Telegraph Lane], which turned to the left and north, and

immediately fell into the main London road, which had been climbing from the valley
below ... The Old Road suffered no deviation, plunged into a wood, and reappeared
just at the summit of the pass, perhaps a quarter of a mile further ... and we left the
valley of the Itchen to enter that of the Wey.

At that time, 1910, at the upper end of Brislands Lane, there were perhaps four bungalows among the farm buildings and nursery, and today there is a house called Pilgrim's Way.[15] The transformation happened when the road became Blackberry Lane. An Alton court in 1935 decided that traffic on this route had precedence over vehicles along Lymington Bottom, the current main road. Belloc's 'little town' consisted of twenty-seven buildings, twenty of them bungalows, six private houses (half uninhabited, possibly under construction) and a 'lock-up shop'.[16]

In the latter months of 1909, Worthington visited observatories in the United States when the opportunities to view Mars were particularly good. He spent a month with Percival Lowell, the owner of the now revered Lowell Observatory in Flagstaff, Arizona.[17] Lowell was famous for his observations of the Martian canals, having published three books on the subject in the previous fourteen years.[18] Lowell believed that he had mapped an advanced Martian civilisation that had transformed the planet into a complex network of canals to bring precious water from its polar icecaps.

'That Mars is inhabited by beings of some sort or other we may consider as certain as it is uncertain what those beings might be ... Each canal joins another, which in turn connects with a third, and so on over the entire surface of the planet. This community of construction posits a community of interest ... The first thing that is forced on us in conclusion is the necessarily intelligent and non-bellicose character of the community which could thus act ...'[19]

At the beginning of his visit to Lowell, Worthington 'could not see [the canals], but by the end of the trip he could!'[20]

Worthington's self-imposed workload from 1910 until the opening of the Four Marks Observatory in November 1913 begged the question of where he found the time. He spent Christmas, with a New Year return, with Lowell at Flagstaff. For three years, he toured the world's finest astronomical observatories and 'managed to throw four solar eclipse expeditions into this itinerary' including Port Davey, Tasmania in 1910, Vavau, Tonga in 1911, and Portugal in 1912.[21] In the steamship era, this was a truly remarkable undertaking. He entertained Lowell at his family's home at Wycombe Court, made a speech the same month at the Royal Astronomical Society (RAS) on the rotation period of Uranus, and began planning for a self-financed eclipse expedition to Brazil which proved to be a 'soggy disaster'.[22]

James Worthington, left, in Tasmania, 1910. His observations were 'completely defeated' by the weather. *University of Southern Queensland*

Worthington then decided to join the famous husband and wife explorers William and Katherine Routledge on a trip to Easter Island, due to depart from Falmouth in March 1913. His father paid the £500 fee, but the Routledges' conditions were unacceptable. Worthington resigned and was sued with an unknown outcome.

In the midst of this frenetic activity, Worthington, in 1912, bought two impressive second-hand telescopes, a 10-inch Cooke refractor and a 20¼-inch Calver Newtonian, each priced at £550, for his Four Marks observatory. The same year, two large white domes appeared in Blackberry Lane to house them. If Worthington had not pulled out of the Easter Island expedition where would he have found the time to manage this major project?

In identical press coverage spread across the whole country, Worthington announced he had decided to 'erect an observatory in the most favourable site he could find in Southern England' and 'after much journeying and long investigations fixed on Four Marks as the finest spot available'.[23]

Placing the buildings in Medstead, although they were at the northern tip of Ropley parish, Worthington admitted to a cost of 'many thousand of pounds'. Over 600 feet above sea level and more than twenty miles from any manufacturing town, with the atmosphere unaffected by any strong artificial lighting, the Four Marks complex was 'both in finish of instruments and in general facilities ... probably the finest private observatory in England'. There were six telescopes, the two largest housed in domes twenty-four and twenty-two feet in diameter. Other instruments included a visual prominence spectroscope and two Steinheil photoheliographs. These were joined from late 1914 by a 4-inch Alvan Clark refractor to be used as a guidescope for long exposures with attached cameras. The whole comprised 5½ acres, including paddock, grounds, cottage and a small residence.

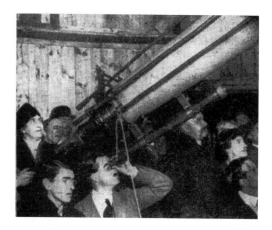

'At Medstead, there has been opened what is probably the finest private observatory in the country. It has cost many thousands of pounds. It is the property of Mr James H. Worthington, a member of the London Astronomical Observatory.' The photograph gives an idea of the size of the giant telescope. *Teesdale Mercury, 19/11/1913*

A launch picture shows at least eleven people crammed into one of the domes. One of them may well have been Professor Alexander Bickerton of the London Astronomical Society, a controversial maverick not unlike Percival Lowell. Bickerton was born in Alton in 1842 and has 'largely disappeared into obscurity'. In his twenties, he developed a gift for science teaching in London. He said that 'to instruct the Londoner you must make your class as entertaining as a music hall and as sensational as a circus'. His sheer enthusiasm landed him the post of Chair of Chemistry at the University of Canterbury in New Zealand where he taught a young Ernest Rutherford, who remained a life-long friend. Bickerton invented *The Theory of Partial Impacts* to explain the origins of new stars.

The observatory just after completion, looking up to Blackberry Lane, in 1912. The current 'Observatory', number 37, is in the background, right. © *Alresford Heritage*

Many prominent members of the astronomical world visited the Four Marks Observatory, possibly Lowell who was still convinced by his Martian canals, but certainly W.H. Steavenson and John Earle Maxwell. Steavenson was a prodigy who, aged seventeen, had independently discovered a new comet. He was elected a fellow of the RAS in the next year. Steavenson described the average 'seeing experience' at Four Marks as 'unusually good for this country'. He made four drawings of a complete rotation of Jupiter and two observations of Ganymede, 'the third satellite'.

The Great War began eight months after the Observatory's opening. Worthington did not serve, aged thirty, but his brother Nigel did. In one of those quirks, Nigel was an officer in the same regiment as my maternal grandfather, the 3rd Dragoon Guards, and fought in the same actions. Nigel got the Military Cross while my grandfather, a trooper, received a permanent piece of shrapnel in his neck, which he let me feel when I sat on his knee.

One has the sense that Worthington soon tired of the Four Marks Observatory. There was a rumour of an affair with a poetess, the wife of a colleague; the war thwarted travel plans and he spent time in London working on a book, *Poetry Prose, Paint and Pencil*, 'with an astronomical bias'.

In October 1914, Worthington wrote two letters to the British Astronomical Association (BAA) Council welcoming members to use his telescopes at Four

Marks for up to three months at a time to further their own research. He suggested that members simply told him what they would like to do by visiting the Observatory before eleven in the morning during the next few months when he would be staying there. He advised that four trains a day travelled from Waterloo station to Medstead, taking around two hours for the fifty-mile trip at a cost of 5s 9d (£0.29) for a third class return ticket. The observatory was a mere ten minutes' walk from the station and that any traveller could have a bedroom and, if coming alone, the local *Windmill Inn* could provide a meal. However, due to the 'arduous handling' of the instruments, he advised observers to come as a group of two or three in which case his kitchen staff would provide all meals.

Many of the Association's keenest observers took full advantage of the generous offer. The 10-inch Cooke refractor proved the magnet. Visitors included some great names: Steavenson; Gavin Burns, a BAA section director; Captain M.A. Ainslie; Harold Thomson and a teenage Reggie Waterfield, a later director of the BAA Mars Section.

In 1916, Percival Lowell died and belief in life on Mars soon collapsed. Edward Maunder of the Royal Observatory had challenged the prevailing narrative by arguing that the canals were an optical illusion and others, with larger telescopes, eventually ended fifteen years of canal-mania. Worthington's reputation was damaged.

'The canals were the creations of earthlings suffering from a delusion sparked by mistranslation, beautiful maps and mutually-reinforced wishful thinking.'[24]

Worthington spent more time in the United States and, by 1918, was in California almost permanently at a property in Pasadena. He bought a modest holiday residence at Carmel-by-the-sea and married a Californian woman, Ethel Johnson. The couple became an enthusiastic part of the local social scene.

The Four Marks Observatory began a gradual decline in popularity. Young men still visited, but with little, if any, supervision. From 1916, an alternative fine amateur observatory was assembled at Headley Rectory, forty miles from Four Marks, near Epsom in Surrey. It sported a splendid 8-inch refractor and 18-inch reflector. Its owner was the Rev T.E.R. Phillips.

'Many people who had used the Four Marks Observatory now headed to Headley.'[25]

Can one discern a diverging culture between these two amateur installations? The newcomer at Headley was managed by a devout Christian, morally self-confident, principled and of high standards with excellent equipment and increasingly favoured by BAA stalwarts. The pre-war installation at Four Marks had an absentee landlord, was perhaps more hedonistic, less cautious, but embarrassed by its owner's public failure.

Were there two sides to the BAA coin? The obverse showed those born to lead and with birth links to those in power: wealthy, white males with public school and university backgrounds, Darwinists. The reverse, full to the brim with reverends who delighted in doing 'the Lord's work' through a telescope, contained those pleased to stand cheek by jowl with a growing working-class tradition in astronomy, fuelled by the Workers' Educational Association, and a small, but increasing, cohort of pioneering women scientists.

And then, early in 1919, the murder happened.

A small group of young observers, fresh from the war one imagines and possibly deeply disturbed by what they had seen and done, met for a long week at Four Marks to prepare background experiments for an upcoming total eclipse.

I surmise they were contacted by Steavenson, the son of a clergyman, and working at the Royal Army Medical Corp (RAMC) hospital at Millbank. He had just become a captain and was to leave for military service in Egypt for six months the following year. Steavenson asked the young men for a favour. A German acquaintance, related to the Herschel family, now a prisoner of war at Skipton in Yorkshire, had gained permission on an honour pass to come south to visit his Hanoverian relative's old observatory premises in Slough. Steavenson asked if the Four Marks party would accommodate him for a couple of days to try to build bridges through the community of the stars.

There were tensions from first arrival. The young German was boisterously proud of the work of his distant ancestor. William Herschel, the first president of the RAS, had an unmatchable list of astronomical achievements before he died one hundred years before. The visitor was, to put it mildly, a little haughty. He believed the Germans were owed a place in the sun and was bitter about the success of the British Empire. He even said so. Worse, he had been a successful U-boat commander.

His new companions had all lost many friends. They saw the German officer class as bestial Huns who had slaughtered, raped and murdered innocents in the streets of Dinant and Liège and had used gasoline to burn the university library at Louvain with its 300,000 medieval books and manuscripts. U-boat commanders had tried to starve Britain into submission.

It was the end of a long night of difficult preparation. There had been no sleep. The German was up a ladder making a last small adjustment as the sun was coming up. The steps were pushed; the man fell and cracked his head against the Calver reflector. If he was not already dead, a second blow made sure that he was.

The way I came to know this has its own little irony. My grandfather, Alf, the one who was ordered into machine-gun fire by James Worthington's brother, had four daughters, one of whom, Regina, was my mother. Those of you who have read this book's dedication will recognise that *The Four Marks Murders* was written at her request and for her pleasure. She was a resident at Belford House for the elderly in Lymington Bottom. One day she telephoned in some excitement. Not only was I writing this book for her but she had found among her fellow residents someone, let's say 'Peggy', who had a murder story to tell. I was to attend for a private tea to learn everything.

Peggy, in her nineties, now dead, wanted to remain anonymous. Her mother had been a maid-come-cook at the Observatory. She had welcomed the young German to the bungalow in 1919 and shown him to his room. They had not spoken much. His English was halting. He said he had just been to Slough to visit the place where an old relation had once had his own observatory. His name sounded like 'Smitz', pronounced with a 'funny' inflection. He was open that he had been captain of a U-boat and had been captured the previous year. Peggy's mother was upset because she had lost a brother drowned to a torpedo, as indeed had my mother lost an uncle on a destroyer to a mine.

Peggy's mother entered the dome with cups of early morning tea on a tray and saw the 'accident'. She was given two ten pound notes and decided that she could no longer remember the incident. Those Germans were a 'bad lot'. She left the building and never returned. Peggy's mother shared her story many times with her daughter, regretting her silence more as the years passed.

German U-boat records are a well-ordered affair, especially for the commanders. Walter Schmitz, an *Oberleutnant zur See*, of the class year of 1909, was the only possibility. He was born in 1891 in Buer in Lower Saxony near Essen. In his first submarine, a creaky old minelayer, *UC 4*, he sank a couple of British steamers and a navy trawler before being given a shiny upgraded model, *UC 75*. In three voyages, Schmitz sank another eleven ships and damaged two more. That's not completely accurate as his last engagement was with the British destroyer HMS *Fairy*. In May 1918, while escorting an East Coast convoy, Schmitz's U-boat was sighted and rammed by the steamer SS *Blaydonian*. Schmitz surfaced within the convoy and was rammed again by

Fairy which sustained heavy damage to her own bows and sank a short time later about ten miles south of Flamborough Head.[26]

Peggy's mother's story rang true except that Schmitz's death is recorded at Raikeswood Camp for German officers near Skipton. He died on 4 March 1919, three weeks after his death in Four Marks. At that time, an outbreak of Spanish flu hit the camp. Forty-two prisoners died in Morton Banks hospital and a further five in the camp itself.

This was not unusual. About 25,000 German prisoners died of the flu in France. Death rates for British and French prisoners in Germany were around seven per cent and, for Germans held in Britain, three per cent. 'Most significantly, too, these death rates were almost entirely other rank prisoner deaths.'[27] In 2002, scientists Johnson and Müller proposed that the Spanish flu claimed between 50–100 million deaths, between one in twenty and one in forty of everyone across the world who survived the war.[28] The 1918–19 pandemic dwarfed the initial Covid-19 event.

I think what happened is straightforward enough. Schmitz's body was taken out into the five acres and buried. It will still be there. His hosts returned to their work, perhaps little bothered by the outcome. Schmitz never returned from his honour leave and, rather than fill in lots of embarrassing paperwork, it was decided to add him to the flu casualties.

Anyway, that's my reasoning.

I also suspect that word got back to Worthington in California and he immediately put his observatory on the market. From September, the property was prepared for an October auction by Edwin Fear and Walker from their Winchester showrooms. It was a complete sale: land, bungalow, residence 'with full equipment, instruments and two domes'.[29]

The property was bought by Henry Oggier in December 1919, a fifty-five-year-old Swiss national.[30] Oggier was variously described as a valet in 1911, his wife of four years, Alice, acting as housekeeper at Cumberland Court in Kensington High Street, London, and, in 1901, as a legation messenger in Victoria Street, London, a diplomatic district.

One wonders at the source of Oggier's money, sufficient to buy a reasonably-sized country property.[31] Cumberland Court is an imposing building, now top-rate, serviced flats. The owners were not 'at home' during the 1911 census, common enough among many of the Court's other apartments with varying numbers of servants. Could it be, unsupported speculation only, that in his rush to rid himself of the observatory, Worthington, gifted, or part-gifted, the property to his valet after some years of valued service, allowing him to quit the country for America with problem solved and conscience eased?

Intriguingly, in early 1926, W. Watson & Sons advertised a 'very fine' 10-inch Cooke refractor at £350 as an 'exceptional price to avoid storage'. This was the 'murder weapon'. Perhaps Oggier who seemingly received all equipment with the domes and the house intended the refractor for a retirement hobby. Tiring after a few years, or needing the money, he placed it for sale.

The Cooke was bought by former BAA president, Walter Goodacre, who installed it at his Finchley observatory the next year. By then, Steavenson was the youngest ever BAA president. He said that any BAA member who visited Goodacre's observatory would 'certainly have the opportunity of looking through a very fine telescope. I shall never forget the magnificent views of the Moon and the planets which I obtained with it many years ago'.

After Goodacre's death in 1938, the big refractor moved to the Mills Observatory at Dundee where it can still be seen today. William Steavenson, 'one of the foremost amateur observers of the twentieth century', died in 1975. James Worthington lived to be ninety-five, dying in Florida in 1980.

In 1939, at the 'Observatory', 37 Blackberry Lane, the bungalow was occupied by James McW. Johnston, a retired china merchant, and his wife Isabelle. Living in the main residence was John G.A. Allen, a retired electrical engineer and a member of the RAF Observer Corps. Henry Oggier, the valet, now retired, and his wife Alice, were living next door at 'Swiss Lodge', probably named for his birth country, and also presumably living off rents.[32] Swiss Lodge no longer exists and may have been a small home built on part of the property.

Oggier died in 1942 in a Basingstoke Hospital leaving effects of £368 3s 8d, a good sum which may have included the property.[33] It was bought by Emily Martha Messenger who died in 1945.

Betty Mills in her history of Four Marks recalls that the igloo-liked domes fascinated local children. No one had ever been inside, but 'it was said that they had been used by an astronomer' … and that she was told that 'they had been demolished at the start of the 1939–45 war because they were considered too much of a landmark for the enemy'.

Perhaps, also, the domes' destruction may have come about because of the death of their valet owner in 1942 and the wishes of Emily Messenger, the new occupant.

The circular fishpond fills the site of the larger observatory in 2020. The smaller observatory is the circle behind with an ash tree in its centre.

ENDNOTES

[1] Aëtius, *Placita Philosophorum*.

[2] *NASA, 15–95, 28/9/2015*.

[3] This is a conjectured route. For alternative ways for a pilgrim king to pass over the Four Marks ridge via either Wield and Medstead (Fearon, *Canterbury) or Ropley to East Tisted to Pelham Place near Rotherfield Park (Curtis, Alton), see 'Conclusion'*.

[4] Henry I, 1101; Henry II (many times); John, 1204, 1217 (four times, Rathbone, *Medstead); Henry VIII (frequent); Charles I, 1635; Charles II, 1669; James II, 1684 (Curtis, Alton; Wood, Historical Britain)*.

[5] Cartwright, *Pilgrim's Way*.

[6] Chapman, *Victorian Amateur Astronomer*.

[7] *Journal, BAA, Vol. 21, No. 130, 1910*.

[8] Chapman, *Victorian Amateur Astronomer, quoting 'Sir John Herschel on the choice of the Standard Length', The Leeds Intelligencer, 31/10/1863*.

[9] In this book, Chapter 15, 'Pub with No Body'.

[10] Thomas, *Pursuit of Spring*.

[11] Belloc, *Old Road*.

[12] Cartwright, *Pilgrims' Way*.

[13] Jackman, *Transportation*.

[14] Chapter 11: 'Honey and blackberries'. Mills, *Four Marks*.

[15] Chapter 19, 'Gradwell's nursery story'.

[16] Census, 1911.

[17] In 2011, the Lowell Observatory, established in 1894, was named one of 'The World's 100 Most Important Places' by *TIME* magazine. It was at the Observatory that the dwarf planet Pluto was discovered in 1930.

[18] *Mars*, 1896; *Mars and its Canals*, 1906; and *Mars as the Abode of Life*, 1908.

[19] Lowell, *Mars and Its Canals*.

[20] Mobberley, 'Quest'.

[21] Mobberley, 'Quest'. Lomb, private email, 2020.

[22] Mobberley, 'Quest'.

[23] *West Sussex Gazette*, 13/11/1913; *Portsmouth Evening News*, 8/11/1913; *Yorkshire Post and Leeds Intelligencer*, 10/11/1913; *The Teesdale Mercury*, 19/11/1913; *The Daily Telegraph; The Observatory magazine; The Astronomical Society of the Pacific; Popular Astronomy;* Science magazine.

[24] Wills, *JSTOR resources, 8/10/2015.*

[25] Mobberley, email, 26/6/2020.

[26] uboat.net.

[27] Jordan, *Epidemic Influenza.*

[28] Johnson and Müller, 'Updating the Accounts'.

[29] *Hampshire Advertiser*, 13/9/1919, 20/9/1919 27/9/1919, 11/10/1919.

[30] House deeds, 37 Blackberry Lane.

[31] 1901 and 1911 censuses.

[32] 1939 Register.

[33] Probate Register.

Reading list:

Belloc, Hilaire, *The Old Road* (1911; Jefferson, North Carolina, USA 2015)

Cartwright, Julia, *The Pilgrim's Way from Winchester to Canterbury* (John Murray, London 1911)

Chapman, Allan, *The Victorian Amateur Astronomer: Independent Astronomical Research in Britain 1820–1920* (Gracewing, Leominster 2017)

Fearon, Henry, *The Pilgrimage to Canterbury* (Associated Newspapers, London 1950)

Hampshire Advertiser, 1919

Langland, William, *The Vision and Creed of Piers Ploughman* (c. 1370–90; Reeves & Turner, London 1887, Project Gutenberg, Vols 1–2, 2013)

Lowell, Percival, *Mars and its Canals* (Macmillan, London 1906)

Marriott, R.A., 'BAA instrument no. 93', Instruments and Imaging Section, British Astronomical Association

Mobberley, Martin, 'James H. Worthington (1884–1980): A quest for totality, observatories & Martian canals', *BAA Journal*, Vol. 128, No. 6, 2018, pp. 331–346

Mosely, R, 'R.L. Waterfield and Four Marks Observatory', *BAA Journal*, Vol. 98, No. 33, 1988, pp. 164–165

Stanley, Arthur Penrhyn, *Historical Memorials of Canterbury: The Landing of Augustine; The Murder of Becket; Edward the Black Prince; Becket's Shrine* (1855; Cambridge University Press 2018)

Thomas, Edward, *In Pursuit of Spring* (1914; Laurel, Holt, Wiltshire 2013)

4 SMUGGLERS AND THE VICAR
Turning one's back in Ropley

MONKWOOD
1825   BODY COUNT: 0

If you wake at midnight, and hear a horse's feet,
Don't go drawing back the blind, or looking in the street,
Them that asks no questions isn't told a lie.
Watch the wall, my darling, while the Gentlemen go by!

Five and twenty ponies,
Trotting through the dark –
Brandy for the Parson,
'Baccy for the Clerk;
Laces for a lady; letters for a spy,
And watch the wall, my darling, while the Gentlemen go by!

'A Smugglers' Song', *Puck of Pook's Hill*
Rudyard Kipling[1]

Samuel Maddock climbed into the pulpit at St Peter's in Ropley and gazed down at his flock. The church was full as rich and poor came to the Sunday evening service to inspect their new vicar. The atmosphere was tense. Maddock glanced at his wife, Elizabeth, sitting in the front pew with their four daughters wearing new laced dresses. He took a deep breath and plunged into the lion's den.

'Welcome all of you to the House of God. His is a house where all are welcome who truly repent their sins. How many of you present here this evening in God's House truly repent their sins? Why should I challenge you on this day of welcome? I challenge you for you live in the village of Ropley that is known across the county for its sins. Indeed, many say that this place is built on sin.'

You could have heard a pin drop.

'What sins might we seek to address in Ropley? We must surely start with a sin of excess: the sin of drunkenness. Strong liquor is not the refuge of the God-fearing. It is the companion of the Devil-worshippers. Moderation in everything. In the wake of this sin comes the enrichment of the unworthy; it brings poverty, violence in the home, children exposed and moral depravity.'

By now, the silence was deafening.

'And what does this craving for strong liquor lead to, my Christian friends in Ropley? I will tell you. It leads to an organised refusal to obey the law of the land. It leads to a devotion to contraband and its bedfellow, smuggling. And what follows, as sure as this evening is followed by night? Why theft from people and from the elected government, by a collapse in the rule of law and, yes my Christian friends, it leads to treachery, to blackmail, to intimidation and to murder.'

A few individuals stood up and left, one shaking his fist and shouting profanities. The trickle grew into a river of argument and dissent and, by its end, the church was half empty.

Maddock's last words followed his congregation out of the door.

'The devil may be in London, my friends,' and then louder, 'but he's nearer than that. He's in Hampshire.' A pause, then, 'He's even nearer still – he's in Ropley.' Maddock leant over the pulpit, 'He's in this church, my friends.' And, finally, in a whisper, 'The devil is in our hearts, in yours and mine, and we must resist him.'

Women wept. Children were confused and frightened. The remaining faces displayed either anger or hope. It would take many years before the church was ever full again.

Out in the fine spring evening, the early leavers mixed with a steady stream walking or riding towards Monkwood. Word of Maddock's sermon floated through the crowd. Among this community, the new pastor was soon 'intensely disliked and regarded with whole-hearted aversion and hatred'.[2] The destination was a small clearing in the woods laid out like a fair.[3] Deliveries received yesterday from the south coast were on offer: wine, gin and brandy, silk, lace and fine handkerchiefs, perfumes, items for gambling like ivory dice and back-woven playing cards, sugar, chocolate and the increasingly sought after oilskin bags of tea.

Britain had to pay for its constant wars of the eighteenth century and for the final defeat of Napoleon at Waterloo. Amidst the fighting and the conquest of new lands, expanding trade brought exotic commodities. The difficulty of levying productive taxes on income and wealth to offset the national debt meant that import duties had to take a large part of the burden.[4] As more revenue was required, more items were taxed. By 1760, 800 items were taxed at import and a further 1,300 were added in the next fifty years. At its height, smuggling was believed to account for up to a third of all trade in England. In 1816, 370,000 gallons of gin and brandy and 4,200 yards silk were seized. In addition, 875 smuggling ships of all sizes were taken, but smuggling was so profitable that one undiscovered run in three was enough. The quantities of imported goods were extraordinary; a single smuggling trip could bring in 3,000 gallons of spirits – Illegally imported gin was sometimes so plentiful that the inhabitants of some Kentish villages were said to use it for cleaning their windows. And, according to some estimates, four-fifths of all tea drunk in England was not duty paid.

Into the nineteenth century, illegal trade along England's coast grew at a prodigious rate. What had previously been simple small-scale evasions of duty turned into an industry of astonishing proportions, syphoning money abroad, and channelling huge volumes of contraband into the southern counties of England. It was a great irony that the cost of beating Napoleon allowed the French to make great profit by abetting smuggling into England.

Apart from the public's strong demand for contraband, other factors encouraged tax evasion. The Customs Service was weak and under-staffed. Frequently, full scale battles with fatal casualties between the smugglers and excise officers involved hundreds of men. The second line or defence, the Revenue Service of Riding Officers and Dragoons, set up to seize smuggled goods once they had been landed clandestinely, was far from efficient. In 1736, smuggling was made a felony. Carrying firearms was a capital offence. Even when offenders were brought before the courts, the third line, the local magistrates, were often lenient as local law officers were sometimes beneficiaries. One can track the complicity of the judiciary by the low levels of punishment meted out.

In Ropley, no case ever made it to court.

The villagers' hatred of Maddock 'grew more and more pronounced until a regular system of persecution arose, and all was done that could be devised to molest and annoy him and his family'.[5] At first, following his opening salvo in 1818, incidents were petty. On Sundays, youths sat on the boughs of the great yew tree in the churchyard, which spread at that time as far as the porch, challengingly drinking alcohol. Mrs Maddock bought a new silk dress. During the evening service, black ditch mud, hidden in the dusk, was coated over the stile she would climb on her way home. The dress was spoilt. One Sunday morning, a pail of night water was thrown at the Maddocks and their children on their way from the doorway of what is now the blacksmith's house, but missed. Another Sunday, the Maddocks were greeted at the church by an effigy of a vicar hanging by the neck from a bough of an elm tree.

By October of the first year, the dissent had spread to Bishop's Sutton, which was a part of the responsibility of the parish of Ropley. Two publicans, John Lacey of Ropley, and Tom Baker of Bishop's Sutton, with John Ivy of Ropley, went to divine service at the parish church and 'uttered oaths and curses and pursued other most indecorous conduct.'[6] Their case was deferred to the next Quarter Sessions against a bond of £50. The *Hampshire Chronicle* hoped that the 'example made of these three young men will be a warning to others not to interrupt any clergyman in the discharge of his parochial duties, nor to disturb any congregation assembled for the worshipping of Almighty God'. It may have helped that one magistrate, Captain Duthy, was Maddock's nextdoor neighbour. It seems the case never got to Winchester.

Through these incidents, and many more, Maddock stood his ground.

Why did Ropley, which included most of modern Four Marks, become the centre for inland smuggling operations for the South of England? No other village away from the coast has such a concentration of verbal and written record backed by open rumour and known locations for hiding contraband.

France was the producer of most of the smuggled items and the French Government often encouraged the illicit trade. Hampshire and Dorset, across the Channel from France, were the greatest smuggling counties. While Kent was closer to London, the biggest market, its coast was often exposed and watched. The coastal areas of Hampshire and Dorset were favoured by the smuggler for their indentations and because they were less well guarded. Cornish and Devon coasts were more treacherous. Once landed at, say, one of the many creeks of the harbours at Langstone, Emsworth (supposedly then by a tunnel under Tower Street and into the cellars of Trentham House or to the Smugglers' Rest and on to a notorious pub near Nore Farm Avenue[7]) and at Chichester (to be hidden in old gravel workings off Brandy Hole Lane[8]), there were unsophisticated cart tracks heading north up river valleys and across open country.[9]

The profit was made by reaching a sales outlet far away from the coast at less cost than the retail price in England minus the price paid in France. Widely differing margins are quoted depending on circumstance and time, the amount of tax and the distance travelled and the number of men involved. Reports suggest up to 500 per cent might be available for expenses and to cover the profit needed to be made at every handover.

There were many varieties of business arrangement. As an example, brandy was sent neat to be re-distilled or diluted in England. It was despatched from source in France in small barrels, tubs, specially designed and made so that a man could carry two in a harness, one on his chest, the other on his back. The filled tubs were bought then transported to the French coast. A vessel was ready to take them part-way to England where a mid-Channel transfer to an English boat would occur. The tubs might be unloaded defiantly in broad daylight, or in a secluded cove or be attached to a raft and floated deep into a harbour. After unloading, the tubs were hidden until local purchasers could take their share. The majority, still unsold, were then loaded onto carts and taken inland to a distribution point. At each stage, until trust was established, it was cash on the nail. At the inland centre, everything needed to be rehidden until firm contracts were made for onward distribution to a customer, or another intermediary, probably in a major town.

The important point here for Ropley is that tubs of brandy did not arrive unordered or unexpectedly. There was a plan: gold coin in France supplied by London merchants and desperately needed by Napoleon to fight the British; money to be paid at the shore; tubs collected by carts or pack-animals sent for the purpose; a chosen and prepared route inland, much more expensive to cover than a sea voyage; hiding places ready around Ropley; and 'fences' alerted in Alton, Guildford, Reading and Winchester and, it is reported, as far as Bristol, Gloucester and Worcester.

The route taken to Ropley was from the harbours at Langstone, or adjacent coves, then to Titchfield and up the Meon Valley through Soberton, where a vault close to the chancel door at St Peter and St Paul was used for concealment, before cutting over to Cheriton and East Down Farm, near Sutton Scrubs in fox-hunting territory, a staging post used to keep an eye on the activities of the authorities.[10] Cheriton is also known as a gin smuggling route as many bottles from Holland have been found in contemporary cottages.[11]

The transportation and concealment needed at Ropley was so extensive that almost every able-bodied man was used to some degree and to some purpose. For the agricultural labourers on near starvation pay, it was a chance to take their families above the bread line. It is no coincidence that the men of Ropley played no part in the hunger riots of 1830.[12] Women were an essential part of this 'land smuggling', although playing a peripheral role. They sold, transported or hid contraband in their homes or about their person; they provided protection, alibis and assistance.[13]

Those few villagers outside the group were encouraged, as Rudyard Kipling put it, to '*Watch the wall, my darling, while the Gentlemen go by!*'

'Watch the wall, my darling …'. *Ogden's cigarette card*

There can be little doubt that all knew. The *Hampshire Chronicle* was full of reports.[14] A smuggling sloop called the *Elizabeth and Kitty*, with a boat attached to her, and a cargo consisting of 190 tubs of foreign spirits, seized by the *Vigilant* and *Scourge* revenue cutters : a smuggling vessel, the *Duck*, of Cowes, seized by *Vigilant* revenue cruiser off the Needles : eighty tubs of foreign spirits seized by a boat of the *Hound* revenue cutter near Brighton : the preventive[15] boat off Hamble fell in with a smuggling vessel which, after being boarded, was rescued by three other gallies, and the man who had boarded was thrown overboard : a cart laden with smuggled spirits was left at an inn yard near Romsey while the driver got refreshment and some persons made free with four tubs of brandy : William White and another man were indicted for raising signals [whistling] to a smuggling boat for the purpose of warning it. On hearing the whistle, men carrying tubs dropped them and ran. Nineteen tubs containing brandy, rum and Geneva [Dutch gin] were found: forty-four casks of contraband spirits seized at Pedlar's Barn, near Lymington, by the coastguard. One of the smugglers was taken, but shortly afterwards rescued.

As the smuggling trade grew, so did the rewards and the risks. 'An exasperated government applied increasingly severe penalties for smuggling and, for their part, the smugglers responded with escalating violence.'[16]

Sir John Cope's Parliamentary enquiry of 1736 highlighted the audaciousness of the gangs:

> *The smugglers being grown to such a degree of insolence, as to carry on their wicked practices by force and violence, not only in the country and remote parts of the kingdom, but even in the city itself, going in gangs, armed with swords, pistols and other weapons, even to the number of forty or fifty, by which means they have been too strong, not only for the officers of the revenue, but for the civil magistrates themselves who have not been able to put a stop to these pernicious practices, even by the assistance of regular forces as have been sent to their aid. The sloops and boats appointed for preventing the running of goods have likewise been beaten off by a greater number of armed men on board smuggling vessels ... The number of custom-house officers who have been beaten, abused and wounded since Christmas 1723, being no less than 250, beside six officers who have been actually murdered.*

The most vicious of these groups of smugglers was probably the Hawkhurst Gang, named after their base in Kent, which terrorised the country people along the southern coast as far as Dorset. After losing a battle with the villagers of Goadhurst, near Tunbridge Wells, the gang collapsed, some of its members turned informers, fourteen were arrested and seven were hanged on The Broyle earthwork in Chichester in 1747.

But, again, why Ropley as the northern centre of the Hampshire smuggling trade?

There are a number of logistical and geographical reasons. Ropley was more than twenty miles inland, well away from regular revenue searches. It was a remote dispersed community, off the turnpike, and could be reached by little-travelled paths. It was beech wood country with a large number of country houses and farms with cellars and out-of-the way fields, reaching to isolated places in current day Four Marks at Brislands, Cobb, Headmore, Hawthorn, Kitwood, many at Maddock's arrival already 200 years old. The area was a steady day's journey, finishing after dusk without having to climb the Four Marks ridge. The village also enjoyed the active connivance of the clergy, for instance, Maddock's predecessor, William Evans, in position for seven years, allowed free use of the church and its tithe barn, as did his partner-in-Christ at Medstead. It was also a convenient, neutral and discreet meeting place for the men from the cities who financed the smuggling operations to meet and agree terms.

It was Ropley for all of these things, but also one more which was the greatest.

The gentry at Ropley were the organisers, the syndicate and the moneymen behind the whole route from the coast to the village and onwards into the major towns. One needs first to look for men who got rich quickly and lived comfortably in the big houses. The trade was carried on 'with a high hand in Ropley for many years'.[17] These men also ran the church and the local courts. They were the stalwarts of the community that the authorities turned to in time of trouble and need.

Just as the squires demanded the best brandy, so, too, their daughters expected the best French lace. Tilling the rich soil a little way inland made many a farming fortune. The immediate ancestors of those who now live a quiet and honest life of industry, prominent in their community, gained their wealth by illicit profit as criminals.

Among them, Major John Lavender, of Ropley Grove, a much-respected Justice of the Peace, a churchwarden and a subscriber to the Hunt, stands tall. Lavender was everything that a respectable country squire ought to be except that he was also a smuggler. He lived some seven dwellings from Maddock.

One noon, Revenue Officers arrived requesting Squire Lavender to sign a search warrant for what is now Smugglers' Cottage in Monkwood where contraband was thought concealed.[18] Lavender offered them dinner. Meanwhile, his groom was sent to warn the cottage where the goods were lowered into a 200-foot well. When the Revenue Officers arrived, they found 'nothing for the Service', the official phrase in their journal for a fruitless search.[19] This story is covered at length in Hagen's *Annals of Ropley*.

In 1928, the owner of the Ropley Grove, Vice-Admiral Wilfred Henderson, found under the stone floor of his dining room, a brick-lined, seven-foot cubic chamber, empty apart from earth and rubble, a storage place for contraband.[20]

What is even less well known is that Lavender's cousin, also John, a blacksmith, lived on Portsea Island among the smugglers and a short distance from Langstone Harbour. He was rich for a blacksmith and owned several houses in Hanover Street. Here is the underlying reason why Ropley was the northern centre of the trade. The Lavender cousins managed the opposite ends of the land corridor.

Maddock it can be seen was a brave, but exposed man. He had decided to challenge his entire village from the very livelihood of the poor to the extreme wealth and comfort of the rich.

It wasn't long before an attempt on his life was considered which, one has to assume, was sanctioned on high. *'Will no one rid me of this turbulent priest?'*

A great deal of secret plotting, as was afterwards discovered, took place amongst the young men at *The Five Bells*, now turned into a cottage, at the top of the village near the pond. This public house was also known as 'Hell Corner'.

The *Five Bells* public house, *Hell Corner* – now a home in Ropley – where the plot to kill the vicar was hatched.

Marianna Hagen, nextdoor neighbour to the Maddock family, tells the story:

A young man who then worked for Mr Maddock was one of the conspirators, but he was good-natured and of a kindly heart. He was one of the few who liked and believed in Mr Maddock, and it was much against his will to be drawn into the plot. But he was afraid to stand alone. He determined, however, to save Mr Maddock from the threatened danger, were it possible, to do so, come what might of his interference.

Every Friday evening, a little service used to be held in a cottage at Charlwood about two miles from the vicarage, conducted by the Vicar, to which he and Mrs Maddock used to drive.

One day, this man came to Mr Maddock saying, 'I beg of you, sir, not to go to the Cottage meeting at Charlwood next Friday.'

'For what reason?' enquired the vicar.

'I can't say more, sir, but I do pray you not to go. There is danger in it.'

Mr Maddock was not to be put off, especially as the young man could give no reason. However, he begged his wife not to accompany him, but she was as firm as her husband, saying, 'We will go together, whatever it may mean. If there is danger I must share it with you.'

The evening was dark and ominous looking and heavy storm clouds lowered overhead. On the long hill at Monkwood there is a steep declivity leading down from the high road into a lane. The sides of it are covered with blackberry bushes, wild flowers and bracken; there is no rail or fence to protect against a fall. At this spot, as the sequel showed, a number of conspirators were concealed, and their intention was to jump out suddenly as soon as the vicar appeared, cut the traces and hurl his carriage down this declivity into the lane below, trusting that in this way his neck might perhaps be broken, or that at the least he might receive some very serious injury.

At the very moment of action, there came a flash of lurid lightning, so vivid that it seemed to rend the heavens and a clap of terrific thunder followed it instantly. Some say that a thunderbolt fell.

'Never was such a flash seen before,' said the men afterwards.

The men were terribly alarmed and conscience stricken, believing that the Heavenly Powers had intervened to save their victim. They rushed up to Mr Maddock, confessing all and begging for his forgiveness.

No date is given for the attempted murder. It is the only story in this book which does not have a body if you dismiss all those who died in the smugglers' battles on the south coast. There were numerous instances of whole communities uniting and taking up arms to reclaim cargoes that had been seized by the revenue. The difference between murder and attempted murder could be small.

The trade did not stop over night. Ropley's criminal influence under the guidance of Lavender and his cronies was extensive and the local people continued needy. 'During the eighteenth century the practice of smuggling possessed attractions for many Hampshire people ... There are many traditions of smuggling adventures, hairbreadth escapes and the capture of contraband goods with tales of caves, secret cellars beneath cottages, and stores of spirits, tobacco and other smuggled goods as far north as Ropley.'[21] Neighbourhood caves, with locations since lost, may be a stretch of the imagination but they may signify holes dug in embankments and old quarries. The list of hiding places is too long to ignore.

In and around the village, the church tower and the tithe barn at the Old Parsonage were regular storage spaces. The younger Mr Duthy of Ropley House covertly encouraged the smugglers and lent his father's horses at night. When Captain Duthy got to know this he turned his son out of the house. Ropley House was built upon the foundation of a much older house. During renovations, a flight of steps was discovered 'leading down no one knew where'; a villager described a 'Mediterranean' passage leading to across to the old school.

One man from Monkwood, Henry Prior, obtained a cart-load of whisky kegs at Portsmouth and was about to depart when the custom-house got wind and gave chase. Prior galloped the thirty miles to Ropley and arrived safely with his kegs which were hidden in the big beech wood on Monkwood Hill.[22]

Just beyond Lyewood House, a narrow lane drops down right into a gorge while the Petersfield Road continues up the hill. This is Smugglers' Lane and on the right near its bottom is the white-walled house called 'Smugglers' with its deep well and whose occupants were alerted by Lavender.

In Medstead, contraband was stored in the church tower.[23] The *Castle of Comfort* was hazarded as a smuggler's pub.[24] One needs to ask the purpose of the large, hollow buttress in the sizable cellar of the old *Lymington Arms* on Lymington Bottom Road, now with a blocked entrance under the floor of Clementines fruit and vegetable shop. Goatacre Farm was thought a smuggling centre with its cave, wherever that may be, a sister to another between the village and Wivelrod. A secret room was found in the chimney of an old South Town house.[25]

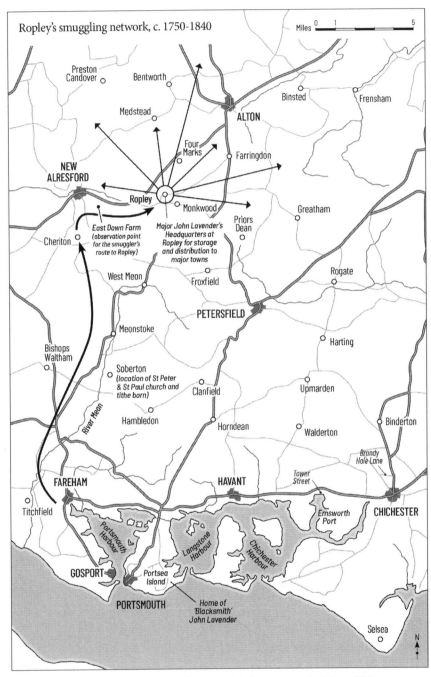

Ropley's smuggling network, c. 1750-1840

The Hampshire smugglers' secluded inlets and their route up the Meon Valley to a look out at East Down Farm near Cheriton. Then on to the distribution headquarters at Ropley with many scattered hiding places in the village and in the surrounding area. Note the homes of the Lavender cousins.

Two wells were used as dumps in Preston Candover with a cave near one reputed big enough to accommodate a coach and horses.[26] The tower of Alresford church was used for storage while, remembered a late rector, 'the vestry was considered a particularly safe place as it was certain that no one would enter it from Monday morning till Saturday night'.[27] There is a 'Brandy Mount off East Street in Alresford; a Brandy Mount Cottage in Cheriton; a dung heap, long gone, and used for storage where the Bighton road joined Winchester Road; at West Tisted, a 'nest with forty eggs in it', a dell with forty tubs at the bottom; hiding places at Herriard Park and the little church of Nateley Scures, near Hook.[28]

John Lavender died, aged sixty-five, in 1840 and was buried by Samuel Maddock. The family tombstone is at the east end of the north transept of St Peter's Church. Despite Maddock's vehement objections to Lavender's secret trade, there is no evidence that he ever denounced the criminals in his village to the authorities.

Marianna Hagen, Maddock's nextdoor neighbour, determined that the vicar gradually won over the people of Ropley. 'He was a good man and a just; one who was not afraid to rebuke the wrong-doer and to stand firmly for the cause of God and true religion … and lived to overcome entirely all dislike and opposition, and become the beloved of his parishioners, who learnt to respect and honour him greatly.' Maddock was a born humourist and storyteller. With early medical training and a basic knowledge of the law, he became central to the village's life. 'I be going down to Mr Maddock,' was the cry on many occasions of difficulty.

What made Maddock remarkable in his stand against smuggling was that he took on more than than his own village flock. He also found that his predecessor was deeply embedded in the trade giving over the church tower and its tithe barn to Lavender and his men. Maddock was unable to turn to his fellow priests for support for, in almost every direction, they were mired in the business of concealment and freely lent their own churches for the purpose.

When Maddock died, aged eighty-five, a local street was named after him. All the schoolgirls had bonnets with black ribbon round them and black capes or shawls were worn in his memory for six months.

But, to add some perspective, the years soon after Major Lavender died saw the benefits of peace. In 1842, Prime Minister Robert Peel reintroduced income tax which foreshadowed less reliance on import duties. Britain adopted a free-trade policy and in three acts from 1842 to 1846, 1,200 items were freed of duty.[29]

Within ten years, large-scale smuggling was just a memory. There was no longer any need to kill the vicar. In 2014, St Peter's Church was largely destroyed by fire.

ENDNOTES

[1] See Pooks Hill in Chapter 3, 'The elf and the archbishop'.

[2] Hagen, *Annals*.

[3] Mason, *Ropley*.

[4] Hogarth, *Ropley Smuggling*

[5] Hagen, *Annals*.

[6] *Hampshire Chronicle*, 2/11/1818.

[7] Reger, *Emsworth*.

[8] *Chichester Post*, 11/8/2018.

[9] Hare, *Secret Shore*.

[10] Platt, *Guide to Smuggler's Britain*. 'East-down farm' mentioned in Duthy, Sketches of Hampshire, 1829, as being near a wood called Sutton Scrubs from which Waller's forces were forced to retire before the Battle of Cheriton.

[11] Morley, *Smuggling*

[12] The *Swing Riots*. See Chapter 9, 'Knowing One's Place'.

[13] Platt, *Smuggling in British Isles*.

[14] *Hampshire Chronicle*: 22/3/1819, 22/3/1819,17/1/1820, 24/2/1823, 24/2/1823, 24/7/1826, 29/11/1830.

[15] The 'Preventive Waterguard', also known as the Preventive Boat Service, was formed in 1809 to combat smuggling.

[16] Hare, *Secret Shore*.

[17] Hagen, *Ropley*.

[18] Morley, *Smuggling*. Hagen, Ropley.

[19] Story confirmed by local resident, George Hale.

[20] Letter from Henderson, 7/10/1928. Henderson was appointed to command the 1,500-strong First Royal Naval Brigade to help defend Antwerp at the beginning of WWI. The Brigade was cut off. Rather than surrender to the Germans and become prisoners of war, Henderson led his men across the border into Holland where they were interned for the duration. He was ordered not to escape.

[21] Shore, *Hampshire*.

[22] Or Henry Price of Monkwood, story from James Smith, Ropley.

[23] Platt, *Guide to Smuggler's Britain*.

[24] Townsend, *Smugglers' Pubs*.

[25] Moody, *Short History of Medstead*.

[26] Platt, *Guide to Smuggler's Britain*.

[27] Curtis, *Alton and Villages*.

[28] Mason, *Ropley*.

[29] May, *Smugglers and Smuggling*

Reading list:

Hagen, Marianna S, *Annals of Old Ropley* (No publisher, 1929)

Hare, Chris, *The Secret Shore, Tales of Folklore and Smuggling from Sussex and Hampshire* (South Dows Society, Pulborough 2016)

Hogarth, Peter, 'Ropley in the Age of Smuggling', No. 84, www.alresford.org

Mason, Frederick, edited, *Ropley Past and Present, A Brief Story of a Hampshire Village* (Scriptmate Editions, London 1989)

May, Trevor, *Smugglers and Smuggling* (Shire, Oxford 2014)

Moody, Nellie, *A Short History of Medstead* (1932)

Morley, Geoffrey, *Smuggling in Hampshire and Dorset 1700–1850* (Countryside Books, Newbury 1994)

Platt, Richard, *The Ordnance Survey Guide to Smugglers' Britain* (Cassell, London 1991); *Smuggling in the British Isles, A History* (History Press, Stroud 2011)

Rathbone, Lorents, *A Chronicle of Medstead* (1966)

Reger, A.J.C., *A Short History of Emsworth and Warblington (Havant Borough History Booklet No. 6)*

Townsend, Terry, *Hampshire Smugglers' Pubs* (PiXZ Books, Wellington, 2016)

5 ROMAN REMAINS
The coming of the Saxons

AD 407 BODY COUNT: PERHAPS 29

The historical narrative for Roman Britain comes to a dramatic halt in AD 410, for in that year the diocese was formally cut off from imperial protection and became increasingly alienated from the distant chroniclers of Rome's fall. Likewise, as payment ceased to reach the remnants of the imperial army stationed along the British limes [frontiers], coinage ceased to enter the archaeological record, and we are left without that method of dating new structures and settlement. The tumultuous events of 406–10 – the last in Britain to be detailed by Roman historians – therefore deserve close scrutiny for they resulted in a Britain that is both remarkable for its bold initiatives for independent rule and self-defence and frustratingly elusive of the historian's grasp.

Snyder, *An Age of Tyrants*

Communus sat with his three-legged stool tilted against the slatted timber wall of the inn. Across the gravel road stood a chair bodger, one foot in the gutter, the other moving at a steady pace to make a leg from local beech wood. There was a cluster of pottery shops in the market square; one shop had a saucy sideline in genital-shaped pottery to tickle the passing military trade. If Vindomis was famous for anything other than its wine, it was the pots from the local woodland estate that the wine went into.[1] People were out shopping and gawking.

Vindomis [Neatham, near Alton] was a civilian settlement across the river from a major mansio, a military staging post where despatch riders changed horses and rooms were available for those on official business.[2] Next to the bodger was a small beer house, an awful drink to the Romans, but gaining in popularity with a cosmopolitan audience. It was late September with a strong afternoon sun. The tavern was doing brisk business.

Communus was a strong man, a wrestler years ago, and a successful commander, but in the wrong army. He watched as another column of sweating soldiery sang their way into view, lifting their voices a little, as they glimpsed the brick-walled mansio with aisles half an *actus* long.[3] Next door was levelled ground suitable for their cluster of eight-man tents to be assembled for an overnight stop.

Two *optios*, seconds-in-command from an earlier group, having settled their men and been released by their *centurions*, blocked the sunlight. One hooked a stool and sat down, his hobnails sparking on the flint floor.

'Mind if we join you?'

The soldiers picked at their teeth with sharp animal bones. The innkeeper arrived as they settled and half-filled two large, dark beakers with deep red wine. The beakers wore graffiti scratched by previous drinkers. Communus nodded for a top up. A grey jar of spring water was placed on the table with some flat spelt wheat bread and a bowl of goat's cheese and hard-boiled eggs.

'It's the *Balisca* grape,' offered Communus. 'We brought it over from Gaul ten years ago and we're trying here. That's why this place is called *Vindomis*, mansio of the wine country. It stands being drunk young, but needs some water.'

'You know your wine? Where are you from?'

'I came with the wine from Bordeaux. My master has a villa less than ten miles from here where he grows vines and hopes to make a lot of money. I am here to buy 1,000 vine stocks for him. We are expanding.'

'Not a good time to be putting *denarii* into this country,' suggested the younger optio. 'We're from the XXth Legion and we've just marched fifteen miles from *Calleva* [Silchester].[4] We're mostly from Germany; some of the old-timers are from Spain. We know we're going to *Noviomagis Regnensium* (Chichester) tomorrow, that's another short hop of about twenty miles. We'll be taking a *cortia*, no doubt, squeezed in with 1,000 tons of cargo and evil-smelling oarsmen who don't know their left from their right. That is if Saxon raiders don't keep us in harbour.

'I wonder how much of the Roman Army will be left in Britain by next year.'[5]

'We've got a new leader, a general called Constantine,' explained his comrade. 'He was a common soldier like us and we voted him in last year because we hadn't been paid. We wanted a strong man, but we liked the history in his name and we made him Western Roman Emperor so he's your new emperor, too.'[6]

Communus looked surprised.

'Never heard of him, then? You will soon. It takes time. He needs a few victories. We tried two others as leader before him, but they were hopeless and so we got rid of them. I'll wager Constantine will send us to Gaul to try to pull everything together, but that leaves you guys to your own devices. Who knows if we'll ever come back?

'You'll need to look to your own protection.'

The men threw a few games of dice. Communus tried hard not to win too much. The conversation became more gloomy as the *optios* thought about their coming voyage and who and where they would be fighting and how it was all going to end up. One or two more good battles and they might get promotion or, as time-servers, receive some allotment of land near their homes. It was always the same story with every aspiring and ageing soldier.

His two acquaintances left, tossing a *sesterce* on the table, and made for the flint-built bathhouse, the stones flashing in the sun. Communus sat glumly watching the legion's mule trains plod endlessly past. If his Roman masters were pulling out of Silchester, how long would it be before Chichester was vulnerable? Here he was sitting with 2,500 civilians on a strategic crossroad from *Londinium* [London] to *Venta Belgarum* [Winchester] and about halfway between Chichester and Silchester. He had been to Silchester once to buy grain in a bad winter. There must be another 10,000 people living there. And London, a city of more people than could be imagined, and a place most men locally had only heard of but never seen. What prizes to leave open!

Picking his way through the local gossip, Communus started to count other potential enemies. Everyone knew the Saxons were making 'hit and run' raids on Britain. The Romans had recently built a line of watchtowers along the 'Saxon Shore' from the Great Bay [the Wash] to *Portus Adurni* [Portchester] to give early warning. From the last century, forts had been backed by cavalry, which provided the Roman army with much needed mobility. But the cavalry had left. Who would man the towers now?

Last year, massed armies of the Angles, Jutes, Saxons, Friesians and Franks crossed a frozen Rhine and devastated the newly settled provinces of Gaul that lay open before them. With no effective Roman response, these pagans nibbled away at the British shoreline sensing weakness. The government feared a barbarian invasion across the channel and believed they would receive little help from their imperial rulers.[7]

The Scotti tribe from Ireland had already made substantial landings in the northwest; beaten back, yes, but they were getting bold again and attacking ports in the southwest.[8] Right in the north, the painted Picts, although badly beaten by Germanicus years ago, still hated the Romans and thirsted for revenge. 'Restless barbarians could not neglect the fair opportunity ... if the walls and stations of the province were stripped of the Roman troops.'[9]

None of these enemies formed regular large armies that could be brought to the decisive pitched battle that the Romans needed. They were loose, fluid, mobile hordes, able to leak through a hundred small gaps, concentrate against major weaknesses or disperse and disappear. The defenders may have packed the hardest punch. But where to punch?[10]

And then there were the enemies at home. Most of his workers on the estate were Celts, *Belgares*. Winchester had been their capital before the Romans came 400 years ago and swept up the river from the estuary at *Clausentum* [Southampton].[11] You never knew with *Belgares*: one minute they were happy and respectful then, the next, they claimed one of their many Gods was insulted and 'surly' wasn't the word for it. Most of them probably hated him and, if it wasn't him that put their backs up, his lord and master was guaranteed to attract trouble.

Publicis Gauis Germanicus, a right mouthful, was a barbarian, captured, made slave, ferocious fighter, freed for his bravery, and rose to high command in Stilicho's army. Stilicho was the Vandal-born chief military commander of the western emperor Honorius. In 398, in Scotland, Germanicus led the final assault in the full-scale war against the Picts with such ferocity that his enemy was 'broken and Britain secure'.[12] Didn't he let everyone know it!

For his services, Germanicus was allocated 100 grids of empty wood and scrub on hills to the south of Neatham on the road from London to Winchester. He was desperate for further official recognition. His plan was to create the best wine estates in the country so that his wealth could buy a high place in the government. He was already constructing the private army and relationships he might need. He had no patience, no respect for others, beat his wife, daughters and house servants and, worse, he hated Christians. For Communus, that was a particular problem.

Most Romans were polytheists, willing to allow the like-minded Celts to worship their own similar traditional gods and goddesses, so similar that temples were often dedicated to both the Celtic god and the Roman equivalent. In contrast, Romans destroyed the Druids because of their political and social influence and now they were intolerant of Christians with their dangerous ideas of unity. At times, persecution swept across the empire. St Alban, the first British Christian martyr, was executed a century before in Verulamium. Aaron and Julius died also, but little was known of them. Emperor Constantine granted Christians freedom of worship; three British bishops attended a church council in *Arelate* [Arles].[13] But that wasn't how it was on the ground. For Germanicus, religion and self-advancement were two sides of the same coin.

An hour later, Communus made a decision. Even Germanicus would see the wisdom of putting off the purchase of wine stock. In case of trouble, a lot of money might be saved. He went to the factor to arrange a promise to purchase in a month, still just enough time to plant.

He gathered his men, with the horses and their cart loaded in one corner with provisions, and fought off protestations and fear of the anger to come when they returned without a large number of stocks. The cart trundled over the settlement's triple ditch while the men wrinkled their noses against the smell of the small brass foundries in the rough chalk hovels. They passed the small white cemetery outside the walls. The road dipped to the ford and then gently climbed for a mile to the *Haligburna* [Holybourne] stream.[14] A pond was fed by several chalk springs rising from a green sand outcrop. This was a potent healing place denoted by rags hanging from the trees. Communus swam briefly with his head under water for the soreness in his eyes. His men sat, watched and joked for a while, as they had no belief.

The party stopped again at the river's source, another collection of springs haphazard on a hillside covered in late wild flowers. Water from here was not medicinal, but it was good tasting.

Germanicus had a carting arrangement with an old farm with a large villa near the source and the men called in briefly to deposit some stores.[15] Communus had been inside only once. It was the previous winter when the *hypocaust* provided a welcome relief from the snow. He joined other guests in nipping between the warm *tepidarium* and the hot *caldarium*. A maidservant oiled him thoroughly and then scraped him clean with a *strigil*. He spent a long time admiring the floor mosaics of African animals and birds and many strange fruits. The owner had brought in an artist from a place near the coast, the largest palace north of the Alps that had burned down and was abandoned.

The upward road was two carts wide, with its base of gravel and clay packed solid by the irregular traffic. Its cambered flint surface showed the care taken in construction. The way zig-zagged at first then climbed straight and true through a large wood. Out of sight in the thick trees, there were occasional sounds of animals – wild bulls, cows or boars – showing no thieves were lurking. The wolves were quiet and asleep.[16] Just over the summit, much beech and oak had been cleared for cultivation by Communus and his workers. This was the start of the site of the latest vineyards. Communus had spent several days persuading Germanicus that by offering some of this land to the labourers, they would get more land, better cleared in quicker time.

Many tracks led on either side to form grids, twenty by twenty-five actus, in a method of land division called centuriation.[17]

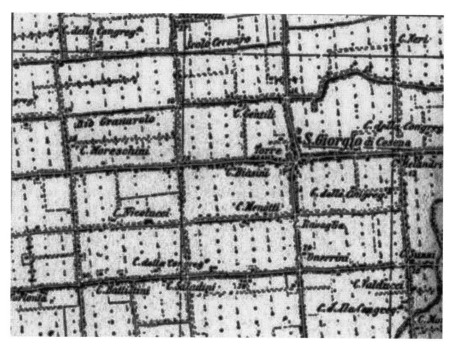

Centuriation near Cesena, Italy, in a late nineteenth century Italian military map. *commons. wikimedia.org/w/index.php?curid=1666714*

Communus remembered standing on a central viewpoint, the *umbilicus agri*, when the first trees had been cleared and taken to fuel the heating at his master's villa. The land in front was called the *ultra*, *citra* behind, *dextera* to his right and *senistra* to his left. The visiting surveyor began to trace the grid using a *groma*, making two road axes perpendicular to each other. So far, they had laid down some fifty squares, *heredia*, each divided in two, the amount of ground that could be ploughed in one day by a pair of oxen.

The memory of his hard and fruitful work brought him some pride. Communus pulled his horse to watch the cart toiling upwards. It was then that the arrow hit him from behind in the left shoulder blade and he slipped to the ground.

✿ ✿ ✿ ✿

One of the Pilgrims' Way routes takes a track from the road junction on the bend at Kitwood, passes through a kissing gate, crosses a small meadow and then on to the large ploughed field that reaches towards and around Old Down Wood. This depleted wood was once part of the great Andreasweald Forest that extended into Sussex and part of Surrey. Alice Holt, the home of extensive Roman potteries serving Neatham and its crossroad trade via a spur road, and Woolmer, wolves' marsh, are the only extensive woods that remain locally. Near Four Marks, Dogford Wood, Charlwood, Winchester Wood and Cheriton Park are other vestiges. Old Down has been cut into since Roman times leaving sharp-edged boundaries where wood has been converted to farmland.

One spring about five years ago, green barley shoots had begun to show. It was a regular walk. Two days before, I had discussed war poetry with my grandson and the power of the flag as a symbol. What would make thinking men rush across an open field into well-directed fire? Ahead of us, tall aged trees edged the wood, the centre ripped out to be a plantation of fir. At the heights against empty blue sky, ravens and buzzards scrapped noisily for territory. I suggested an experiment. My grandson was to run as fast as he could towards Old Down, all the time hearing the stutter of several machine guns aimed at him and his fellows. He set off. After thirty yards, he fell to the ground waiting for me to catch up.

'I was really frightened,' he gasped.

Today, *Misty*, the greatly missed retriever, waited patiently, field side, for my call. The path had been turned as every year and needed the feet of walkers to re-establish it in an attempt at a straight line, everyone unsure of the route to the far destination. Dozens of skylarks rose and sang. Unusually for these times, four lapwings scratched about. In the mid distance, the heads of two roe deer peered apprehensively. I gave a scarecrow signal and *Misty* dashed for her treats.

Two thirds of the way to the wood, I saw the Roman roof tiling. Given the terracotta texture and size, and with experience, the tiles are unmistakable. My find was a generous piece of an *imbrex*, a half pipe enlarging towards one end. I moved it and worked around with my fingers, fending off *Misty*, and found the corner of a *tegulae*, flat, oblong with one raised ridge still attached. *Imbrices* and *tegula* work together to make waterproof rooves, the pipe of the *tegula* fitting snuggly as a joint over the upward raised edges of two flat *imbrices* side by side. These pieces were not rough-cast local manufacture, but had been produced by skilled craftsmen.

I moved them further into the field, out of sight of casual passers-by. When I came back with carrier bag a week later, they were gone. Not even *Misty* could find them.

Archaeologists build palaces from broken pottery, coins and tesserae. My lost find intrigued me.

First, the tiles had no business there. This was an open field with a foot-beaten earthen track. In the 1930s, the field was itself wooded, stretching to Kitwood hamlet. There were no houses except at the field edge, all new; none of them used a copycat Roman roof. They had no sign of cementing or holes in the tiles to be used to combat today's high winds and planning regulations. Nor was this a track where any builder's rubble had been used to toughen up the pathway.

Second, the tiles had a deeper, semi-glazed surface, which was not normal and were part-engrained with soot. Both fragments had been in a fire.

Does one associate the Romans with Four Marks?

Perhaps, if I should tell you there are 138 proven Roman sites within ten miles of the village.[18] There are a string of probable Roman villas along the high ground between Farnham and Alton. The area around Alton is claimed to have had the highest concentration of Roman villas anywhere in the UK apart from the Cotswolds. Elaborately constructed villas have been found in mainland Hampshire at Abbot's Anne, Bitterne, Bramdean, Crondall, Itchen Abbas, Liss, Porchester, Rockbourne, Thruxton, Twyford and Winchester. Smaller, but substantial properties have been found at Ladyplace Gardens in Alton, north of Bighton Wood, Wyck Place in Binsted, Colemore, Coldrey at Lower Froyle and at Martyr Worthy; then there are earthworks at Stoner Hill (past *The Trooper Inn*) and Stroud.

There are seemingly only three known traces of centuriation in Roman

Britannia, two in Sussex and one on the road from Chawton Park Wood towards Winchester, recently uncovered and under detailed investigation.[19] The ground falling away to the southwest was, potentially, a major agricultural clearance. There is a high concentration of ditches and boundaries parallel and at right-angles to each other stretching from Medstead to Four Marks and out to New Alresford, Tichborne and Cheriton. Based on the vineyards at Neatham, and with current day similar businesses at Winchester, Hattingley in Lower Wield, Hurstbourne Priors, Itchen Stoke and East Meon, grapes may have been one of the likely intended crops.

The London to Winchester road has long been suspected, but only recently is on the edge of being confirmed.[20] William Camden wrote in 1607 that 'from this place [Alresford] to Alton there goes all along a Roman Highway, part of which makes a Head to an extraordinary great Pond here at Alresford'.[21] In 1690, John Aubrey saw 'all along, a perfect Roman way from Aulton to Alresford'.[22] After cutting across Alton, with perhaps a deviation near the modern library, the road begins its climb at Ackender Wood with a large terrace and joins Chawton Park Wood through a zig-zag. A broad ditch runs for a third of a mile up a narrow valley to the summit of the downs and enters a centuriation of estate roads.[23] Although not particularly hilly, except at Chawton Park Wood 'all the constructional evidence identified is associated with sloping ground' often with pure and mixed ager terraces.[24] The next investigations are scheduled and will draw more definitive lines.

Roman coins are ubiquitous in the wider area: 106 were found at Neatham in one dig; a low value dupondius at Holybourne; of Augustus at Selborne, of Faustina at the *Golden Pot*, of Valentinian at Bentworth as well as coins of Carausius in Selborne and Claudius II in Alton and Commodus at Shalden Green and Constantine at Anstey. Most important for this story are bronze coins found in Medstead of Antoninus Pius (138–161) at Field View, Homestead Road (1949), Constantine the Great (306–337) at 'Larchwood', Paice Lane (1943), Constantine II (337–340) at Lymington Bottom Road (1963) and three suspected Roman coins found on land adjacent to Cedar Stables behind Castle Street (1993).

Then there is Roman pottery found at Bentworth, an amphora at Hattingley, greyware and New Forest ware at Nutley, an imbrex at Old Alresford, tesserae at Axford and a probable aqueduct from the Candover Valley to Winchester via Itchen Abbas and Kings Worthy.

The following year, I heard a late morning ring at my doorbell and a casual acquaintance invited me to the boot of his car. Inside was a large lump of Roman hypocaust broken in two, several flat square tiles held together by layers of rough cement. At the break, on the underside of one tile was the unmistakable 'Z'-scrape made by the mason. I gave my findings.

Hypocaust under the floor of a Roman villa in Vieux-la-Romaine, near Caen, France. *commons.wikimedia.org*

'What's it worth?'

'Nothing at all except to a museum or an archaeologist who might want to dig where you found it. They are not rare. These piles of bricks held up the floor of a villa and allowed hot air to pass around and perhaps up through vents to provide an early and excellent form of central heating.'[25]

'Nothing?'

'I'll buy it for a fiver if you tell me where you found it,' I said.

He thought briefly. 'No, I'll see if I can get a better offer.'

'OK. Best of luck. I'll still buy you a pint next time I see you if you tell me roughly where it's from.' His muddy Alsatian was watching me closely through the back window.

'Well ...'

'How about near Old Down Wood? Where the track from Kitwood goes across the big field?

'Yeah. OK.'

Six months later, I was in the *Castle of Comfort* and got a slap on the back.

'I'll take that pint now,' my acquaintance said with a big beam on his face. As I handed over the glass, he announced, 'And I got £10 for that lump of stone. Sold it him over there with the cocker spaniel. He wanted to put it together with a Roman coin he'd found.'

We wandered over and got into conversation. The man, unshaven, wearing jeans and a dirty T-shirt, was a detectorist and wanted to be careful. He had found his coin on its own two inches below the surface in a field. He didn't have permission to search there and he didn't want to give up his find. He also wanted to go back and have another look.

'Can I see it?' I asked and he fished it out of his pocket. It was gold, a solidus in good condition, of the Emperor Honorius. 'Minted in Thessalonica,' I said. 'It's unusual around here. It's come a long way. You're a lucky boy.'

'You know something about Roman coins?' he asked. 'What do you think it's worth?'

I turned it over a few times. His eyes were sparkling.

'Tell me roughly where you found it and I'll give you my best guess. Perhaps somewhere near my mate's tiles that you bought?'

He nodded.

'Over five hundred and double that on a good day.'

His face went pale.

Solidus of Honorius, 393–423, minted in Thessalonica 393–395, which fetched about £500 in auction in 2020. *coinarchives.com*

I now knew quite a lot about 'my' villa. It was far beyond the rustic building of a traditional farmer. The site was close to the current village pond and offered a sweeping view over Alton Lane up to the Four Marks ridge. It was connected by a centuriation estate road through a massive area that was being cleared for farming on the Alton to Winchester road. The villa was modelled on a Roman building with a courtyard and enjoyed central heating where a fire was lit in a furnace and the hot air circulated under the floor.

A hypocaust was expensive. It burned large amounts of wood, of which there was plenty being cleared nearby. You needed slaves to keep loading fuel into the furnace. Only the rich could afford them. Wealthy 'late' villa owners also had mosaics and wall paintings and panes of glass in their windows. If you wanted to see one in Hampshire, the best was the Rockbourne villa near Fordingbridge.

The burned tiling suggested either an accident or a deliberate burning. The hypocaust was charred as well which could have been from its own fire, but the burning was mostly on the floor side. I speculated no accident.

Flavius Honorius Augustus came to his throne as a child in 393. His reign was precarious and chaotic, held together by his principal general, Stilicho. The Roman soldiery left Britain around 407 and when Honorius executed Stilicho the following year, the Western Roman Empire was near to collapse. Although Honorius reigned until his death from oedema in 423, I deduced that such a valuable coin as a golden solidus would not have come into the country after 407.

Perhaps there had been some cataclysmic event at Old Down Wood in the very early years of the fifth century?

✽ ✽ ✽ ✽

Germanicus was in the vanguard of a new landed elite who realised that they could no longer depend on the Roman government for advancement, and no longer saw the cities as the exclusive means to display their wealth and power. They turned to patron-client relationships to build a loyal body of supporters, with whom they eventually seized control of their districts.[26] As the Romans left, they increasingly stepped out of the shadows to take the reins of government in an independent Britain. The term most often used to describe them was *tyranni*, 'tyrants', and after 410, according to Saint Jerome, the island was 'fertile of tyrants'.[27]

Germanicus lay on a couch enjoying the late sun while fingering his torque of gold and contemplating a boar with crackling skin as it was slowly turned over charcoal by a slave and basted with olive oil by another. His eldest son, Publius, lay close by making inroads into a flagon of wine. Figs, walnuts and grapes were to hand. In the background, he heard his younger children playing.

His peace was shattered when a cart driven at pace rumbled in the yard after scattering fallow deer and pheasant from the edge of the wood.

'Saxons,' shouted the driver. Germanicus rushed over to see Communus lying with a broken arrow in his back. He picked up the fletching, four flights of swan feather, leather-bound.

'Saxon,' he agreed. He called for his wife to tend to Communus and some servants to carry him inside. His young children were ordered to the cellar. Publius was sent to round up the men and he sent two fast riders by little-used estate roads to alert Neatham. He then collected his armour and sword and looked to the defence of his property.

The Saxons' watery homeland was fast sinking beneath the sea, coastal settlements were being abandoned to the elements, and a class of seaborne warlords had arisen who offered an escape through violence and robbery.[28] From twenty years before, barbarians penetrated into the soft, rich hinterland of the southeast of England. Here they broke up into small bands to plunder at will. When sated, they headed home with herds of cattle, columns of slaves, and wagons piled high with booty. Many Roman units disintegrated in the chaos of defeat, and the countryside filled with deserters and bandits.[29]

In the first attack, Publius, young, inexperienced and anxious to prove himself to his father, sought little cover. He was struck by two arrows, one through the left eye which killed him. Germanicus cradled the body for a moment and then led his men in a headlong, rage-driven charge. Within five minutes, the fight was over. Fifteen Saxons lay dead and dying, six felled by Germanicus, and three others were captured. He took the captives, wounded or not, to his son's body and beheaded them one by one.

Six other Saxons in the treeline took flight along the path to the pond and to the south. Germanicus broke the news to his wife, left a small guard, gathered his men and horses and followed the running men. He caught them within a mile and slaughtered them.

As he stood among the bodies, heaving for breath, he saw the flames and smoke rising from his home. By the time he returned, the place was fallen brick and ashes. Communus, the few guards and most of the livestock, were dead. His wife and children had disappeared and were never found.

Nor, indeed, was his gold torque, lost somewhere in the fighting. In the dying light, he buried his son alongside Communus and two of his own men outside the wood under a small mound.

ENDNOTES

[1] Whaley, 'Optical Survey', 2007. Powell, 'Neatham: Excavation', 2008.

[2] Proof that Neatham was Vindomis is not conclusive, but it is increasingly likely based on recent archaeology, Margary, *Roman Roads*, and on Number XV, *The Antonine Itinera* from *Calleva Atrebatum* (Silchester) to *Isca Dumnoniorum* (Exeter).

[3] 1 actus = 120 pedes (feet) = 35.5 metres. The Roman foot (pes) = 296 mm. The Roman mile, the *mille passus* = 5,000 pedes.

[4] *Calleva Atrebatum*, thirty-nine miles from Chichester.

[5] Constantine III, a pretender, withdrew most (if not all) capable Roman troops from Britain in his bid for empire in 407, leaving the island independent but virtually defenceless … About the year 410, Rome officially recognised its loss of Britain … when the beleaguered emperor Honorius informed the Britons that they must defend themselves (Snyder, *Age of Tyrants*).

[6] Gibbon, *Decline and Fall*.

[7] Salway, *Roman Britain*.

[8] Salway, *Roman Britain*.

[9] Gibbon, *Decline and Fall*.

[10] Faulkner, *Rise and Fall*.

[11] Shore, *History of Hampshire*.

[12] Claudian, *On the Consulship of Stilicho*.

[13] Eborius of York, *Restitutus of London and Adelius of Caerleon*.

[14] *NEHHAS Journal*, Vol. 3, Part 3 (9), 'River Wey Crossing'.

[15] Graham, David, 'Archaeological Investigation: Ladyplace Gardens, Alton', 1988; altonbiddig.uk, Liss Archaeology, 2018–19.

[16] *Hampshire Notes & Queries*, Vol. VI.

[17] *NEHHAS Journal*, Vol. 3, Part 3 (10–11A).

[18] *Ordnance Survey*, 'Map of Roman Britain'. www.archiuk.com, accessed 5/2020.

[19] NEHHAS.

[20] See the excellent debate in the Hampshire Field Club Proceedings: Calow, 'Investigation', Weston, 'Roman Roads' and Whaley, 'Roman Roads'.

[21] For the Alresford Great Pond see in this book 'Conclusion'.

[22] John Aubrey, 1626–1697, was an English antiquary, natural philosopher and writer, perhaps best known as the author of the *Brief Lives* and as the discoverer of the Avebury henge monument. Also, Daniel Defoe, 1724, 'the great Roman Highway which leads from Winchester to Alton' and Thomas Cox, 1738, 'a Roman Highway' from Alton to Alresford.

[23] *NEHHAS*, FAB 1, 20.

[24] *NEHHAS Journal*, Vol. 3, Part 1.

[25] Fagan, 'Sergius Orata'.

[26] Snyder, *An Age of Tyrants*.

[27] Jerome, *Adversus Jovinianum*.

[28] Faulkner, *Decline and Fall*.

[29] Faulkner, *Decline and Fall*.

Reading list:

Calow, David, 'Investigation of a possible Roman Road at Bighton and Medstead', *Proceedings of the Hampshire Field Club Archaeological Society*, 53, Spring 2010, pp. 8–10

Dark, Ken, *Britain and the End of the Roman Empire* (Tempus, Stroud 2000)

Fagan, Garrett G., 'Sergius Orata: Inventor of the Hypocaust?', *Phoenix*, Vol. 50, No. 1, 1996, pp. 56–66

Faulkner, Neil, *The Decline and Fall of Roman Britain* (Tempus, Stroud 2000)

Gibbon, Edward, 'The End of the Western Empire', *The History of the Decline and Fall of the Roman Empire, Vol. IV* (The Folio Society, London 1986)

Jones, Michael E., *The End of Roman Britain* (Cornell University 1996)

Margary, Ivan D., *Roman Roads in Britain*, Vols 1&2, third edition (1973)

Ordnance Survey, *Map of Roman Britain, 10 Miles to One Inch*, 4th edition (Southampton 1978)

Powell, Andrew B., with many contributors, 'The Romano-British Small Town at Neatham: Excavation at the Depot Site, London Road, Holybourne, 2008', *Proceedings of the Hampshire Field Club Archaeological Society*, 69, 2014, pp. 49–81

Salway, Peter, *Roman Britain, Oxford History of England* (Oxford University Press 1991)

Smith, J.T., *Roman Villas: A Study in Social Structure* (Routledge, London 1998)

Snyder, Christopher A., *An Age of Tyrants, Britain and the Britons A.D. 400–600* (Sutton, Stroud 1998)

Weston, David, 'East of Winchester – 1', *Proceedings of the Hampshire Field Club Archaeological Society*, 49, Spring 2018, pp. 21–24

Whaley, Richard, 'Optical Survey of the Mansio at Neatham', *North East Hants Historical and Archaeological Society Journal* (NEHHAS), No 104, Autumn 2007; edited, *Roman Road Abstracts*, Version 6.1, NEHHAS 2014; NEHHAS, Vol. 3, Parts 1–3, 'Collected Reports on the Roman Road: Winchester to Guildford', revised 2014–15; 'East of Winchester – 2', *Proceedings of the Hampshire Field Club Archaeological Society*, 49, Spring 2018, pp. 25–26

Wilde, James, *The Bear King* (Bantam, Transworld 2020)

6 DEBRIS
Calling in at Four Marks

LONDON
2020   BODY COUNT: 1

The body of Abidemi Afolayan was found early in the morning sitting against the door of a backstreet bar, the *Fu Manchu*, in Clapham in south London.[1]

Afolayan, a man possibly in his late twenties, was very dead. His throat had been deeply slit and his life's blood was spread wide around, soaking his torn jeans. Garish slave beads from his ripped necklace were stuck fast in the congealed pool. Half a dozen string charm bracelets hung loose on his left wrist. His tired, dirty T-shirt carried the standard picture of Che Guevara of distant memory, but lightly overprinted with a recipe for a *Cuba Libre*. One trainer, a cheap imitation *Nike*, sat alone three yards away. For a bonus, Afolayan's cheeks had been slashed so that his teeth could be seen on both sides of face. His tongue was missing never to be found.

The bar owners, more interested in clearing up before the day-time vegetarian trade arrived, told the police they didn't recognise the body. He had certainly not been in the bar that week. He would never have got in dressed like that. They did say that he looked Nigerian.

The police were less than enthusiastic. They had three unsolved stabbings on their books already, all young black men, but there seemed little connection with Afolayan's death. Their caseload had the hallmarks of local bravado killings which suggested that retaliation in a tight community was likely. These three would get priority to try to stop further bloodletting. With Afolayan, the matter shrieked of organised crime, drugs or illegal immigrants. It promised a week of boring desk work with little chance of a result.

Personal papers found in the back pocket of the jeans said that Afolayan came from the town of Ijebu Ode in western Nigeria. There was a street address.

To the investigating officer's surprise, she received a return email from the

Lagos police the next day. To no one's surprise, Abidemi Afolayan was alive and well, a car mechanic, and living at his mother's home. His papers had been lost, stolen it seems, two months before. He had no criminal record and had never left his home state. In a surprising aside, the Nigerian email added that Afolayan was a Yoruba, a Christian and that his first name translated as 'born during his father's absence'.

Even the pathologist's report sounded half-awake. The body was undernourished with several sets of old bruises. Three ribs were still unmended. The last food had been a beef burger with onions, no chips. The teeth were in poor condition for a man of, say, twenty-eight. He died about six in the morning, two hours before he was found. Death was by exsanguination caused by a forceful, slow cut to the neck 'like it was done with relish while looking into the man's eyes'. It was likely the cheeks had been sliced first.

The detective checked the scanty possessions of 'Mr Nigerian 2' one last time: a grimy handkerchief more like a rag, a wallet with three one-pound coins, the travel papers, the wrist bands and necklace pieces in a plastic bag, a small black cross and, deep and rolled in the bottom of the brown evidence bag and missed first time around, three receipts for £29.99 each for single overnight accommodation from a Travelodge in some place called Four Marks.

The officer called the hotel by the number on the receipt and was diverted to an automated booking system. She logged in to the main site and learned that the company's number one priority was the safety and security of their customers and teams. 'TravelodgeProtect+' was their programme of cleaning and social distancing measures to keep everyone safe.

The Four Marks hotel was five miles south of Alton in Hampshire on the A31 with no dinner facility. While all standard double rooms featured a 'comfy king size bed with four plump pillows and a cosy duvet,' she read, 'guests can enjoy a variety of food and drink choices within a short car journey from the hotel'.

She finally forced her way through the system to a head office number in Sleepy Bottom, Thame, after an abrupt call to Goldman Sachs, the Travelodge chain's owner. The information then came quickly: the three invoices were for three single stays each seven days apart in February and March 2020. Each was pre-booked the day before and paid with a credit card. No breakfast had been taken. No car had been logged. The hotel security cameras showed the dead man alone.

The credit card led nowhere other than a warren of organised deceit and theft.

Nothing came back from Organised Crime or Customs at Southampton.

The detective spoke to her boss and proposed a visit for an overnight stay to check all the security footage for three months. The boss thought about it for a second and said, 'No'. There wasn't the budget and there was precious little likelihood of finding anything out.

Hampshire police didn't see it as a local case. The murder had occurred in London. All their officers were busy on coronavirus duties, checking the local pubs and on crowd control in Bournemouth.

The crime file gradually worked its way to the bottom of the tray, which is where it now rests.

ENDNOTES

[1] *Clapham Junction e-news.*

7 SENDING A MESSAGE
The loneliness of the semaphore station

TELEGRAPH FARM, TELEGRAPH LANE
1830   BODY COUNT: 1

George Ogbourn's first thought was of an abrupt end to his career, a preoccupation that haunted him on cold nights as he wrestled with the rough cloth in his truckle bed. Failure weighed and shamed. A lowly officer of impoverished family, fifty-five years old, with no chance of advancement or prospect of marrying into a redeeming fortune. 'Og' was far away from the male comforts of the wardroom and, happily, those of his wife. There was no friendship to aid him in crisis.

What was before him on the skyline of Windmill Hill was clearly a crisis. He sat on a flint wall backed by a quickset hedge next to a sagging wicket gate and cursed his luck, but mostly he cursed his handyman.

As a midshipman in 1815, Ogbourn had scraped a pass in his examination at Portsmouth to become a lieutenant in His Majesty's Navy.[1] That year, he married Elizabeth Paddick at St Mary's, Portsea.[2] Within two years, he was glad to spend most of his time monotonously patrolling the Mediterranean Sea lanes for enemy sails. His sole moment of prominence came when, as a midshipman, the lowest of the low, he served aboard the British sixth rate frigate, *Dido*, a slip of a ship, with nine-pounders to prick the revolutionary fleet. *Dido*, in company with the slightly better armed, *Lowestoffe*, was sent to patrol outside Toulon.[3] Off Minorca in 1795, on a steaming June morning, they met with two superior Frenchmen, the 40-gun privateer *La Minerve* and the 32-gun frigate *L'Artémise*. In the short fight, *La Minerve* was captured and *L'Artémise* fled, her captain later being relieved of command for fleeing the battle.

Aboard *Dido*, Ogbourn was ordered to carry his severely wounded and blood-gushing first lieutenant, Richard Buckoll, from the deck to his cot. Buckoll partly recovered and became a 'lucky' post-captain, amassing a fortune in prize goods. He remained grateful for Ogbourn's service. In 1798, he sailed his refitted sloop *Serpent* for Africa, picking the midshipman from the unemployed pool at Portsmouth. In April, after an illness of eight days 'owing to his dreadful wounds', Buckoll died at sea. Ogbourn was one of four pall bearers in a colourful procession, led by 'blacks continually firing', who took Buckoll to his grave by Fort Acre at the mouth of the Great Fish River.[4]

Ogbourn was left, bitterly resentful, without a sponsor for his mediocre skills. He was often shunned by his peers, some nervous of his preference for male company. When Napoleon was sent to the island of Elba in 1814, Ogbourn thought his naval world had foundered. When, next year, he became a lieutenant, he cheered on the emperor's escape and bewailed the victory at Waterloo. He had no war to fight, no prize money to gain, and, unwanted in a peacetime navy flooded with unemployed lieutenants, he drifted, begging for work. His basic half pay was five shillings a day, which he steadily drank.

His seeming last chance came in 1827 when, unexpectedly, he was appointed to command one of the new semaphore stations on a planned branch line from Admiralty House on Whitehall, London to Plymouth.

Ogbourn raised the bottle brought home that evening from the *Windmill Inn*.

'To good old Captain Buckoll,' he slurred, 'who went and died and let me down even though I saved him.' Draining the dregs, he added, 'Here's to me, that never got a fair chance in the damned navy.' And, lastly, throwing the glass against the half-cellar wall of the station and looking to the heavens, 'And here's to you, Sam Claythorne, you bastard, who've finished me off.'

Silhouetted against a thousand stars and lit by a rising moon, the handyman's corpse shifted in the slight wind. Claythorne was hanging by his neck from a rope attached to a sturdy, outstretched, signalling arm, his hands tied behind his back and his dark woollen trousers dropped to his ankles. Ogbourn sat and idly watched the body sway to and fro, trying to decide what to do. There was no hurry; there was no housing along the ridge; the nearest property was Pies Farm on the road down towards Farringdon. The farmer's candles had long been snuffed.

After an hour, Ogbourn was cold and sobered. Tied hands and trousers at half-mast suggested that Claythorne had been caught at his old games with a local woman. Someone had taken exception and followed him home, probably from the beer house in Kitwood. Claythorne's wandering hands had been the reason why the widow who did the cleaning had left the station the previous year and why it was now such a mess inside.

Ogbourn shrugged at the inevitability of it all. He fetched the ladder, climbed to the flat roof, pulled the ladder up behind him and stepped up till he was side by side with Claythorne's face with its wide open bloodshot eyes. He flicked his knife and cut. The body landed in a tangle. A few bones snapped followed by a few more as Claythorne was kicked off the roof. Ogbourn covered the heap with a tarred canvas and went to bed. In the morning, he used the semaphore to send a message back up the line to Chatley Heath from where they redirected his report to Portsmouth. Then he just sat and waited.

Much of this murder in 1830 is based on two sources: a study of England's semaphores by ex-signalman Tom Holmes, published in 1983, and a dusty history of the *Board of Inquiry* which followed Claythorne's death, still tied in 2007 in its original cream ribbon. Records of naval inquiries are stored with those for Courts Martial in the Admiralty section of *The National Archives* in Kew by the River Thames.[5] Perhaps because of the unusual nature of this case, and maybe because of the Inquiry's findings and decisions, the documents were found uncategorised at the back of a file held in the naval library at Portsmouth.[6] The file purports to deal only with the mundane matters of requisition and supply of stores to the semaphore sites.

One could, therefore, suggest that the description of Ogbourn's encounter with a trio of flag officers in January the following year was carefully mislaid and, because the events were unknown to the public at large, never sought after. To understand the story, to give it context, it is best to return to Napoleon and his triumphal march into Italy.

At the end of the eighteenth century, revolutionary France was surrounded by enemies from the Netherlands to Austria and from Prussia to Spain. The cities of Marseilles and Lyon were in revolt; the British fleet blockaded Toulon. The French had fervour and belief and two technical advantages, contrasting sides of the same coin: first, their foes were uncoordinated with inadequate lines of communication while, second, France had developed a method which allowed the rapid transmission of information and orders. The system was named after its inventors, the five Chappe brothers, led by Claude, an Abbé and an engineer. Two moving arms were connected to the opposite ends of a third middle rotating arm. The apparatus and its many twins were fixed on top of purpose-built brick towers placed about ten miles apart.

The first line from Paris to Lyon in 1792 was a sensation. Within a few years, the Chappe network had 556 stations over 3,000 miles. Its international reach included Amsterdam, Perpignan, Strasbourg, Milan and Venice. Messages that once took four days on horseback could be relayed in less than four hours. The Chappe system became Napoleon's military ace, its code compressing messages and keeping them secret.

The Chappe towers played an essential part in the revenge planned by the Count of Monte Cristo in Dumas' later novel. He described the mechanism as 'like the claws of an immense beetle … the various signs should be made to cleave the air with such precision as to convey to the distance of three hundred leagues the ideas and wishes of a man sitting at a table'.

Embarrassment at the British Admiralty was considerable where horses and despatch vessels were still the norm for delivering and receiving instruction. A drawing of a 'Chappe' and a coded alphabet were found on a French prisoner in 1794. The Admiralty's rapid response meant forty-eight signal towers were erected from the next year along England's south coast. They communicated by balls and flags, which gave signals, but only with fixed meanings. The breakthrough was a system that allowed words to be spelled out. After vigorous competition, fifteen shutter telegraph stations invented by Lord George Murray, another clergyman, were placed the same year between London and Deal, Chatham and Sheerness. These machines opened and closed their shutters in combinations that produced sixty-three options. A line

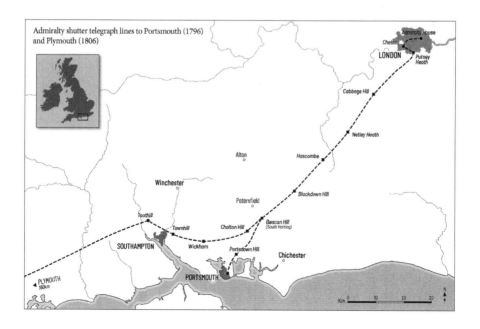

Admiralty shutter telegraph lines to Portsmouth (1796) and Plymouth (1806)

from London to Portsmouth was introduced in 1796 and in 1806 to Plymouth, both as temporary wartime measures. The budget for each station was £230.[7]

Neither shutter line came close to the ridge at Windmill Hill. The nearest station, number eight, was the branch point of the lines to Portsmouth and to Plymouth, sited within the bronze age fort on Beacon Hill in West Sussex.

The lines were discontinued when Napoleon was broken and despatched to the island of Elba but, with his escape and arrival in France in 1815, only six months had passed before the Admiralty demanded the re-establishment of the shutter stations. Seven weeks later, with the Duke of Wellington's victory at Waterloo, the Admiralty announced a plan for a permanent system of stations to Portsmouth based on a semaphore, machines with movable arms and, the following day, tabled an act enabling the purchasing of one-acre sites.[8] The semaphore was the third technological development in less than twenty years: from horse riders to 'ball and flags' to shutters and now to semaphores. The shutter stations to Portsmouth were closed in 1816 and the land returned to their original owners.

In 1818, Thomas Goddard, the purser of the Royal Yacht *Royal George*, in his fifties, was appointed to find sites for the new semaphore and his deliberations are available at *The National Archives*.[9] He describes how 'sometimes drenched with rain, and very often terribly scratched by thorns and briers, he forced his way to the top of likely hills and there, perilously perched on a ladder held by his two riggers, scanned the neighbouring heights for the most suitable site for a station'. Often, he found that the background at the old shutter sites prevented semaphore arms from being seen and he condemned most of them as unsuitable.[10] The new semaphore line with fifteen stations was completed in June 1822 and cost £3,000 a year to maintain.

Finally, for those more interested in Ogbourn than the history, the story reaches the Four Marks semaphore in the modern Telegraph Lane or, as it was then, the Ridge Field at the top of Farringdon Common.[11] In 1822, Goddard was sent to survey a branch line to Plymouth. The following year, he submitted a list of sites, but money was scarce and the project was shelved until 1825. It was a slow business, the Admiralty could only afford three stations a year and Goddard found negotiations with landowners difficult, 'always baffled' by their recalcitrance. At that rate, Plymouth would not have been reached until 1837.

Goddard ordered thirty semaphores at £83 11s 6d each of the same pattern and type already in use on the Portsmouth line. The new branch line diverted

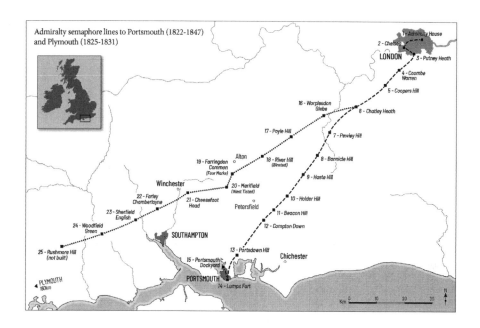

Admiralty semaphore lines to Portsmouth (1822-1847) and Plymouth (1825-1831)

1 - Admiralty House
2 - Chelsea
LONDON
3 - Putney Heath
4 - Coombe Warren
5 - Coopers Hill
16 - Worplesdon Glebe
6 - Chatley Heath
17 - Poyle Hill
7 - Pewley Hill
Alton
19 - Farringdon Common (Four Marks)
18 - River Hill (Binsted)
8 - Bannicle Hill
9 - Haste Hill
Winchester
20 - Merifield (West Tisted)
22 - Farley Chamberlayne
21 - Cheesefoot Head
10 - Holder Hill
Petersfield
11 - Beacon Hill
23 - Sherfield English
24 - Woodfield Green
12 - Compton Down
SOUTHAMPTON
25 - Rushmore Hill (not built)
13 - Portsdown Hill
Chichester
PLYMOUTH 180km
15 - Portsmouth Dockyard
PORTSMOUTH
14 - Lumps Fort
Km 0   10   20   30

at Chatley Heath near Cobham. Farringdon Common was the fourth station along, sandwiched between River Hill at Binsted, built by Mr Harding of Farnham, now a home, and Merifield (Merryfield), West Tisted, a four-storeyed octagonal tower of which all that remains is a faint cellar trace. The sites, which were often near turnpikes, were marked with boundary stones bearing the Government's broad arrow, the one at Farringdon Common dated 1826.[12]

The Farringdon Common station was built for £987 by a young William Dyer whose premises were in Alton High Street.[13] The land was bought from the Chawton House estate, occupied since 1826 by Edward Knight, the third eldest brother to Jane Austen for whom he provided the cottage in Chawton where she wrote many of her works in her last years. Knight's local estate, one of three, was almost 400 acres and sat on the Gosport turnpike. As well as four children, the household comprised in 1851, a butler, coachman, footman, page, groom, housekeeper and six various maids. The rector of Chawton, a younger brother Charles, lived next door. Knight's son and heir, also Edward, was later to be the figurehead of the railway line from Alton, through Four Marks, to Winchester.[14]

Lieutenant Ogbourn took over as a caretaker superintendent in 1829 with an extra 3s a day over his half pay.[15] He was allowed £1 a year for stationery and £4 for petty cash within his quarterly maintenance account of £20.

Farringdon Common Semaphore Station, c. 1970, now Telegraph Farm, Telegraph Lane, Four Marks. The original living quarters and semaphore room remain but the semaphore tower was reclaimed by the Navy. The room on the left had its roof re-slated when it became a fever hospital. The windows of the half underground rooms are visible. The house was sold in 1982 and bungalows were built on adjacent land. *Southern Newspapers Limited*

His handyman, Claythorne, was recommended by the Navy at 32s a month. Claythorne was forty-eight and walked with a slight limp. A handymen's average age was forty-five, some were pensioners, some had been wounded; they all needed to be able to read and write. Many sought their positions as a relief from rough seas, flogging and the press gang. Widow Oakley worked and slept in the kitchen from Monday to Friday, paid out of Ogbourn's allowance. A grandson brought a trap up from Farringdon to fetch her home for each weekend.

Three further stations from Winchester to Woodfield Green at Downton were completed by September 1831 and that was the end of it. Of, perhaps, thirty-five stations, only eight were built. 'Old Mrs Visibility', as the Navy knew the Admiralty, was having a re-think about the cost and about sending messages visually. Electricity was, at last, about. The Plymouth line came to a full stop although the Portsmouth line continued for another sixteen years.

The Four Marks semaphore, many miles short of Plymouth, was never used in anger. In truth, apart from initial training and testing, it was hardly used at all. For Ogbourn and Claythorne, this was all known within weeks of moving in. The line's coming closure, the halt to building, was common

A painting of Putney Semaphore Station, c. 1827, second along from the Admiralty. *National Maritime Museum, Greenwich*

Notice that work was to start on the Winchester Semaphore Station in 1829. It was completed in May the following year. *Hampshire Chronicle*

Monday, April 6th, 1829

Winchester. — The Commissioners of the Navy are about to erect a new line of semaphores, in order to accelerate the communication with Plymouth. The eminence called Chestford Head, near this city, has been selected as one of the stations, on which a residence will shortly be built for the accommodation of the officer and men to be stationed there.

discussion in the newspapers. The rain came through the flat roof in the first serious downpour and Bill Dyer had to be threatened out of Alton to conduct repairs. The Farringdon Common tax collector came for his £2 for the first year's occupation for which Ogbourn had not budgeted, the money destined for Squire Knight who may have sold the land, but had not completely let go. The two men were trapped and became veritable smallholders, bored, and waiting for the day when Ogbourn would revert to half pay and Claythorne would be out of a job.

The other truth was that they disliked each other from the first time they met. It was a tension they kept from the Admiralty for fear of losing their positions. It was not a feeling they kept from each other. The rancour festered over the next twelve months and Ogbourn's authority all but disappeared. The commonest causes for dismissal of handymen were insubordination and drunkenness and Claythorne specialised in both. After a few months, he tried to force himself on the Widow Oakley on his return from the beer house and she ran shrieking into the night. Ogbourn threatened him, but received a mound of spite and invective in return and felt he could do no more.

The Inquiry at Portsmouth into Claythorne's death was inconsequential. The corpse was whisked away by a party of marines. If the departure was noted, it was only by the locals at the *Horse and Groom* at the bottom of the hill on the Gosport turnpike. The marines' three-hour lunch celebrating their unexpected day release was talked about for years to come. Their horses and covered waggon waited patiently outside. The body was never mentioned again.

The two months Ogbourn waited for his hearing reduced him to a wreck. The board's officers plainly noted that they considered for a while committing him to an asylum. His weeping self-pity and spilling out of unwanted, unmanly details lost him any support he may have had. He was admonished for his lack of leadership, kept his half pay and disappeared on a nameless mission to die in 1850.

LIEUTENANTS.   113

Names.				Seniority.
James Lawrence ...	...	...	...	18 *Mar.* 1815
Edward Willis Ward	...	...	...	do
Henry Tryon...	...	...	...	do
John Hall (B)...	...	...	...	do
George Ogbourn	...	...	...	do
John Harvie ...	...	...	...	20 *Mar.* 1815
James Stanes...	...	...	...	do

George Ogbourn, still a Lieutenant in 1831 after sixteen years' service. *The Navy List*

It was decided that further enquiry was unlikely to achieve any result. The 'accident' happened on naval property and was therefore outside the responsibility of any local authority. Publicity for such an incident was not sought at a time of a slightly embarrassing line closure. Also, the powerful Edward Knight was wanted by the Navy to assist in other plans.

Elizabeth Ogbourn heard that the station was unoccupied. She applied to the Navy and was given permission to move in to safeguard the property while she chased her missing husband for support. Aged forty, childless, she shared semaphore in the early 1840s with her brother John, an agricultural labourer, and Charles Bone, a blacksmith.[16]

In 1847, every semaphore crew on the Portsmouth semaphore line received their redundancy notices, but the Plymouth branch had withered long before. All the masts were dismantled, including the murder arm, and warehoused for some future use.[17] Ogbourn's station was sold back to the Chawton Estate, now managed by the second Edward's son, Squire Montagu Knight. The site was worked as a smallholding until about 1896. River Hill House at Binsted was also sold back to its estate and was leased to Captain Bainton RN, famous for his cucumbers grown in 'new-fangled' greenhouses.

Elizabeth Ogbourn moved to Newton Common, living on a navy pension, taking with her 'servant' Charlie Bone as a gardener. She died in 1857. In one of those little twists, Bone then moved to Priors Dean and worked as a blacksmith for William White at Locks Cottage, shortly to become the *White Horse Inn*.[18]

The story of Claythorne's demise is finished, but not that of the semaphore station.

In 1839, permission was given to the London and Southampton Railway to build an extension from Bishopstoke, now incorporated with Eastleigh, to Gosport so long as it passed 'outside the fortifications', and to change its name to the London and South Western Railway (LSWR) Company. The company's southern branch to Gosport, opened later, was the line from Alton to Winchester passing a few hundred yards from the abandoned semaphore station.[19] The Knight family of Chawton Estate had a significant financial interest in Alton's railways. The Gosport line began in November 1841, but owing to mishaps did not start operating until February the next year.

The Admiralty immediately wished for an electric telegraph line to be installed between Nine Elms in London (Waterloo was not then built) and Gosport. In the next year, 1845, Cooke & Wheatstone produced their advanced two-wire single needle telegraph. Wires were laid following the railway tracks into the Royal Clarence Victualling Yard at Gosport, from whence one of the first submarine cables ever laid in this country passed under the harbour to King's Stairs.

It is of passing interest that the Knights, therefore, sold and rebought the land of the semaphore station from the Admiralty and then profited from the LSWR's rental to the Admiralty of the space for the semaphore's replacement telegraph system, the fourth new signal technology in less than fifty years.

By 1881, Ropley saw its first telegraph clerk, nineteen-year-old Thomas Akaster from Portsmouth, lodging with a railway porter's family in Gasson Lane off the turnpike. One of his jobs was to deliver telegrams throughout the parish; he was soon to be using another invention, the bicycle.

During the nineteenth century after the semaphore's closure, the smallholding was known as 'Semaphore Farm', later changed to 'Telegraph Farm', which it remains to this day. It is a misnomer perhaps linguistic creep sought a more powerful word.

From February 1896 until the end of 1912, Alton Rural District Council rented the building for £25 a year to establish a District Isolation Hospital to deal principally with scarlet fever. Many children from the Four Marks school were patients. Isolation staff had a beer allowance or money in lieu.

The extended Wyeth and Langridge family worked the farm, variously of twenty-five, thirty and fifty acres, from around 1920, still remote with no other houses in the lane. 'Cousin Beatrice' Sharp used to watch the cows along the verges to help out with the food supply. The 'trig point' at 700 ft is in the next field, one of some 6,500 triangulation pillars built in the 1930s to hold a theodolite and used by the Ordnance Survey to map the country.

An autobiography of 1932 mentions 'little' Semaphore Farm: 'We used to deliver milk round the village with *Tinker* pulling the trap. There was a shiny urn on the cart with a measure which was used to fill the customers' utensils.'[20]

Local stories claim that the semaphore site was, in the very early days, used as a beacon. Local historian, Betty Mills, is adamant there never was an ancient beacon. Beacons were either used to rally troops to defend the realm or were a 'one message' device, not suitable for repeat signalling.'[21]

However, you can't put a good story down. There were three beacon fires. The first two were for the Queen's silver and diamond jubilees and the second, in 1988, for the Armada celebrations.

But, it still should be Semaphore Farm in Semaphore Lane.

ENDNOTES

[1] *The Navy Chronical*, Vol. 33. *The Navy List*, 1815, 1820, 1831, 18/3/1815.
[2] *England marriages*, 1538–974.
[3] Winfield, Rif, *British Warships in the Age of Sail 1714–1792*.
[4] Campbell, John, *Naval History of Great Britain*, Vol. 7.
[5] *The National Archives*, Kew, ADM/178.
[6] *Royal Navy Library*, Portsmouth, Supply/SEM/e247/1833/g/2, access 2007.
[7] Holmes, *Semaphore*.
[8] 55 Geo. III C.128.
[9] *TNA*, ADM 359/37A/91.
[10] Holmes, *Semaphore*.
[11] Leigh, *Chawton Manor*.
[12] Hudleston, 'Semaphore Telegraph'.
[13] 1841 census.
[14] See Chapter 1: '*The Battle of the Shant*'.
[15] For a description of the semaphore station and its operational routine, see this chapter's appendix.
[16] 1841 census.
[17] *The Times*, 31/12/1847.
[18] See Chapter 15, 'The Pub with No Body'.
[19] See Chapter 1, 'Battle of the Shant'.
[20] Cornick, *Early Memories*.
[21] Mills, *Four Marks*, pp. 25–26.

Reading list:

Cornick, David, *Early Memories of Four Marks* (No publisher, undated)

Dumas, Alexandre, *The Count of Monte Cristo* (1844; Penguin, London 2003)

Holmes, T.W., *The Semaphore, The Story of the Admiralty-to-Portsmouth Shutter Telegraph and Semaphore Lines 1796 to 1847* (Stockwell, Ilfracombe 1983)

Hudleston, Captain R., 'The Coast Signal Stations and the Semaphore Telegraph', *Journal of Society for Nautical Research*, July 1911

Wyeth, Gerald, *Four Marks School Boy's Memories* (No publisher, undated)

Appendix: The Admiralty's standard semaphore station

The Admiralty issued seventeen regulations for the management of each semaphore that were strict, but not onerous, and concerned the drawing of cash, preservation of the house, requisition of stores, transfer of stores and a caution 'to grease and oil the working parts of the machinery from time to time'. The two telescopes pointing up and down the line were not to be left for five minutes while on duty. One man was to sleep at the station for security. A journal was kept and forwarded weekly to the Secretary of the Admiralty. The semaphore room was to be swept every day and the floor washed once a week in winter and twice weekly in summer.

The building was an ordinary-looking, slate-roofed, poor country bungalow of four rooms, about 13 x 11ft, with fireplaces and fitted corner cupboards; half-cellars had a sunken walkway round and windows. The brick and stucco walls were 17 inches thick. There was a washhouse with a bucket toilet away from the house.

The semaphore room was 8ft x 7ft 9in. With a ladder outside, access could be gained to the flat lead roof where a hexagonal hollow mast made of six planks bound by iron rings protruded. Measurements were taken from the semaphore room floor to the spindle of the mast's lower arm, 30 feet high above the building.

Each arm was made of deal, 8 feet long and 16 inches wide. If Thomas Goddard wanted the arm higher he had to build a taller house, or second best, a higher mast. There were two semaphore trees, each with its own arm, one above the other, and both could rest unseen inside the hollow mast. Each had seven positions: at rest and three either side, to the left or right, set at equal 45 degree gaps, say at 1.30 pm, 3.00 pm and 4.30 pm. The arms were attached by rods to crank handles in the semaphore room. The device gave a total of forty-eight signs (seven by seven, minus one when both arms were at rest) and these were allotted the twenty-six letters of the alphabet, ten numerals (0–9) and twelve standard words like 'fog' and 'not clear'.

A message from the Admiralty to Portsmouth took less than fifteen minutes. It was claimed that the hour of noon could be signalled from London and an acknowledgement from Portsmouth received in ninety seconds.

A second book of local memories states that 'the kitchen, scullery and dairy were built below ground level approached from the road side via a steep narrow winding stone staircase. The three downstairs rooms had sash-type windows looking out onto curved brick walls. These damp pits were the home and graves of frogs and toads that accidentally fell in … The windows could never be opened. These underground rooms were dark and sombre even on the brightest days as my grandparents were reluctant to have the electricity laid on … When the wind blew and the doors were open, there was a high risk of the paraffin lamp causing a fire.[1]

'The scullery contained a very old-fashioned brown stone sink, the waste water being collected underneath in a bucket and poured down a grating at the bottom of the steps to run into a dell on the opposite side of the lane. The single cold tap was supplied by an overhead galvanised water tank that was filled daily using a hand pump and detachable long tin pipe at the top of the stairs, the water being extracted from the water tanks in the garden which collected the rain water from the roof of the house, barn and stables.

'There was a large brick, bread oven and copper built into the corner of the scullery. The kitchen contained a black leaded cast iron grate which provided a modest degree of heating, and oven hot plates for cooking and heating five irons together with a fender and coal scuttle. All the floors, and in the dairy, were large stone slabs. There were marble shelves in the dairy for coolness.

'All these rooms were partially below ground with no damp course and the earth resting directly against the exterior walls. There was always a damp, dark smell and the plaster and wallpaper refused to remain in place, even the white, water-based distemper applied to the walls tended to flake off shortly after being brushed on. Upstairs was approached via a set of steep wooden stairs and had three bedrooms and a lounge, no bathroom. In the depths of winter, a stone hot water bottle was filled from a kettle or a heated brick wrapped in a cloth.'

ENDNOTES

[1] Wyeth, *Four Marks Memories.*

8 FANNY AND THE WOLF
Fanny Adams and the Hangman

WINCHESTER
1867   BODY COUNT: 1

The murder and dismemberment of eight-year-old Fanny Adams, seduced from near her home in Tanhouse Lane and taken to a large hop garden, was a very close Alton affair, the only murder in the area in living memory. It is little wonder that local feelings ran high and a mob was on the street.

Fanny lived with her parents, George and Harriet, with her paternal grandparents next door, people with their roots in the town. The hop garden was owned by William Dyer, George Adams' employer and a successful builder.[1] True, her convicted murderer, Frederick Baker, was a twenty-nine-year-old Guildford man, but he lodged in the High Street with boarding housekeeper, Sarah Kingston, next door to Dyer and four doors away from his uncle, William Row, a watchmaker. Baker had worked for twelve months for Alton's pre-eminent legal figure, William Clement, whose prestige offices were in the same road.

After drinking with fellow clerk Maurice Biddle in the *Swan Inn*, Baker was arrested in Clement's office by Superintendent William Cheyney from the police station on Butts Road, then smuggled out of the back door for fear of the mob. Fanny's body parts were collected from fields near Flood Meadows and from the River Wey. The remains were taken to a doctor's surgery in Amery Street, recently *The Leathern Bottle* restaurant, to be stitched together for her father to identify. The inquest took place at *The Duke's Head* (now *The George*); the committal proceedings were held at Alton Town Hall In Market Square. Fanny's mutilated corpse was buried in the town cemetery on the Old Odiham Road where her tombstone, erected in 1874, paid for by voluntary subscription and carved by Dyer, is kept spick and span to this very day.

If there has been one crime that has dogged sleepy-old Alton's reputation, it was this wanton killing in 1867. 'The most practised or the most callous pen can hardly write with patience of a poor little child playing with her companions in a hop-garden, and thence ravished away by a human wolf, and gnashed to mere fragments in his maw.'[2]

Look up any brief history of the town and, within a paragraph or two, the story of Sweet Fanny Adams leaps out. In truth, Alton's amateur historians relish the notoriety and its gory details because otherwise, apart from the 'old history' of the Romans, Saxons and the Cavaliers, there is very little to declare apart from beer and railways.

Yet, at the heart of the story are two men from that part of Ropley that became Four Marks in 1932. Amid all the mass of leaflets, newspaper and internet articles and books written since, this connection has lain undiscovered.[3]

Why pay so much attention to this particular child murder? Two reasons, I suggest.

First, three years before, George Purkess, a London publisher began to specialise in cheap, true stories of crime, accident and domestic disaster. His bold idea was the creation of *The Illustrated Police News, Law Courts and Weekly Review*. The *British Newspaper Archive* calls it the first and most long-lasting Saturday penny newspaper. It combined sensationalism with two hugely popular Victorian genres: the police newspaper with accurate factual reporting and the illustrated journal, pioneering the use of engravings drawn from true, or as near true as possible, likenesses of participants in the crime of the week. *The Police News* was the forerunner of today's tabloids.

On 5 December, the journal was at Winchester for the trial. Its front page was titled 'The Alton Murder! : The Trial and Condemnation of Frederick Baker'. The engraving showed a calm, well-dressed young man surrounded by a wreath of hops. Within, further pictures included the house where the victim lived, the gate leading to the 'hop garden' and a centrepiece of simple, innocent Fanny with long dark tresses, a virginal smock and a poor-girl's dyed straw hat. This last engraving has been borrowed and used endlessly until the present day.

The Police News gave the murder oxygen that would have been impossible just five years before. *The News* also covered Baker's execution in sickening detail (to most modern tastes) and reprised the story in a 1934 edition.[4]

Second, was the thrilling and appalling mutilation of Fanny's body and its casual, disrespectful link to the Royal Navy. *The Police News* may have been sensational in its presentation, but its court reporting was backed by several

Engraving: Fanny Adams.
The Police News, 30/12/1867

Engraving: Frederick Baker.
The Police News, 30/12/1867

dozen other newspapers. In any event, the language used by the prosecutor, Montagu Bere, a battle-hardened recorder of the Southampton and Bristol legal circuits, hardly needed embellishment. The facts given here, few disputed, are a composite of reports in *The Police News* and three other newspapers whose staff attended: a more discreet *The Daily News* of London and the Hampshire papers, the *Advertiser* and the *Chronicle*.[5]

A string of witnesses told briefly of their searches. Thomas Gate saw the head resting on two hop poles with the trunk 'about sixteen yards away'. The body was 'cut open and cleaned'. Charles White, an engine driver who lodged on Vicarage Hill, was with Gates and agreed. He picked up a girl's hat from a hedge. Harry Allen, a coachmaker, collected a heart and an arm hidden by hedge clippings in an adjoining field. He then saw the lungs. Shoemaker Thomas Swain found the left foot amidst clover. Police Constable Joseph Waters was on a bridge over the Wey when he noticed an eye at the bottom of the river; his colleague, John Masterman, found the second eye lying on the river bank. Another officer, John White saw a ten-inch knife nearby. Alton house painter William Walker produced a four-inch flintstone, covered with blood, hair and small pieces of flesh, which he had first taken home before he surrendered it and it was designated as the murder weapon.

One couldn't make it up.

The awfulness got worse when the doctors examined the pieces of the corpse. Louis Leslie, the Alton divisional police surgeon from the Royal College of Surgeons, said vermin had already been at work on the head in the summer heat. The skull was fractured. The right ear was severed and there were several cuts including one that extended 'from the forehead above the nose to the end of the lower jaw'. The whole of the contents of the pelvis and chest were completely removed. The vagina was cut out and, along with the breastbone, was never recovered.

It is a disturbing thought that these bones, at least, may be lying quietly beneath one of the half-million-pound homes on the new Redrow housing development at Hop Field Place.

Added to the publicity surrounding the murder, and the hanging of Baker at Winchester, this collection of body parts was given eternal recognition by the cruel wit of the Royal Navy.

In 1869, British seamen received new rations of tainted tinned beef or mutton with almost universal disapproval and suggested that the meat might be the butchered remains of Fanny Adams.[6] Her name became slang for mediocre meat, stew, scarce leftovers and, finally, anything of little value. The large containers doubled as mess tins, still known as 'fannies'. The expression developed into 'Sweet Fanny Adams', then 'Sweet FA', and, by World War II, to 'Sweet Fuck All' – nothing at all, something worthless.

Sadly, this coarse euphemism may be Fanny's true legacy and the reason for her worldwide fame. The name was already in the public domain with a popular novel published in 1790: *The love, joy, and distress, of the beautiful & virtuous Miss Fanny Adams; that was trapped in a false marriage to Lord Whatley.*

Baker always protested his innocence until after his death when it was leaked that he had written a letter of apology and confession to Fanny's parents, read to them by the vicar, the Reverend Octavius Hodgson, and this, apparently, quashed any lingering doubts. Baker denied any sexual motive or violation. This was hinted at by the prosecution during the trial although never brought to the fore except when the jury heard briefly that Baker had been rejected by a woman to whom he was engaged. Baker wrote that the crime was committed in 'an unguarded hour and not with malice of forethought'. He had become enraged at her crying, 'but it was done without any pain or struggle'. The weight of evidence was compelling if largely circumstantial, described by the judge as 'almost exclusively, presumptive evidence'.

Baker was noticed and spoken to by several witness near the scene including Fanny's frantic mother who did not think of Baker, a solicitor's clerk, as a potential murderer. Later, Baker admitted carrying Fanny off into the field where most of her remains were found. He had spots of blood on his clothes and carried two pocket knives which he had washed of blood stains. He admitted paying Fanny's two playmates, her younger sister Lizzie and a friend, Minnie Warner, three halfpennies and suggesting they went off into town to buy some sweets.

The last entry in Baker's diary read, '24 August, Saturday – Killed a young girl,' which has two possible and opposite meanings. He had been drinking. Two absences from work that day were noticed, the first, it was suggested, when Fanny was killed, the second, some hours later, when he returned to cut up the body. Drinking at *The Swan* with Biddle while the town was in turmoil, Baker suggested things could look bad for him if a body was discovered. He thought to leave on the Monday. It was suggested finding work would be difficult to which Baker suggested he could always become a butcher.

Amid all the emotion and stupid comments, there remained no direct proof that Baker had wielded the stone that had crushed Fanny's skull. As Samuel Carter, the defence counsel, pointed out in his summing up, cutting up a dead body is not murder. Carter was a last-minute replacement for John Coleridge, MP, great nephew of Samuel Taylor Coleridge. Perhaps Coleridge would have made a difference; he later became Attorney General and Lord Chief Justice.

There is good reason to suggest that if Baker were tried today, he may not have been found guilty or, if he were, it would have been a question of insanity decided by a series of psychological reports. Baker was held in prison for over three months. The trial in the Castle at Winchester took two days and the jury just fifteen minutes. The sentence was prescribed. The state hanged Baker eighteen days later on Christmas Eve.

Before he came to trial, Baker was already guilty in the minds of the people of Alton and those across the country who read *The Police News*. The inquest held by Deputy Coroner Robert Harefield three days after Fanny's death was in a pub directly across from Baker's place of work, full of local, excited people. The decision was that Fanny had been murdered by Baker. Fanny's death certificate stated the cause of death as 'injuries inflicted by Frederick Baker (Murder)'. The parish register of the death had a footnote, 'Cruelly murdered by Frederick Baker'. *The Police News* claimed, 'The atrocity of this murder created the most profound sensation and indignation against the accused man, not only in the county in which it was committed but throughout London …

'We have no desire to dwell on the sickening narrative of a crime which must be familiar to all, or to give a minute recapitulation of the evidence. It is a circumstance worthy of notice, and one that reflects credit on the public sense of decorum, that although this crime is one of the most sanguinary, the most atrocious, and the most exceptional, under almost every aspect, that has been perpetrated within our time, its frightful particulars have met with little public discussion, and a general though tacit wish has been expressed that the abominable thing should be got rid of – that the criminal and the crime should be withdrawn as soon as was practicable from the public cognisance.'

It would seem there was little room for doubt or space for a fair trial before a crowded courtroom hearing the evidence for the 'first' time.

The defence counsel picked at some of the evidence. All agreed that Baker was calm when talked to in the street, in the pub, at his arrest in the office after the crime and at the police station. He always denied involvement. He had been drinking alcohol during the day. Minnie Walker was carried into court and declared that Baker had been at the same spot the previous Saturday to the murder when he had also chatted to young girls. Dr Alfred Swaine Taylor of Guy's Hospital discussed at length the 'very small' spots of mammalian blood on Baker's clothes and on only one of his two knives, 'neither of which could have cut through bone'. The blood could have come from a claimed nosebleed.

Leslie, from the College of Surgeons, described in detail the numbers of cuts to flesh and bone. Under cross-examination, he said, 'I believe it possible to dismember a child of this age with a knife, but it is not probable. I think a larger instrument must have been used. Still I think a man with undisturbed possession of a hop-field, might with either of those knives have effected the dismemberment of a child eight years of age in an hour about half an hour after death ... I think the person who did it could choose his position and need not be much marked with blood.'

How embarrassing must it have been for Alton's senior lawyer William Clement that he employed a child murderer for almost a year? Clement came from a large legal and banking family; the bank was in joint ownership with Jane Austen's brother Henry. William's father, Thomas, had 'considerable land and properties at Steep' and was a descendant of Rothercombe Farm in Petersfield. He was a 'solicitor of considerable eminence and extensive practice'. William's brother, Benjamin, had a naval career that sounds like the source for C.S. Forester's tales of Horatio Hornblower.[7] He was the part-inspiration for Austen's *Mansfield Park* and is commemorated by a large stained glass window in the chancel of the church of St Nicholas in Chawton.

Clement's offices seem a loose affair on the Saturday of the murder, a normal working day. There was none of the Dickensian constraint that might be expected. Baker came and went as he pleased, drinking freely and meeting workmate Biddle in the inn. Biddle was an eighteen-year-old junior clerk. Clement's servant, Sarah Lawrence, said she saw Baker after the murder, noticed no blood or anything extraordinary. Another clerk, Frederick French, who took a two-hour afternoon dinner saw 'nothing out of the way' about Baker. Clement's chief clerk and actuary to his savings bank was William Trimming, aged sixty-eight, an employee for 'thirty or forty years', and perhaps not ideal to keep order in the office. Clement himself was seventy-six and died two years later. By 1871, Trimming retired to Selborne.

This defence was but diversionary hot air because, although Baker, 'perfectly calm and self-possessed', had pleaded innocence, the real defence, prepared against an expected finding of guilty, was that Baker was insane.

It was a difficult trick to ride two horses set in opposite directions.

Frederick Baker lived with his parents, Frederick and Ann, in South Street, Guildford, now Sydenham Street and the house under a multi-storey car park. Witnesses testified to his sobriety and others to his heavy drinking. He was a man who lost control when he succumbed to a bout. His father was a journeyman tailor. There was an older daughter, Mary Ann. Frederick the elder, a 'sharp-looking old man, dressed in black with a white neckcloth', was the first witness for the defence. He described his son:

He was always a nervous child, was troubled with sickness and pains in his head, and was continually under the care of a doctor. He was always bleeding at the nose. So weak was he that he was not sent to school until he was about twelve. He was long ill of the typhus at sixteen. I sat up with him fifteen nights myself. After that he always continued complaining of his head. We put him in the office of Mr Smallpiece, solicitor, where he remained five years. He often came home and said his duties were more than he could bear. From his birth, he was twenty-six years under my roof and I never knew him to drink intoxicating liquors ... He said that he would go and drown himself ... When I saw him [last year) in the service of Mr Clement his appearance and demeanour struck me with horror ... Before that [we] had been on a steamer in London and his manner was such that I watched him, being afraid he would jump overboard.

The father confirmed his son had been a member of a Literary Institute in Guildford for twelve years. He was secretary to a debating society, director of a penny savings bank and a Sunday school teacher. He had never heard of any charge being made against him. Again one senses the drunk, a man of contrasting, but co-existing characters.

The sister, Mary Ann, said, 'I am three years older than him and I have always lived at home. From his childhood he was very weak. The effect on his mind through the breaking off of his engagement was very bad. I remember that he was very unhappy when he saw the young woman with another man. He was very despondent and he … would have destroyed himself had not a young man saved him.'

Alfred Johnson, a Guildford bricklayer, said in one conversation that 'his manner was so strange that I thought he was out of his mind because I have a relative the same way'.

Others testified that Baker's mother's family had a history of mental illness and one cousin was currently in Fareham county lunatic asylum and 'unlikely to come out'. A Guildford police sergeant described how Baker had rushed towards a canal before being stopped. A surgeon said Baker's mother had died of consumption and his father had an attack of acute mania, becoming violent and trying to hit his daughter with a poker, and had delusions. There was a 'taint of deadly insanity in the family'.

Around Christmas 1864, Baker left Guildford without giving a reason. The prosecution sensed a sinister reason, but did not chase it out. Where Baker went is not known, but he did spend one night in January 1866 in the Lambeth Workhouse. One report was that he lived rough and begged for his food.[8]

The arguments on the evidence rowed back and forth, but neither the prosecution nor the judge gave any credence to a claim of insanity. The wanton strewing of body parts about a field did not signify illness. Mr Justice Mellor thought the crime was probably 'for the gratification of lust', although no evidence was given which pointed to this. He 'utterly refuted the doctrine that the enormity of the crime was any evidence of the state of mind of the criminal'. However, he did allow the jury the right to consider insanity, but urged that they should not use any discontent with the death penalty to lead them to use insanity to 'escape' it. The learned doctors disagreed fundamentally about the possibility of Baker suffering from homicidal mania or any other form of mental illness.[9]

Arresting officer Superintendent Cheyney suffered severe cross examination as there were several discrepancies between his account in court compared to what he had said in front of the Alton magistrates.[10] Despite this, Cheyney did well after the affair. By 1881, he had moved to Gosport where he lived at the police station with his family and six lodging constables, and another next door. He had four prisoners in the cells including two privates in the Royal Marines.

Eighteen days later, early on a Tuesday morning, Frederick Baker was taken to the hangman.

A vast crowd began to gather in front of the wall and shrubbery which form the boundary of the gaol; people flocked from all parts of Hampshire and the neighbouring counties and long before eight o'clock the assemblage numbered at a moderate computation as many as five or six thousand persons, who upon the whole were mostly well behaved and orderly; indeed the spectators did not strike us as being composed of that rough class which generally predominates in a thorough London mob. A large proportion were women.'[11]

Winchester prison, opposite the current Royal Hampshire Hospital, was opened for inmates from 1849. Its up-to-date equipment included a hand crank, a box with a handle, that prisoners were made to turn for punishment. A warden could adjust the amount of effort needed by turning a screw on the side of the box which is why, today, prison officers are known as 'screws'. It was not a busy place for hangings: it held thirty-eight. Executions in England were public until 1868 when the law mandated that they took place privately and within the prison. Baker was the last man publicly killed at the gaol. The work was conducted by William Calcraft, one of the most prolific of British executioners, who carried out, perhaps, 450 hangings in a forty-five-year career.

EXECUTION OF BAKER.

**Full Particulars will be Published Imme-
diately after the Execution, with**

ILLUSTRATIONS.

ONE PENNY.

Calcraft is fundamental to this story. It is important to understand his background and his way of working and of making money. He was a cobbler who used to add to his income by selling meat pies on the streets around Newgate Prison on hanging days. During a sale, he met the City of London's hangman, John Foxton, who recruited him to flog juvenile offenders and, later, to be his assistant. After Foxton's death in 1829, the government appointed Calcraft the official executioner in his place.

Some considered Calcraft incompetent for his reliance on the common short-drop hanging, a fall of only three feet, in which a condemned was slowly strangled to death, rather than the later long-drop in which the neck was immediately broken. Because the condemned could take several minutes to die, Calcraft, 'renowned for his bad taste', would sometimes dramatically pull on legs or climb on shoulders in an effort to break the victim's neck. It has been speculated that Calcraft used these methods partly to entertain the crowds, sometimes numbering 30,000 or more. For his antics, Calcraft was in great demand around the country.

Calcraft supplemented his income by selling sections of the rope used to hang his victims at five shillings an inch; hence the expression, 'money for old rope'. Perhaps, parts of Baker's rope may still exist.

In his later days, Calcraft usually worked without an assistant, a highly questionable practice as the objective was to work at speed without incident. Approved assistants were paid for by the authorities. In private arrangements, people paid Calcraft to be in close attendance, sometimes posing as his assistant, but having no training at all. Calcraft was allowed to keep the clothes and personal effects of the condemned, which he often sold in advance to Madame Tussauds of London for dressing the latest waxwork. An artisan attended Baker's death at Winchester Gaol, took a death mask, and within ten days the clothed likeness was put on display in the 'Chamber of Horrors' in Baker Street.[12]

If Calcraft had been a 'royal personage or an eminent statesman he could hardly have been treated with greater consideration'.[13] Prison governor, Henry Baynes, was on hand to meet him at the railway station. Calcraft arrived with only one piece of hand luggage, a carpetbag containing a new rope, a white cap and some restraining straps for the arms but not for the legs. In the Calcraft style, Baker was to be allowed to dangle and kick.

This was the time of Fenian atrocities, bombings and murders, and Calcraft was nervous of executing members of the Irish Republican Brotherhood because of threats he had received. He came fresh to Winchester from the public execution, at a fee of £30, of William Allen, Michael Larkin and Michael O'Brien, who became known as the 'Manchester Martyrs'. These three Fenians had been found guilty of the murder of a police officer and were hanged together. Most accounts claim that Allen died instantaneously from a broken neck, but the Catholic priest in attendance, Father Gadd, reported that 'the other two ropes, stretched taught and tense by their breathing, twitching burdens, were in ominous and distracting movement. The hangman had bungled! Calcraft then descended into the pit and there tried to finish what he could not accomplish from above. He killed Larkin!' Father Gadd refused to allow Calcraft to despatch O'Brien in the same way and so for 'three-quarters of an hour [he] knelt and held the man's hands within his own, reciting the prayers for the dying.'

In 1870, in his last years, Calcraft, after many refusals, agreed to tell his life story.[14] An unnamed journalist reworked the memories into a series of articles that have recently been released as a facsimile book. Calcraft freely admits to his loss of nerve and recognised that 'the indignation of the populace was very great and there was another general cry-out for [my] dismissal, and the abolition of the hangman's office'. His editor noted that, 'Calcraft's popularity as a skilful hangman began to decline, and his want of strength and nerve was often commented on.' Some City of London alderman wanted to pension him off.

The Police News noted of Frederick Baker's guilt that, 'One or two paragraphs have appeared in one or two of the papers intimating that the execution would be postponed, pending an inquiry into the prisoner's state of mind. It is to be very much regretted that the press, or rather a portion of it, should lend themselves to a show of silly, misguided persons who are always persistent in their endeavours to turn aside the "Sword of Justice" and to render nugatory the laws of England.'[15]

When Baker was requested to submit to pinioning, he displayed 'great firmness and evinced no trepidation while it was being performed'. He walked to the drop above the main gate 'unassisted and without portraying the least emotion'. Calcraft put the cap on Baker and adjusted the rope. Prolonged prayers lasted two minutes which 'deeply effected' Baker. 'A quivering motion was observable in his frame, his knees began to tremble and his hands were closely clutched together.'

The drop fell open. Baker, probably guilty, but a man who was convicted on mainly circumstantial evidence, fell half out of sight. He was a man pre-judged

As promised, full particulars with illustrations, immediately published, of the execution
of Frederick Baker in Winchester before a crowd of thousands. William Calcraft is at the
noose. His 'assistants' are waiting below the trap. *The Police News*, 28/12/1867

by the community and those who tried him. In today's age, he would surely
have spent his remaining days in an asylum.

Here is the crux of this story. In the pit, stood two men, brothers in their
twenties, who had paid Calcraft for their 'ringside seat'. Baker was seen to
struggle for about a minute as his 'quivering body swung in the bright morning
air'. There was no quick route for Calcraft to get below to grab the legs to end
another botched job and he shouted to his customers to pull as best they could.
They did what they were told and took a leg each.

The two men lived at Kitwood, then in the northern part of Ropley parish.
They told family that they were incensed at Baker's crime. Their plan was to
take off Baker's hood after the drop, look into his eyes and to spit on his face.
The plan was ill thought through for Baker's head and shoulders were in plain
view of the crowd.

This is the murder of which I write. Not the murder of Fanny Adams.
Not the judicial murder of a convicted Frederick Baker by an authorised if
incompetent hangman. But the wilful common murder of a lunatic by two
men from Four Marks who paid for the privilege.

How do I know this? I knew well the grandson of the youngest man in the pit who lived in Four Marks until his death twenty-five years ago. He told me the story on the condition that I never mentioned their surname for his own young grandchildren still lived locally. My friend knew too much intimate detail for it to be other than true. I watched his emotion as he told the long hidden family secret.

George and Harriet Adams, Fanny's parents, stayed on in their Alton home for a few years, but reportedly, Harriet found the pressure and association too much. The family moved to Ravenscroft Road in Beckenham, Kent, where George continued as a bricklayer. By 1891, through to 1901, now in their sixties, only daughter Elizabeth Ann, aged twenty-nine, stayed with them, Fanny's playmate on the day of the murder. After the death of his wife, George returned to Alton where he died in 1912.

George and Harriet Adams and their other children, 1870s. *Tilyfloptoo*

Withheld from this story until now, is one other pertinent fact; kept back because it was not disclosed to Baker's jury.

There had been another child murder, in June the year before, in a field near Guildford. Jane Sax, aged seven, was on an errand from Shere to Gomshall. She was attacked by a man who stabbed her in the throat, partially severing her windpipe and cutting her tongue. On her deathbed, she identified twenty-one-year-old James Longhurst, who was later hanged for the crime. This was a 'local' crime of such similarity that it must have been read about and discussed by all and sundry.

George Shaw-Lefevre, later Baron Eversely, a solicitor wrote to the *Law Times Journal:*[16]

Some few people, and amongst them the writer, doubted at the time if the guilt was sufficiently established by the chief evidence, if not the only evidence, of identity being that of the dying child, who more by signs than words identified the accused. At the present a horrible impression has been created that the lad Longhurst was innocent, and that the Alton and the Guildford criminal are identical, the party accused at Alton [Baker] having, it is reported been resident in Guildford when the offence was committed. Steps should now be taken by those in power to probe this matter to the bottom [in case] the law has fatally erred.

An editorial statement in the *Journal* concurred.

Longhurst suffered a terrible execution. He protested his innocence. It took five officers to hold him down to be pinioned. The affair was badly botched. He struggled violently at the end of the rope.

The executioner was William Calcraft.

Another letter, written by the gaol schoolmaster, appeared via the clergy in which Longhurst admitted guilt and begged forgiveness. One does wonder at the convenience of these last-minute, dictated admissions which absolved the authorities and silenced the doubters while comforting the parents.

Neither of the hangings of Baker or Longhurst received a mention in Calcraft's *Recollections*.

ENDNOTES

[1] As a young man, William Dyer built the semaphore station, discussed in the previous chapter, '*Sending a Message*'.

[2] *The Police News*, 31/12/1867.

[3] Cansfield, *Sweet FA*. Hampshire Genealogical Society, 'Who was Sweet Fanny Adams?'. McCloskey, *Killed a Young Girl*. Curtis Museum, 'True Story' and Rice, Alton Paper 20, 'What's in a name'. Mukerji, 'Sweet Fanny Adams', *Hampshire Family Historian*. Sly, *Hampshire Murders*.

[4] 22/11/1934.

[5] *The Daily News*, 6/12/1867; 7/12/1867. *Hampshire Advertiser*, 7/12/1867. *The Hampshire Chronicle*, 14/12/1867.

[6] The conventional view is that it was tainted mutton, but careful research by McCloskey, *Killed a Young Girl*, p. 179, suggests it was Pussers Bully Beef, preserved and canned by the Royal Navy Victualling Yard at Deptford which was first issued to the fleet in 1867, the year of Fanny's death.

[7] *Royal Navy Biography*.

[8] McCloskey, *Killed a Young Girl*.

[9] *ODNB*, J. Hamilton, 23/9/2004.

[10] *The Police News*.

[11] *The Police News*, 28/12/1867.

[12] Catalogue item 223, 1868 catalogue.

[13] *The Times*, 1/5/1873.

[14] Calcraft, *Life and Recollections*.

[15] *The Police News*, 28/12/1867.

[16] McCloskey, *Killed a Young Girl*, p. 167.

Reading list:

Calcraft, William, unknown biographer, *Life and Recollections of Calcraft, the Hangman* (London 1880; Gale Digital Collections 2020)

Canfield, Peter, *The True Story of Fanny Adams* (Canfield, Soldridge 2004)

Curtis Museum, 'True Story' and Rice, *Alton Paper 20*, 'What's in a name'

Dernley, Syd, with Newman, David, *The Hangman's Tale, Memoirs of a Public Executioner* (Pan, London 1989)

Hampshire Genealogical Society, 'Who was Sweet Fanny Adams?'

Illustrated Police News (and others), 'The Trial and Condemnation of Frederick Baker', London, 1867

McCloskey, Keith, *Killed a Young Girl. It was Fine and Hot: The Murder of Sweet FA* (2016)

Mukerji, Jenny, 'Sweet Fanny Adams', *Hampshire Family Historian*

Sly, Nicola, *Hampshire Murders* (History Press, Cheltenham 2009)

9 KNOWING ONE'S PLACE
Transportation and the Swing Riots

NEW SOUTH WALES, AUSTRALIA
1833   BODY COUNT: 1

Throughout the south and west of England late into 1830 agricultural workers undertook acts of violent, local protest. Hampshire was, with Wiltshire, the most troubled county in Britain. It is now evident that 'many events went unreported and the full extent of rural protest was greater' than official records.[1] Anger was widely directed: against new machinery, rapacious landlords, the local church and far-away tithe holders supported by a hated tax, the lack of employment, the declining price paid for labour and the rising cost of bread and beer.[2] The air was full of recrimination, crops destroyed and machinery and buildings that symbolised repression burned.

The country's landowners had gone too far and were in fear of loss of their historic authority, particularly in the setting of wages. Their natural allies, the local clergy, reeled from personal attacks and, in some cases, took up arms to fight their flock. The garrison at Winchester was emptied as mounted troops raced to Hampshire's small towns to suppress discontent. Within months, ten local men, most from Headley and Selborne, were sentenced to death although not one hanged, at least for their first crime.

This collection of discontent became known as the *Swing Riots* although a single name could never encapsulate the complexity of hunger, hatred and disparate targets. 'Swing' was derived from Captain Swing, a fictitious name often signed to the threatening letters delivered to farmers, magistrates and parsons in the dead of night. The Captain became the shady figurehead of the rising.[3]

Dr William Curtis, who founded the Curtis Museum in Alton, rode across the hill at East Worldham on his way to Kingsley when he was stopped by some 300 excited rioters.

'Oh, Mr Curtis,' they said. 'It is a pity you were not at Headley when we broke into the Workhouse. You would have laughed if you had seen the tiles fly. Tell the people in Alton to look out as we are intending to attack the Workhouse and Breweries after we have been to Selborne.'[4]

Headley workhouse today, re-named Headley Grange. *John Owen Smith*

The threat contained farce. Abraham Crowley bought the larger of Alton's two breweries in Turk Street from the Baverstock family in 1821. He managed an extensive business on the Basingstoke Canal including flyboats and wharfs on the Basingstoke Canal for delivering goods to London. He was married to Charlotte, Curtis's eldest sister. Abraham's two brothers married two of Charlotte's sisters. The Hawkins family owned the other, the *Swan Brewery*, housed in longstanding premises behind the *Swan Inn*, which could be reached from Turk Street via a small lane.[5] As well as the *Swan*, their empire included the *White Horse* (then the *Black Boy*), the *Windmill*, *George Inn*, *Crown Inn* and *Duke's Head* and, later, the *Golden Pot*, *King's Head* and *Tumble-down Dick* plus fourteen others in villages around. The Complin family ran a third brewery in Holybourne High Street.

When Curtis got to Alton, he went straight to his brother-in-law and raised the alarm. A messenger was sent to Winchester to ask for protection. Alton citizens, perhaps 140, town gentry rather than men of the soil, were sworn in as special constables. Crowley's old hop store on the corner of Turk Street became a guard room. Packets of hops were arranged around the fire as seats. No wonder Curtis later joked that he was well received when he delivered sausage rolls and home-made gingerbread nuts to the men between the night's patrols.

A troop of thirty Life Guards, the senior British regiment, arrived and were quartered at the *Crown Inn*. The regiment of 'upper-class soldiery' was feared by working men. Caroline of Brunswick, estranged wife of George IV, died in 1821, weeks after being refused entry to her husband's coronation. She was loved by the public. Her funeral procession, passing through London on its way to her native Germany, was eventually forced to change route by the crowds. Stones and mud were thrown at the military. The Life Guards were 'sanctioned in firing their pistols and carbines at the unarmed crowd. Screams of terror were heard in every direction. The number of shots fired was not less than forty or fifty,' and two people were killed.[6]

Up to 1,500 men gathered from all the villages about Alton, but 'became disorganised' at the news of resistance. Gestures were made instead. The labourers and their local leaders acted openly and fearlessly because they 'expected that their protest would be tolerated'.[7] Rioting and protest had a 'certain historical legitimacy' because both rulers and ruled understood that disorder and even violence were part of a popular culture.[8] The Heighes brothers broke a threshing machine at Wyck in Binsted, an 'established way to put pressure on an employer using new technology';[9] there were assaults and robbery at Farringdon and Greatham; and disturbances at Liphook. Rioters set fire to a public house and a barn at Newton Common.

A hand threshing machine.
J. Allen Ransome, The Implements of Agriculture, 1843, Rural History Centre, University of Reading

The mob that met William Curtis at East Worldham may have been disingenuous, but they were accurate. At Selborne, the occupants were turned out of the Union workhouse, the fittings and furniture burned or broken and the roof pulled down.[10] The unloved Reverend William Cobbold was forced to sign away part of his tithe rights. In repayment, he later fought tirelessly to halt any thoughts of pardons or leniency. It was a similar story at Headley where the Reverend Robert Dickinson was forced to agree a reduction in his tithes to £350 a year. At his village workhouse, the mob 'rushed like a torrent into every room'. This was an institution that required its inmates to be badged 'HP' in metal letters for 'Headley Poor'. For up to ninety minutes, windows were torn out, the stairways broken, ceilings pulled down. Up to 50,000 tiles were stripped from the roof.

Ten years before, in August 1823, William Cobbett passed through Selborne and noted that the summer had been so cold and wet that hop bines had 'scarcely got up the poles and the leaves were black, nearly, as soot and covered in lice'.[11] The hops were bad everywhere and 'their failure must necessarily be attended with consequences very inconvenient to the whole of a population so small as this'. A farmer told Cobbett that there could not be a 'more unhappy place in England' than Selborne. A shot was fired through the window at the vicar, possibly because of his lawsuits against the people. When this history is added to the tithe revolt and the attacks by the Reverend Sir John Rivers at Martyr Worthy, and the great disagreements with the Reverend Samuel Maddock in Ropley in 1818, there is more than a whiff of anti-clericalism to add to the anti-tithe movement.

This was not the first time Alton was threatened by an agricultural riot. In the previous century there were minor skirmishes against turnpike roads, not as bad as the destruction of gates and tollhouses elsewhere, and, in 1800, field workers marched, as in many places in the county, in protest against their 'distressed condition'.[12] 'Labour was abundant, work was scarce in winter, and wages were low.'

These circumstances were urged as a reason for the enclosure of the common lands which, by increasing the area under cultivation, afforded increased employment for the people. The bulk of the agricultural Hampshire population remained practically untaught. Consequently when labour-saving devices, such as the threshing and turnip cutting machines, were first introduced, the labourers who found employment in the winter by threshing corn with the flail, as their forefathers had done from Saxon times downwards, were too ignorant to see anything in such an innovation except ruin for themselves and their families. Machines were smashed and other acts of lawlessness committed.[13]

Writing from Ropley to Hampshire's Lord Lieutenant, John Duthie added his voice, 'The year will long be remembered by the excessive dearness of every article of life. The grievous pressure induced ... make it the duty of every man to endeavour to trace out the productive causes of the overwhelming evil.'[14] After diagnosing the problem, Duthy was clear that he had 'no hesitation in saying that this master-mischief is the War'.

Although, in 1830, the mob cried off, the local hop workers assembled near William Complin's brewery at Holybourne to try to get higher wages because the 'present allowance was really insignificant' to support their families.[15] Complin, who ran several public houses, was under direct threat from the wider rioters angry at an employers' conspiracy to reduce wages. He met with other farmers who reversed their decision and agreed to 'give a reasonable price for their labour'. The *Hampshire Chronicle* reported that the 'men appeared perfectly satisfied, and return to their work'. The newspaper couldn't resist betraying its own sympathies as it observed that 'the conduct of the men towards their employers was orderly and respectful. They declared they did not intend to join with any persons not belonging to the parish, and only requested as much as would enable them to live.' Perhaps the men's public position was not surprising with the Life Guards waiting nearby.

The labourers' statement implies two sorts of separation: one with other agricultural labourers come into the hop fields for seasonal work; the other with events perpetrated nearby, but by others. They were wise to differentiate, especially because of what followed in the months either side of Christmas.

With regard to the first, the dispute did not end with the meeting with Complin and his fellow farmers. Two days later, the Life Guards faced off a large mob, partly from the hop fields, that gathered outside the *Swan Inn* in Alton's High Street. This was the same inn where three years before in more genteel times, Mr Joseph Smedley, in Thackeray's *Vanity Fair*, stepped from his fast carriage, a post-chaise, during a journey from Southampton to London and 'imbibed some of the ale for which the place is famous'.

The angry men were led by Robert Maggs from Gloucestershire, a convicted petty criminal, a felt-hat maker, and a man experienced in the earliest bouts of trade unionism, an activity almost unknown in Alton. Maggs had moved to the area that summer, worked the hop fields when the picking started in September, and stayed at the *Lymington Arms*, the local inn for travelling hatters, at Lymington Bottom Road, once in Four Marks, now in Medstead.

As to events elsewhere, a recent analysis identified 3,283 incidents during the unrest in the countryside.[16] Open dissent began in Kent, another 'hop' county, in November 1830, spread into Sussex and parts of Surrey in the same month, then moved outwards by way of Berkshire, Hampshire and Wiltshire before heading westward and northwards. The highest concentration of lawlessness fell south of a line drawn between Hampshire and the Wash.[17]

Events reported in Winchester through November and December included 'evil-minded and dishonest men wandering about in predatory hordes exacting money and provisions from several gentlemen and farmers'; the moving of the 47th Regiment from Portsmouth and the 3rd Dragoon Guards from Southampton to guard the centre of the city; a mob of 300 at Avington where special constables led by two reverend gentlemen attacked with bludgeons and took fifty prisoners ('this instance of prompt and successful resistance, being opposed to a lawless mob, cannot be sufficiently applauded'). A large group of men rioted at Itchen Abbas; at Martyr Worthy the mob set about the rector, Sir Henry Rivers. Five hundred men extorted money from the inhabitants of Swathling and Stoneham where fifty-three were taken; prisoners were brought in from Basingstoke; money and provisions were taken from Littleton; threshing machines were destroyed at Wickham, Botley, New Alresford and Durley; men rioted in Upham; at Swanmore and Soberton 'many who have hitherto borne excellent characters have been carried away by the madness of the moment'; at Stockbridge, men with clubs and staves demanded a reduction in tithes and two sovereigns; at Lower Wallop, a wage rise of twenty-five per cent was agreed with local farmers; there were large gatherings of land occupiers and owners at Titchfield and Hambledon and, at a meeting at the *Swan Inn*, Alresford, 'the whole of the male population' voluntarily came forward to form horse and foot patrols. The county gaol held over 200 prisoners charged with having riotously assembled and destroyed machinery at Rockbourne, Basingstoke, Andover, Weyhill, Upper Clatford, Fordingbridge, Romsey, Buriton and Wickham.[18]

The historian George Rudé was at pains to point out that the wider business involved threatening letters, assaults, robberies to tithe, enclosure and food riots and that in 'every one of the twenty-five counties affected, there was rick-burning, and the firing of farms, barns and country mansions'.[19]

The Hampshire newspaper letter columns were full of the worthy lamenting the state of affairs and declaring the reasonableness of working men wishing to earn enough to feed their families. The establishment and the legislature were somewhat tougher:

> *Every friend to good order and the well being of society must deeply lament the existence of an insurrectionary spirit among a portion of the agricultural labourers, which is fast spreading, and if not timely checked, will be productive of the most serious results to the country at large ... A Royal proclamation offers a reward of £50 on the conviction of every person guilty of acts of outrage and violence, with His Majesty's pardon, if the offence shall be made by an accomplice. £500 are offered, to be paid on conviction of any person for secretly setting on fire ricks of corn, hay, buildings, or other property in the countries of Hants, Kent, Wilts, Berks, Sussex and Surrey ... Let then the misguided men who, in an evil hour, have listened to the pernicious counsels of designing individuals, and gone astray, quickly reduce their steps and return to their peaceful avocations, lest they be destroyed by their faithless associates ...'[20]*

Alton was a hop town and was vulnerable to agricultural disharmony. The crop was grown all around by a large permanent workforce. In season, the kilns worked through the night. The breweries were large employers and their product, beer, was acknowledged, with bread, as essential to the health of the labouring man. Hop gardens started at Holybourne church with hop kilns near the big farmhouse, Twitchens, and stretched up Holybourne Hill to the many farms around Binsted. Will Hall, recorded in the Domesday Book, lay to the west of Alton. Its farm in the early nineteenth century was in a valley near the source of the River Wey where 600 acres of wood, hops, and arable and pasture land rose gently to the north. William Gunner, its farmer, wrote:

> *Of all the crops the farmer has to do with [hops are], the most interesting, causes him more anxiety, requires more attention, costs more to produce and perhaps oftener fails than any other, but at the same time no crop has paid so well.[21]*

Hop poles, twelve to fourteen feet high, were placed with four roots to each pole on small mounds in rows wide enough to allow a small wagon. Cuttings were planted in the spring. A foot from the bottom wires connecting with strings to guide the plants. The regular labourers in the 1830s were joined for the four or five weeks of the picking season by a large team of casual workers. Some were local families, but there were also gypsies and travellers and people from far afield. For a month, starting about eight in the morning because of the dew, men with poles pulled the hops down for placing in big baskets marked with seven black rings, each a full bushel to be noted by the tally man. The hop bines were rough and make hands sore in the wet. Each night, the crop was dried on hair mats in oast houses heated with fine coal and coloured by sticks of brimstone.[22]

The other main ingredient was barley, steeped in pure Wey water, and spread on the floor to germinate. Sprouted cereal was kiln dried to stop further growth and then roasted in maltings.

Private houses were licensed to brew their own beer from 1830 and these new premises provided a ready supply and a meeting place for dissenters. In 1577, there were nearly 20,000 taverns, alehouses and inns in England and Wales. In 1840, there were nearly 50,000 brewers, reduced to 25,000 by 1880.[23]

When the gypsies were in Alton for the picking, the centre of the town was often bedlam. Ponies were paraded at raucous sales in Market Square. Because of the fights, some pubs had a besom broom tied to their sign to signify gypsies were not welcome.

Last night there was the most awful row among our Irish party. They fell out among themselves and fought like bulldogs – men, women and children. They knocked each other down with hop poles and fought as if they would kill each other.[24]

Robert Maggs began his proselytising sitting in a wagon sent each day to Ropley to take out-of-town pickers to Holybourne and Binsted. He was a tall man of forty years, full bearded and wearing, as befitted his profession, a natty top hat. His constant companion, always at his feet, was a spaniel of amiable disposition, but doubtful parentage. Maggs had a rhythmic pace of voice which people who knew him called mesmerising. He came from an extraordinary concentration of South Gloucestershire villages that, from the mid-sixteenth century, housed almost a thousand apprentice-trained felt-makers. These men made the base felt hood which was then worked into the latest fashion by Bristol finishers. At that time, 'no man of whatever station would be seen about without his hat.'[25]

From the seventeenth century, felt-makers were among the first bodies of men to begin the slow process to trade unionism. Felt-makers fought bitterly into the nineteenth century with government and employers to control workers' rights. This was chiefly achieved by managing the apprenticeship system and, thereby, entry into the trade. Militant hatters were responsible for the entry of the word 'strike' into the English language.[26]

Maggs spent one year at hard labour in 1825 for picking up, he said, a silk handkerchief in a Bristol street and keeping it.[27] From then on, he was a firebrand and a radical. Early in 1830, his association was in dispute with the hatmaker firm of Christy. These disputes were often resolved in the favour of the party with the longest pockets. One way of alleviating the financial burden was for the Hatters' Association to send some of its men 'on the tramp', a long-standing and well-organised system whereby men toured the country on foot to find work. 'Tramping' is a word which has gone down in the world. In times of industrial action, the system had great benefit. The men carried with them a personal, endorsed 'blank', a card which gave their credentials. Each man was given a set amount in shillings to cover his journey over an agreed number of days. The tramps stayed at turnhouses, often public houses run by retired hatters, where cheap food and accommodation was pre-arranged. There were many hundreds of these stations marking employment routes across the country. The *Lymington Arms* was an option on one of the lesser-trod routes from Gloucestershire to Winchester and Southampton.

A tattered hatter's blank issued by the Associated Feltmakers of Winterbourne, 1810. The tramping hatter is welcomed to the turnhouse by the publican and his wife, who holds a pot of beer. The scene is decorated by sheep, beaver, rabbits and hats, the animals whose fur and wool was used to make felt hats. The hatter's personal details are written on the back. *Bristol Record Office, 43454/1, PicBox/7A/Trade/1, 23/2/1810*

The agricultural workers drawn to Alton's hop fields for work had none of the organised background of Maggs and his fellow hatters. They could not believe the independence held by combinations of craftsmen standing against domineering manufacturers. How different was the lot of the hop pickers, little skilled, when grouped before all-powerful landowners and farmers? To keep employment, agricultural labourers needed to show respect, indeed subservience, to their 'betters'. Local experience of self-help was limited to benefit societies, clubs really, founded on a sharing basis and held at the *Duke's* and *King's Heads* public houses. Hampshire's Friendly Society was founded only five years before in 1825.

Behind Maggs outside the *Swan Inn* stood, perhaps, 200 jeering, mocking men: gypsies, layabouts, homeless wretches and others from neighbouring villages who would be gratified just to receive last year's pay rates. Facing them in two lines across the High Street were twelve Life Guards, armour glistening, white plumes perfectly groomed, all with swords drawn. A bloody fight seemed inevitable.

The young officer, from a family with large estates in Northamptonshire, called for the 'rioters' to disperse or he would order his troopers to charge and to clear the street without mercy. To make his point, he moved his men ten yards closer and halted. There was a two-minute staring match.

Maggs' spaniel had seen enough. He yapped forward towards the stamping horses. The captain trotted forward alone, waved his sword and sliced the dog in two.

The protestors ran.

That was the end of Alton's last demonstration. Maggs was easily identified as the leader and found the next day at the *Lymington Arms* with a bellyful of Crowley's beer. He was arrested without a struggle and taken to Winchester.

The government of the Duke of Wellington had been well warned of the likelihood of trouble. In the *Political Register*, radical politician and writer, William Cobbett, commented:

The time is at hand when it will become a choice of labourers, certain death from starvation, or the chance of death by rope or gun, and, be assured, my Lord Duke, that Englishmen will prefer the latter. Think, then, betimes, of the consequence of parish after parish combined till there be half a country in commotion.[28]

One of the ways the authorities tried to stop opinions like these reaching the poor was by an artificially high Stamp Duty on newssheets. In July, Cobbett decided to publish the comment section of the *Register* separately as 'Twopenny Trash' (Politics for the Poor). In July he wrote to 'The Working People of England':

> *The great and general cause of these unnatural crimes [arson] is the extreme poverty of the people; or in other words the starving state in which they are. The natural consequence is discontent; that leads to resentment. No man can suffer what he deems a wrong without feeling anger against somebody ... that anger will vent itself in acts, whenever he finds himself able to act. Though he might not get redress by such action, he gets revenge.*

Lord Carnarvon of Highclere Castle wrote to Lord Melbourne, the Home Secretary, stating that Cobbett's papers were distributed all over the neighbourhood and had 'undoubtedly caused the incendiary spirit'. Cobbett blamed those in society who lived off unearned income at the expense of hard-working agricultural labourers.[29] The government charged Cobbett with seditious libel. In the trial at London Guildhall in July 1831, Cobbett discredited the case against him and to the government's great embarrassment was acquitted.

By the end of 1830, 1,000 men awaited trial, 2,000 across the country. Melbourne accused local magistrates of being lenient. In Hampshire, and four other counties, he appointed Special Commissions to try offenders outside the usual court schedule. The first of these started in The Castle in Winchester on 20 December. Sir John Vaughan, Baron of the Exchequer, was the chief judge, assisted by Sir James Parke and Sir Edward Alderson. The Duke of Wellington, in his capacity as Lord Lieutenant of Hampshire, also sat on the bench.

Badly-scared and indignant, the landowning class would have its reckoning. Juries were selected from a list of twenty-three gentlemen, thirteen of whom were baronets or knights, and lasted, with a break of two days for Christmas, through until the end of the month. Judge Alderson said, '[We] do not come here ... to inquire into grievances. We come here to decide law.'[30] His toughness brought its reward when his daughter, Georgina, joined the aristocracy by marrying Robert Gascoyne-Cecil, 3rd Marquess of Salisbury.

The severity of the Winchester court can be seen in its unprecedented use of transportation in comparison with other counties. Two-thirds of those tried at Winchester were convicted and more than half were transported, mostly for seven years. Those who were sentenced to death had their sentences commuted to transportation for life. The total number of transportations was 152.[31]

One man, Robert Maggs, was tried *in camera* for 'leading, provoking and instigating a riotous assembly'. All that is known is that he pleaded not guilty, but said nothing in his defence. He was in court for less than ten minutes. His crime carried a mandatory death penalty. In a display of petty cruelty, Maggs heard that his sentence had been commuted as he approached the gallows.[32]

There is background to the government's attitude which does them no credit. The Webbs, socialist reformers, noted that, 'Under the shadow of the French Revolution, the English governing classes regarded all associations of the common people with the utmost alarm. In this general terror, lest insubordination should develop into rebellion, were merged both the capitalist's objection to high wages and the politician's dislike of Democratic institutions.'[33]

The plethora of Combination Acts, which followed the French Revolution, was part of a stream of restrictive legislation against the working man organising his forces.[34] Three junior ministers masterminded Press propaganda. One of them, Bristol-born Francis Freeling, ran the Post Office from 1797–1836 and through it a large national spy network that opened private letters at will.

Francis Place, another social reformer, said the new laws were 'not so much the consequence of the desire to keep the people in an abject state of subjection to their employers, as of a persuasion that they enabled those employers to get their work done at less expense. Justice was entirely out of the question; the working man could seldom obtain a hearing before a magistrate – never without impatience and insult; and never could they calculate on even an approximation of a rational conclusion.[35]

The Times was quite clear that 'one of the first acts of the Imperial Parliament would be the prevention of conspiracies to raise wages. 'All benefit clubs and societies are to be immediately suppressed.'

None of this was helped by the severe depression of the years following the close of the Napoleonic War and two years of bad harvests. The new order included 'landowners, bourgeois capitalist farmers, and the rest, including small farmers and labourers'.[36]

Cleric Edward Tufnell claimed that the masters 'are always and everywhere in a sort of tacit, but constant and uniform combination, not to raise the wages of labour above their actual rate ... We seldom, indeed, hear of this combination, because it is the usual, and one may say the natural state of things. Masters too sometimes enter into a particular combination to sink the wages of labour even below this rate. These are always conducted with the utmost silence and secrecy, till the moment of execution, and when the workmen yield, as they sometimes do without resistance, though severely felt by them, they are never heard of by other people.'[37]

Greedy landowners took advantage of lean times. The response of the agricultural labourers, the form it took and the exact reasons were local, but it was a movement and was the beginning of a fundamental change in the British way of life. The men of Holybourne, Binsted and the rest were a part of it. They took whatever means were to hand. When arguing doesn't work, what is left for the hungry: threats, bullying, theft, assault and burning?[38]

Early in February 1831, Robert Maggs was taken to the hulk *York*, moored at Gosport. York was a 74-gun ship converted to a prison hulk in 1819. Typically, she confined about 500 convicts. In company with five other men sentenced at Winchester (Robert Holdaway, Matthew Triggs, John Heath and James Harding for the Headley Union, and James's brother, Aaron, for the Selborne Union), Maggs sailed within two weeks on the *Eleanor* for New South Wales. The voyage took 126 days with 205 people aboard including a missionary for the Aborigines. The ship re-provisioned at the Cape of Good Hope and took on three more prisoners.

The Surgeon Superintendent, John Stephenson, wrote in his Journal, 'No set of men perhaps under similar circumstances ever suffered less from disease.' However, after leaving the Colony, 'the vessel was very laboursome and shipped such quantities of water that it was frequently necessary even in a fresh breeze to have the hatches battened down for two or three days together, leaving only sufficient space for one person to pass up or down.'

The *Eleanor* arrived in Sydney Cove on 26 June. The 'Swing Rioters' from Hampshire joined representatives of 'nearly every protest movement known to the British government'.[39] Australia received members of most working class discontent: frame-breaking Luddites in 1812, East Anglian food mobs in 1816, members of the Pentridge Rising near Nottingham in 1817, the Cato Street Conspiracy in 1820, radical weavers from Scotland in 1820 and Yorkshire in 1821. Still to come were rioters from Bristol in 1831 and Wales in 1835, the Tolpuddle Martyrs in 1834, and more than 100 Chartists, the working class movement, between 1839 and 1848 – all part of 130,000 men, women and juvenile offenders.[40]

Maggs was quickly assigned to Captain John Brabyn at Clifton Hill in Melbourne.[41] Brabyn, a man in his seventies, had a colourful past. He was a bodyguard to the Duke of York in Flanders and saved his life when the duke's horse was shot from under him. He turned down a knighthood from King George III, but was given his commission with the New South Wales Corps in 1795. He was one of six magistrates involved in the 'rum rebellion' in 1808 which imprisoned Governor William Bligh in Australia's only military *coup d'état*.

Maggs' talents as a hatter were recognised and he was allowed unusual freedom to visit the homes of Brabyn's male friends and fellow officers to take measurements for new headwear. It was on one of these trips in 1833 that Maggs was drinking near the port with two lags when, as they said later, 'Maggs stiffened, started muttering to himself, wouldn't talk to us and started drinking swiftly.' After 'an hour of strange behaviours', he got up and 'silently left'.

Two days later, the alarm was raised. The body of Major Archibald Cuthbert-Smythe, attached to the Melbourne Volunteer Rifle Regiment, was found early in the morning near the door of his residence in Richmond, stabbed in the back and neck several times. A small black horse with a star on its forehead was missing. So was Robert Maggs. Five pounds was offered for his apprehension with a further two pounds for the horse.[42]

Maggs was caught upcountry with the horse within the month.[43] No charge was ever brought for the murder of Cuthbert-Smythe, presumably more difficult to prove as it was unwitnessed. However, horse stealing was a capital offence so justice would still be served. Maggs maintained his customary silence under questioning and admitted nothing.

He relented only as he made his second journey to the gallows and realised that, this time, there would be no escape. The chaplain bent his head to hear any last words which might save the man's soul. He was disappointed and confused.

Maggs whispered, 'That man killed my dog. It woren't right. It woren't necessary. I loved my dog.'

Maggs was hanged in August. There was no 'drop'; he was left to swing and wriggle for ten minutes.[44]

ENDNOTES

[1] Kent, *Popular Radicalism.*

[2] Tithe was a long-established system of local landholders being required to pay a tenth of all produce, often swapped for money. A rector was due both the 'great' or rectorial tithes (corn, beans, peas, hay and wood) and the 'small' or vicarial tithes (the remainder). A vicar was due only the small tithes, the great tithes going to some other holder, in the case of Selborne to Magdalen College, Oxford.

[3] 'Swing' may have been a reference to the swinging stick of the flail used in hand threshing, the country skill being replaced by threshing machines (wikipedia).

[4] Curtis, *Alton.*

[5] Hurst, *Breweries.*

[6] *The Guardian,* 18/8/1825.

[7] Gash, *Aristocracy.*

[8] Palmer, *Police and Protest.*

[9] Hobsbawm and Rudé, *Captain Swing.*

[10] Smith, *Workhouse riots.*

[11] Cobbett, *Rural Rides.*

[12] Shore, *Hampshire.*

[13] Shore, *Hampshire.*

[14] Duthy, *Observations.*

[15] *Hampshire Chronicle,* 29/11/1830

[16] *Family and Community History Research Society,* 2005.

[17] Hammonds, *Village Labourer.*

[18] *Hampshire Chronicle, 29/11/1830.*

[19] Rudé, 'Rural and Urban Disturbances'.

[20] *Hampshire Chronicle, 'Summary',* 29/11/1830.

[21] *Journal,* William Terrell Gunner, 18/8/1850.

[22] Fenwick, *Hops and Breweries.*

[23] Wood, *Historical Britain.*

[24] 28/9/1850.

[25] The history of the hatters, trade unionism and Robert Maggs, in particular, is taken from an unpublished PhD thesis, 'Felt Hat Industry'.

[26] *Annual Register,* 1768.

[27] Gloucestershire Quarter Sessions and Assize Court between 1818-1848 (GA, Q/Gc/5/1-7, 6/1) .

[28] *Political Register,* 23/10/1830.

[29] Fox, *Berkshire to Botany.*

[30] Hobsbawm and Rudé, *Captain Swing.*

[31] Wallis, 'We do not come …'.

[32] *Hampshire Chronicle,* 21/12/1830.

[33] Webbs, *Trade Unionism.*

[34] *Treasonable and Seditious Practices and Assemblies* Bills (1795); in the wake of naval mutinies, the *Seduction from Duty and Allegiance Act* (1797); two Newspaper Publications Acts (1798-1799); Administering Unlawful Oaths (1797); and an Act for the more *Effective Suppressions of Societies established for Seditious and Treasonable Purposes* (1799).

[35] Wallas, Pace.

[36] Poole, 'Forty Years'.

[37] Tufnell, *Character.*

[38] Hawkins, 'Review of Captain Swing'.

[39] Hughes, *Fatal Shore.*

[40] Frost, *Botany Bay*.

[41] *New South Wales Advertiser*, 10/3/1833.

[42] *New South Wales Advertiser*, 10/3/1833.

[43] *New South Wales Advertiser*, 31/3/1833.

[44] *Sydney Gazette*, 1/9/1831.

Reading list:

Chambers, Jill, *The Hampshire Machine Breakers: The Story of the 1830 Riots* (Self-published 1969)

Curtis, William, *A Short History and Description of the Town of Alton* (1896; Noverre Press, Binsted 2012)

Duthy, John, 'Observations on the present high price of provisions', *Letter to the Lord Lieutenant and inhabitants of Hampshire* (1800; Gale Ecco reprint, 2020)

Fenwick, Paul, edited, *Hops and the Breweries* (Memories of Alton Project 2017)

Fox, Norman, *Berkshire to Botany Bay* (Littlefield, Newbury 1995)

Frost, Alan, *Botany Bay, The Real Story* (Black, Collingwood, Australia 2012)

Fruen, Brenda, 'A Rural Ride Through The Hard Parishes: A Study on the Mid Hampshire Chalklands Prior To The Swing Riots', *Proceedings of Hampshire Field Club Archaeological Society*, 54, 1999

Gash, Norman, *Aristocracy and People, 1815–1865* (Harvard University Press 1981)

Hammond, J.L. and Barbara, *The Village Labourer, 1760–1832: A Study of the Government of England before the Reform Bill* (1911; London, Longmans, Green 1995).

Hampshire Chronicle, December 1830

Hawkins, J., 'Review of Captain Swing', *Historical Journal*, 12, 1969, pp. 716–17.

Heal, Chris, 'The Felt Hat Industry of Bristol and South Gloucestershire 1530–1909', EThOS, British Library, 2012

Hilton, Boyd, *A Mad, Bad, and Dangerous People? England 1783–1846* (Oxford, Clarendon Press 2006)

Hobsbawm, E.J., and Rudé, George, *Captain Swing* (Pimlico, London 1969)

Hurst, Jane, *Alton's Breweries* (No publisher, undated)

Hughes, Robert, *The Fatal Shore* (Harvill Press, London 1987)

Kent, David, *Popular Radicalism and the Swing Riots in Central Hampshire* (HCC, Hampshire Papers, No. 11, 1997)

Palmer, Stanley H., *Police and Protest in England and Ireland, 1780–1850* (Cambridge University Press 1988)

Poole, Steve, 'Forty Years of Rural History from Below: Captain Swing and the Historians', *Southern History*, Vol. 32, 210, pp. 1–20

Rudé, George, *The Crowd in History, A Study of Popular Disturbances in France and England, 1730–1848* (Wiley, London 1964)

Shore, T.W., *A History of Hampshire, including The Isle of Wight* (Elliot Stock, London 1892)

Smith, John Owen, *One Monday in November … and Beyond, The Selborne and Headley Workhouse Riots of 1830* (Self-published Headley Down 2002)

Tufnell, Edward Carleton, *Character, Object and Effects of Trades' Unions* (1834; reprint New York, Arno Press, 1972)

Wallas, Graham, *The Life of Francis Place 1771–1854*, revised edition (London, George Allen & Unwin 1918).

Wallis, Rose, 'We do not come here … to inquire into grievances; we come here to decide law', *Southern History*, Vol. 32, 210, pp. 159–175

Webb, Sidney and Beatrice, *The History of Trade Unionism* (Longmans, Green, London 1898)

Wood, Eric S., *Historical Britain, A comprehensive account of the development of rural and urban life and landscape from prehistory to the present day* (Harvill Press, London 1995)

Appendix: Table of 46 men local to Four Marks and Alton tried after the Swing Riots

Place	Surname	First name	Age	Riotous assembly	Thresher breaking
Alton	Maggs	Robert	40	•	
Bighton	Butcher	Isaac	23	•	
Bighton	Hibberd	William	47	•	
Binsted (Wyck)	Heighes	Thomas	29		• (1)
Binsted	Heighes	William	30		• (1)
Farringdon	Gibbs	Thomas	25		
Greatham	Kingshott	John	35		
Headley	Bicknell	William	23	•	
Headley	Bright	William	22		
Headley	Harding	Thomas	32	•	
Headley	Heath	John	42	•	
Headley	Holdaway	Robert	38	•	
Headley	James	Henry	38	•	•
Headley	Marshall	Thomas	21	•	
Headley	Painter	James	36	•	
Headley	Robinson	Thomas	67	•	
Headley	Triggs	Matthew	38	•	
Itchen Abbas	Blackman	James	36	•	
Itchen Abbas	Cannings	John	20	•	
Itchen Abbas	Carter	George	28	•	
Itchen Abbas	Cook	Thomas	30	•	
Itchen Abbas	Cooper	John	57	•	•
Itchen Abbas	Hampton	George	25	•	
Itchen Abbas	Hitchcock	Henry	19	•	
Itchen Abbas	Hopkins	Christopher	22	•	
Itchen Abbas	Horn	James	18	•	
Itchen Abbas	Illsley	David	50	•	
Itchen Abbas	Lawrence	George	21	•	
Itchen Abbas	Mullins	Henry	19	•	
Itchen Abbas	Oliver	Benjamin	34	•	
Martyr Worthy	Bolter	William	60		
Martyr Worthy	Coleman	George	22		
Martyr Worthy	Grantham	William	36		
Martyr Worthy	Holt	George	25		
Martyr Worthy	Over	George	24		
New Alresford	Bown	Benjamin	26		•
New Alresford	Camis	James	19		•
Selborne	Bennett	Robert	16	•	
Selborne	Bone	Henry	31	•	
Selborne	Cobb	John	27	•	
Selborne	Harding	Aaron	41	•	
Selborne	Hoare	Thomas	36	•	
Selborne	Hoare	William	39	•	
Selborne	Newland	John	39	•	
Selborne	Smith	Benjamin	23	•	
Selborne	Trimming	John	25		

1: Value £25, of Robert Shotter & Edward Baigent 2: On Mary King: one sovereign, bread, cheese & beer
3: On Ann Parker 3s 6d 4: On Sir Henry Rivers, Rector 5: On John Dagwell 6: Forcing Rev Cobbold to sign
tithe reduction of £300 7: Mobbing Rev Cobbold 8: Painter never sailed, was pardoned in 1833 and went home to Kingsle
HL = Hard labour

Destroying Selborne & Headley Union	Assault & robbery	Acquitted / discharged	Death	Transportation (commuted)	Prison (months)
			•	Life	
		•			
		•			
				7 years	
		Reprimand			
	•	•			
	• (2)	•			
• (Head)		•			
	• (3)	•			
• (Head)			•	7 years	
• (Head)			•	Life	
• (Head)			•	Life	
• (Head)			•	Life	
• (Head)	• (2)		•	1 year HL	
• (Head)			•	7 years (8)	
• (Head)		•			
• (Head)			•	Life	
					1M
		•			
					1
				7 years	
					1
					1
		•			
					1
		•			
					1
		•			
					1
					1 HL
	• (4)	Pard 1833	•	14 years	
	• (5)		•	7 years	
	• (4)				1
	• (4)				1 HL
	• (4)				1
					18 HL
					18 HL
• (Selb)		•			
• (Selb)					12 HL
• (Selb)					24 HL
• (Selb)			•	Life	
• (Selb)					24 HL
• (Selb)					24 HL
	• (6)				6 HL
• (Selb)					6 HL
	• (7)				

10 DRUGS AT THE BUS STOP
Looking after the youngsters

FOUR MARKS
2019   BODY COUNT: 1

The murder of a young man snatched from near the bus stop at the parade of shops on Winchester Road in Four Marks is the one, among all the others in this book, in which I have least confidence. I have no documentary proof, but only word of mouth evidence. To my knowledge, the police have never been called to find a missing person. No body has ever been found.

And yet, paradoxically, this murder is one where three people, all alive today, were prepared to come forward, identities hidden, and swear that it did happen. What's more, there was unanimity in their reaction to the unintended death: sadness that a young person lost his life, but little or no remorse because everyone felt that a greater good had been served and a terrible warning message had been sent. They believed that a chilling lesson needed to be forced into the face of the small drug-dealing community that infests the towns and villages of north Hampshire.

At the end of the day, I am a believer. If I were not, I would not have written this chapter. You can read the evidence and decide for yourself.

It was early spring last year. My request for Four Marks murder stories had been shared with friends and acquaintances for over a year. I was used to crank calls so the suggestion of a night-time, blindfolded, pick-up in a car by three unknown men was no surprise.

Like any sane person, I refused.

I got the second call thirty minutes later. The three men still wanted to talk to me. The meeting could be in any way that I was happy as long as it would mean that I could never identify them, their car or the place where we met. The caller explained their need to guarantee their secrecy. We hassled for five minutes until we agreed a plan. After all, as the man on the phone said, they already knew my name, phone number and where I lived. If they wanted to do me harm, why go through the charade? My collection was set for eight the next evening. Their mobile number was unavailable when I checked. They were using an untraceable 'burner' phone.

The process we followed was a bit farcical, but it worked. I never saw my driver, his car or the house he took me to. We drove for about fifteen minutes, turning right far more than turning left. By the traffic volume, we were on the Winchester Road three times. I am sure we never left the village. The blindfold came off in a fitted, fake-oak kitchen, *Wren*, I think. The blinds were down; anything vaguely personal had been removed, including a couple of pictures which left slight dust-marks on the walls. It was a new house. There was little traffic noise, more a distant hum. We sat around a white plastic table with four stools, probably brought in for the occasion. I was the one without a mask because I had to take notes. The three were dressed head-to-toe in black, including their own masks which had crude cuts for their eyes and mouths. Their accents were bland, everyday south of England, no Hampshire. They were incomers, but then so was almost everyone else in Four Marks.

They started their story, one man taking the lead, another interposing when he felt something had been missed, a fact or an emphasis, the third speaking only once.

First, they asked me to explain about my book. What experience did I have in writing books? Why was I doing it? How many stories had I got? Did I have a publisher? When would it come out? How would I sell it? Did I have any official support?

I was able to answer the personal questions, but told them they would have to trust me on the publication. I had lots of help from people far and wide, many eminent experts in their subjects. The replies had been gratifying particularly because of the unusual subject.

Satisfied, they moved on. They had a problem. They had tried to deal with a local drug problem among Four Marks teenagers. Their own children were under threat. They were part of a wider group, some dozen parents who had been frustrated by police inactivity and so three sub-groups had met anonymously and separately to decide what to do. There was a Chinese wall between their deliberations.

This group had acted first and a young drug dealer had died. He was being beaten, 'not too harshly', to put the fear of God in him. He just died.

'It was a heart attack,' said one, in a way that made me think he would know.

The body was taken 'fifty miles away' and buried. 'It'll never be found other than by absolute chance.'

'So, what's the problem?' I asked.

'The problem is,' said the leader, 'that we wanted to frighten him off. Use him as a deterrent. We wanted word to get back to whoever was supplying him that there was an, err, vigilante group in Four Marks, that was going to fight back. We wanted them to know that we wouldn't be looking to the police. We were taking direct action.'

The third man spoke for the only time in the hour-long session.

'We would do it again if we had to, and again, and again, until they stopped.' There was a determination in his voice. He was convincing. I thought his child had been hurt. I also thought he was the one who had been doing the beating.

The leader came to the point.

'We had to get rid of the body to stop any chance of being incriminated. To be honest, we panicked a bit. If we had had time to think we may have gone about it another way.

'To our surprise, nothing happened. There was no hue and cry. No strange cars cruising around looking for their boy drug dealer. No one was asking after the missing lad.

'We have some friends in the police, people who are disgusted about where officers are told to spend their time. They checked for us. There was nothing going on. No investigations.

'We are desperate that word gets back to the drug pushers about what has happened. We don't want them to think their boy had just done a 'runner'. We didn't want him to die, but once he had died, we wanted to use that to frighten them some more. We couldn't do that unless the story came out in another way, separate from us. If it did come out, we could take advantage of it. Draw attention to it. We have some ideas on how to do that.'

'Might even help your sales,' said the second one, with a chuckle.

'Not really the point,' I replied, 'but, if I can cut through your immediate emotions and fears, I am prepared to write the story if you can do more to persuade me this isn't a hoax.'

'Let me try,' said the main man.

Most of the local children go to Perins secondary school in New Alresford. It's got academy status. About a year ago, we started to pick up stories of an increase in overt drug taking among school pupils. Children were offered the first pill free. Small groups in the later school years were easily identified and the principal names passed on to staff. One teacher was made liaison. Our children told us that pills were being openly taken and sold. Needles were seen in use in the toilets. There was debt and a rise in thefts from changing rooms and purses to pay for it. Some individual pupil's academic and sporting performance evidently fell off. There was a rise in abusive and insolent behaviour. We were told that there was extra vigilance and the matter was 'in hand'.

We are not suggesting that Perins was any better or worse than any other non-city school. We believe that Perins' staff were largely successful in what they did. However, rooting out the inner core of drug users is probably almost impossible. Parents of the children who were implicated were often in complete denial and took criticism of their offspring as a personal insult, threatening legal retaliation. At least one boy was expelled and a couple of others left the area.

It was probably partly because of actions at the school, but perhaps also because of the increase in cheaper drugs from Southampton, and from outside the county, that sales moved to outside the school grounds. A number of youngsters, not pupils, started pushing their trade at the places where children gathered for the morning school buses.

One particular boy, Billy, perhaps seventeen years old, frequented the new shelter opposite the Indian restaurant two or three days a week. Perhaps he had another venue on the intermediate days? He always wore a bulky, knee-length, black Puffer jacket, which went unnoticed in the cold weather.

He was watched for three days, pictures were taken, and he was seen to hand packages to five schoolchildren. At least once each day, he drifted amongst the crowd murmuring a question as he went. Most of the youngsters ignored him or turned their backs. There was nothing threatening.

We passed the information on to the police and waited. Nothing happened. Apparently, there was a resource issue. We waited. Apparently, there was a major operation in Winchester. We waited. Enquiries were proceeding at the supply end of the chain.

That's when we held our meeting and established three groups to look independently at how best to deal with 'Billy'. Our group already knew that each morning after the school bus had left he walked to the bakery, bought a coffee, read a motorbike magazine and waited for the next regular bus towards Winchester. The next day, as he came out, two of us took him from either side, we let him glimpse a toy pistol that we pushed in his stomach and we walked him over to our waiting car with its engine running. As we pushed him in we put a hood over his head, like yours, and shoved him to the floor.

'I hope you washed it,' I offered.

'Don't worry.' The first man smiled, I think. 'You got a brand new one.'

We sat him on a chair in a garage, took off his jacket, shoes and trousers. His white socks had holes in them. We tied him up and played some games with his mind while he was still blindfolded. We suggested we might slice him up a bit. We ran the blade of a kitchen knife over his legs. He wet himself and started shaking. We put our masks on then took his off while we held the knife in front of his face. He was very white. One of us slapped him twice on each side of his face.

We asked him the same questions again and again. What was his name? Where did he live? Who supplied him? I think we had scared him so much, he was petrified. He couldn't move and couldn't speak. He just sat there shaking.

Then he just died. One groan. His face went red. Five seconds and he was gone. Too many drugs? Too much stress? Perhaps he was going to die soon, anyway?

There was a long pause for personal reflection.

The second man took up the story. 'To our surprise, he had no phone. He had no wallet. He had about £200 in notes which we put in a charity box. He had about twenty little bags each with five blue or red pills. We burned them. Then we buried him. We had a talk. Then we called you.'

'We did keep watch at the bus stop for a few days,' picked up the leader, 'but no one unusual showed. Our children said that Billy just stopped turning up. We've been back once a week since and there's nobody new.

'We just want to keep it that way.

'Will you write the story as one of your chapters?'

I looked into their eyes one by one. I decided they were telling the truth.

'Yes. I'll write it. Do you want to see it before it goes to print?

'Listen, Chris, we never want to see or hear from you again. Put your hood on and we'll take you home.'

It was only after I heard their car drive away with its lights off and I stood near my front door that I wondered if I was now guilty of being an accessory after the fact. But then, I would be reporting what happened – in my own time.

11 HONEY AND BLACKBERRIES
Aftermath of the Battle of Cheriton

FOUR MARKS
1644   BODY COUNT: 3

The group of five men, foot soldiers in the Royalist army under Lord Hopton, slumped with their backs against a flint wall. A breeze from the north licked off their perspiration. The failing sun was behind them: an unseasonable warm day towards the end of March was rapidly losing its heat. It was 1644. One of their number twisted, raised his head and searched the fields for signs of pursuit.

'Nothing yet,' he muttered.

'May be we got away with it,' said another.

For the last three hours, cut off from their regiment, the musketeers had run for their lives through open fields, then slowed and crossed the country more carefully using Bramdean Common, small woods and hedgerows for cover. The men headed north and east to miss Ropley and, especially, to stay away from the King's Highway and other local tracks leading from Alresford to Alton. With such pains to be unobserved, they had travelled only three miles. In the first fading of the light, they found a quiet, unlit, farm cottage near Lyewood. Unfed for twenty-four hours, their brief discussion determined a low risk. Inside, they found three flat loaves of unleavened bread set aside to cool for an evening meal. They took two and dashed for the wall where they now rested.

The oldest of the men, about fifty, their captain, John Pinchin, with a full grey beard to hide a vivid facial scar, noticed bees amongst the early clover.

'I've heard stories about the fine flowers that grow around here,' he offered. 'The soil is very good this side of the ridge.' He watched the bees and their lazy, laden departures, then got up and slunk away to return five minutes later with a stone layered with honey.

'To go with the bread,' he said. 'With my thick gloves, it was easy. Bee-keeping flourishes here; they used to make mead. My grandfather often sent for some because he said that William the Norman bought Ropley honey from his kinsman, Gilbert de Gascoigne, who held the land.'

John Pinchin, of the manor of Shalden, northwest of Alton, had declared for King Charles from the beginning of the war. With his son, Rupert, two landed retainers and four volunteers, he had since marched back and forth across Sussex and Hampshire. They were selected for membership of a small Hampshire trained band, sent wherever was thought necessary, being men 'sufficient, of able and active bodies; none of the meaner sort, nor servants; but only such as be of the Gentrie, Free-holders, and good Farmers, or their sonnes, that are like to be resident'.[1] The Crown realised that recent advances in military technology made it impossible for each man to bear the best weapons without a higher degree of individual and unit training.

In February 1643, Pinchin and his men had been back at Alton, a place they knew well from market days, and watched from behind houses in Lentern Street as 1,500 Royalist horse attacked a small Parliamentary reconnaissance party. Their approval turned to horror as a large field gun was discharged into Prince Rupert's advancing cavalry at very close range with devastating effect.

The following December, the Royalists, Pinchin among them, returned to Alton to set up a garrison. One early dawn, they suffered a surprise attack by men who had taken a devious route from Farnham. Most of the Foot were surrounded in the churchyard of St Lawrence. Their colonel, Richard Boles, died sword in hand in the pulpit refusing to surrender. Some 100 men were buried in a pit just outside the north wall of the nave; a further 500 were captured, most of whom switched sides. To this day, the church door bears scars from cannon ball and shot. Pinchin and a small band slipped away. One of his retainers, so close to home, faded into the night; a volunteer was felled by a musket fired from behind the church wall; another was left in Alresford, probably to die, as he had a leg 'all but severed by a vicious pike thrust'.

Their retreat halted at Winchester. The Royalist survivors spent the winter in the stronghold, regrouping, recruiting and being reinforced by a detachment of the King's main 'Oxford Army', almost doubling their strength in comparative safety as bad weather prevented serious action.[2] Each musketeer was armed with a matchlock musket with a barrel four-feet long, 'the bore of twelve bullets rowling in', a rest, bandelier, head-piece, sword, girdle and hangers for the charges. The rest, with a point placed in the ground, carried the heavy gun's muzzle while the musketeer took aim.[3]

Left, the door of St Lawrence Church, Alton. 'At the time of the fight it stood at the west end. A loophole for a musket and the scars of pike thrusts still adorn this historic door.' Right, the pulpit in which Colonel Richard Boles was killed. 'In 1644, it stood in the centre of the church. Bullet marks, with the lead still in them, can be seen on the inside walls of the church.' *Both photographs, Bryan Boyd, from Adair, Cheriton 1644*

Matchlocks were a usefully rugged weapon in action. Even if a mechanism was broken, the musket could still be fired by placing the match in the priming pan by hand. Its disadvantage was that huge amounts of matchcord were required. Even on a march, file leaders had to keep one alight so that the cords of the file could be lit quickly if attacked. Lighter muskets that did not need a musket-rest were supposedly on the way, but Pinchin and his men never saw any.

During the whole of this war, a great deal of military traffic passed between Alton and Winchester: scouts, baggage, message takers, retreating soldiers one way, reinforcements the other. Necessarily, any movement had to cross the ridge at or near a yet-to-exist Four Marks.

The best road map for the period was published by John Ogilby in 1675 and was dedicated to the 'High and Mighty Prince', Charles.[4] What a difference thirty years can make. It is a beautiful strip map; Plate 51 shows the route from Bagshot to Southampton. The direction is unambiguous. After leaving Alton, with Chawton off the road to the left, the road climbs the ridge between the 53rd and 54th milestones, dissecting Chawton Park Wood. This is the King's Highway: there is no sign of any track to the south which developed in the

Musketeer's equipment: Hats and Montero caps, bandoleers and tools, muskets. *Roberts, Soldiers of the English Civil War.* © *Bloomsbury Publishing*

(1) **Present**: Remove your right to the thumb hole, the second finger to the tricker, with your left hand fixe the fork of the rest to your musket and your thumb against the fork, and the pike end of the rest on the ground. (2) **Give fire**: Lift up your right elbow and place the but end of your musket within your shoulder near your breast, the small end appearing a little above your shoulder standing with the leg foremost and the knee bent and the right leg standing stiff. (3) **Dismount your musket**: Bring your musket and rest to your right side and carry both in the left hand only. (4) **Uncock your match**: Take the match from the cock with the thumb and second finger of your right hand holding the musket and rest in the left hand only. *Directions for Musters, 1638*

next century into a turnpike and became, in turn, the basis for the A31. The highway to Winchester was the road taken by the iron-wheeled carts, horses and thousands of infantry, passing south of Medstead and north of Ropley to Bishop's Sutton.

The Parliamentarians held two musters locally outside of the villages, both in 1643, one at Bentley Green and the other some two miles south of Alton just off the highway to Winchester. One historian argues this would have been at or near Four Marks, but the distance suggests somewhere on Chawton Common.[5]

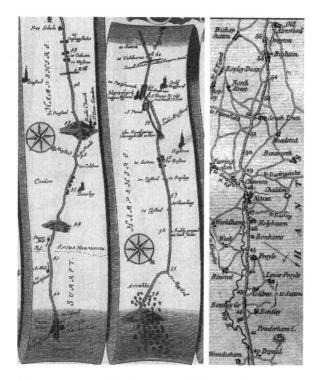

Left, two strands of Ogilby's map, 1675, from Farnham
through Alton to Alresford, and, right, Paterson's map of
1785 with milestones.

Entering the Shrave and dropping down into Alton today, one has to imagine
many thousands of Parliamentary troops camped in full view.

In March 1644, the Parliamentary commander, Sir William Waller, leading
10,000 men, including 3,000 from *The Southern Association* of Kent, Surrey,
Sussex and Hampshire, advanced from Arundel up the river valley to East
Meon where, on the 26th, he held a rendezvous for his whole army. Hopton
moved Royalist forces out of Winchester determined to prevent Waller from
taking an open road to threaten London.

While the two sides skirmished around the Meon, Waller sent a strong force
of horse and foot to take Alresford and to cut Hopton off from his base at
Winchester. It was a literal race which the Royalists just won. Pinchin and his
men, and others bringing up the rear, were stationed with their muskets in the
upper windows of *The Swan* and watched horsemen sweep to and fro without
being called to fire.

The next day, the Royalists moved to Tichborne Down, where there is a golf course today, and engaged in several skirmishes, but, all the time, waiting while Sir George Lisle took 1,000 musketeers and 500 horse towards Cheriton where he could observe the Parliamentarian camp.[6] Two riders raced back to Hopton in Alresford shouting that the Parliamentarians were retreating, delighting the men sitting round their evening fires.

Lisle's assessment was wrong. Overnight, Waller held a Council of War and decided not to retreat, but to give battle. At dawn, he sent his City of London Brigade into Cheriton Wood and then ordered an advance which checked Lisle's outriders.

It was then that Pinchin's final battle began. The full Royalist army of 6,000 moved into position. Pinchin's small group was bunched with a thousand other musketeers led by Lieutenant-Colonel Matthew Appleyard, a 'soldier of known courage and experience'.[7] Together with a battery of guns, the men were ordered to take the wood.

> *The morning was very misty ... Appleyard advanced towards the Enemy; But the bodyes of our men no sooner appear'd on the topp of the Hill, but the Enemy shewed how well they were prepared for us, and gave fire very thicke and sharp, which our men very gallantly received and return'd ; But the Lord Hopton foreseeing that our party could not long hold out upon so great a disadvantage, and observing an opportunity to cast men into the wood upon the flanke of the Enemy, he drew off one division of the musketeers, and commanded them to run with all possible speede into the wood upon the [Parliamentarians'] flanke, where there was likewise a crosse-hedge to cover them, which they had noe sooner done, and given one volley from thence but the Enemy fell in disorder; and began to runne and Appleyard with his party pursued them, and had the execution of a part of them through the wood, and possest himself of all their ground of advantage, and tooke a horse Colours and some prisoners, but none of their cannon, for they being light gunns were drawen off.[8]*

After 'hot fighting', musket on musket and hand-to-hand, Pinchin and his comrades prevailed. They found themselves on the far east of the wood with a poor view over the battlefield. Word spread that young Sir Henry Bard, against orders, had launched his regiment of foot against Parliamentarian cavalry and was overwhelmed and destroyed.[9]

Pinchin waited with foreboding as the horsemen guarding his own flank were sent forward to set right Bard's impetuousness. With their cavalry gone,

Pinchin and those around him, directly commanded by Captain John Tirwhit, stood the brunt of a Parliamentary counter-attack and were forced out of the wood. The bulk of the musketeers fell back to the ridge behind the wood, but several small groups were left in the open without squares of pikemen to guard them. The large, painted, white silk ensign of Tirwhit's unit, signifying 'Innocence or Puritie of Conscience, truth, and an Upright Integritie without Blemish', bobbed out of sight.

Felt-hatted and without armour, the isolated musketeers could 'only defend themselves at close quarters by upturning their muskets and using them as clubs'.[10] It was among these bare fields that the greatest casualties occurred to Tirwhit's command as the cut-off infantrymen were attacked on two sides by rampant Parliamentarians on horse and foot.

The wood was lost. The way back to Alresford was blocked and, in any case, the town would likely soon be taken and burned. Although Hopton retreated with his main force intact, it was a great defeat. The remaining Royalists fled in every direction 'pursued for some miles by the victorious round-heads'.[11] Pinchin told his men to throw down their heavy muskets and rests and to run. Their only path was northeast on a roundabout way towards Alton where perhaps they could make their way through the few enemy left in the town to reach Shalden and temporary safety.

Bread and honey finished, Pinchin called his son and his men around him.

'We must keep moving,' he told them. 'We must assume pursuit by some of Parliament's zealots. We can try for Basing House across open country, but we will have to cross the roads which will be thick with baggage trains and pickets.

'The better plan is to make for Shalden and home where we will be sheltered and hid. It will not be difficult because I know this ground; I used to ride right here with the King's hunt. There is risk nearer Alton, but we know that place as well as anyone.

'What say you?'

The men agreed on Shalden.

'Let us depart.'

Pinchin's chosen route was up the road to Lyeway and on to Kitwood. Travelling across country to the lane by Brislands Farm, they could join the old Pilgrim's Way from Winchester to Farnham, crossing the ridge near a windmill.

When they reached the pilgrims' route, they found an abandoned grassy road which ran away, clear and empty for a couple of miles.[12] It was, perhaps, twenty yards wide and guarded by rough hedges. There was no evidence of marauding landlords. It was treeless, wide and neglected. It had an abominable surface. Pinchin and his men had to pick their way from one dry place to another over the enormous ruts which recent farm carts had made. Almost at the wood lining the ridge, there was an abundance of barren blackberry and furze bushes and a small lake, a Saxon mere.

The men paused for five minutes' respite. As they rose in the gloom to gain the ridge, they heard several shouts. Pinchin and his retainer slipped into the undergrowth, but his son, Rupert, and the two volunteers were not so quick. They were surrounded by sweating Parliamentary soldiery with swords drawn.

The words exchanged were not recorded, except that the name of the leader of the pursuers, Richard Kiddle, was clearly heard. The spot was well identified because John Pinchin described it in a written complaint, full of disgust and indignation. The men were standing on the right hand side of what is now Blackberry Lane almost at the rise before the road disappeared into the wood to reappear on the ill-frequented track that long after became The Shrave.

What happened is not in doubt. Kiddle claimed that he was infuriated by the loss of two comrades at Cheriton that morning and recognised Rupert from the extravagant red plume in his hat. The group rushed forward and pierced their captives with their swords before Pinchin even thought to make a futile rescue. The three men were each skewered twice, three times, and then stripped of their red tunics, weapons and purses and left white on the road as the last light of the day slipped away.

The murderers moved off towards Alton, throwing unwanted metal helmets and armour plates into the bushes, singing bawdy songs, laughing, leaving two tearful men to place their dead in a deep ditch and to cover them with stones, chalk and flint.[13]

From the distance given to the edge of the wood, the side of the road and the site of the old mere, it is possible to give an approximate modern-day position among three Blackberry Lane houses: Magpies, Briarfield and Brymere. There is no record of the bodies being recovered later, a journey that would have been dangerous for Pinchin. The armour might also be waiting to be found deep in a garden vegetable plot.

There it might have ended except for the two documents that tell the story and its consequences.

John Pinchin and his retainer made their way into Alton and, in the heart of the night, passed the churchyard where they had fought their dreadful encounter three months before. They went up a brief track where two tanning houses bordered the Wey river, fresh from its source. At its end, the clouds shifted and a bright moon lit their path up a long deserted hollow to their remote village. Pinchin was welcomed by his wife and young children in a mood that changed from delight to horror as he told them his news.

The next day, Pinchin wrote in anger and in sorrow to Sir Andrew Potley, Major General of Waller's Foot, a veteran of Swedish service, at Farnham Castle. Potley's Yellow Coats were Pinchin's direct adversary at Cheriton Wood so presumably some respect existed although there is no evidence that they knew each other or ever met.[14] Only excerpts from the letter remain, but it lays a direct complaint against Kiddle and his companions for murder:

> *There was no heate of battle But onlie the wearisumme resultte of foote soldiers of the Kinge after Cheriton. There was noe fighte; But quarter arsked which brought onlie slaughter.*[15]

Pinchin's letter received no reply for he had not given an address. He may well have heard that Kiddle was arrested and brought before a Council of War at 'Phernham' on 26 April, less then a month later. Kiddle was accused of 'Running away from his Cullors [Colours]'. The council's president was Andrew Potley.[16]

Witnesses, Patrick Gourdon and James Plenty of Winchester, said they knew Kiddle well and saw him and others walking to a village near Alton to 'take of a drink'.[17] Kiddle with William Childe and Richard Luckis then left their colours and went towards Basing House.

There was no mention of the three deaths in Blackberry Lane.

On 3 May, Potley handed over the presidency of the council, which still sat at Farnham, to James Wemyss, general of artillery.[18] The council 'adjudged that Kiddle being accused of Running away from his Cullors, and proved against him by two witnesses, for such his offence shalbe hanged by the neck until he bee dead, Saveing unto our Generall his further will and pleasure.'[19]

Wemyss authority was based on an article of war to which all soldiers in Waller's army had sworn:

> *That no officer or soldier shall ransom or conceale any prisoner or prisoners, but within twelve howres shall make them knowne unto the Generall or others authorized to receive*

them, That from henceforth you better observe the returne of such prisoners as you shall take into the hands and custody of my Marshall Generall, where they are to take the Covenant before such tyme as you shall intertaine, or take them upon ymployment, all which you are better to observe upon payne of such punishment as in the article is expressed. Bee it also, that if any officer or souldier shall wilfully faile to appeare at the Rendezvous at the houre or tyme appointed, hee the said officer shalbe forthwith cashiered, and taken from his charge, and the souldier ymprisoned.

And it is further declared that no souldier upon any pretence whatsoever shall dare to stay behind or straggle from his Colours upon payne of Arbitrary correction.

Given under my hand this Thirteenth day of March 1644.

William Waller

It seems that under the article, Kiddle should have been imprisoned, but perhaps justice in Farnham in the days following the Battle of Cheriton, with Potley's guiding hand, followed another course.

In 1651–2, two acts authorised the confiscation and then sale of all the manors, lands, estates, tenements and hereditaments, except rectories and tithes, which had been forfeited to the Commonwealth for treason. Parliament needed a 'considerable sum of money for carrying out the services of the Commonwealth', mainly for the navy, and intended to borrow £600,000 against the security of these lands 'of the said Traytors'.

The list for the county of Southampton on 18 November 1652 had thirteen names including John Pinchin of Shalden.[20]

What happened to the double-broken family is not known. A search of the nineteenth-century censuses shows the Pinchin name scattered thinly around England, but none in Hampshire.

The manor of Shalden was ceded at the beginning of the nineteenth century to the Knight family of Chawton. In 1840, it was sold on by Edward Knight (Chapters 1, 4 and 12).

In retrospect, the defeat of the Royalist army at Cheriton was a turning point of the Civil War and, for importance, deserves a place alongside the more famous and bloody battles of Edgehill, Marston Moor and Naseby. The King's dream of taking the whole of Hampshire and threatening London from the south were stopped. Sir Edward Walker, the King's Secretary at War, declared that the disaster 'necessitated His Majesty to alter the scheme of his affairs, and in place of the offensive to make a defensive war'.

ENDNOTES

1 Roberts, *Infantry*.
2 Haythornthwaite, *Civil War*.
3 Roberts, *Infantry*.
4 *Illustration of the Kingdom of England … Principal Roads, Duckham, 1939 edition.*
5 Godwin, *Civil War in Hampshire*.
6 Spring, *Battle of Cheriton*.
7 Adair, *Cheriton*.
8 Hopton, *Bellum Civile*.
9 Brereton and McKenna, *Journal of the Civil War*. Haythornthwaite, *Civil War*.
10 Adair, *Cheriton*.
11 Duthy, *Sketches of Hampshire*.
12 Belloc, *Old Road*.
13 There is a story of a second, nearby massacre of a small group of fleeing Royalist soldiery on the same day. The tale has been handed down, but no written evidence has been found. These men retreated to a sparsely guarded ammunition dump behind the *Castle of Comfort* public house in Medstead. The 'Castle' was the guards' lodging, their 'comfort' was the ammunition store. As the defeated men arrived from the Cheriton battlefield, a strong force of Waller's men followed close behind. This time there was a hard fight and no prisoners were taken.
14 Spring, *Battle of Cheriton*, p. 5, claims that this Potley was not Andrew, but Major General Christopher Potley, 'an obscure officer'.
15 *Extracts of the Papers of Sir Andrew Potley concerning the Swedish Wars*, unnamed editor (University of Stockholm 1932), pp. 22-23. The bulk of the book is in Swedish.
16 Adair, 'Court Martial Papers of Sir William Waller's Army, 1644', No. 2.
17 See Adam de Gourdon, this book, Chapter 13: '*Murder on the King's Highway*'.
18 Potley left Waller's army under unusual circumstances. The day after the fight at Cropredy Bridge, near Banbury, while he was attending a Council of War, the floor collapsed and all Waller's officers tumbled into a cellar. Waller and James Holbourne, no lightweight, fell on top of Potley, leading to his retirement (Adair, *Cheriton*), p. 186.
19 Adair, 'Court Martial Papers of Sir William Waller's Army, 1644', No. 5.
20 *An Additional Act for Sale …, 1652:* Henry Fowel, Abbots-Ann; Anthony Gosling, Morestead, Dr Laney, Petersfield, James Mallett, Portsmouth; John Pinchin, Shalden; John Unwyn, Ennington; William Budding, Clinton; William Chamberlain, Nash; Thomas Chamberlain, Lyndhurst; Anthony Hide, Woodhouse; James Linkhorn, Bowyet; Miles Philipson, Throp; Swithin Wells, Eastleigh. To these were added estates of Sir Charles and Sir John Somerset, Sir Richard Tichborne and the manors of Blendworth, Catherington, Chalton and Clanfield.

Suggested reading:

Acts and Ordinances of the Interregnum, 1642–1660 (HMSO, London 1911): An Additional Act for Sale of several Lands and Estates forfeited to the Commonwealth for Treason (11/1652)

Adair, John, 'The Court Martial Papers of Sir William Waller's Army, 1644', *Journal of the Society for Army Historical Research*, Vol. 44/180, 1966, pp. 205–226; *Cheriton 1644, The Campaign and the Battle* (Roundwood Press, Warwick 1973)

Brereton, Sir William, and McKenna, Joseph, editor, *A Journal of the English Civil War: The Letter Book of Sir William Brereton* (1646; McFarland & Co, Jefferson, North Carolina, USA 2012)

Godwin, George Nelson, *The Civil War in Hampshire (1642–45) and the story of Basing House* (1882; Kindle 2020)

Haythornthwaite, Philip, *The English Civil War 1642–1651, An Illustrated Military History* (Arms and Armour, London 1994)

Hopton, Ralph, edited Healey, Charles E.H. Chadwyck, *Bellum Civile, Hopton's Narrative of his Campaign in the West (1642-1644) and other papers* (c. 1647; Somerset Record Society Vol. XVIII 1902; Forgotten Books 2017)

Ogilby, John, *Britannia, Vol. 1, An Illustration of the Kingdom of England and Dominion of Wales; Description of the Principal Roads* (1675; Duckham, London 1939)

Roberts, Keith and McBride, Angus, *Soldiers of the English Civil War I, Infantry* (Osprey, London 1989)

Rushworth, John, 'Historical Collections: Essex's and Waller's armies, to June 1644', in Historical Collections of Private Passages of State: Vol. 5, 1642–45 (London, 1721)

Spring, Laurence, *The Battle of Cheriton 1644* (Stuart Press, Bristol 1997)

12 TROLLS ARE BAD PEOPLE
Internet justice

FOUR MARKS
2018   BODY COUNT: 1

I didn't write this chapter. It came to me ready written by someone in Four Marks who was responding to my requests for tips about village murder stories. I'll call him Charlie.

Charlie left me to do whatever I wanted with his story. He agreed an edit and I changed a handful of words.

Charlie used to live in one of the new builds on the large estate off the Winchester Road, Goldcrest Way I think it was. He was one of the first people to move there. I met him twice, verified what I could and then took him at his word. He told me that the whole affair caused him to have bad dreams. He wondered if writing it down would mean he could sleep again. He's now long gone and far away; Canada, I think.

I wouldn't tell you anyway.

It was a worm that caused the break-up of my second marriage; a worm so inconspicuous, so unattractive, that I cannot remember what it looked like.

'Any sensible adult would have sorted it out without a fuss,' my wife warned me.

I lost my first wife and my two children in a crash near Herriard. A lorry took us from the side. My wife was driving. I spent an hour trapped with the bodies before I was cut out. I had an operation in Basingstoke to remove ruptured discs in my back. I soon got a reputation at work for heavy drinking. For the next thirty years or so, I was probably not a nice person. I took business risks and some people got hurt. I was a poor friend, unreliable, selfish. I enjoyed, mostly, a string of casual relationships, but never got close to another marriage.

I retired with a healthy bank balance and aimless. I toured Sri Lanka, building the holiday around visits to the ancient royal capitals of Anuradhapura and Polonnaruwa, each steeped in Buddhism and architecture.

My guide at Anuradhapura fell sick over lunch on the first day. Harshani,

Sinhalese for a 'delight and a joy', was the last minute replacement and joined me that evening. She was in her early thirties with a degree in English, a vision of graceful movement, and was tolerably knowledgeable about Buddhism, but knew nothing about architecture and not much more about the city ruins. I spent more time looking at her than at moonstones or stupas.

Her parents lived in a mean two-bedroomed house on the outskirts of Columbo, not a good place to park a car. I didn't like them from the start and I was sure the antipathy was reciprocated. He was monosyllabic, sly, slow to respond, always watching from under heavy lids. There was a brittleness about the mother's caring, as if it was an act for my consumption. I found it remarkable that an English degree had come from this environment. Harshani asked me for money and I paid for everything, and, I suspect, quite a lot more. There was no sign of work, of love, within the family, visible mementoes, or visits from relatives.

We married in a local pseudo-Christian ceremony two weeks later, low-key, few flowers and even fewer friends. I was uncomfortable throughout thinking of my dead first family. I just wanted to get Harshani away.

There's no fool like an old fool. Harshani was keen to live in England and, after some brief posturing from British immigration she got permission, but only because one grandparent was supposedly Scottish, not because she was married to an Englishman. We moved into a new house in Four Marks. From the first day, she investigated everything I owned. Knick-knacks full of memories moved to her dressing table; others disappeared and enquiries were met with a blank face and dismissive shrug. As well as some changes to the kitchen, her first major demand was a large television system with four speakers and subscriptions to every channel possible. On my own, I had seldom watched; now, the set was on every waking hour.

Harshani was quickly pregnant and insisted on going home to Sri Lanka to have the child. It was decided she would travel alone and that I would join them as soon as news came of the birth and bring them back to England. After regular phone calls, Harshani announced the birth of our daughter, Sammi. There was no need to come to Sri Lanka. Could I pick them up at the airport at the end of the week?

It was a stilted reunion; I was confused and disappointed. Sammi cried constantly, had a string of never-ending ailments and clung to her mother for attention. This was, of course, my fault for forcing Harshani to live in England which was freezing and awful with tasteless food. My contact with the child was deliberately limited. To be honest, it was almost as if Sammi was someone else's offspring. Within a month, there were daily rows: Harshani could shout louder and hold any grudge far longer than me. Most of the time I didn't understand how I had failed and caused such misery. By the time Sammi was one year old and getting about under her own steam, I was a foreigner in my own house.

I was taking an early morning phone call. The doorbell rang as I walked to and fro. A determined man with big ears and an odd haircut and clutching a clipboard loomed large.

'You do realise,' he challenged, 'that you have rare worms living on your verge. They are in great danger if not cared for. You need to act responsibly.'

'What on earth are you talking about?' I spluttered.

'Your worms,' replied the man, 'your precious worms. You need to safeguard them for future generations. Are you happy if I arrange this?'

'Yes, yes, whatever.' And I firmly, and I hoped politely, closed the door.

Two days later, a circle of flat white wooden stakes appeared on the grass by the front gate. Somewhere in the middle lurked my dismal family of worms. A large sign was attached with staples to the nearby telegraph pole. The owner of the property had agreed preservation measures for a rare worm. No grass was to be cut, nor any car parked, within a metre of the marked worm area on financial penalty. It took only a week for a delivery vehicle to flatten the stakes. I then forgot to tell the gardener that no mowing was allowed outside the gate and he trimmed the whole verge. I remonstrated and he retaliated, behind my back, by pulling the sign down and sticking it in the black waste bin.

The green bin in Four Marks, as one slowly learns, is for rubbish destined for the municipal dump; the black bin contains recyclable material in line with the local council's green policy. I found two seedy gentlemen checking my black bin watched over by Worm Man bearing his clipboard. They had discovered the discarded white sign, badly torn.

I suppose I shouldn't have made the personal comments I then did. I took the bin down the garden and lit a fire with the contents. Within half an hour, a police car arrived to deal with a complaint about dangerous smoke. I pointed to the bonfire, faintly visible forty yards away with its smoke drifting across an empty building site.

'You can tell the waste disposal people hiding behind their hedge that they should brush up on bonfire law.'

'Sir, I wouldn't like to get the impression that you are not taking this matter seriously.'

'Which matter? Let me put it this way. I've had three thefts from my garden shed and garage in the last two months, all reported, and this is the first police visit I have ever had. At least I now know what you take seriously.'

Worm Man had his clipboard held high as a shield in case of attack.

'Not a very neighbourly attitude,' said the smaller of the seedy ones, inspecting the discarded sign. 'First off, you're destroying council property by ripping off the sign thereby showing disdain for your public authority. Then you go and put it in the black bin when it should have gone in the green one. And you've gone and squashed the worms and thrown the stakes God knows where.'

'The stakes are in the green bin,' I offered. 'They were run down by a delivery van. Do you have the right to come onto my property and rummage in my rubbish?'

Worm man could hold back no longer. 'It's not rubbish,' he yelled, 'and you agreed I could put it up.' You get to that time in life, driven by bitter experience, when the truth of the old adage about stopping digging when you are already in a deep hole becomes a lifeline.

'You'll get a letter of admonishment,' he declared in capital letters, 'and the council will review your service provision. You won't get away with this.'

'Please leave my property,' I responded, 'and you can take your rubbish with you.'

There were eleven follow-up letters of increasing severity over three months.

This background is not meant as an excuse for what happened. I am still deeply ashamed about it. As I came in from my worm skirmish, Harshani attacked my cantankerousness, my trouble-making, my always picking fights with reasonable strangers, about trapping her away from her own mother, of not caring for her or Sammi. Harshani had a piercing tone, capable of reaching deep into my consciousness and festering there. Two days later, without respite, I lost it. I hit her. Not a punch, you understand, but a solid, powerful slap. She wasn't big and I am. She stumbled across the room and hit her head with a crack on a skirting board. I thought I had killed her and I had to push Sammi off as I tried to give her attention.

Harshani was groggy when she came round, her speech slurred, and I rushed them both to A&E. There is no one so low as a wife beater in the casualty department of a provincial hospital staffed, it seemed, entirely by female nurses and doctors. I was open about what had happened. No recriminations were made directly to me. In fact, no one spoke to me at any length. Harshani was taken straight to X-ray while a scowl-faced social worker on night duty took Sammi into care, behind my back and without discussion. That made me lose my temper and the police were called.

Harshani and Sammi came home a week later and for a while we received daily visits from social workers and district nurses, always female and working in pairs, to check that my wife and daughter had received no further beatings. All talks took place with me firmly excluded from the room. My opinion was never asked.

Harshani announced that she wanted a divorce and that she was taking Sammi back to Sri Lanka. She was scared for their lives. If I paid her money for Sammi's health and education, she would go quietly. One part of me was still in shock at what I had done. I gave in almost immediately, sold some shares, and gave her a third of all the money she knew about. The next day she left in a taxi for, I thought, the airport. There was no contract, no written agreement, no access rights, no contact address, just emptiness.

When the social workers next came to check on Harshani, I told them she had gone home. Their faces shone disbelief. An embarrassing difficulty was that I didn't have her parents' contact number in Colombo. To my pleasure, Harshani had always looked after the relationship and the phone calls.

Then the police arrived. After a brief interview, they walked the garden, prodding loose earth, looking for busy worms. I spent the next night in a noisy, smelly cell in Winchester. Harshani's phone was switched off. No flight records for the pair could be found. Lengthy enquiries were initiated in Colombo. The parents' house was vacant.

How much time you can spend with a person and still have no idea who they really are?

I was never formally charged, but was warned not to leave the country. I had to surrender my passport. After a month, no trace of Harshani and Sammi had been found. The only slight evidence in my favour was that all their clothes had gone, all pictures disappeared and a significant sum in cash had been drawn from my accounts. But, as the detective inspector said, 'That could mean one thing or the other, couldn't it, sir.'

The investigation was not closed; there were no inquests as there were no bodies. It became a cold case.

I wondered if I had been the victim of an elaborate confidence trick. Was the scheme set up before my arrival in Sri Lanka? Had my guide in Anuradhapura actually been sick or had he spent the morning assessing a possible 'mark'? Was Harshani all the time waiting around the corner for her lonely, gullible and elderly prey to be delivered? Was Sammi really my child? Was she really Harshani's child? My mind started to swim; the truth, what truth, floated beyond reach, never coming into focus.

The mistakes I made with facts, with memories, when talking to the police came home to haunt me. I have one piece of advice for anyone arrested, 'Say nothing.' Police interviews are about false friendship, deliberate misunderstandings, and entrapment. You make your choice: be a fool, lie to yourself that the world is good, and bare your soul. But, if you do, you will lose as I did and everyone and everything might be destroyed. You begin to see the world for what it more often is, a nasty place where you are unimportant and unrespected, a statistic to be used.

The police leaked many details of the disappearance of my little family to the press. I thought it was a blatant and vicious attempt to force me to error, perhaps through an emotional reaction. For two days, journalists and photographers camped at my gate doing terminal damage to any worms which may have poked their noses above the turf. I regularly saw cameras pointed at my windows. The doorbell rang and rang till I disconnected it. The chimes were replaced by loud rappings. I complained to the police, but their only interest was in a confession. I closed the curtains, lived from fridge and freezer, and withdrew from the outside and read. My contacts were through the computer and the post-box, which contained only more books, invoices and hate mail.

At first, I read the hate mail avidly. The notes contained intimate details unknown to anyone who had not read, or spoken to someone who had read, the police interview reports. Here was a conflicting subject: someone in the police force was fostering a hate crime, for I was surely hated. Some letters were classic melodrama: green ink, capital letters, pasted magazine cuttings, lurid half-truths, complete lies and drastic threats. God appeared a lot and often provided a personal guiding hand. It took several weeks to tire of the sadistic rubbish; further letters were placed in a cardboard box, unopened.

It was from one of these notes that I first realised I was a subject of widespread condemnation on the internet. I had found YouTube by occasional accident, but had never Twittered or been on Facebook or Instagram. In fact, I was so ignorant of social media that I hardly recognised its existence or purpose. I didn't have my first personal phone until I was in my forties and driven by business. I preferred privacy. I didn't value public sharing.

However, I was prompted now to investigate social media. I wanted to see how it all worked at first hand. I opened Facebook and Twitter accounts, placing the minimal amount of personal information. I was introduced to what I have seen since several times described as 'the Twentieth Century gangrene' that is 'killing us, mind and body'. As someone said, 'I wish we could uninvent it altogether.'

As word spread of my electronic availability, I was plunged into the court of Facebook and Twitter, charged as a murderer and an abuser and suffered the attack of the 'isms': ableism, classism, homophobia, racism, transphobia and worse. To be accused is to be guilty: a 'digital Salem'.[1] All that mattered was that I was accused with enough force. Denizens of the internet with minority opinions have power over anything they choose not to like. I was left in the poorest of positions as, while there was no evidence of what happened to Harshani or Sammi, there was sufficient public information about to encourage legitimate speculation as to foul play. If one added police leaks, malicious fire-stoking and a general hysteria, I really had nowhere to go.

What was clear was that retaliation was equivalent to throwing fuel on the fire. For someone like me, male, white and over sixty, any response would be amplified, twisted, held as evidence and used to convict. I was used to handling critics, other than the police, by reasoned argument so I had no idea how to handle a Twitterstorm.

Slithering through this freedom is the 'troll', the anonymous generic given to a very broad church ranging from bullies to amateur philosophers, from the mildly offensive to the illegal, to knights of the internet who see themselves acting in the public interest to expose hypocrisy and stupidity. At the core are those who cannot be argued with, who do not care which subject is chosen. They are the gutless, the inept and the plain sick whose lives are spent scanning the horizon for any offence with the intent to crush debate or variety. Their enjoyment is pure malice.

Trolling is not going away anytime soon. It has been a central feature of online life since the mid-1990s. An increasing desire for digital affirmation is leading more people to share their most intimate and personal lives online, often with complete strangers: what we like, what we think, our sins, where we are going. The more we invest of ourselves online, the more there is for trolls to feed on and the more likely we are to be hurt.

As a result of my study, I decided to fight back against my hate mailers, but finding trolls is difficult. Many use proxy servers to mask their internet addresses and they have dozens of accounts with different names for each platform they use. If they are banned or blocked by a particular site, they re-join under another name.

I set up, easily, fake Facebook and Twitter accounts, explored the settings and was taken aback by the potential volume of information collected by Facebook. An account's index shows twenty-four categories with at least thirty-six further sub-categories. One user wrote that she found 324 MB of data collected by Facebook after twelve years of membership that took forty minutes to download. Facebook knew every personal contact and the identities and contact details of all parents, siblings and cousins. It was the 'huge' list of contacts and friends which shocked the most. Years before, she had downloaded a Facebook ap to her phone and allowed it to synchronise with her phone contacts. 'Basically it sucked up all the contacts in my phone and stuck them on a contact list'; numbers lost years ago, boyfriends, people met in crises, relationships ended unfairly or in anger, all permanently recorded by Facebook and shared with whom and at what price?

Data is actually not numbers, but friends, relationships, memories, ups and downs, life's dilemmas, successes and catastrophes. And then there was every Facebook 'like', cookies collected through web browsing, Uber taxis, Google maps following every movement, pizzas ordered.

You can never escape your past. Social media providers always know where you were through your phone and also where you are now. For ordinary people it is already too late. You can only try to limit them learning much that is new.

I went back to first principles. I downloaded all of the aggressive postings and tweets onto a spreadsheet, noting the source, date and content and I added the new items that came each day. Then, with some enthusiasm, I opened my box of hate mail and entered that also, but included franking information and physical characteristics, like the use of green ink. Across all three sources, I developed another spreadsheet that noted each 'fact' dealing with my crime and which communications included it.

I love a chase; the pursuit of connections that are not immediately apparent. What I saw was that there were fewer humans challenging me than I thought.

I was looking at over 500 items, but with a reasonable degree of certainty there were a maximum of thirty-two perpetrators and, excitingly, a minimum of twelve. While there was some ingenuity in the content, there was also a laxness, probably through an over-confidence, a surety that their identity would not be uncovered. Of the twelve, it seemed likely that eight were camp followers, trolls in it just for the fun and hurt.

Catfish, or fake accounts, persuade people to join a witch-hunt by setting up dummy profiles and interacting with themselves, not just talking to themselves, but also following themselves. They make 'friends' of themselves on Facebook and 'like' and 're-tweet' their own tweets on Twitter. This incestuousness can also give the game away as careful investigation of their 'Following' and 'Follower' lists shows the degree of interaction and high level of support that is indicative of a 'fake'. I confirmed this by using the *Tweepi* website to go to the very start of these catfish Twitter accounts. When people follow themselves they mostly start it very early on and so their initial followers repay attention and can reveal interesting information that was thought long buried.

I was left with four primary targets and I re-concentrated my efforts on them alone, their letters and their Twitter and Facebook posts.

The mail showed a variety of media. For instance, one was my green ink specialist, but that person also used magazine cut outs and stencilled capital letters. Envelopes for these four also showed a pattern. While their posting points were spread, it looked probable this was deliberate. I placed all of them on a wall chart with four differently coloured pins. There could be no mistake: three were local, two from Four Marks, and one from north Hampshire. The fourth was centred in Reading, while none of the letters actually came from the town. As new insults arrived day by day, there was no serious deviation.

I went back to the letters cut from magazines by three of my trolls. Two of them used glossy paper that seemed similar; one was more basic, but heavy-duty paper, possibly a cheaply produced, limited circulation publication. A visit to the newsagent provided a clutch of likely candidates. In fact, the answer was simple to spot, the glossy papers came from two cooking magazines aimed squarely at women at home; the paper product was my own village magazine, the *Four Marks News*. The cooking magazines did not necessarily imply that the writer was a woman, but if it was not then they likely lived with a woman who did not mind her monthly magazine being cut up. An order for recent back numbers of the three publications showed that the cut outs were used within the month of publication, not treasured possessions, but possibly bought for the purpose by people who knew each other.

I then stood back from these accounts and assessed them. Genuine online account holders place their own needs, prosperity and self-image at the forefront of what they do. These accounts had glaring omissions of expression of personal interest. They had one purpose only: to denigrate me, the 'murderer'. There was no attempt to hide their intent; they were on a crusade.

Why would they care? Troll fakers have a weird motivation and so exhibit weird behaviours. It doesn't seem weird to them, but to perceptive onlookers it appears as a branding. As these people think their own behaviour is normal, they are not aware how many abnormal clues they leave.

Unless intent on confusion, one of my four was less well-educated, probably achieving no more than a few lower GCSE examination pass marks; one I felt sure had a degree, probably in a specialist vocational subject. Two frequently used formal trite expressions which suggested a bureaucratic background that was not in senior management. These two almost always posted their messages after six o'clock in the evening, which suggested a return home from work. My bet was that for one of these, English was a second language. All showed a paucity of imaginative word use; their vocabulary was limited. And all four were slapdash with word choice, spelling mistakes (some defining errors were always repeated) and grammatical construction. One was left-handed. The likelihood was that two did not write regularly, say as part of a job. That suggested they were non-clerical, non-management, possibly in manual work or out of work altogether. Perhaps this general laziness extended to their computer or phone controls?

After some hours of speculation, I reasoned that these were not four casual trolls. If not co-ordinated, or known to each other, they knew of my case personally or directly through another who did. My money was on a male police officer or associate from north Hampshire and a graduate female social worker working locally, one of whom knew the person in Reading, who was possibly out of work. One of the two people in my village knew me or Harshani and Sammi. I felt the connection had to be with Harshani who had made no local friends that I knew of: so a female who worked in a local shop she visited or, perhaps, and more likely, someone who worked in or around the local medical centre. Could one of them be Sri Lankan?

Before pounding the streets, I travelled out-of-county to Esher and bought for cash a low-level laptop and used it to develop further false email, Twitter and Facebook accounts. I joined the criticism and added additional juicy insights, suggesting insider knowledge. I let my outpourings increase in vitriol, especially when I saw a drop-off in contacts from my four main suspects.

After four weeks of steady self-establishment, I hit gold. One of my suspects asked me on Facebook to be a 'friend'. I had been building to 'pinging' them and asking for a chat with the intention of gathering their IP address, the numerical identifier of their device, be it a computer or mobile phone. You can only gather an IP address while the personal interaction of a chat is in progress. At other times, Facebook is the channel, or stands in the way of, a contact with another user. Here, you use a 'netstat' command covertly whilst chatting, standard fare on Windows, and then type the IP address into a purpose-built website to give a location, which may be the device's actual location or may be that of its internet provider.

I accepted the hand of friendship and began a careful correspondence. What I now had was an IP address based in Basingstoke in north Hampshire. It was, I hoped, the policeman who was intrigued by how I knew what I knew. Facebook friends for their false account were limited, but one was in Reading and clearly family.

I placed a formal subject access request to the police for all of the papers about me connected with my investigation. I explained I was preparing my defence against a possible charge. When these papers arrived, within the month, I listed every policeman connected with the case, which produced seventeen names. I then cross-checked these names with the Basingstoke voters' register. There were only two matches and I could remember one of them clearly, a constable, foul-mouthed, unbelieving, and who evidenced an immediate dislike of me. I recorded both addresses. I had a bundle of social work papers, medical reports, formal warnings and instructions for meetings, and, similarly, found four women who lived around Four Marks.

Calling on my waste disposal expertise, I checked the days for rubbish collection in Basingstoke. To their credit, green bins were for recyclable material. In the early morning on the day of emptying, I set out for the homes. At each address, I checked the names on letters and packages in the bins, found my targets, and emptied the contents into large black plastic bags.

In Four Marks, I needed to empty only one bin outside a bungalow in Winston Rise as it contained near the top a cooking magazine with letters cut out.

Back home, I sorted through my bags and confirmed my two trolls.

Detective Constable Ray Strange of Hampshire CID, whose bin also included a confidential paper relating to my case which he had copied and taken home. Strange had a disabled younger brother in Reading whom he supported, paying £300 a month towards his rent. They met every weekend, followed the local football team in season, went fishing otherwise, and did their drinking at *The Village* at Station Hill and drank Carling Black Label. Strange ran a pub tab and paid through his credit card. Social worker Janet Brimsmore had several photo printouts in her bin and I recognised her straightaway as the woman who had taken Sammi into care. She was Sri Lankan by birth, had a BSc social work degree from Portsmouth University, and was forever posting pictures of her latest culinary creations.

The next night I drove back to her home, parked outside, accessed the Wi-Fi, and, as I hoped, found that she didn't log off her system and had no password connected with it. Within five minutes I was in and browsing her personal Facebook page. I saw an individual I knew: Worm Man. They were more than just friends. They showed a combined interest in me through their conviction that I had murdered a precious worm and both Harshani and Sammi. Their co-ordinated trolling was laid bare in email correspondence.

I then bought another laptop, loaded it with pictures of my targets culled from their bins, and added two false Facebook and Twitter accounts. I discarded my old laptop in a municipal tip having put a six-inch nail through the hard drive. Strange's computer was password-protected, but his brother's in Reading was not. As an anonymous 'Concerned Citizen', I posted on the brother's and Brimsmore's covert and open accounts, and sent emails to their entire contact lists, especially their work comrades, and to the press. I made explicit accusations of each other's complicity in computer trolling, based on confidential work papers and knowledge. They had targeted and unfairly pinpointed a man who had lost his family and had been driven into seclusion and deep depression. I added damning written evidence, facts and pictures. I then destroyed this second laptop and burned all of my evidence.

The results could not have been more dramatic or immediate. The disclosures made national news. Photographers parked in front of the four homes. Following an internal police investigation, Strange was fired. His brother was taken into a sordid care home.

I left Worm Man to sweat, sending him a few weeks later a birthday card with a worm on the cover, wishing him health, and signed anonymously in a combination of green ink and cut out letters. I hope that the rest of his life was miserable and lonely.

After two weeks, Brimsmore took a drug overdose and died in agony. I was interviewed, of course, but the coroner offered me an official apology.

Did I cause her suicide? Of course, I did. Was it murder? I'm not sure.

ENDNOTES

[1] After the Salem witch trials in the 1690s.

13 MURDER ON THE KING'S HIGHWAY
Trouble with the Common Market

CHAWTON PARK WOOD
1248   BODY COUNT: 1

Ye, through the pass of Aultone
Poverte might passe
Withouten peril of robbynge,
For where poverte may paas
Peace followeth after.

Peace is robbed in the Pass of Alton on his way to Winchester Fair
Piers Plowman, William Langland, c. 1350

Richard Squirrel found a stranger murdered in the Pass of Alton in 1248. Although Squirrel was the first to find the body, he was not suspected of involvement and nothing more is known of him. The villages of Alton, Medstead and Chawton, that bordered the crime scene, were fined by a judge sitting in Winchester early the next year for putting insufficient effort into an investigation.[1] It is no surprise that the murderer was not identified as he was likely protected by a swathe of co-conspirators.

The Pass of Alton was the way through today's Chawton Park Wood, then called Alton Forest, a declared nest of murderers and robbers who drew on their local communities for sustenance, hiding places and tight lips. Lumbering wagons were vulnerable as they ground slowly through thick beeches up to the ridge. This was the best place to attack merchants and lonely travellers making their way between Alton and Winchester on the London road. Assaults had been reported regularly for many years. For instance, in 1237 or 1238, a servant of a foreign merchant, Hector Arras, was robbed passing through the neighbourhood. The king ordered the bishop in Winchester to return the merchant's chattels which were found at Southampton.

I put forward five primary suspects, none of them named before, for your consideration during this chapter as the murderer in the case of Squirrel's gruesome find: John Barkham, John de Bendinges, Richard Bennet, Walter Bloweberme and Adam Limesy. Please read on and make your choice.

Who the stranger was or where he came from was probably never discovered. Evidently not local, nor even distantly local, he seems to have been travelling alone. No other bodies were found and no one came forward to report an attack. There was nothing on his person to give clues to his identity, which suggests he had been stripped of anything useful. Was he walking or riding? If there was a horse, it would likely have been carrying valuables and been taken by the bandit. What remained of the dead man's clothes might have suggested a man of some small status, a merchant or someone about more than local agricultural business. If he been a peasant, one suspects the matter would not have taken up the time of a visiting judge of a senior medieval court, a 'justice in *eyre*', who rode a circuit from county to county hearing cases.[2]

One other robbery in the Pass later that year became notorious for the theft of today's equivalent of £100,000, for embarrassing the king, Henry III, and for threatening trade relations with western Europe. This was a sensitive matter because Henry had braved strong English criticism in allowing foreign merchants free movement of their goods within his prosperous realm. Dozens of wealthy men from Alton, Medstead, Ropley, West Tisted and Selborne and surrounding estates openly defied him at Winchester Castle by either directly or indirectly refusing to name the perpetrators.

The story has often been repeated in histories of the era, but little discussed locally other than to note that a consignment of wine destined for the king at Winchester was also stolen at the same time. This story is untrue and comes from a misreading of the original accounts.[3]

Contemporary historian Matthew Paris wrote a notable and over-excited review of the robbery in Latin.[4] This work is often quoted without criticism to the present day. Paris's contribution was reviewed in considerable depth by Michael Clanchy in 1978.[5] Clanchy valiantly supports Paris, especially his accusations against the corrupt local gentry, but at the end Paris stands accused of exaggeration, conflation, hyperbole and allowing his own sentiments, like anti-papacy, more a rant against authority that theologically based, to intervene.

Paris's biographer, Richard Vaughan, concluded in 1958, that the man was a likeable 'humbug and a hypocrite'.[6] He deplored the 'splendours of the world yet revelled in them ... The king suffers just as much from his tirades as does the pope.' Vaughan found Paris a great read, an excellent raconteur and 'his gossip is often inspired even when it is worthless and malicious'. It is necessary, therefore, to read Paris warily when he discusses the robbery and to travel also with Clanchy and others to the original material.

Squirrel's discovery was at the same place as the later robbery, likely within a mile of the Four Marks boundary stone, and just a few months later. We are entitled to speculate whether our assassin was one of the band finally dealt with for this second felony.

Ralph Wauncy was ordered by the king to oversee an enquiry concerning the Alton robbery and met a wall of resistance. The enquiry was headed by the experienced knight, Henry de Mara [de la Mare]. Little progress was made other than blaming unnamed outlaws. People were arrested, then released by their peers. With Wauncy and Mara having failed, Henry now looked to the justices of the general circuit, *eyre*, who were due in Winchester in January 1249. These justices, although headed by the formidable Henry of Bath, encountered the same difficulties. Twelve jurors from all the Hampshire hundreds, including those from Alton and adjoining Selborne and Odiham, were summoned to appear, but refused to give up the names of the perpetrators, in some cases their own names.

Here is an abridgement, with many emendments and cautions, of Paris's account. Conversation as a whole is imagined by Paris, which, of course, does not mean that it is not sometimes nearly accurate. Parts in double quotes are disputed.

As Lent drew near, two merchants of Brabant [from Belgium and Holland] *came to the king in Winchester to make a complaint 'mingled with lamentations and tears', 'Most peaceful and just king, we were passing through your territories, which we believed to be peaceful, to prosecute our trade, when we were attacked on our journey, undefended as we were, by some freebooters and robbers, "whom we know by their faces, and whom we found at your court," who basely and robber-like took from us two hundred marks [£133 6s 8d] by force; and if these men presume to deny the charge, we are prepared, with God for our judge, to discover the truth by the ordeal of single combat against them.'[7]*

'The suspected parties were therefore taken [but after trial in the county were released]. What wonder is it? The country was suited to them for the whole of it was infected with robbery.'

The merchants pressed their charge and importunately demanded their money [from] *the king who began to be disturbed.*[8] [He asked his advisers for a solution.]

[The king was told the situation was the same all over England.] *'For very frequently are travellers robbed, wounded, made prisoners and murdered. We wonder that your justices in eyre, whose especial duty this is, have not cleansed this country of such a disgrace. We believe, therefore, that these robbers, who abound here beyond measure, have craftily entered into a conspiracy that no one of them shall, on any account, accuse another.*

'Henry de Mara, your justiciary, was here, with his colleagues, and did no good. Those persons whom he had appointed as inquisitors were confederates and abettors of robbers.

'We must, therefore, deal cautiously against such many-shaped traitors, that cunning may be deceived by cunning. For great numbers of traders, especially those from the continent [travel from Kent or London through the Pass of Alton to visit Winchester and its market]. *"The men who have been robbed declare that if the money … is not restored to them, they will forcibly reclaim it by seizing all property belonging to the merchants of your kingdom in their country"* … *The duke of Brabant, whose friendship we desire, will, and not without good cause, treat you with disdain.'*

The king summoned the bailiffs and free-men of [Hampshire to the Great Hall and in front of the bishop] *and with a scowling look said to them, 'What is this I hear of you? The complaint of despoiled persons has reached me. It is necessary for me to listen to them. There is no county or district throughout the whole extent of England so infamous as* [Hampshire] *or polluted by so many crimes. Even when I am present, robberies and murders are committed.*

'Nor are these crimes sufficient; "but even my own wines are exposed to robbery and pillage, and are carried off in stolen carts by these malefactors, who laugh and get drunk on them."

'How can such proceedings be any longer tolerated? To eradicate these and similar crimes, I have appointed wise persons to join me in ruling and guarding the kingdom. I am only one man, and do not wish, nor am I able, to support the burden of managing the whole kingdom without the aid of coadjutors [assistants].

'I am ashamed and wearied of the foul stench of this city and the adjacent districts. I was born in this city and never was so much disgrace brought on me anywhere as here.

'It is probable, and I must believe, nay, it is now quite clear, that you, the citizens and inhabitants of the province, are infamous accomplices and confederates.'

The king then suddenly exclaimed in a loud voice, 'Shut the gates of the castle. Shut them immediately.'

[The bishop intervened.] *'Stay, my lord, stay a little, hear me patiently. There are in this castle some strangers, good men and of pure fame, and friends to you, whom it does not become you to shut in.'*

Twelve persons were elected from amongst the local citizens who were sworn to give the names of any thieves whom they knew. These men were taken to a private place where they were closely guarded.

After a long deliberation, they would not mention any of the names of the thieves which greatly displeased the king for he was well aware that they knew something of the plans of the robbers.

Infuriated, he said, 'Seize these deceitful traitors, chain them, and throw them into the lowest dungeon, for they refuse to speak, and conceal what they ought to make known. They are doubtless excommunicated by their bishop. See how they give these [robbers] *their favour. Select me twelve others who will* [tell] *me the truth.'*

[The new men heard] *that the former twelve were imprisoned and condemned to be hanged ... After a long and secret consultation,* [they came back] *and disclosed the thefts and other crimes of many persons of whom a great many belonged to the neighbouring districts, especially to Alton.*

[Some men took advantage of the crowd and escaped.]

Many of the inhabitants of the district who were formerly considered good men, with rich possessions, and some whom the king had deputed as bailiffs ... "and some even who were superintendents of the king's household, and crossbow-men in his service," were made prisoners and, being proved guilty, were hanged ... Some, however, took refuge in the churches [like St Swithun's], *and others suddenly and secretly took to flight, and* [were never heard of again].

Those who were taken were more closely questioned and confessed "that they had committed unheard of robberies and murders". [About thirty who were clearly proved guilty were hanged and about the same number] were imprisoned, awaiting a like punishment. [By his latter book, *Historia Anglorum*, Paris said the number hanged was one hundred.]

Those who belonged to the king's household, when about to be hanged, said, 'Tell the king that he is our death and the chief cause of it by having so long withheld the pay which was due to us when we were in need. We were obliged to turn thieves and freebooters, or to sell our horses, arms, or clothes, which we could not possibly do without.'

"[When he heard this,] *the king was touched with shame and grief and gave vent to his sorrow in protracted sighs.*"

Winchester and the whole of that county incurred an indelible stain of infamy and opprobrium from these occurrences.

There is no doubt the local jurors were corrupt and used their positions to try to free guilty men. Two of the three principal accused, John de Bendinges and John Barkham, were men of knightly status, and at least twenty of the sixty-four persons indicted as accessories were freemen of the Alton region.[9] One of the appointed officials who so displeased Henry was Richard Kitcombe, a Selborne juror, identified as from the Four Marks hamlet of Kitwood with lands worth more than £30. He was hanged when found guilty of supplying a pig and two sheep to the outlaws in the wood close to his home. 'Whether he had acted entirely of his own free will is doubtful as the unidentified outlaws obtained food by force and intimidated local people.'[10]

For those found guilty, or thought guilty, a range of punishments was available to the king and his courts. For those caught red-handed, hanging, imprisonment, fines and banishment were the most straight forward. Others could be left to be routinely tortured and to rot in infested jails as they waited for trial. Of those charged with being principals in the robbery, or of being corrupt jurors, twenty-five were found guilty, twenty-five were acquitted, twelve were remanded in custody for lesser offences and two had no verdict recorded. Of those found guilty, thirteen were outlawed in their absence, two escaped the country, one, Clement Driver, was committed to the bishop as a clerk convict and nine were presumed hanged.

As always, there was one rule for the wealthy and another for the poor and insignificant. There were always two types of crime in play. It was one thing to steal from someone of similar rank where honour could often be settled by apology and payment. It was entirely another matter to step across the social barriers and steal, upwards, from the king or, less drastically, from one's social superiors as, say, a labourer from a knight. Stealing downwards, as today, was of much less importance especially in the eyes of a judiciary chosen to support their own class.[11]

The harshness of criminal law was mitigated where gentlemen were concerned. Destitute aiders of the robbers were sentenced to death while the principals escaped. Alice Gosepaun, with no chattels, was hanged as was William Godshill who pleaded that he had been compelled to act as the gang's messenger. Compare this with Cecily Colemore who offered 100 marks to have a special jury, which then acquitted her. Clergy were exempt from the death penalty.

'The king's justices seems to believe that wrongdoers should indeed be punished with equal severity, but that did not mean that all punishments should be the same. Each malefactor must offer an equivalent recompense to the king for his offence. Gentlemen like Bendinges and Barkham had lands which the king could confiscate and despoil whereas a poor man or woman had nothing to offer except their own person.'[12]

One of the difficulties for early law enforcers was the lack of any experts in forensic medicine or pathology. Accusations could be denied. Torture might be inappropriate. The aim of trial by battle was to establish the truth by divine intervention: God would ensure that the innocent party triumphed.[13] Battle was once the routine procedure in an accusation of felony when the accuser undertook to prove his allegation 'by his body'. It was essentially an 'ordeal' similar to surviving a hot iron or ducking in water.[14] Giving battle was not seen as a simple matter of the physically superior or more expert fighter winning; the court would sometimes give the stronger party a handicap such as requiring him to fight with a hand tied or standing in water. This was the route offered by the Brabant merchants to embarrass the king and coerce him to take action over their loss.

A widespread variation of trial by battle was a direct predecessor of today's 'turning State's evidence' where a convicted party, someone who had acknowledged their guilt, turned 'approver', or accuser. By naming his co-conspirators, an approver could hope to escape the noose and accept, for instance, banishment. Complex rules applied and if any of those 'fingered' was found to be not guilty, then the approver's sentence would be carried out. It was a process seen to have merit by the court because it broke up bands of lower-class robbers by making them inform on each other. Appointing, and paying and equipping, approvers was a power reserved to the king and a few close advisers.[15] 'At a less theoretical level, the royal government used the approver as a prosecutor and intimidator where no better proof could be obtained.'[16]

The attempt of an approver to save his skin led to a trial by battle if the claim was refuted by the accused. 'The defendant entered the field first and taking the approver by the hand denied the accusation word for word. The approver repeated his accusation and swore that it was true. The duel proceeded until one was killed or cried "craven". If the accused was defeated and not killed, he was hanged.'[17] A day was then set for the approver to fight his next accused, and the next, and so on. Outcomes were often complicated by the exchange of money, bribery and interventions by friends of either party.

The eyre roll that contains this story of robbery at the Pass of Alton is seen as remarkable for two reasons.

First, it records two combats where separate approvers, Walter Bloweberme and Reynold Sutor of Scotland, fought duels and won, a third combat where the outcome is unknown through damage to the record, and a fourth where the approver withdrew after the accused offered battle.

Second is that on the frontispiece of the roll membrane is a drawing of Bloweberme, on the right in profile, in combat with an accused Hamo Stare, three-quarter face. To the left, Stare is hanged on a gibbet, standing on a stylised hill, after losing the fight. The men's names are inscribed above in black ink.18 The picture is therefore the earliest known, and perhaps only, representation of a trial and its sentence following a crime committed in the Four Marks environs.

Walter Bloweberme, right, in trial by combat with Hamo Stare following the robbery at the Pass of Alton. Stare lost and was hanged, far left, before his body was placed in a gibbet to rot, probably at Gibbet Copse at the head of the Pass, 1249. *Curia Regis Roll, Hampshire Record Office*

The combatants are not using the ordinary weapons of the time.[19] Approvers were provided with special outfits, usually at the crown's expense.[20] Fortunately, the bill survives for equipping one of the combats in the Hampshire eyre as it was charged to the bishop of Winchester's Waltham account and recorded on his pipe roll.[21] *It specifies the following:*

Purchase of two shields	*13s 4d*	
Emending the same	*8d*	
Purchase of two staves	*3s 0d*	
Purchase of white leather, felt and linen cloth for armour and tunics	*8s 3d*	
Wages of armourer to make and equip	*2s 0d*	*£1 7s 3d*

The fight is fact, not conjecture. The question now becomes, 'Where did it take place?'

Approvers associated with the Alton Pass robbery were assembled, unusually, at Winchester instead of Newgate in London. Combats mostly took place on 'mean ground' or at the place of the crime. The crime was at the Pass of Alton near where the current foresters' cabins stand off the car park at the head of Chawton Park Wood. Alongside the car park is the still-named Gibbet Copse of which little is directly known. Leigh, in his *History of Chawton Manor*, says, without source, that the 'gallows' at the copse had tumbled down by 1280.[22] The date suggests a strong association with the robbery of the Brabant traders in 1248 and its consequences.

Could Bloweberme's trial by battle have taken place near the car park off Boyneswood Road or, in any event, was the gibbet the last resting place of Stare's body. Gibbetting was a gruesome process, much used with smugglers and highwaymen, whereby the corpse of a hanged felon was taken to a remote but prominent spot, sometimes the scene of the crime, and there suspended in an iron cage from a high post and left to rot with no hope of a Christian burial. The act signified deterrence rather than detection. Increasingly gory punishments were inflicted on those convicted of [felonies] to deter and scare all those who passed.[23]

[A full list of those accused does not offer much in the context of this book. Also the record is occasionally obscure and there are contradictions, especially in Paris's account. In an appendix to this chapter, I have gathered details of the principal robbers and included those who were local to Four Marks or were unusual in some way.]

Royal serjeants had been appointed to keep guard of the Pass in June

1248, but had failed to protect the Brabant merchants.[24] In September, in the immediate aftermath of the robbery and at the time of the annual St Giles Fair held at Winchester, a stronger force was sent. A king's serjeant, William of Woodham, the bishop's reeve from Highclere and various Welshmen, presumably Welsh mercenaries, passed through Bishop's Sutton on their way to guard the Pass for visiting merchants.[25] The common assumption, including by Paris, is that the Brabant merchants were on their way to Winchester, but an alternative suggestion is that their destination was the annual Alresford sheep fair, regularly attended by Flemish dealers who preferred to stay in Alton rather than the inferior local inns.

Following the eyre, there was a slew of action, all well intentioned, but seemingly to little effect.Next summer, the way through the Pass was ordered to be widened by the felling of the thick beech trees to a width of 200 feet, an arrow shot, on both sides of the road, but it did not happen. In 1251, a writ was sent to all sheriffs across the country warning them of highwaymen in 'passes'. The sheriff of Hampshire was especially instructed to have 'diligent and cautious investigation concerning certain men of Winchester and Alton'. 'Several men' from each nearby village were ordered to keep watch on their

nearby pass. The men of Alton given this duty quickly asked the king to send more armed men to assist them. The following year, Ellis Rochester, a professional soldier, was granted all the land in the Pass once belonging to the hanged William Pope. Further grants were made to Rochester in 1255, 1257 and 1259, 1269 and 1271.

In 1261, the king complained that his baggage train had been robbed in the Pass. Action was finally taken to prepare for the felling of the trees. The woodland in the Pass was surveyed and valued in 1262 by William

'The Pine Walk', Medstead, c. 1900s: The remains of the King's Highway?

Wintershall. With the king taking a close eye on progress, an enquiry at next year's Hampshire eyre was told that robberies and homicides were committed 'even daily' in the Pass by 'foresters and shepherds'.

The Second Barons' War from 1264 to 1267 intervened. A number of barons led by Simon de Montfort sought to force the king to rule with a council rather than through his favourites. After initial successes, de Montfort broadened the social foundations of Parliament by extending the franchise to the commons for the first time. At that time, he held Henry and his son, Prince Edward, captive. The war also featured a series of massacres of Jews by de Montfort's supporters, including his sons Henry and Simon, in attacks aimed at seizing and destroying evidence of baronial debts. Edward escaped and took command of the royal armies, eventually freeing his father. After a rule of just over a year, de Montfort was killed at the Battle of Evesham and his body grossly mutilated.

De Montfort's surviving son, and other barons and knights including Adam de Gourdon, previously mentioned as known to some of those convicted during the 1249 eyre, continued the fight. Gourdon, now an outlaw disinherited from his lands, was a nobleman, once Lord of Selborne and Bailiff of Alton. His stronghold was the wooded country between Farnham and Alton, particularly the castle of Barley Pound in the Crondall countryside, 'one of the best examples of a ring and bailey fortress in the county'.[26] Barley Pound is halfway between Powderham and Bentley Castles, probably Barley Pound's defensive siege fortifications.[27]

There are many accounts of the terror that Gourdon with his 'band of eighty men' wreaked on the Pass of Alton, the Hampshire countryside and wider afield, one story often springing from another with embellishment.[28] Charles Dickens called him the 'last dissatisfied knight in England'.[29] Gourdon was undoubtedly a thief and a murderer although some would like to make him Hampshire's Robin Hood.

What happened next is hotly disputed as to style and place and has passed into legend. Prince Edward, ex-prisoner of Gourdon, decided to track the renegade down and stop the nuisance. Some might suggest that this was more likely to be unfinished business from Edward's days in his captivity. To suggest that the pair were unknown to each other disputes the facts. A hand-to-hand combat ensued, in noble tradition, some say in a dell east of Long Sutton, near Alton. The prince leapt a barricade and engaged Gourdon in a long encounter

in which both were injured. Edward either offered Gourdon his life during a
pause or spared his life at the point of a sword.

Adam de Gourdon presented to the Queen, 1267. *The English School*

Gourdon agreed and was taken to meet Edward's mother, Eleanor, that evening
in Guildford. Gourdon became a faithful and princely adherent. Meanwhile,
Gourdon's men were slaughtered.

> *I am Adam de Gourdon, a noble free;*
> *Perchance thou hast heard my name?*
> *'I have heard it, I trow (quoth the prince), and thou*
> *Art a traitor of blackest fame.*
> *Yield thee to me!' But the outlaw cried,*
> *Now, if thou knowest not fear.*
> *Out with thy sword! By a good knight's word,*
> *I will give thee battle here.*
> *'Come on!' cried that prince of dauntless heart* [and much more of the same ...] [30]

Descendants of the Gourdon (Gordon) clan claim that Adam's family assisted
Scottish king Malcolm Canmore in his overthrow of the usurper Macbeth
in 1057. Adam was killed in 1296 at the Battle of Dunbar fighting his old

adversary and supposedly new best friend, Edward 'Longshanks' Plantagenet.[31]

Hostilities over, Wintershall, who had conducted the 1262 survey of the Pass, was ordered to go back in 1269 and take the trees down. The king offered up his ninety-five acres of hunting land. Ellis Rochester was granted the woodland on condition that he felled the trees and brought the land under cultivation.

The bishops of Winchester and Oxford, together with Robert de St. John [seen by some as an obstructionist], *and the tenants who had rights of common therein, met before the king's justices, and surrendered all their title and claim therein, in order that the woodlands might be grubbed up, and brought into a state of cultivation; and the king, by the deed before mentioned, granted his own demesnes in the neighbourhood, in order that a royal road, spacious, wide, and good, might be forthwith made from Alton to Alresford. There seems but little doubt that the old road, which now indeed consists chiefly of green lanes, still wide and spacious, and which runs from Alton, by Chawton Wood and several solitary farms, through Bighton, to Old Alresford, is Henry's 'royal road'.*[32]

William Leigh and Montagu Knight, in their history of Chawton Manor, explained that the 'Pass of Alton' lay on the estate.[33]

In a grant by John de St John in the 14th year of Edward II, land is described as extending 'towards Mundchamesrude on the West' and abutting 'on the highway by the Pass of Aultone on the North'. In a grant of 17th of Edward II, part of the land is described as lying 'next Le Paas between the land of the Chaplain of the Chapel of Chawton and the land of John le Knyght'. In the next reign, one of the parks at Chawton is said to be next to the Pass. In 1605 the accounts of John Knight contain, 'Payd more to John Trymmer for hedging at Parke against the passe way upon the dytche xxd.' An enclosure joining the old upper road by Chawton Park is still called 'Pease-way Close'; and a continuation of this road in Medstead is known as 'The Pace-way' (Paice Lane) ... The word 'Pass' is used in the sense of a 'road or passage'.[34]

Beneath part of Paice Lane, about four feet deep and to the right of it, is a hard surface – thought to be the road.[35] Why this route? At the beginning of the thirteenth century, Godfrey de Lucy, bishop of Winchester, took up his residence at Sutton – since known as Bishop's Sutton.[36] 'He obtained leave to build a dam at Alresford, thus enlarging the pond which was then large enough to reach to the Palace, but it has since shrunk to one-third its size. The Bishop was permitted to make a road across the dam, connecting New and Old Alresford, as the ford was useless since the dam was made. The road of Henry III was constructed to meet this one of Bishop Lucy, thus allowing Henry to travel to his beloved Winchester more directly.'[37]

Despite his drastic actions, the king still found extreme difficulty in preventing the local community closing ranks around criminals. The lawlessness went on. In numerous instances, the juries would not indict, or pronounced acquittals and many of those accused fled or escaped. In 1272, Adam de Gourdon was escorting prisoners to Winchester jail but lost them to outlaws in the Pass. In 1280, he was ordered by King John to give back Hawkley Mill stolen from the bishops of Winchester.

The Statute of Winchester in 1285 laid the blame for another increase in crime on local jurors who refused to accuse people of their neighbourhood of felonies especially when the victims were strangers. Nothing had changed. Clearing space as a security measure along commercial roads was made law across the country.[38] The Statute provided that the 'highways leading from one market town to another shall be enlarged, where as wood, hedges or dykes be, so that there be neither dyke, tree or bush, whereby a man may lurk to do hurt, within two hundred foot on the one side and two hundred feet on the other side of the way.'[39] 'It was this limited idea of keeping open the free passage for the King and his subjects that the Common Law sought to realise by holding someone responsible for the maintenance of every public highway.'[40]

It was a start, but a slow one. In 1318, Thomas Fisher of Breckles accused someone for their part in the robbery of £14 in silver and a horse belonging to William Micklepayn of Winchester which took place in the Pass of Alton.[41]

ENDNOTES

[1] *Hampshire Record Office*, Curia Regis Roll, JUST 1/776, parent roll, and KB 26/223, detached membrane; additional transcripts by Meekings, C E F, and Hector, L C, 1949; and text by Bissche, Edward, 1654.
[2] In 1221, six justices went on *eyre* (or circuit) in the western counties.
[3] Clanchy, 'Highway robbery'. Clanchy is Professor Emeritus of Medieval History at the Institute of Historical Research, University of London and Fellow of the British Academy.
[4] Paris, *Historica Anglorum*.
[5] Clanchy, 'Highway robbery'.
[6] Vaughan, *Paris*. Vaughan was an expert on the Middle Ages and an accomplished linguist in thirteen languages. He was a university professor in three different countries and a leading ornithologist.

7 A medieval token from Nuremburg in Bavaria, exchangeable for money, was found recently by a metal detectorist between the railway line and the route of the King's Highway.

8 Probably Thomas Wales (Walloon?) and Reyner Lewe (Britnell, *Pipe Rolls*).

9 Haverkamp and Vollrath, *England and Germany*.

10 Clanchy, 'Highway Robbery', Introduction.

11 Chapter 9, this book, 'Knowing one's place'.

12 Clanchy, 'Highway Robbery', Introduction.

13 Clanchy, 'Highway Robbery', Introduction.

14 Neilson, *Trial by Combat*.

15 Hamil, 'King's Approvers'.

16 Clanchy, 'Highway Robbery', Introduction.

17 Hamil, 'King's Approvers'.

18 Clanchy, 'Highway Robbery', Introduction.

19 Clanchy, 'Highway Robbery', Introduction.

20 Hamil, 'King's Approvers'.

21 *Hampshire Record Office*, Winchester Pipe Roll, m.28: Meekings in Wiltshire Crown Pleas 1249, 91.

22 Leigh, *Chawton Manor*.

23 Hare, *Secret Shore*.

24 The post of Serjeant at Arms was formalised in the late thirteenth century when Edward I formed a bodyguard of twenty men. They performed a wide variety of administrative and judicial tasks directly for the king, from tax collecting to making arrests.

25 Britnell, *Pipe Rolls*.

26 Munday, 'Outposts of an outlaw', citing Williams-Freeman, *Field Archaeology*.

27 Bentley Castle is a name given to the site by archaeologists (Stamper, 'Siege Castle').

28 Malham, *History of England*. Trimmer, *History of England*. Shore, *Hampshire*. Smollett, Urban, et al, *Gentleman's Magazine*, 1821. Mills, Four Marks.

29 Dickens, *Child's History of England*.

30 Bute, *Lays and Ballads*.

31 history.wdgordon.com/gordon10.htm (2020). *Dictionary of National Biography*.

32 Duthy, *Sketches*. 'Duthy appears to have had access to documents which cannot now be traced' (Moody, Short History of Medstead).

33 Leigh, *Chawton*.

34 This view is supported by Janin, *Medieval Justice*: 'Highway robbery at the Pass of Alton: "Pass" refers to a track cleared through a forest, not a defile between the hills.'

35 Moody, *A Short History of Medstead*.

36 Duthy, *Sketches*.

37 Duthy, *Sketches*.

38 Jackman, *Transportation*.

39 Act 13, Edward 1, c. 5.

40 Webbs, *King's Highway*.

41 Musson, *Public Order*.

Reading list:

Britnell, Richard, *The Winchester Pipe Rolls and Medieval English Society* (Boydell, Woodbridge 2003)

Carpenter, David, *Henry III, 1207–1258* (Yale University Press, 2020)

Clanchy, M.T., edited, 'Highway Robbery and trial by battle in the Hampshire eyre of 1249', in Hunnisett, R.F., and Post, J.B., *Medieval Legal Records, edited in the memory of C.A.F. Meekings (HMSO, London 1978); From Memory to Written Record, England 1066–1307,* third edition (Wiley-Blackwell, Chichester 2013)

Coates, Richard, *The Place-Names of Hampshire* (Batsford, London 1989)

Curtis, William, *A Short History and Description of the Town of Alton* (1896; Noverre Press, Binsted 2012)

Dictionary of National Biography

Duthy, John, *Sketches of Hampshire; embracing the architectural antiquities, topography, etc, of country adjacent to the river Itchen; ...* (1839; British Library 2020)

Gentleman's Magazine, and Historical Chronicle, Vol. 91, Part 2, pp. 205–209, 1821

Giles, J.A., Rev, translated, *Matthew Paris's English History, 1235–1273,* Vol. 2 (c. 1250) (1853; Scolar Select reprint 2020)

Gover, J.E.B., *The Place-Names of Hampshire* (MSS, English Place-Name Society 1961)

Haverkamp, Alfred, and Vollrath, Hanna, editors, *England and Germany in the High Middle Ages: In Honour of Karl J. Leyser* (German Historical Institute, London 1966)

Hamil, Frederick C., 'The King's Approvers: A Chapter in the History of English Criminal Law', *Speculum,* Vol. 11, No. 2, April, 1936, pp. 238–258

Janin, Hunt, *Medieval Justice: Cases and Laws in France, England, and Germany: 500–1500* (McFarland, Jefferson, North Carolina 2004)

Jackman, W.T., *The Development of Transportation in Modern England* (1916; Frank Cass, London 1962)

Malham, John, *Grand National History of England, Civil and Ecclesiastical, from the Earliest Period of Genuine Record to the Year 1815* (Thomas Kelly, London, 1815)

Moody, Nellie, *A Short History of Medstead* (1932)

Munday, Linda, 'Outposts of an Outlaw, Adam de Gourdon and the Crondall Castles', Hart Heritage 5, *Hampshire Archaeology,* 2018

Musson, Anthony, *Public Order and Law Enforcement, 1294–1350* (Boydell Press, London 1996)

Neilson, George, *Trial by Combat* (1890; BiblioLife 2008)

Rathbone, Lorents, *A Chronicle of Medstead* (1966)

Shore, T.W., *A History of Hampshire, including The Isle of Wight* (Elliot Stock, London 1892)

Smedley, Menella Bute, *Lays and Ballads from English History* (Lumley, London 1856)

Stamper, P.A., 'Excavations on a Mid-Twelfth Century Siege Castle at Bentley, Hampshire', *Proceedings of the Hampshire Field Club and Archaeological Society*, Vol. 40, pp. 81–89, 1984

Trimmer, Sarah, *History of England* (Grant and Griffith, London 1869)

Vaughan, Richard, *Matthew Paris* (1958; Cambridge University Press 1979)

Wood, Eric S, *Historical Britain*, A comprehensive account of the development of rural and urban life and landscape from prehistory to the present day (Harvill Press, London 1995)

Appendix: Local robbers, suspects and corrupt jurors

* William Arundel, son of Hugh, Lord of Upton Grey. Acquitted, but ordered to 'find sureties to stand to right if the Brabant merchants wish to proceed against him'.
* William Arundel from Upper Wick, near Selborne.
* John Barkham, a principal robber. Lands forfeited. Pardoned with de Bendinges on the same terms. He was pardoned a second time later that year at the request of Henry of Almain, the king's nephew.
* John de Bendinges, a principal robber, fled 'fearing for himself'. He fought in Wales in 1245 and 1246 and may have been one of the king's serjeants 'protecting' the pass. Lands, fields, pastures, woods, gardens and houses near Odiham were forfeited and laid waste. Forty pounds passed to the 'king's works at Windsor'. Twenty thousand shingles were ordered from de Bendinges' woods to roof royal buildings. Probably the whole sum of the stolen money was recovered from him. He was pardoned (but his property was not returned) in 1254 at Meilhan-sur-Garonne in Gascony at the request of Guy de Lusignan, Henry's half-brother. It is likely that the merchants knew the monies had been recovered and this explains why they were determined to claim compensation. The king made a second visit to Winchester and, after protracted negotiation, Thomas Walloon was given £16 early in March and, twelve days later, Reynar Lewe received £106.
* Richard Bennet, a principal robber.
* Walter Bloweberme, approver, convicted ten accused, six at Guildford and four in Hampshire; one by combat against Hamo Stare, and three by flight, including Henry Clop who left the country. Bloweberme also accused two men who were acquitted by jury and another, presumed acquitted. He was tried the following year, 1250, before justices in Westminster, when he turned approver again and accused twenty people, twelve in Canterbury and eight in St Albans where a robbery was alleged. Bloweberme is presumed hanged.
* Ellis Blunt supplied food to the outlaws.
* John Boarhunt, accused, corrupt juror, of Burhunt Farm, near Selborne. Foreman of the Selborne jurors. Fined 40s.
* John and William Bullock, probably of Bullocks Farm near Odiham. William Bullock was an Odiham juror. Charged with corruption. Fined 100s.
* The canons of Durford Abbey in Rogate, Sussex, were implicated by a

message delivered by the outlaws to their cellarer. William the abbot and others accused of homicide in 1249. Outlaws hid in the abbey.

* Thomas Clerk, clergy, of Priors Dean, wrote letters for the outlaws. Claimed 'his clergy' against punishment although he was married and had a lay fee.

* Henry Clop escaped to sanctuary rather than fight Bloweberme for which Bishop's Waltham's hundred was fined 66s 8d.

* 'Master Geoffrey', formerly the king's cook. Deprived of his royal lands in Mapledurham near Petersfield in December 1248 [which showed that the king knew of the robbery before the Hampshire eyre in 1249].

* John Harvest, indicted of aiding the robbers. Acquitted, but turned approver later and was hanged.

* Gilbert and son, William, Hattingley, probably from the hamlet near Medstead. Charged with harbouring.

* Henry King of Priors Dean. Property worth more than £6. Hanged.

* Richard Kitcombe of Kitwood (now in Four Marks) one of the electors of the Selborne jury. Hanged.

* Richard Lacfeud, one of those who escaped from the crowd at the Winchester Castle.

* Adam Limesy whose chattels were seized and passed to the bishop of Winchester. West Tisted inheritance. Pardoned at Bordeaux at the request of Edward, Henry's eldest son. In the Hampshire eyre of 1256, he disappeared and was suspected of homicide and was outlawed once again.

* Miles Merchant, and his son, with a house in Alton belonging to his wife. He had twenty-five shillings.

* John Otter, connected with Selborne Priory and a confederate of Adam Gourdon.

* William Pope, approver, obtained about fifteen convictions, and was the only one actually named (many times) by Paris. Crucially, Pope owned most of the land in the pass. The main robbers set out from his house and for this the jurors found him guilty and he was sentenced to hang. Paris claimed Pope was 'abounding in household goods, so much so, that, on examining his house after he was taken, there were found about fifteen casks full of wine in his cellar'. Pope may have been reprieved after losing his goods. Clanchy has great difficult in disentangling Paris's version from the facts in the record. A royal writ dated September 1249 states Pope left the country either, suggests Clanchy, because he became an approver or because he

escaped. At the same time Pope's wife, Joan, was 'granted a quarter of corn from his chattels'.

* William Scot, approver with Robert Winchelsea. Both lodged in Winchester Castle gaol, suspected of robbery. Cases unproven. Permitted to go to the Holy Land in 1253.
* William Sinclair of knightly status.
* Hamo Stare hanged and gibbetted after losing his trial by battle with Bloweberme.
* Reynold Sutor, approver, accused three men who were acquitted by juries, a woman whose verdict is unrecorded and an accused who accepted the challenge. Sutor's fate is unknown.
* Robert, alias Nicholas, Winchelsea. See William Scot, above.

14 CARE OF THE INNOCENTS
Birth, death and ethics

FOUR MARKS
1950s   BODY COUNT: WHO KNOWS?

My mother had three sisters, all of them at one time or the other nurses. Ethel stands out for me, round-framed glasses, dark hair slightly unkempt hanging down to the shoulders. Earnest, friendly, caring, deeply religious. Unmarried till late in life, she took up district nursing after the war and, in the 1950s, covered a large area of Somerset, based on Wiveliscombe. It seems she was known in every run-down cottage on every farm near every village in the county. She had an early black Ford Anglia and attacked the high-hedged, country lanes without fear by assuming little oncoming traffic, but peeping her horn at every corner. It was also a way of announcing her arrival.

'Peep. Nurse is here. Peep.'

Late in life, she showed me her maternity record book with over 2,000 entries, delivered at all hours, almost all single-handed, often by candlelight, while family members scattered for hot water and clean linen, or sat waiting on hard chairs with hands clenched in worry.

Ethel reckoned she delivered about three babies a week for over fifteen years.

'They seemed to like two in the morning.'

One time, I put her to the test as we walked down a Somerset High Street. Every child we passed, perhaps two dozen, said, 'Morning, nurse.' Two girls even curtsied. Ethel named every one, their address, where they were born and what they were doing now. There was a wave and a personal comment for each young person.

'Forty-nine of my mothers were taken to hospital before the birth for complications,' she told me, with a heavy emphasis on the 'my'. I only lost eight babies on my own, apart from stillbirths, and two mothers. Two of those babies were my fault, but the families refused to make a complaint although I told them what happened.'

No one had a phone. The eldest child was trained to cycle or run to the nearest shop, pub or rich house. Everyone had nurse's number prominently displayed. Often, she would slow the car to pick up the messenger trudging their way back up a hill to home.

It feels now that I spent almost the whole of many summers as a boy in short trousers sitting beside her with her black Labrador, Kelly, in the back, tongue hanging out of a window, as we drove to her appointments. I don't know why I was there rather than with my parents, but I loved it. Every house, some none to clean with chickens strutting around the flag-stoned kitchens, had cake, home-baked biscuits and lemonade. While I waited, I would talk to the old people sitting in the sun on a bench near the porch or play with the children and their pets or help with the farm animals. Everywhere there were neat rows of healthy vegetables standing proud in the red earth.

Pregnancies and babies were the centre of Ethel's life, then the chronically ill and people recovering from accidents and hospital operations, and, of course, the slowly dying. Her objective was to keep hospital beds available for the most needy. She didn't keep a log of deaths. The worst for me was the screams from the diabetics. In those days, in my imagination, the needles were four inches long, thick and very painful.

It seems like Ethel never bought food. In the runner and broad bean seasons especially, my job was to place the gifts carefully on the back seat then, when we were out of sight, Ethel would stop and I would move the vegetables, fruit and meat into the boot, out of sight, so as not to offend anyone and always leaving her 'special bag' uncovered. The storage space was usually shared with skinned rabbits, a ham or two and joints of chicken. When we came to the poorer families, often on the outskirts of a large village, I would select a load for redistribution. The one thing I couldn't stand was the smell of hare.

Ethel was a natural and wicked storyteller and led her audience through every revelation. Her tales often had a black side and many would not fit well with today's cautious sentiments. But she was honest and people already knew her innate kindness.

Ethel told, one day, of a frantic call about a young man who had been missing over night. He had mental health problems and was on suicide watch. She raced to the family farm and, after a brief discussion with a brother, drove to a local hilltop much visited by courting couples. They found the man dangling from a rope tied around a bough. He had died late the night before and was stiff from *rigor mortis*. Ethel held the man's ankles to keep him still while the brother climbed the tree to cut the rope. As the body was released, Ethel found herself staggering round the hill carrying the upright stiff corpse, fearful of letting go, waiting for the brother to catch up.

She once visited a dim cottage occupied by two elderly sisters. One of them had died during the day and was laid out on her bed, the room lit by a single candle. Ethel checked the body over and moved to the kitchen for a cup of tea. She heard a noise behind her, turned, and there stood the 'dead' sister who had been woken by a noise. Apparently, she lived for another two years.

One routine visit to a pregnant woman turned into a nightmare as a slightly undersized baby was born. Then another. And another. It was a case of checking, snipping, washing and wrapping and moving on to the next. After two hours, Ethel and the mother were exhausted. Ethel placed the infants in the mother's arms. One, two, three, four and sat down in the rocking chair only to shoot bolt upright.

'I thought there were five. You've only got four. You did have five babies, didn't you?'

'I don't know,' wailed the mother. 'I thought I was only going to have one.'

Ethel searched the room. A cry from the sofa led her to the fifth, hidden beneath a discarded blanket.

'I was sure it was five,' she told her audience.

Ethel came to visit me in Four Marks in the early 1990s while in her seventies. We went for a Raj Railway Lamb at the *Four Marks Golf Club* and she tossed her tales out like onion bhajis. As we laid down our cutlery, an elderly lady from the next table stood up and came over.

'I couldn't help but hear your stories,' she told Ethel. 'When I realised what you were talking about, I couldn't help but listen. I hope you don't mind. They took me right back to when I worked for a while as a district nurse around Four Marks. My name's Doris.'

There was nothing for it, but to leave the two of them at the table to rummage over old times. I retired to the bar with Doris's husband. He was an old soldier and had many stories of his own.

Doris invited Ethel for lunch two days later and I did the ferrying. I picked Ethel up from West Tisted and she was unusually quiet on the trip back to Four Marks. I let her be, thinking she was just tired, but she continued withdrawn through the evening and went to bed early. I took her in her customary cocoa.

A District Nurse visits Alton's hop fields, 1960s. *QMI Heritage*

She was sitting in bed holding her rosary beads muttering her prayers with her cherished bible near to hand.

'If you want to talk about anything, I will be in all day tomorrow,' I told her.

She nodded, clearly elsewhere, and I closed the door.

The next day, about eleven, she looked around the door of my study. Would I like a cup of tea? I smiled, nodded, and moved to a more comfortable chair to wait whatever was to come.

'In amongst all the happy times, some memories aren't so good,' she said. 'We had a glass of wine with lunch yesterday. You know I hardly ever drink. I think we remembered too much. Doris told me some of the things she did, things she thought it best to do at the time, things she thought afterwards maybe she shouldn't have done. She talked of two buildings she visited in Blackberry Lane, almost opposite each other. One was a nursing home for the elderly, the other a maternity home where young mothers who lived far away came alone to have their babies. Meeting me brought a lot of it back. Things like that had been safely locked away where they belonged. We should have left them there.

'It was almost exactly the same for me, the things she did. We spent a lot of the time crying. Her husband got cross because he didn't know what was going on. I was pleased when you arrived to take me home.'

I think it must be difficult in 2020 to understand the independence of being a district nurse in the early 1950s. Nowadays, a nurse's world is closeted in quality and diversity and safety practices. Sometimes, Doris and Ethel would go more than a week without seeing a medical colleague. They were supposed to have formal meetings every two weeks but, in the mad rush of travelling the countryside, these meetings were easily postponed. If there were no serious cases, encounters with doctors might be passing visits at some minor emergency or an intense hour of a procedure conducted on a kitchen table with no time for side chat. Visits to the pharmacy were flying affairs as pills, needles and bandages were restocked. More time might be spent with the local petrol pump attendant than an understanding colleague.

Today's 'home professionals' have a *Code* full of standards and behaviour for nurses, midwives and nursing associates – a booklet of wonder if it had been issued immediately after six years of war.[1] Despite all the clear instructions, and they are very clear, there are no easy answers, no set of ordered rules that 'once the relevant information is fed into an algorithm or computer out will pop the answer'.[2] What ethics provide is a common base: a set of moral issues that lead to a set of moral commitments that can be discussed in an understood and respected moral language. As a dilemma presents, these ethical principles should be considered 'before coming to our own answer or to choose between them when they conflict'.

One set of suggested guidelines is summed up as respect for four principles 'plus attention to scope'. They are not everyone's complete cup of tea, but then what cup of tea suits everyone?

Respect for the autonomy, the independence, of patients is fundamental. People must have the right to choose treatments, to make their own decisions based on what they have been honestly and openly told. There must be no attempt to deceive. Promises made must be kept. Information given must be kept confidential. However, one person's right to autonomy must not be allowed to override the autonomy rights of others.

Trying to help patients means bringing the best skills, training and communication to bear. The next two principles must be weighed separately and at the same time. The benefit that is done must be greater than the harm that might follow from taking a course of action. There is a need to be clear about risk and probability of both benefit and harm so that, sometimes highly personal judgements can be made.

The fourth principle is another balancing act. It requires treatment to be fair in the allocation of scarce resources, respect for what people believe to be their rights, and an understanding of what is rightfully theirs under the law. This is a minefield in which an individual's moral, religious, philosophical and political beliefs can vary widely. Nurses need to tread carefully for there is no justification for imposing one's 'own personal or professional views about fairness on others'.

'Attention to scope' recognises that despite all of the agreement that may be inherent in the moral agreements, two nurses may still 'disagree radically about to what and to whom these moral obligations are owed'.[3] There are many pitfalls here. Two issues are of dominant importance for nurses: Who falls within their principles of respect? Who and what has an acknowledged 'right to life'?

As a 'for instance' only, does the obligation to distribute scarce resources fairly apply to everyone in the world? Future people? Just people in our own countries? Who or what has rights? Do animals and plants have rights? (Imagine Doris and Ethel's reaction to this question.) What about the right to life of embryos, foetuses, new-born babies, severely mentally-impaired children, patients who are permanently unconscious or even brain dead?

Today, principles like these lead to simplistic statements in the nurses' *Code*. Consider statements like 'respect, support and document a person's right to accept or refuse care and treatment', or 'act as an advocate for the vulnerable, challenging poor practice and discriminatory attitudes and behaviours relating to their care' or 'take measures to reduce as far as possible, the likelihood of mistakes, near misses, harm and the effect if it takes place'.

In the *Code*, there are 109 exhortations like this spread over twenty subject areas. To an outsider like me, there is more than a hint of protection of the organisation alongside that of care for the nurse and patient, more of an eye to enforcing disciplinary procedures and bringing a ready defence against legal action.

It was of great interest to me to read an article on Chinese medical ethics which discussed a work by Sun Szu-miao, a famous Taoist and alchemist in the seventh century, on the 'absolute sincerity of great physicians'.[4] He emphasised the necessity of a thorough education, rigorous conscientiousness and self-discipline, and explained that compassion, *tz'u*, and humaneness, *jen*, were the basic values of medical practices. The similarities with today were overpowering.

Despite all this modern preparation, where do the concerns of modern nurses lie? A study within the last ten years in the USA says that every day almost two-thirds of nurses have concerns about protecting patients' rights and about their ability to give informed consent to treatment. While only eight per cent worry frequently over beginning-of-life decision-making, for a quarter there are frequent concerns over what to do when near the end of a life.

These latter two areas were where Ethel and Doris's historic distress lay. I suspect they would have been overwhelmed by the *Code* and seen it, at the end of the day, as a wordy substitute for common sense and 'doing the right thing'.

District nursing had its roots in 1859 when William Rathbone, a Liverpool merchant and philanthropist, employed Mary Robinson to nurse his wife at home during her final illness.[5] When his wife died, Rathbone decided to engage Robinson to go into one of the poorest districts of the city and try to relieve suffering and 'to teach the rules of health and comfort'.

I furnished her with the medical comforts necessary, but after a month's experience she came to me crying and said that she could not bear any longer the misery she saw. I asked her to continue the work as agreed for another two months. At the end of that time, she came back saying that the amount of misery she could relieve was so satisfactory that nothing would induce her to go back to private nursing, if I were willing to continue the work.

In 1860, Rathbone wrote to Florence Nightingale who advised him to start a nurse training school and one was built, attached to the Liverpool Royal Infirmary, by 1863. Manchester, Derby, Leicester and East London soon followed, then Glasgow and Dublin. It took time, experimentation and organisation for the training of the new district nurses to become established. The work coincided with great advances in medical science and new ideas about the emancipation of women into paid occupations.

Ethel reminded me of her frequent visits to what was then Tone Vale psychiatric hospital near Taunton, the second Somerset Asylum which opened in 1892, the first near Wells having become overcrowded.

'People forget why it was there in the middle of nowhere,' said Ethel. 'Incest was a real problem in the out-of-the-way villages. The authorities didn't want to give the problem its proper name, but there were so many young people with severe mental difficulties. They suffered terribly and no one in the families could handle them.

'Many times when I left a new birth, I knew the baby would be dead by morning. Sometimes, I would have a cup of tea, hearing the whispers, knowing what was going on. I was then given a tiny bundle wrapped in a piece of cloth and told the baby had just 'gone to Jesus'. I kept a holdall in my boot so that I could take them away.'

At that information, I caught my breath with long-ago memories about the 'special bag' among the beans and rabbits.

'I marked them all down as stillbirths,' she continued. 'Those innocents were buried in unmarked corners of the churchyards. Everyone kept quiet. No questions. We were trusted that the right decisions had been made.

'Doris had a small bag in her boot as well.'

The other half of Doris and Ethel's dreadful memories that had rushed to the surface concerned their role as angels of mercy, or angels of death as some might say without recognition or forgiveness. I had seen Ethel perform this part twice with my own family members. I had no doubt that this form of euthanasia was done with complete regard to reducing suffering in a person with but a short time to live. There was no gain, no hidden element of unsavoury personal power. They were doing their work as they saw it.

I don't know if pain-killing or calming injections were administered, not serious in a well person, but with the known side-effect of quickening death in a sick one. I do know that Ethel would pull a chair close by, hold the dying person's hand and would talk directly into their ear, inaudible unless you were very close, keeping up a constant, monotone, monologue, urging them to embrace death, pointing out the end of pain, the inevitability, the release, the meeting again with parents and other loved ones.

When I have seen lingering death, there has always seemed to be a struggle between the body, which has had enough, and the mind wanting to fight on. You could argue that Edith and Doris's role was to reconcile these conflicting views.

I believe that Doris, in Four Marks, and Ethel in Somerset were one and the same: sensible, loving nurses who would do all for their patients when they brought them into life and when they helped them leave it.

Today's nurses are, of course, still lauded for their caring, but there has been great change in their work structure and freedom to act.

ENDNOTES

[1] N&MC Code.
[2] Gillon, 'Medical ethics'.
[3] Gillon, 'Medical ethics'.
[4] Tsai, 'Ancient Chinese medical ethics'.
[5] *QNI.*

Reading list:

Gillon, Raanan, Medical ethics: four principles plus attention to scope, *British Medical Journal*, Vol. 39, pp. 184-188, July 1994

Jones, Thomas M., 'Ethical Decision Making by Individuals in Organizations: An Issue-Contingent Model', *Academy of Management Review*, Vol. 26, No. 2, 1991, pp. 366–395

Nursing and Midwifery Council, The Code, 29/1/2015

Queen's Nursing Institute, 'William Rathbone and the beginning of District Nursing'

Royal College of Nursing, Principles of nursing practice, 2020

Tsai, Daniel, Fu-Chung Thai, 'Ancient Chinese medical Ethics and the four principles of biomedical ethics', *Journal of Medical Ethics*, Vol. 25, 1999, pp. 315–21

Ulrich, Connie M., et al, 'Everyday ethics: ethical issue and stress in nursing practice', *Journal of Advanced Nursing*, Vol. 66, No. 11, 2010, pp. 2510–2519

15 THE PHAETON, THE BOY, AND THE FAKE AND DREAM CANALS

Driving without any care or attention

FOUR MARKS
1798   BODY COUNT: 1

Alton is a long and low town and the main street has no church in it until it begins to emerge on to the concluding green, called Robin Hood Butts. I could as well have gone through Medstead as through Ropley to Alresford, but I went by the Ropley way, and first of all through Chawton. Here the road forks at a smithy, among uncrowded thatched cottages and chestnuts and beeches ... I took the right hand road and had a climb.

Edward Thomas, *Pursuit of Spring*, 1914

Joseph Hill of Romsey was a man in a hurry. His fortune and reputation was at stake and, like all men of business on the cusp of important decisions, he wished to be in several places at the same time. Hill was a surveyor working to fulfil a great dream: to connect the waters of the River Itchen above Winchester and through to Alresford with the recently opened canal at Basingstoke. With one stroke of a pen on his map, barges loaded at Southampton would be able to travel to the River Thames and London. From London, the whole of the country lay open.

Hill was fortunate to be an engineer in the early 1790s at the time of canal mania. Those with money sought new places for investment. Because of Napoleon, returns from Government stocks were in decline. The low price of wheat discouraged the enclosure, some would say theft, of even more common lands away from the people in the countryside. The great manufactories pumped out their smoke and demanded coal and raw materials be brought to their doors and their finished goods be taken to the city markets. The answer to all these problems was canals and more canals; forty-two, just opened, had

197

attracted £6½ million with the prospect of large returns. Hill's own surveys, estimates and reports for the Southampton and Salisbury (S&S) Canal had been roundly endorsed by the management committee in 1794 and he was ordered to 'use his utmost exertions to carry the line into full execution'.[1]

In the eighteenth century, the transport of goods depended on two principal sources of power, the wind, useless away from the estuaries, and the horse. Using bridle paths, the greatest load that a pack-horse could carry was three hundredweight. A heavy waggon, moved by a team of horses on soft road, was limited to a ton. The burden could be doubled if the road surface was macadamised. In coalfields, a horse harnessed to a waggon mounted on rails was able to pull eight tons. A horse could be most effectively employed on a towpath hauling as much as thirty tons in a river barge or on the placid waters of a canal up to fifty tons.

Providing canals could be built at reasonable cost, then great numbers of them would be far more efficient than the manifestly inadequate road network.

The year was 1798. Joseph Hill intended that the S&S Canal would soon join the River Itchen at Southampton. If he could forge a new way from the Itchen through to the Thames, he would bring great profits to his employers and renown to himself.[2] Hill had spent the last week around Alton working his way along potential routes for his new canal. His landowning hosts declared quickly for one of two camps. The gentry and farmers of this part of Hampshire were either devoutly for the new waterway or implacably opposed. Devising a practical route depended on advantages explained, promises made and money expected. Many side deals were arranged as pet projects and slices of countryside were protected. Cash always upstaged zeal when it came to land.

To allow Hill to scour the route, he favoured his own two-horse, four-wheeled phaeton. His high perch over the five-foot rear wheels enabled a wide view of the contours of the countryside and there was plenty of space for his maps and the tools of his trade.[3] He was one of a very select company of people who could afford the luxury of money and time to travel. The height of his carriage also gave the owners of these expensive vehicles the nickname 'high flyers'.

Hill paid his two-horse toll of six pence at the Butts, the last until he left Alresford.[4] He turned his phaeton left onto the well-maintained turnpike, which descended through the Meon Valley to the forty-eight milestone at the highwater mark on Gosport beach. At Chawton forge, he turned right and began the slow, two-mile climb up Ropley Hill to what, well over a hundred years later, would become Four Marks.

The old road to Winchester, 1920, ran along side the right side of the Butts, then Chawton Park Road, and through Chawton Park woods. The turnpike toll house was situated where the trough is today, centre. The turnpike ran on the road to the left, along Winchester Road and through Chawton. By Jane Austen's House, the turnpike forked at a forge. The left route, the premier road, carried straight on, past the church and, at the cemetery, turned left for Gosport. The right fork formed the Winchester turnpike up the hill to Four Marks. It is easier to imagine these crossroads, at the Butts and in Chawton, before the Alton by-pass and with no Chawton roundabout with its slips to the A31 and A32.

To Hill, this road, passing beside the long woods at Chawton Park, gave every example of why canals were needed. It was the main road from London to Winchester and yet it was deeply potholed and rutted with collapsing edges. It made travel dangerous. Serious injury and death from tipped carriages were common. Satirist Jonathan Swift confessed that he preferred to begin journeys on a Sunday because he would have 'freshly' heard 'the prayers of the church to preserve all that travel by land and water'.[5] Those who travelled in the eighteenth century needed to invoke every aid for a safe arrival.

Apart from sheep, the way was unfarmed, colonised by unruly gorse and bracken. A few off-road, run-down barns might be seen without the rain. A small team of fish-laden horses with their panniers stuffed with the day's catch from some small port dashed past on their way to the capital.[6] A mile along, pauper women and children, employed by the turnpike trust, stood back as Hill went by, then slowly resumed working the roads, picking, breaking and placing stones and pebbles. In one instance, a man and his wife with more than ten children, several very young, sheltered under an oak tree as he passed.

The phaeton was held up by a gang of thirty-strong pack-horses, laden with bricks, their leader carrying a warning bell.[7] Herders had allowed the slow-moving beasts to spread across the road and were oblivious to the shouts from the faster vehicle behind. Many in the country took the view that the wheeled carriage was an intruder on the highway, a disturbance of the existing order and a causer of damage. Villagers rarely, in a lifetime, travelled further than a day's walk from home. Even in 1817, Hazlitt considered that country dwellers were 'out of the world', so different was their way of life from townsmen.[8]

Since the last century, laws limited the number of horses that could pull a waggon, thus limiting the size of a load. By 1741, loads over three tons were forbidden and low-width wheels with thin rims closely regulated.

As Hill reached the summit near the windmill, he paused to let his horses rest and took a drink at the alehouse. He had arranged a change of animals at the *Anchor Inn* in Ropley because he had a meeting that evening at the *White Hart* in Winchester.

Here on the crest, he was at the very point of his challenge: how to get his waterway across this ridge. The stretches from Alresford to reach Ropley and from Alton to the Basingstoke Canal, the latter opened for three years now, presented small problems.[9] But the hill remained. He had decided not to try to skirt it, but to tunnel through the chalk.[10] The longest water tunnel to date was at Sapperton, almost 2¼ miles, on the Thames and Severn Canal at Cirencester, finished ten years before.[11]

How high he made staircase locks climb before starting the tunnel would directly affect the tunnel length. The Four Marks tunnel could be anything from three to five miles, unheard of distances. The problem within the problem was how to get water to the barren summit and to store it there to refill the locks as traffic passed through. A considerable steam pump would be needed to raise the water for recurring use. He had found one at Boulton & Watt in Birmingham.

Tunnels were not Hill's favourite pieces of engineering. His difficult partner, George Jones, had worked on the successful Greywell Tunnel on the Basingstoke Canal, but had a disastrous involvement with the Sapperton Tunnel, where his incompetence when mixed with alcohol had been exposed. Miscalculation over the severity of canal engineering problems were legendary. The formidable difficulties and cost increases at Sapperton had been noticed with alarm in every canal company boardroom.

Now, Hill had severe difficulties with his own tunnel near Southampton on the S&S. Bad ground and water in the digging had dogged him since 1795. Three shafts had been sunk but, by June last year, less than a third had been competed. At Christmas, the committee had lost patience with Hill and Jones and called in John Rennie, the great engineer, to make an inspection.

The meeting that evening was with senior directors of the S&S to hear Rennie's thoughts before they were presented to the full board in Southampton.

Hill urged his pair to a trot and took the long downward slope to the old Lymington stream. He hoped that the plans in his chart box would impress the money men and save the day. The road was empty, more furze, more bracken. He realised that his musings had let the horses move to a dangerous canter. The high phaeton swayed precariously in the ruts. As first, he thrilled to the risk, a do or die rush to a meeting which would decide his future.

At the cross way where the road began a short climb, a wild pig streaked across the road, startling the horses, putting them into headlong flight. Hill could do no more than stretch back with the reins and hang on. He sensed a figure as a blur close to his leading wheel. The phaeton leapt. There was a cry, a crunch, and the spatter of splintering wood. Hill was thrown clear as the carriage on its side ran on thirty yards until the horses tired and stopped. Two broken wheels settled in the wake. There were no onlookers. No sounds apart from the distant heavy breathing of his horses, one of which had begun to graze. The rain stopped.

Hill was badly bruised. The carriage was wrecked, possibly beyond repair. His chart box lay open and some of his drawings began to smudge in the wet. The boy's body was badly mangled, the head partly detached and the legs pointing in opposite directions.

One horse had a broken leg. The other, tangled in its harness, kicked wildly when Hill tried to get near. He trudged the two miles to Ropley Soke where he found help. A cart was harnessed for the climb to the accident. Nothing had changed, no grieving parents, but the crows were already at work on the body. The boy was unknown and taken to the tithe barn. The next day he was buried without ceremony in the paupers' corner at St Peter's in Ropley with just a wooden cross at the grave head. One could easily miss the entry in the parish burial register. It is below the bottom margin of the page, tucked under a florid recording of a recently interred senior citizen, 'Pauper boy, unknown, died on the turnpike, 3 March 1798.'

Hill, of course, missed his meeting that afternoon in Winchester, but he did arrive at the company's offices in Southampton the next afternoon. His body ached as he skipped through Rennie's report.

In respect of the work already done it is by no means completed, those parts that are likely to stand are ill framed and seem to have been done with little care or judgement … In joining the different lengths of arching together they do not in many places agree, sometimes one length is sunk more than another … At the west end of the tunnel, a part of the sheeting for about sixteen yards has already risen up and the tunnel has sunk about a foot. The whole of this length must be taken out and done anew … The bricks I have examined are unsound, there is too much sand in the clay … The sand that has been used for the mortar is perfectly unfit for the purpose, being little better than clay.[12]

Hill had no option but to resign before the shareholders took their revenge. He handed in his designs and charts and left the canal business forever. By June, Rennie found that George Jones had made improvements, especially with the tunnel, but it was too little, too late. In August, the men were due a month's wages and the money ran out. Shareholders refused to stump up. John Rennie condemned the tunnel and the S&S slid towards bankruptcy.

A young vagrant had lost his life. Hill escaped censure for what, in today's terms, would be death by dangerous driving under the effects of alcohol. The S&S collapsed and, although it did mate with the Andover canal and also reached Southampton and the Itchen Navigation by an amended route, it never joined with Salisbury which had to be content with the River Avon to Christchurch and the lost dream of a connection to Bristol. However, it was not the end of plans to join the Itchen with the River Wey and the Basingstoke canal.

Here is local historian John Duthy writing in Ropley in 1839.

Many abortive plans have been projected in later years for restoring this navigation, and continuing it, through Alton and Farnham, to join the Wey and Thames; but difficulties constantly arose; hills interposed which were to be tunnelled at great expense; funds were not forthcoming; and the character of the country and neighbourhood, along the course of the projected canal, presented an obstacle still more discouraging than any physical one, being occupied almost entirely by an agricultural population, and destitute of sufficient trade or manufacture to give support to such an undertaking. Yet could it be effected with any prospect of remuneration to the projectors, there is little doubt that a canal carried along the course alluded to, would materially benefit all the vale of Itchen between Alresford and Winchester; not only by the facility it would afford for the transport of all weighty and bulky articles, but also by the collateral advantages to be derived from the formation of a clearer and deeper channel for the river, whereby an opportunity would be given for carrying off water more briskly and effectually from the contiguous meadows; an operation not only productive of much additional value to the soil, but materially conducive to the health of the neighbouring population.

One can only wonder at the effect today if any of these logical, but perhaps wild, schemes had come to fruition. Between the Winchester Road and the Mid-Hants railway line south of Four Marks, a long stretch of locks might reach towards North Street with the car parks and cafés proper to a major tourist destination. On the north side of the tunnel, the longest in England, Alton, its

What might have been on the climb from Ropley to the mouth of the projected canal tunnel under the Four Marks ridge in the 1790s. The main flight of sixteen locks at Caen Hill on the Kennet and Avon Canal.
Arpingstone, commons.wikimedia.org/w/index.php?curid=1808864

prosperity buoyed by canal traffic, would be home to pleasant, domesticated wharves transformed by pleasure craft, restaurants, museums and craft shops.

To understand why this did not happen, it is best to start with England's riverways.[13] Without improvements, many extensive stretches of river remained unnavigable even before they petered out at, for instance, the feet of the Pennines as the new industrial towns looked down. Most Acts for improving river navigation were obtained to reach further inland. Rivers received earlier and more focused attention than any road. There was a period of great Parliamentary activity between 1662 and 1665 when a number of river improvement Acts were passed. In Hampshire, the need to import coal and to export agricultural produce prompted Acts to make both the Itchen (1663) and the Avon (1665) navigable. In March 1663, a Bill got as far as a second reading in the Lords to make various rivers open to barges to London, including Farnham and Petersfield and also from Southampton to Winchester and Alresford.[14]

An Act in 1665 invested powers in a group of seven *undertakers* to make the *'Itchin or Itching ... Navigable and Passable for Boats, Barges, Lighters and other Vessels'*. Improvements consisted of cuts across meanders and the provision of locks to maintain depths, and took place over many years. Farmers often fought the changes fearing for their profits as barges made available routes to cheaper markets. By 1710, the Itchen Navigation was virtually complete as far as Winchester.[15] 'Little, however, could be done to control the vagaries of the weather: floods in the spring, ice in the winter and droughts in the summer.' Weirs, dams and mills blocked many rivers making continuous navigation difficult. Then there were dumped ballast, the destruction of riverbanks and the cost from tolls and pilfering from river barges. In 1752, after an Act for preventing robberies on any navigable river, thirteen thieves were sentenced to transportation.

There is a great local historical tradition that the Itchen Navigation, that part of the river which could carry commercial traffic, was once used to extend from Winchester to the heart of Alresford. This wistful theory often involved descriptions of canal wharves in the town served by a flow of laden carts servicing the market and the country around. It was a story promulgated by Duthy and, later, by many others.[16]

Motorists driving from Old to New Alresford travel over near 500-yards of causeway on top of a dam which was constructed in 1189 by Godfrey de Lucy,

Bishop of Winchester. The great pond he created, now Alresford Pond, was to be his extensive fish larder.

Here is Duthy's view again.

The farther object of this public-spirited prelate … [was] by deepening the channel of the Alre and Itchen, by conducting the springs to a common current, by regulating its supply from this vast reservoir, and by use of other artificial aids, de Lucy rendered the stream navigable from Alresford to Winchester, as well as from thence to Southampton, for barges and flat-bottomed boats. The upper part of this canal between Alresford and Winchester has for ages been destroyed and all communication by water interrupted; yet some vestiges of its course, the lake and the imperishable causeway, together with ancient records and documents connected with the subject, all afford indisputable testimony of the wisdom and beneficence with which this great bishop of Winchester dispensed the revenues of his diocese.[17]

What led Duthy, and the others, to reinterpret the fishpond as a reservoir to regulate a canal's water flow were the 'ancient records and documents' to which Duthy refers. A purported charter, which King John granted to de Lucy, allowed him the right to take tolls on goods carried on the canal.

The charter is a fraud and was thoroughly debunked by local historian Edward Roberts.[18] Independent examinations exposed the charter as 'spurious' and a 'forgery'.[19] There was no canal, just a fishpond feeding a river with its three mills.

In 1802, all five of the Itchen Navigation acts were brought together under one new bill which dealt with traffic over twenty and below forty-five tons from Blackridge at Winchester to Woodside 'where the sea flows up'.[20] The Act's seventy-one clauses were detailed in order for the waterway to become 'public and navigable': fixing tonnage rates, appointing commissioners, setting improvements to be completed, and acknowledging petty privileges and the rights of the two owners, George Hollis of Winchester and Harry Baker, linen draper, of Pall Mall, Westminster. No mention is made of any navigation above Winchester and certainly not to Alresford. However, what the Act did do, without saying so directly, was to clear the way for canal development north to Alton.

While what little resource was available was applied to river navigations, little attention was paid to the country's roads although they were undergoing a great increase in usage.[21] There was a paid increase in foreign trade, the growth of manufacturing and local distribution centres and a steady substitution of pasture for arable production. The pitiful state of the transport routes can scarcely be imagined. In the seventeenth century, a journey by coach was a hazardous affair. It was not unusual for a journey from Portsmouth to London to take as long as four days.[22] In 1750, the inhabitants of Horsham in Sussex petitioned Parliament for an improvement in the 'road' to London since it was only suitable for riding on horseback.[23] Those wishing to drive a coach to the capital were obliged to go first to the channel coast before taking the only serviceable road via Canterbury. In many cases, only pack-horses could be used.

Daniel Bourn, writing in 1763, claimed that thirty or forty years before the roads had looked 'more like a retreat of wild beasts and reptiles than the footsteps of man'.[24]

Roads were repaired by the parishes through which they passed.[25] The will of John Knight of Chawton in 1559 bequeathed ten shillings 'to the mending of the highe waye'.[26] Both parish administrators and their surveyors were lax and there was widespread ignorance of proper repair methods. A new system for organising road maintenance for almost the next 300 years was established in 1555, but it could not deal with the problems created by the increasing volume of traffic.[27]

Most road labourers were local men employed on a semi-permanent basis or hired casually. While not working on the roads they were employed in agriculture. So long as local farmers remained the chief beneficiaries from these labours, there was some sense in maintaining 'their' roads.

'Once the road took on the characteristics of thoroughfares linking distant centres of production, it was unjust to expect farmers and labourers to work unrewarded mainly for the benefit of strangers.' Even in the 1770s, carriages and waggons apart, some 150,000 turkeys and 750,000 sheep were driven each year to Smithfield. John Scott of Amwell remarked in 1778 that those 'devoted feathered legions, at certain seasons of the year, bespread the surface of the roads on their way to the all-devouring metropolis.'

Initially, turnpikes, with their gates, tollhouses and tax collectors, were regarded with suspicion both locally and at Westminster. Of the forty-one road bills proposed between 1664 and 1713, thirty-nine per cent were defeated. However, in the next sixty years only fifteen were defeated. As traffic volumes continued to rise, parishes found the turnpike became the recognised way to gain assistance.

A writer in 1754 said, 'It is but too notorious a truth that as soon as a turnpike Act is obtained, all the parishes through which the road passes consider the Act as a benefit ticket and an exemption from their usual expenses and elude the payments of their just quota towards the reparation of the road, by compounding the trustees for a less sum or by doing their statute labour in a fraudulent manner; and in both these cases they are generally favoured by the neighbouring justices and gentlemen for the ease of their own estates only.'[28]

In 1753, an Act was passed to allow turnpike trustees to take over one of the roads from Alton to Winchester, which in essence many years later became the current A31.[29] At that time, only thirteen main routes leading from London were virtually complete; the nearest to Four Marks was that from London to Portsmouth (A3) and Chichester.

ANNO QUADRAGESIMO SECUNDO

GEORGII III. REGIS.

Cap. 111.

An Act for explaining, amending, and rendering more effectual several Acts of the Sixteenth and Seventeenth Years of the Reign of King *Charles* the Second, and of the Seventh and Thirty-fifth Years of the Reign of His present Majesty, relating to the Navigation of the River *Itchin* in the County of *Southampton*.   [26th *June* 1802.]

WHEREAS by an *Act* made in the Sixteenth and Seventeenth Years of the Reign of King *Charles* the Second, intituled *An Act for making divers Rivers navigable or otherwise passable for Boats, Barges, and other Vessels*, the River *Itchin* alias *Itching*, in the County of *Southampton*, was made navigable and passable for the Purposes therein mentioned, and under the Restrictions therein contained, from a certain Place called *Blackbridge*, near the City of *Winchester*, in the County of *Southampton*, to a certain Place called *Woodmill*, in the same County; to which Place the Sea flows up; and the said Act was explained and amended by Two Acts, one of which was passed in the Seventh Year and the other in the Thirty-fifth Year of the Reign of His present Majesty: And whereas, under and by virtue of the Provisions or Regulations of the said Acts, the Proprietors of the said River are exclusively appointed to be the Carriers on the said River, at certain [*Loc. & Per.*]   22 F   Rates

Anno vicefimo fexto

Georgii II. Regis.

An Act for repairing and widening the Roads leading from a Place called *Bafing-ftone*, near the Town of *Bagfhot*, in the Parifh of *Windlefham*, in the County of *Surry*, through *Frimley* and *Farnham*, in the fame County; and from thence through *Bentley, Hollyborn, Alton, Chawton, Ropley, Bifhop's Sutton, New Alresford*, and *Mattingley*, otherwife *Matterley Lane*, to the City of *Winchefter*, in the County of *Southampton*.

Two pieces of legislation which set the pace for water and road transport in the Itchen valley in the 19th century: the 1802 Act to make the Itchen 'navigable and passable' to Winchester and the 1753 Act to repair and widen the road leading from Basingstone, near Bagshot, through Alton, Chawton and Ropley to Winchester, a turnpike which eventually formed the basis of the A31. *Parliamentary Archives*

The road chosen to be improved branched from the Gosport turnpike at Chawton and went through the wasteland at the ridge at Four Marks before dropping down to Bishop's Sutton and New Alresford. The long-standing villages at Medstead and Ropley were ignored. After Mattingley, 'three several branches which all lead into the said city', Winchester, were specified. These were not new roads: the Act only required repairing and widening of one of the existing roads between the two centres, but this choice was seen as the cheapest and easiest to do the job. Some 250 of the great and the good were appointed trustees making for interesting management meetings.

Being part of the great Road from the Cities of London and Westminster ... are, from the Nature of the Soil, the narrowness thereof in many places, and by reason of the many heavy Carriages frequently passing along the same, become very deep and ruinous, and dangerous to Carriages and Travellers; and cannot, by the ordinary course and method appointed by the Laws of this Realm, be effectively amended, widened, and kept in good Repair; Therefore, to the Intent that the said Roads may, with all convenient Speed, be effectually amended, widened, and rendered safe and commodious, and, from time to time, kept in good repair ...

Little remains of the local turnpike system. There is a small, but interesting, exhibition in Alton's Curtis Museum. Alton's toll houses have long gone, but one of the typical octagonal buildings with conical roofs that allowed the keeper to see in both directions still exists on the Selborne Road. A maximum of three toll gates were specified between Alton, New Alresford and Winchester, although additional choke points were allowed to stop travellers slipping off to the side and round the main tax collection points. Known toll points include the Butts, Pound Hill in Alresford, Matterley (Staples Green at the crossroad to Ovington), Shortsledge at Chilcomb, before Winnall, just after the *Golden Lion* on the final approach to Winchester. A later toll house, after 1824, still exists coming south out of New Alresford. In 1830, the toll gates at Alresford (which produced £300 in the previous year) and at Shortsledge and Winnall (both £272) were offered at auction at the *George Inn* in Winchester.[30]

Despite the considerable sums of money spent on the turnpike roads, many of them could not be sufficiently repaired because of the excessive weights and the poverty of the surface.[31] As a contemporary example, the turnpike leading from Hertford to Basingstoke in 1752, received revenue of about £300 a year.

However, interest on £1,200 at four per cent, £190 a year in salaries, and other bad management, took the net amount left to be spent on the road, fourteen miles long, to only £60. Unearned salaries were reduced to £55. Penalties were brought in on weights carried and charges per hundredweight legislated in an Act that was amended the year after the 'Four Marks' turnpike opened. Waggons with wheels nine inches broad were exempted from toll payments for three years and the number of horses related to wheel sizes were legislated. Tolls could be raised by one-fourth if revenues were insufficient.

It may be that the new toll road stayed unpopular with locals for many years because of the tolls. The tithe map of 1845 shows the two ways to Alton were, then, via Hussell Lane and Beech, and the old King's Highway through Chawton Wood, Medstead and Bighton to Old Alresford and across de Lucy's embankment. 'As late as the end of the nineteenth century, there are tales of the men of Medstead, often with their wives or daughters riding pillion behind them going to Alton through the Wood.'[32]

In 1819, John Macadam was appointed surveyor general of the turnpike trusts. One of his first jobs was to upgrade the Alton to Gosport turnpike and he was often seen in Alton as the road through the town was improved, a 'formidable undertaking', by his pauper and paid labourers.[33] This work, significantly, did not apply to the Winchester road. Macadam had invented a new process whereby the roadway was trenched to a fixed depth. All the large flints and gravel were broken small enough to run through

The Alton Machine left Alton at 0600 every morning reaching London the same night. In 1750, this was considered a marvellous feat. The *Alton Machine* was an immense, clumsy vehicle, drawn by six horses, the coachman had four in hand and the postillion rode a pair of leaders. The half-price passengers were not carried on the roof, but literally in a large basket, slung behind. The name 'machine' became common and hence stage coach horses were called 'machiners'. Curtis, *Alton*, from Knight et al, *The Land We Live In*, Vol. 1

a wire sieve. The ground was made good and these broken stones placed on top
and well rammed.[34] Turnpike speeds more than doubled as people travelled in
safer conditions.

Despite the gradual improvements of the local turnpikes, the formidable array
of canal devotees refused to give up.[35] Despite, the failure of Joseph Hill's plans,
the objective was always to achieve the holy grail of linking the English Channel to
either the Basingstoke Canal or to the upper Wey Navigation. A mass of schemes
sought supporters with sufficient power to push them through Parliament. The
number requires far more space to detail than is available here. Any successful
canal had to link a major industrial centre with a great port and Basingstoke Canal
had neither. Foremost in planners' minds were the continuing wars with France
which brought demands to move urgent supplies from London to Portsmouth
without risk at sea from the French fleet and accompanying privateers.

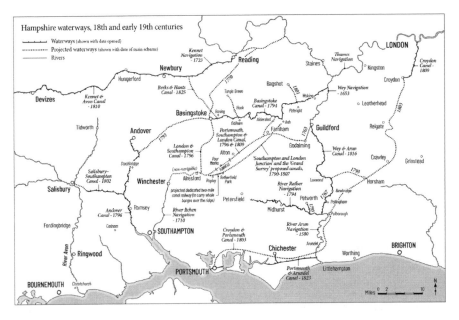

Three more schemes travelling north from the Itchen Navigation to Alton
caught either the public's imagination or opprobrium. Over fifteen years, the
Hampshire Chronicle was full of meetings for and against, petitions, arguments,
satire and ridicule. Working for the Grand Surrey Canal, William Belworthy,
in 1803, and picking up on work by Ralph Dodd in the 1790s, surveyed from
a lock at Ash, near Aldershot, through Farnham, past Alton to Alresford. The
idea was carried on by Michael Walker in 1807 whose solution to the Four

Marks ridge was a canal from Alresford to Lyder Hill, above Merryfield, from where a rail link would carry canal barges to Rotherfield Park and offering the prospect of a canal flowing through Lower Farringdon to Chawton.[36] Rather than recite the arguments, three contemporary letters are appended in an appendix to this chapter.

Then, in 1807, the idea of a canal under the Four Marks ridge was brought back to the table. The Portsmouth, Southampton & London Junction Canal Company advocated a thirty-five-mile barge canal from the Itchen with a two-mile tunnel to Alton estimated by the promoters to cost £200,000. By 1809, £124,000 had been subscribed. 'However, the Basingstoke Canal Committee judged the likely cost to be twice the estimate and that year the scheme was abandoned, like all the others, on the grounds of expense, the likely lack of water and the problematical amount of trade in times of peace.'[37]

The answer finally came when Lord Egremont placed an advertisement in 1811 inviting those interested in a Surrey and Sussex canal to an exploratory meeting in Guildford. Egremont subscribed personally £20,000 of the original £90,000 capital to connect the upper River Wey to the River Arun, with its port at Littlehampton, and with a westward extension to Chichester and Portsmouth.[38] The whole canal opened in 1823 and was no great success. It was almost entirely closed by 1855.

The Itchen carried its last barge, loaded with coal, just over ten miles from Southampton to Blackbridge Wharf in Winchester in 1869, before finally succumbing to steam.[39] The railway had arrived. There were at least two proposed railway tunnels through the Four Marks ridge, one near the current railway line, the other on a more northerly course through Chawton Park, passing closer to Medstead.

The legacy of these many years of planning and inaction was a period of neglect that led to the state of the local roads today, according to the country survey Brigadier Archie Hughes in 1953. 'Everyone thought the day of the roads was finished.'[40] When the canals arrived, the carriages and waggons on the roads could not compete. When the railways provided the same services, the canals could not compete.

A few months ago, I was standing at the point where I estimated the vagrant boy had been killed by Joseph Hill's phaeton over 200 years ago. I had thought of taking a picture for this book, perhaps showing the slope that Hill had careered down. I soon realised no modern photograph would work. Too much heavy traffic would mask the previous bleakness of the spot. A woman came out of a nearby house and asked me what I was up to. We got chatting and I told her the tale of Hill and his canal. Clare asked if she could read the story. I agreed on the condition that she didn't share it around.

'You know,' she said, 'there was another more famous accident in just this spot in the 1930s, I think, anyway I was told. Lawrence of Arabia was on his motorcycle coming to or from his estate, Moreton, near Bovington Camp. He came off in the dip, but he wasn't too badly hurt.[41] Should have been a warning to him.'[42]

Some weeks later, Clare sent me an email. She said the chapter had greatly touched her, and she had shared it with members of her family, for which she half-apologised. She went with her sister to Ropley graveyard, the church still under repair from its fire, and, unsurprisingly, could find no sign of the corner where the boy was buried.

Clare decided there needed to be a monument and so she thought to give her numbered house a name, perhaps 'The Pauper Boy'. She also asked family and friends for contributions to be given to Barnardo's, the charity which has worked for around 150 years with homeless children. She found that last year in the UK, Barnardo's helped almost a third of a million young people, an eleven per cent increase on the previous twelve months. The family raised just over £15,000.

Clare also sent me a bottle of fifteen-year-old Springbank malt whisky for writing the story. I'm sipping it now and thinking of the dead boy and the canals that never were.

ENDNOTES

1 *The Salisbury and Winchester Journal*, 22/9/1794.
2 *Hampshire Chronicle*, 26/3/1796.
3 Felton, *Treatise on Carriages*.
4 Curtis, *Alton*. www.geogport.ac.uk. *The National Archive*, Q26/3/25.
5 Swift, *Polite Conversation*.
6 Webbs, *King's Highway*.
7 Webbs, *King's Highway*.
8 Bagwell, *Transport Revolution*.
9 *Hampshire Chronicle*, 25/8/1794, gives detailed instructions for those wishing to use the canal which opened on 4/9/1794. Prospective customers were invited to attend meetings at Basingstoke, Crookham and Frimley Wharves.
10 Vine, *Lost Route*.
11 The longest tunnel in England is the Standedge on the Huddersfield Narrow Canal, 3,24 miles, opened in 1811.
12 Southampton Canal Society.
13 Albert, *Turnpike System*.

[14] Vine, *Lost Route*.

[15] Monkhouse, *Southampton*.

[16] For example: Duthy, *Hampshire Sketches*, 1839; Lewis, *Topographical Dictionary*, 1848; *VCH County History of Hampshire, 1900-14;* Robertson, A,J,. *History of Alresford* (Winchester 1937); Beresford, M., 'The Six New Towns of the Bishop of Winchester', *Medieval Archaeology*, Vol. 3, 1959; Hinton, D.A., *Alfred's Kingdom* (London 1977).

[17] Duthy, *Hampshire Sketches*.

[18] Roberts, 'Alresford Pond'.

[19] Deedes, C., Registrum Johannis de Pontissara (Oxford 1924), quoting Charles Johnson, Public Record Office. Keene, D J, 'A survey of Medieval Winchester', *Winchester Studies 2*, 1985.

[20] 42 Geo III, c. 111, *House of Lords Library*.

[21] Webbs, *King's Highway*.

[22] Mills, *Four Marks*.

[23] Webbs, *King's Highway*.

[24] Bourne, Daniel, *A Treatise upon Wheel-Carriages* ... (London 1763).

[25] Albert, *Turnpike System*.

[26] Leigh, *Chawton Manor*.

[27] 2&3 Philip and Mary, c.8. Webbs, *King's Highway*.

[28] *Gentleman's Magazine*, XXIV, p. 395.

[29] 26 Geo2 c.51 (1753) for 'amending' (repairing and widening) the roads leading from Basingstone, near Bagshot, through Frimley, Farnham and 'from thence through Bentley, Holybourne, Alton, Chawton, Ropley, Bishop's Sutton, New Alresford and Mattingley, otherwise Mattingley Lane, to the City of Winchester (Alton Lower District). This Act was renewed, at least, in 1768 and 1817. Modern by-passes and road straightening schemes have changed those parts of the road through population centres (*Parliamentary Library*).

[30] *Hampshire Record Office*, Q23/1/3. *Hampshire Chronicle*, 6/12/1830.

[31] Jackman, *Transportation*.

[32] Rathbone, Medstead.

[33] Curtis, *Alton*.

[34] Macadam, *Remarks on the Present System of Roadmaking*, 1816.

[35] Hadfield, *British Canals*. Vine, *Attempts to Reach the Channel; London's Lost Route*.

[36] Lyder Hill (grid: SU660313) can be found on the road from Ropley to Monkwood in 1759 (Taylor's map of Hampshire).

[37] Vine, *Lost Route*.

[38] Hadfield, *Canals*.

[39] Course, 'Itchen Navigation'.

[40] Mills, *Four Marks*.

[41] he dip on the Winchester Road at the crossing with Lymington Bottom was a great deal deeper at the time. There was a major road improvement scheme to fill it in in 1931 – perhaps as result of Lawrence's accident?

[42] Lawrence died in an accident in another road dip near his home while riding his motorcycle in 1935. A co-incidence no doubt, but Lawrence bought his estate in Wiltshire from cousins, named Frampton. In the 1960s, Johnny Frampton committed suicide by throwing himself down a deep well with a large piece of concrete tied to his ankles. The well was close to Frampton's home opposite the railway embankment on the previous Station Approach and just around the corner from Lawrence's accident. Local men were called to drag the body out. Frampton, an ex-colonial civil servant in Nigeria, was reported sickened by the British government of Harold Wilson siding with the Nigerians against the Biafran people. He predicted the one million deaths that followed, mainly children, the sick and elderly dying from malnutrition. For other Four Marks' involvement in the Biafran war, see Heal, *Disappearing*, and its sequel, *Reappearing*, at the end of this book.

Reading list:

Albert, William, *The Turnpike Road System in England 1633–1840* (Cambridge University, 1972)

Bagwell, Philip S., *The Transport Revolution from 1770* (London, Batsford 1974)

Bogart, Dan, edited with Shaw-Taylor, l., and Satchell, A.E.M., 'The Turnpike Roads of England and Wales', *The Online Historical Atlas of Transport, Urbanization and Economic Development in England and Wales c. 1680–1911*, 2017

Cary, John, *New Itinerary of the Great Roads throughout England and Wales* (Cary, London 1802)

Course, Edwin, 'The Itchen Navigation', *Proceedings of the Hampshire Field Club & Archaeological Society*, Vol. 24, 1967, pp. 113–126.

Cross, Tony, and Smith, Georgia, *Bygone Alton* (Phillimore, Chichester 1995)

Duthie, John, *Sketches of Hampshire* … (1839; British Library 2020)

Felton, William, *A Treatise on Carriages; Comprehending Coaches, Chariots, Phaetons, Curricles, Gigs, Whiskies, &c Together with their Proper Harness, etc*, Vols. 1 & 2 (1796; Forgotten Books, London 2020)

Freeman, M.J., 'The Carrier System of South Hampshire', *The Journal of Transport History*, Vol. IV, No. 2, September 1977; 'Turnpikes and Their Traffic: The Example of Southern Hampshire', *Transactions of the Institute of British Geographers*, Vol. 4, No. 3, 1979, pp. 411–434

Gerhold, Dorian, edited, *Road Transport in the Horse-Drawn Era* (Scolar Press, Aldershot 1996); *Bristol's Stage Coaches* (Hobnob Press, Salisbury 2012)

Hadfield, Charles, *British Canals, An Illustrated History* (1950; David & Charles, Newton Abbot 1969)

Hampshire Advertiser, The British Newspaper Archive, accessed 2020

Hampshire Chronicle, The British Newspaper Archive, accessed 2020

Jackman, W.T., *The Development of Transportation in Modern England (1916; Frank Cass, London 1962)*

Jebens, Dieter & Cansdale, Roger, *Basingstoke Canal* (History Press, Stroud 2008)

Leigh, William Austen, *Chawton Manor and Its Owners* (1911; Forgotten Books, London 2020)

Lewis, Samuel, edited, *A Topographical Dictionary of England* (S. Lewis, London 1848)

McAdam, John Loudon, *Remarks on the Present System of Road Making* … (Longman, Rees et al, London 1827)

Monkhouse, F.J., edited, *A Survey of Southampton and Its Region* (British Association for the Advancement of Science, Southampton 1964)

Paterson, Daniel, *Direct and Principal Cross Roads in England and Wales*, 18th edition (Mogg, London 1826)

Roberts, Edward, 'Alresford Pond, A Medieval Canal Reservoir: A Tradition Reassessed', *Proceedings of the Hampshire Field Club & Archaeological Society*, Vol. 41, 1985, pp. 127–138.

Rosevear, Alan, *Ogilby's Road to Hungerford; Milestones & Toll-houses in the Upper Thames Valley* (Roads across the Upper Thames Valley: 2, 10)

Southampton Canal Society, 'Southampton and Salisbury Canal', www. whitenap.plus.com/sarum, accessed 2020

University of Portsmouth, *Hampshire Canals*; *Old Hampshire Mapped*, www.geog. port.ac, accessed 2020

Vine, P.A.L., *London's Lost Route to the Sea, An historical account of the inland navigation which linked the Thames to the English Channel* (David & Charles, Dawlish 1965); *London's Lost Route to Basingstoke, The Story of the Basingstoke Canal* (Sutton, Stroud 1994); London to Portsmouth Waterway (Middleton Press, Midhurst 1994)

Viner, D.J., 'The Industrial Archaeology of Hampshire Roads: A Survey', *Proceedings of the Hampshire Field Club & Archaeological Society*, 1969, Vol. 26, pp. 155–172

Webb, Sidney and Beatrice, *The Story of the King's Highway* (1913; Frank Cass, London 1963)

Appendix: Hampshire Chronicle: Southampton and London Proposed Junction Canal

28 July 1807, London

Notice of an Act being laid to Parliament for a 'navigable cut or canal' from the River Itchen at the parish of Alresford to the River Wey in the parish of Godalming or to the Basingstoke Canal in the parish of Aldershot to pass through the several parishes and places:

In Hampshire: Milland, St Peter's Cheesehill, St John's, St Peter's Colebrook, St Maurice, St Bartholomew Hyde, Winnall, Headborne Worthy, King's Worthy, Abbots Worthy, Martyr Worthy, Easton, Itchen Abbas, Itchen Stoke, Old Alresford, New Alresford, Bishop's Sutton, Ropley, East Tisted, Newton Valence, Farringdon, Chawton, Alton, Holybourne, Neatham, Froyle, Binsted, Coldrey, Bentley and Aldershot, and, in Surrey, Farnham, Waverley, Elstead, Puttenham, Witley, Peper Harow, Eashing and Godalming.

28 September 1807, Southampton

At a numerous and respectable meeting of the gentlemen of this town and neighbourhood held this day at the Audit-house, in pursuance of a requisition to take into consideration the plan of the above measure, and, if approved of, to support the applications to Parliament:

Samuel S. Taylor, Mayor in the Chair

The following resolutions were unanimously agreed to

That a communication between Portsmouth, Southampton and the Metropolis by means of the junction of the present navigation of the Itchen with the River Wey, or the Basingstoke Canal, is a measure comprehending advantages not less evident than important to the interests of the inhabitants of the ports in question, and the counties through which the line passes, than to those of every merchant, manufacturer and trader in the kingdom.

That of the detention by adverse winds, of ships at sea and in port, bound on voyages to and from the places in question on public service, having been of great and acknowledged inconveniences and detriment to the nation, the junction in question will be, in the opinion of this meeting, the means of effecting a certain and eligible conveyance for Government stores, merchandise, etc, etc, by which these evils in future be avoided; and is therefore become a matter of great public necessity; at the same time as it promises ample compensation to the promoters.

That the plan and estimate made by Mr Michael Walker, engineer, after a full and deliberate survey taken by him in the last and present year, of a line commencing at the wharf of the River Itchen at Winchester, and passing by the towns of Alresford, Alton, and Farnham to the summit level of the Basingstoke Canal; or to the River Wey, at Godalming, appears to this meeting well calculated to answer the purpose desired; and that this meeting do approve of the same.

That for the prosecution of this plan, a subscription be now entered into for shares of £100 each, and that a deposit £2 on each share, be forthwith paid to any of the following bankers:

Messrs Devavnes and Co, Pall Mall
Messrs Marsh, Sibbald, and Co, Berners Street
Messrs Alex Davison, Noel, Templar, and Co, Pall Mall
Messrs Forster, Lubbocks, and Co, Mansion House Street
Messrs Robarts, Curtis, and Co, Lombard Street
Messrs Were, Bruce, & Co, Bartholomew Lane
and the banks, at Southampton

And, in order to securing the accomplishment of so great an object, and that no obstacle should take place in its completion, that 2,000 shares be subscribed for, of which 5% shall be funded in the bank as a permanent stock to be under the control, and for the benefit, of the subscribers.
Samuel S Taylor, Chairman

8 December, 1807, Alton

At a numerous and respectful meeting of proprietors and occupiers of lands and mills, and others, to take into consideration the plan and probable consequences of the above measure.

Present:

The Right Hon Lord Stawell	John William, Esq
The Right Hon Earl Temple	John Marsh, Esq
Sir Thomas Miller, Bart	John Manwaring, Esq
The Marquis of Winchester,	John Charles Middleton, Esq
by Mr Greetham	James Shotter, Esq
Sir Chaloner Ogle	Major Barton
William Harris, Esq, Edward Austen, Esq,	The Rev Mr Miller
by Mr Seward	The Rev C. Powlett
Robert Newton Lee, Esq	The Rev G.N. Watkins
Edward Woolls, Esq	The Rev Mr Sainsbury
James Ward, Esq	

Messrs Chitty, Seward, Knight, Arundell, Eames, Waight, Crump, Goldfinch, Stevens, Lamport, Crump, Trimmer, Baker, Simmonds, Paine, Dowden, Bristow, Attfield, Tice, Lavington, Robinson, Allden, William Eggar, Thomas Eggar, Henry Eggar, William Yalden, Kersley, Goodeve, Simmonds, Stovold, Smith, Hayling Budd, Clement, Samuel Eggar, Bennett, Woolveridge, Worthington, Bernard, Pullinger, Bernard, Hale, Christ. Yalden, Andrews, Smither, Pullinger, West, Stubbs, with many others.

Lord Stawell, in the chair

The following resolutions were unanimously entered into, viz:

That the proposed canal is unnecessary, as the communication between London, Portsmouth, Southampton, and Winchester by Sea is, in the opinion of this meeting, better calculated to answer the purposes both of Government and of individuals, for the following reasons, viz:

Because supposing the advantages attending an intended communication over that by sea to be as great as the promoters of the canal suppose, it should appear that a loss of so considerable a part of our coasting trade, and consequently of the nursery of our seamen, especially too at a moment when our foreign commerce is prohibited throughout the world, will more than counterbalance any advantages which may be expected from coals; articles of commerce and the naval stores being conveyed in barges in preference to ships.

Because the proposed canal must be very frequently short of water, inasmuch as there is already so little water in the River Wey, on the line of the proposed canal, between the Basingstoke Canal and Alton, that there is already insignificant to drive the mills on it in the summer months, which are now obliged to cease grinding on that account, consequently there will be too little water for the canal.

Because the line of the proposed canal and Ropley, is through porous soil, which will never hold water, in a country where there is a great scarcity of water already, so much so, that the cattle are obliged in dry summers to be driven four or five miles for water, from the parishes of East Tisted, Newton Valence, Farringdon, etc, to Alton, and the water, to fill the canal for five miles from Alton to Rotherfield, must be taken from the River Wey at Alton, where this is already too little water.

Because the navigation of the canal will be continually impeded by frost, in the winter months, during which season of the year alone, can the inland carriage of public stores be supposed to be more advantageous to the public, than that by sea, consequently the benefits pretended to be held out to the public by the canal will prove to be fallacious.

That this meeting is therefore of opinion that the present communication by water Coastways, will be the most certain, the most useful, and generally the quickest, and the most to be depended on.

This meeting is also of opinion that another material reason why this canal would not be of public utility, is that there is a hill between Rotherfield Park and Lyderhill Farm, upwards of two miles broad, where the canal is not intended to be cut, and where the proprietors propose to have an iron railway over the hill, so that persons trading on this canal, will be put to the great trouble and inconvenience of twice loading and unloading their goods, at not very trifling expense, and risk of damage and plunder, which will certainly prevent the canal being much used, and from being of that public and general utility which has been held forth to the country.

That this meeting is of opinion that a great number of mills, and a large quantity of dry and water meadow land, so obviously and imperiously necessary to the agriculture of the country on the intended line, will be destroyed by this canal.

That this meeting is of opinion that the public would not be at all benefitted by this canal, whereas the extreme injury to numerous individuals is certain, and it appears that scarce any of the owners or occupiers of land upon this proposed line have either consented or subscribed to its completion, consequently that the canal will be a very unnecessary and cruel violation of private property, without any prospect of proportionate public benefit.

That this meeting is further of opinion, that the freeholds and property of a great body of individuals, ought not to be entered on and cut to pieces against the consent of the proprietors, merely to answer the purposes of gain of a few persons, and, on these grounds, this meeting is determined to resist and oppose the passing of the bill, for the proposed canal, by every lawful means.

That committees be appointed for conducting the said opposition, and the following be of the committee

At Alton, viz:

The Rt Hon Lord Stawell

Sir Thomas Miller, Bart

The Rev Thomas Combe Miller

Robert Newton Lee, Esq

James Ward, Esq

The Rev Noel Watkins

Mr Bridger Seward

At Farnham

John Marsh, Esq

James Shotter, Esq

John Manwaring, Esq

John Williams, Esq

Mr Chitty

Mr G.C. Knight

Mr Crump

Mr Dowden

Mr Newnham

Mr James Stevens

At Alresford

The Rt Hon The Earl Temple

Sir Chaloner Ogle

William Harris, Esq

Major Barton

The Rev C. Powlett

The Rev J. Wright

Mr Waight

Mr William Yalden

Mr Richard Goldfinch

Resolved that a subscription, to defray the expenses of the said opposition, be immediately entered into, and subscriptions be received by the following bankers, at the disposal of the general committee, viz, by

Messrs Praeds and Co, Fleet Street, London

Mr Knapp at Alresford and Winchester

Messrs Austen, Grey, and Vincent, Alton

Messrs Cock and Lamport, Farnham

And Messrs Stevens and Co, Farnham

That the individuals of each local committee be considered as members of a general committee, and that meetings be called from time to time by any three members.

That a meeting of the general committee be appointed to be held at the Swan Inn, Alton, on Tuesday the 18th day of December instant, at eleven o'clock in the morning.

That a surveyor and engineer be immediately employed by general committee, to survey the line of the canal and to report their opinions to the said general committee.

That the resolutions be published in London and in provincial papers.

(Signed) Stawell, Chairman

16 THE PUB WITH NO BODY
Birth, death and ethics

THE SCRAP YARD, HAWTHORN LANE, FOUR MARKS
1962   BODY COUNT: 1

The 'Pub with No Name' at Priors Dean, the highest public house in Hampshire, is one of the county's iconic hostelries. Inside, it's a rambling affair with a large wooden bar that dominates the two drinking rooms. Its proper name was, and still is to some, the *White Horse Inn*. Locals delight in pointing out the empty pub signpost. It stands, oddly, off the top of the road that climbs over the long hill from East Tisted to fall away down Stoner Hill through 'Little Switzerland' and into Steep and Petersfield.

It was at the 'No Name' that a visitor was murdered in 1962. The visitor was there to pay homage to the English poet, Edward Thomas, the pub's most celebrated drinker. Perhaps the killer might have got away with manslaughter with a good lawyer. The death happened almost sixty years ago so those involved are mostly dead. I know of only one still living and I know from close experience that she is now too ill to talk about it. I don't know the name of the murderer, or of the murdered man, but I do know how he died and why the body ended up in the vehicle scrap yard in Four Marks.

Near the start of the Great War, Thomas often walked along the track below the road from his home in Steep and occasionally reached the *White Horse*.

> *The path, winding like silver, trickles on,*
> *Bordered and even invaded by thinnest moss*
> *That tries to cover roots and crumbling chalk*
> *With gold, olive, and emerald, but in vain.*[1]

It is difficult to catch the breath of the place: the loneliness of Priors Dean, the women who gave birth to and nurtured the alehouse, the dramatic late-in-career transition of Thomas from critic and writer to a poet who became the 'father of us all'. Emerging from the story is a barmaid, the 'wild girl', who sparked Thomas to the profession that he had always evaded. Thomas 'remade English poetry' and shared 'significant cultural and political contexts with W.B. Yeats and Wilfred Owen'.[2] Thomas's many admirers make pilgrimages to the *White Horse*, the subject of his first poem, but academia has ignored the young woman who inadvertently played such an important literary role.

In the 1840s, the blacksmith at Priors Dean was William White from Ropley. He was married to Elizabeth,

Edward Thomas, 1905. *Hulton Archive/Stringer*

from Wiltshire, and every year or two they produced another child. The dewpond at their door at Locke Cottage provided water for the forge and was a friend to the cows and visiting horses. Water from the house came from a backyard well, never dry.

> *Between the open door*
> *And the trees two calves were wading in the pond,*
> *Grazing the water here and there and thinking,*
> *Sipping and thinking, both happily, neither long.*
> *The water wrinkled, but they sipped and thought,*
> *As careless of the wind as it is of us.*[3]

The business prospered and, by 1851, William held ten acres and was able to call himself a farmer, which placed him nearer to superior neighbours. His wife died and he remarried, a second Elizabeth, from Froxfield across the turnpike. Elizabeth had another five children. She was also the mother of the *White Horse*.

The land across this part of the Hampshire Downs through Colemore, Froxfield, Privett and Hawkley was all small farms and their workers. The Froxfield Plateau was thought the 'wildest and most beautiful' in the county.[4] Here's William Cobbett in *Rural Rides* in 1823:

The lane had a little turn towards the end; so that, out we came, all in a moment at the very edge of the hanger! And, never, in all my life was I so surprised and so delighted! I pulled up my horse, and sat and looked; and it was like looking from the top of a castle down into the sea, except that the valley was land and not water ... Those who had so strenuously dwelt on the dirt and dangers of this route, had not said a word about the beauties, the matchless beauties of the scenery.

Much of Priors Dean had been medieval rabbit warrens. The soil was good to poor, suited to wheat, oats and sheep, depending on its facing position on the hill. Avaricious landlords enclosed the land after 1800, reduced the Commons, slew much of the beech and increased the land under cultivation. The old woods were once the haunt of charcoal burners.

> *... by that time all trees*
> *Except those few about the house were gone:*
> *That's all that's left of the forest unless you count*
> *The bottoms of the charcoal-burners' fires –*
> *We plough one up at times.*

The area was largely self-sufficient with long-term families and social order, slow and distrusting of incomers. Cobbett's disgust with the rapid growth of towns and the sufferings of the exploited rural poor was in harmony with life around Priors Dean. With the high food prices following the Napoleonic wars, a surge of labourers moved in to live among the ruins and outhouses. Close by Locke Cottage was a wheezing windmill, the nearest thing locally to industrial machinery.

Neighbouring Colemore today is an almost deserted village, hardly worthy of the name; nearby Hartley Mauditt, tucked behind Chawton, lies abandoned, one of over ninety such places in rural Hampshire. Priors Dean and its blacksmith occupied a separated corner of a largely agricultural county.

Edward Thomas was an incomer as were all the foreign landlords at the *White Horse* after the second Elizabeth, as were Thomas's devotees, and all the modern-day, early evening drinkers and diners, more professionals with mobile phones than woodsmen with callouses. Over a hundred years, the few local men who could walk to the *No Name* were driven deeper into the public bar that used to be the smithy.

W.H. Hudson in *Hampshire Days* caught the separation, deep-set in 1903. He went with a friend to find the small church at Priors Dean, reportedly hidden behind nettles:

> *It was an excessively hot day in July … through roads so deep and narrow and roofed over with branches as to seem in places like tunnels. On that hot day in the silent time of the year it was strangely still, and gave one the feeling of being in a country long deserted by man … We saw two cottages and two women and a boy standing talking by a gate, and of these people we asked the way to Priors Dean. They could not tell us … A middle-aged man was digging about thirty yards away, and to him one of the women now called, 'Can you tell them the way to Priors Dean?'*
>
> *The man left off digging, straightened himself, and gazed steadily at us for some moments … When he had had his long gaze, he said, 'Priors Dean?'*
>
> *Then, at last, he stuck his spade into the soil, and leaving it, slowly advanced to the gate and told us to follow a path which he pointed out, and when we got on the hill we would see Priors Dean before us. And that was how we found it.*

One sees the Whites as hard-working people looking to better themselves. William added a wheelwright business to his blacksmith's shop and the ten acres. Elizabeth developed a bakery, a grocery shop and a small alehouse. As the beer shop became established, William's landlord sold the lease to the Southgate Brewery in Winchester, run for many years by the Barnes family, deep city establishment. Their public houses in and around the city were legendary: *The Marquis of Granby, Sun Inn, Northam Tavern, Gardeners' Arms and The Builders' Arms.*

William White died in 1867, aged fifty-eight. The next year, the *White Horse* was offered for let by the brewery with early possession.[5] In July 1870, the Barnes brothers, in difficulties, put to auction all moveable stock: 100 hogsheads, 2,000 gallons of beer, sacks of hops, even their draught horse. Two weeks later, the brewery buildings were for sale or let, an engine house, a mill house, waggon sheds and the private residence.[6]

Elizabeth survived the storm. She was the acknowledged publican in 1871; two of her sons, Frank and Herbert, took over their father's smithy.

The way over Froxfield Plateau was a connection between the Portsmouth and Gosport turnpikes.[7] From 1802, passengers from Alton were picked up daily from the *Crown* and taken 'two miles beyond East Tisted' to turn left 'over

Prior's Dean Common' to the *Red Lion* at Petersfield.[8] The *White Horse* was no coaching inn. No sweating teams of four turned off and threaded down the narrow lanes with passengers demanding appropriate toilets and dinner and wine all to be finished within the half hour. Most regular lines were owned by a consortium of the stagecoach owner and the proprietors of the coaching inns, too high a price for the pockets at the *White Horse*.[9] The obvious halt if one was needed was the *White Horse*'s near neighbour, the *Trooper Inn* at Froxfield, two miles closer to Thomas's home. The *Jolly Trooper* in 1830 did have its roots in the seventeenth century and had the space and size for a service to change horses. The inn became a popular centre for the Hunt, a recruiting centre in World War I, and the village Post Office with its own grocery and bakery business. The *Trooper* was not competition to the *White Horse*; it lived in a different world.

> *Once on a time 'tis plain that 'The White Horse'*
> *Stood merely on the border of waste*
> *Where horse and cart picked its own course afresh.*
> *On all sides then, as now, paths ran to the inn;*
> *And now a farm-track takes you from a gate.*
> *Two roads cross, and not a house in sight*
> *Except 'The White Horse' in this clump of beeches.*
> *It hides from either road, a field's breadth back;*
> *And it's the trees you see, and not the house …*

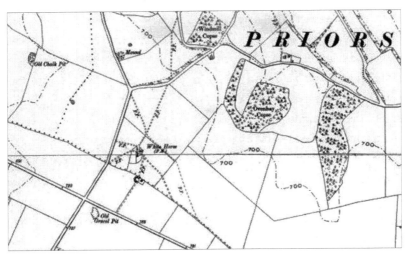

The White Horse *'hides from either road, a field's breadth back': 'all paths ran to the inn'.*

Within three years, Elizabeth remarried to Joseph Saunders, her first husband twelve years her senior, her second ten years her junior. Saunders was a chair turner from Tylers Green, born in Buckland, one among the many craftsmen supplying the great English furniture centre at High Wycombe. He brought with him to Priors Dean a little boy, his nephew, who had to pick up chips to feed the fire of his two-cylinder engine.

'My uncle,' the landlord, told Thomas, 'fell in love, I suppose, with the widow, and married her.' Joseph continued to go about the country sawing timber with his engine. But the beeches overhanging the house were spared.[10]

Elizabeth died, with no record found, and Joseph Saunders left for no known reason for his native Buckinghamshire; he can be found many years later as a widower lodging with a publican near Wycombe.[11]

Job Brown and his wife Charlotte, were installed at the *White Horse* before 1891. Both named Buckland as their birth place, as had Joseph Saunders, born within a year of Job. There was a family connection by marriage, unsolved, between the two men or their wives. As Job Brown was the father of the story-telling landlord, and if Thomas was accurate in his reporting, then Job Brown was the brother of Joseph Saunders.

With Job and Charlotte were three unmarried children, one 'Richard W' and the youngest of whom, 'Minnie K', became the barmaid. There was a six-year-old granddaughter, too, 'Minnie V', known as Violet. She was the daughter of Job and Charlotte's son Leonard whose wife Matilda had died in childbirth in Kingston-upon-Thames.

Job began work as a bricklayer in his home village. By 1871, he was a sawyer in Chawton, perhaps mirroring Joseph's work. His home was 'Four Marks Cottage', opposite the *Windmill Inn* on the ridge. He later ran a pub where he was called to give evidence at the death of a tramp to malnutrition and exposure.[12] Two years later, Job was the landlord of the *White Horse*, in Alton High Street.[13] By 1881, he was a carter in Long Ditton with Hampshire born children. He died as the innkeeper at the *White Horse* in 1891, age sixty-one, of heart failure after an hour and a half of 'heat apoplexy' with Minnie by his side.

The *White Horse* was named by Elizabeth before 1881. The name might have come from a favoured or imaginary horse visitor to the forge or, more teasingly, might have been a twin of Job's tenancy in Alton in the 1870s: a family with two *White Horses* and a new pub sign erected in Priors Dean to Violet's irritation.

A thief took it, fallen on the ground, and threw it in the pond, she explained.

> *'But would you like to hear it swing all night*
> *And all day? All I ever had to thank*
> *The wind for was for blowing the sign down.*
> *Time after time it blew down and I could sleep.*
> *At last they fixed it, and it took a thief*
> *To move it, and we've never had another:*
> *It's lying at the bottom of the pond.*

Shortly afterwards, the 'Pub with No Name' was born.

> *'Did you ever see*
> *Our signboard?' No. The post and empty frame*
> *I knew. Without them I should not have guessed*
> *The low grey house and its one stack under trees*
> *Was a public house and not a hermitage.*
> *'But can that empty frame be any use?'*

It is rumoured that the locals were fed up with fleeting visits by foreigners on their day trips from faraway places. The sign signified a welcome the locals did not share and so they continually got rid of it. They preferred what had always been their private, secluded place in Priors Dean. The pub became the Hampshire equivalent of that remote Welsh bar where all conversation stops as the unwelcome English visitor enters.

In late 1909, Edward Thomas and his family moved to Berryfield Cottage at Ashford near Petersfield so that his children could attend Bedales, a new co-educational establishment. Over the next three years, Thomas produced twelve books of what he often called 'hackwork', dragging himself to the limits of his physical and mental endurance, in order to earn enough money to support the growing family. His biographers are quick to point out that, far from hack, many of these books, like *The South Country*, *The Heart of England* and *In Pursuit of Spring*, remain classics of their genre. Thomas's literary reviews often broke new ground. He was the first to recognise the genius of de Walter de la Mare, W.H. Davies and Robert Frost. Thomas was a close acquaintance of the other literary giants of his time: Hilaire Belloc, who explored locally looking for the

The Pub with No Name and pond. The forge, the public bar, is the building in the foreground.

Pilgrim's Way,[14] Rupert Brooke, John Buchan, Joseph Conrad ...

Thomas spent hours, nights, walking to dawn, on the steep chalky paths around the wooded hangers seeking peace, inspiration or the courage to be a poet. Two or three times a year, he made the climb from his second home, Yew Tree Cottage, a workman's semi-detached house in Steep, to the *White Horse*.[15] In 1914, Thomas described the pub as 'dirty white', looking like a farmhouse which it 'half was', with a lean-to, rick and shed and only one cottage within sight.

> *For who now used these roads except myself,*
> *A market waggon every other Wednesday,*
> *A solitary tramp ...*

On one November trip, he found the subject for his first and longest poem, 'Up in the Wind'. Violet Brown sparked the transition from prose to poetry that he had never dared face. He wrote in prose followed by two poetic drafts.[16] It was an important watershed in English literature. Matthew Hollis, his biographer, wrote, 'Thomas did something extraordinary that he had not systematically attempted in years. He began a poem.'[17]

In December 1914, on the four days following 'Up in the Wind', Thomas wrote 'November', 'March', 'Old Man' and 'The Sign-Post' – 'poems of a quality rare not only in his generation'.[18]

Violet was twenty-nine years old, her hair-half down, a 'wild girl', born near Kingston-upon-Thames, but returned from her 'good' job in Kennington to help run the family pub. In his prose, Thomas called her a 'slattern'. She shrieked. A loud clock ticked, the cabbage bubbled and heaved under a big saucepan lid; the girl poked the fire and bent her back to scrub the bricks. All the while, she told Thomas about the awfulness of the *White Horse* and her 'fat' father, the landlord, who had recently taken over after Charlotte's death.[19]

> *'I could wring the old thing's neck that put it here!*
> *A public house! It may be public for birds,*
> *Squirrels, and such-like, ghosts of charcoal-burners*
> *And highwaymen.' The wild girl laughed.*
> *'But I hate it ...'*

Thomas never enquired after the 'old thing that put it here'. We know that it was Elizabeth White, who died near the time that Violet was born. Thomas, an accidental Londoner himself, born in Lambeth but from Wales, felt that Violet's Cockney accent 'made her and the house seem wilder by calling up ... the idea of London, there in that forest parlour.'

Thomas wrote almost 150 poems in a two-year whirl of creativity that ended when he died on the first day of the Battle of Arras in 1917, aged thirty-nine, 'shot clean through the chest'. His family were told that he had suffered a 'bloodless death' from the blast of a passing shell, a common explanation intended to ease the loss. Men of his age didn't have to join up, but even though he 'disagreed with the fighting he found it unconscionable to do nothing while his compatriots were being slaughtered'. Thomas's first two slim volumes of poetry, written under a pseudonym, were published some weeks later and have never since been out of print.

One must come to Edward Thomas in one's own way and time, if at all. He wrote a review of North of Boston, a work by his great American friend Robert Frost, which many feel, and I agree, could have been written of Thomas's own work.

*These poems are revolutionary because they lack the exaggeration of rhetoric … Their
language is free from the poetical words and forms that are the chief material of the
secondary poets. The metre avoids not only old-fashioned pomp and sweetness, but the
later fashion also of discourse and fuss. In fact the medium is common speech … With
a confidence like genius, he has trusted his conviction that a man will not easily write
better than he speaks when some matter has touched him deeply, and he has turned
it over until he has no doubt what it means to him, when he has no purpose to serve
beyond expressing it, when he has no audience to be bullied or flattered, when he is free,
and speech takes one form or another.*

Edna Longley, who spent her life studying Thomas's work saw him as 'situated
on the cusp of history and on the brink of modern selfhood',[20] one of the
half-dozen poets who 'remade English poetry' in the early twentieth century.[21]
Another writer described Thomas's 'unpretentious lucidity, plain language,
colloquial speech rhythms and a Hardy-like focus on country life and the
natural world'.[22]

One suspects Violet Brown never knew the spark she lit in Thomas and the
shock he then had on English literature. She told Thomas,

> *Here I was born,*
> *And I've a notion on these windy nights*
> *Here I shall die. Perhaps I want to die here.*
> *I reckon I shall stay. But I do wish*
> *The road was nearer and the wind farther off …*

There was a misunderstanding in Thomas's recording of the relationships,
which, believe me, are complicated. Thomas said that Violet had a firm
opinion of her father.

> *… The little boy stayed on.*
> *He was my father.' She thought she'd scrub again –*
> *'I draw the ale and he grows fat,' she muttered –*
> *But only studied the hollows in the bricks*
> *And chose among her thoughts in stirring silence.*

Her father was Leonard and there is no record that he ran the pub. By the time of Thomas's visit, he was long dead. In 1921, the Lion Brewery of Winchester bought the lease of the *White Horse*, together with the surrounding meadows, from Sir Joseph Tichborne for £1,300.[23] The fat landlord was Richard Walter Brown, Leonard's younger brother, who committed suicide at the *White Horse* the next year, aged fifty-three. Richard was Violet's 'fat' uncle, not father. Apart from his early years, he had never left the inn, working as an agricultural labourer, a farmer and assisting in the business.

The circumstances of his death were bizarre. Richard had been 'strange in his manner' for several days, so strange that his niece locked him in the building and slipped out of a window to go for help. When she returned, she found that her uncle had climbed out of the parlour widow and clambered into a rainwater tank. He weighed twenty stone and when men came to get him out they found him wedged and drowned.

The inquest, held at the inn, heard that Richard had been disturbed because two men who had called at the *White Horse* had gone on to kill or mutilate four sheep with a spade and an axe.[24] He was about to be called as a witness at their trial. The connection seems obscure. He claimed he had turned the men away, but at the trial the judge said it 'looked as if there were something wrong'. The accused were both 'mad drunk', but the police suggested 'bad drink'. Perhaps here is the answer for Richard's fear of court, hardly doctored beer, but maybe an illicit still?

Most remarkable about the trial was that the owner of the sheep, William Allee of Colemore, pleaded for the men's dismissal. 'I think this is only a drunken freak,' he said. 'I am willing, if you treat them leniently, to give them work and start them on again … If you can let them go, I will look after them and try and make them honest.' Charges were dismissed.[25]

Minnie Violet Brown did not see her future clearly. She left the pub the year before the suicide and returned to her birthplace to marry William Wickham, thirteen years her junior. Always the wild girl!

Over fifty years later, all was different, yet the same, at the *No Name*. The latest landlord thought to attract more passing motor trade. Misunderstanding the marketing value of the 'Pub with No Name', he paid for a replacement sign with a prancing white horse. The commoners were no longer woodsmen, but skilled decorators, plumbers, electricians and car mechanics who still glowered at the solicitors and business executives across the counter. The landlord was warned by these feral offspring of the old forge.

*There is a post and a wrought iron support, but it is only meant to frame the clouds.
We like it that way. Leave it well alone.*

One large group of regulars came from a Four Marks scrap yard at Dovecot in Hawthorn Lane. The place was built up after the war by Ray Trenchard, a man of great appetites that led to fifteen known children. I need to be careful how I phrase things because there are a lot of descendants still about.

The scrap yard was a wild place, a child's delight, free vehicles to drive at speed on grassy fields and tracks, and few restrictions, especially if Ray was at the betting shop or the pub, which was often. Ray had a solid heart. He employed anyone in need of money; there was always a job to do in the rag and bone business. A young man from Alton who was in a 'financial spot of bother' could often be found staying in the yard. It's fair to say that if 'anything was going on' in the district, there would be someone from the yard close by.

The business began in agricultural contracting and then handled aged agricultural machinery: threshing machines, tractors and harvesters. The end of the World War II also brought in job lots of military surplus, particularly Jeeps, Rolls Royce chassis and dying lorries. Cars that expired on reaching Four Marks ridge were gathered up. Ray's reputation meant that at Hampshire farm auctions unsold wrecks were marked down without question for his standard agreed bid of £1. Vehicles poured in and people needing parts for their old motors soon followed. There was a thriving trade sending metal to recycling centres in Fareham, Poole, South Wales and at Blackbushe Airport.

One early source of wealth was less well known. War surplus extended to munitions, some of them unexploded and 'spare' fuel for military installations. There were more aircraft crashes and bombs dropped around Four Marks than people nowadays imagine. So many enemy bombers flew overhead to London that there was a searchlight battery up a side track off Lymington Bottom Road. Memoirs and recollections are full of stories, including when a damaged bomber staggered at point blank distance passed a local anti-aircraft gun. As the aircraft crew threw out everything they could find to lose weight, the gun commander, with just four shells available, telephoned in vain for permission to fire.[26]

But, there may have been another, more secret, reason for the close attention. Today, there is a still-concealed, underground brick bunker near Red Hill in Medstead. The bunker was known as an ammunition dump and was a reputed designated secondary target.

A landmine fell in a field behind houses in Telegraph and Willis Lanes putting crockery on the floor at Semaphore Farm and tilting the barn. The nursery in Brislands Lane was pushed several feet sideways by a near miss. Mr and Mrs Diamond in Boyneswood Road suffered a direct hit. A German bomber flew low over Blackberry and Alton Lanes, opened its bomb doors, and released a stick of bombs which landed in fields without exploding and 'may well be still there today'. In the woods down Mary Lane, a large crater appeared overnight close to the road. Staff and pupils at the school were showered with glass as three windows were blown in without warning.

Pulsing V1s and steady V2 rockets passed overhead nightly. A V1 was found in the watercress beds in Alresford. A heavy Stirling bomber heading home for Odiham airfield was hit by friendly anti-aircraft fire over Portsmouth. It circled Four Marks in the fog before coming down behind a house in Hawthorn Lane where it blew up in an apple orchard. The crew bailed out, but the pilot was caught by the circling aircraft and was found dead in Headmore Lane. Lasham airfield was swept by machine gun fire during a parade. A German multi-engined plane crashed in Medstead where the bodies were found scattered high in the trees. An air ambulance DC-3 Dakota came down between Four Marks railway station and Boyneswood Road. A *Messerschmidt* just missed the tracks near North Street Farm. A US B-17 Flying Fortress landed in a water meadow close to Alresford Pond carrying a full bomb load.

Local children were enthralled by a real dogfight over Farringdon between Spitfires and *Junkers 88* bombers. A bomb fell in the field opposite the *Horse and Groom*. Men from the pub chased the crew who parachuted from one JU88 which then made a forced landing in an oat field. Another 88 crashed in Rotherfield Park and the crew perished.

A number of high explosive and incendiary devices were dropped on Alton, falling on the town's sawmills and business premises. Two bombs on Anstey housing estate killed five and injured six. Several homes were demolished and a larger number damaged but repaired.

Enemy aircraft not only dropped bombs but sent down leaflets calling for 'surrender'. Strips of metallised foil, known as 'chaff', were thrown into the skies to confuse British radar. This glistening foil festooned the trees, often in Chawton Park Wood, bringing an early Christmas.

I give you all this information because a lot of material fell to the ground. Finds were everywhere. Much of the debris, live bullets, military kit, aircraft parts and bombs, official and unofficial, ended up at the scrap yard.

If this heavenly bounty and misappropriated supplies stacked among the vehicles adds to the impression of lawlessness, then all well and good. You are nearer to the impression I wish to create.

That day in 1962, as the pints were drunk, there was one particularly noisy and unwanted Edward Thomas fan in the lounge bar. He was on a solitary pilgrimage. No one knew him, but let's call him Rupert. He moved to the centre of the room and brayed his addiction. The sound filled every nook which had heard it all before.

Thomas and his poems meant nothing to most of the increasingly angry and red-eyed watchers, one group a collection of petty criminals and workers from the scrap yard. Those that had heard of Thomas hated Gloucestershire in general and still resented being forced at school to learn by heart,

> *Yes, I remember Adlestrop –*
> *The name, because one afternoon*
> *Of heat the express-train drew ...*[27]

The bad boys, the wild ones from the scrap yard club, held court and decided on action. The pub sign would have to go.

One lad from Alton shinned up the post and went to work with a spanner. Rupert appeared and called out in alarm. The sign fell and caught him edge-wise across the head. Was this deliberate? Young troublemakers are often quicker than the rest of us to know what to do in a crisis. Their car for the night, a *Singer Gazelle* with three doors left from a recent fatal accident, was brought up. The large sign went in the small boot which was tied down with string. Rupert lolled on the back seat, brain showing from his dreadful gash, and was driven to the scrap yard, far up and out of sight.

In the morning, after a good night's sleep, preparations were made for a burial. The group leant on their spades and looked at the car. There was no body. There were blood smears which denied any dream. But there was no body. After a search, everyone drifted to the day's tasks, looking about as they went for anything unusual.

At the pub today, there is an 'Edward Thomas Corner' with a carved wooden plaque, erected in 1978 by *The Edward Thomas Fellowship* to mark the poet's centenary, 'that forest parlour, low and small among the towering beeches'.

Sometimes 200 members of The Fellowship come on the first Sunday in March to commemorate his death. To these visitors, they attend the *White Horse*. To the locals, it is the 'Pub with No Name'.

Now, you understand why it is also, to a select and dangerous few, the 'Pub with No Body'.

ENDNOTES

[1] Thomas, 'The Path'.

[2] Longley, *Collected Poems*.

[3] Thomas, 'Up in the Wind', from which all quotes are taken unless noted otherwise.

[4] Harvey, *United Parishes*.

[5] *Hampshire Chronicle*, 12/9/1868.

[6] *Hampshire Chronicle*, 23/7/1870.

[7] Freeman, 'Turnpikes and Their Traffic'.

[8] Cary, *Itinerary of the Great Roads*.

[9] Gerhold, *Bristol's Stage Coaches*.

[10] Prose notes of Thomas. Hollis, *Collected Poems*. Longley, *Collected Poems*.

[11] Census 1891.

[12] *Hampshire Advertiser*, 30/10/1872. Cornick, *Early Memories*, talks of Four Marks House standing opposite the Windmill, 'a private house with quite a bit of land behind it, complete with a couple of dells'. It was knocked down in 1998.

[13] *Hampshire Advertiser*, 8/5/1875.

[14] Belloc, *Old Road*.

[15] Hollis, Jocelyn, *Collected Poems*.

[16] Wilson, *Thomas*.

[17] Hollis, Matthew, *Now All Roads lead to France*.

[18] Cooke, *Thomas*.

[19] *Kelly's Directory*, 1911.

[20] Longley, 'Roads from France', *The Guardian*, 28/6/2008, in Wilson, *Thomas*.

[21] Longley, *Annotated Poems* in Wilson, *Thomas*.

[22] 'Introduction', *Works*.

[23] Sargent, 'A Pub, a Poet and a Poem'.

[24] Arthur Page, 20, and Alfred Warwick, 22 (*Portsmouth Evening News*, 18/12/1922, 14/2/1923).

[25] This attitude to animal death and maiming bears comparison with the reaction to horse deaths in Chapter 17, 'First catch your low-life'.

[26] Cornick, *Early Memories*. Wyeth, *Memories*. Mills, *Four Marks*.

[27] Thomas, *Adlestrop*.

Reading list:

Cary, John, *New Itinerary or an Accurate Delineation of the Great Roads throughout England and Wales* (Thomas Hasker, London 1802)

Cobbett, William, *Rural Rides* (1830; Penguin, Harmondsworth 1977)

Cooke, William, *Edward Thomas, A Critical Biography 1878–1917* (Faber and Faber, London 1970)

Farringdon and Chawton Millennium Book, *The Last Hundred Years, 1900–2000* (Farringdon & Chawton Magazine 2000)

Freeman, M., 'Turnpikes and Their Traffic: The Example of Southern Hampshire', *Transactions of the Institute of British Geographers*, Vol. 4, No. 3, 1979, pp. 411–434

Gerhold, Dorian, *Bristol's Stage Coaches* (Hobnob Press, Salisbury 2012)

Harvey, Thomas, Rev, *A History of the United Parishes of Colmer and Priors Dean* (Privately published 1880)

Hollis, Jocelyn, *Collected Poems* (Amer Poetry, USA, 1988)

Hollis, Matthew, *Now All Roads Lead to France, The Last Years of Edward Thomas* (Faber and Faber, London 2011)

Hudson, W.H., *Hampshire Days (1903; Oxford University Press 1980)*

Longley, Edna, edited, *Edward Thomas, The Annotated Collected Poems* (Bloodaxe, Tarset 2008)

Sargent, Andrew, 'A Pub, a Poet and an Poem', *Newsletter, The Edward Thomas Fellowship*, No 84, August 2020

Smith, Ron, 'Medstead Memories – The wartime years', *www.medstead.org*, 2019

Thomas, Edward, *The Works* (Wordsworth Poetry Library, Ware 1994)

Wilson, Jean Moorcroft, *Edward Thomas, From Adlestrop to Arras, A Biography* (Bloomsbury, London 2015)

17 FIRST CATCH YOUR LOW LIFE

Horse mutilation

FOUR MARKS
1993   BODY COUNT: 1

I walked home early from the pub and noticed the light on in my study, a light I knew I had left switched off. The patio door had been jemmied out of its groove. I slipped in quietly and picked up a black wood *iwisa* – a Zulu souvenir – and walked into the room. A man in his thirties, dark hair, short, clean-shaven, was pushing my laptop into a black plastic bag, which was already, it seemed, quite full. He wasn't fazed to see me, finished his packing and told me to get out of his way.

'You've made a mess of my study,' I accused him. 'And I know you from around the town.'

'So what, you old git?'

I moved towards the house phone.

'You touch that and I'll break your arms. You call the police and I'll come back later with some mates and do you proper.'

'I think I will call the police. This is the fifth time I've had a break-in in the last couple of years. I am fed up with it and that means I'm fed up with you, moron, and the fact that you live off the backs of people who don't steal for a living. And, my dim friend, the people I know will chase you to the end of the world and then eat your children.'

'Stupid idiot,' he lectured. 'Got no kids and I'm not frightened of you. I've got more dangerous friends than you anyway, you old fart. You weren't chosen by accident, you know. Anyway, the police won't come. And if they do call by, they won't bother. They never bother around here. I've been to court and they just let you off, anyway. So you can't do nuffin', scum.'

'Someone, sometime, has to stop a low-life like you. If the police won't do their job, then I guess, sooner or later, someone like me has to step up.'

'You touch me, I'll say you started it and it'll be you what the police arrest.

You'll end up in the nick. I'll get off because they'll send me for counselling.'

'Sadly for you, I think you're right.'

And I hit him on the head with the *knopkierie*. There was a satisfying crunch. I tipped out my laptop and the others things he had taken. I picked him up by his collar and dragged him into the garden then got some plastic ties and bound his hands behind his back. In a pocket, I found his car keys. The vehicle was parked a few yards down the lane with no one in it. I took it into my driveway, bundled him in, collected some things, and drove to a wooded area about a mile away towards Hawthorn.

I cut his clothes off and tied him tightly to a finely shaped oak tree, naked in plain sight of the road. He started to groan as I placed a large card around his neck on which I wrote, 'THIEF'. In the boot of his car, I found five swag bags which I arranged at his feet, hopefully for eventual collection by the owners.

I placed a noose around his neck and waved the free end of the rope in his face. At this point he broke down and began sobbing. Leaning close to his ear, I told him that if I ever heard from him again he would die slowly and in great pain. When I asked for his name, he gave it immediately. He was Sid.

I pretended to take his picture on my phone and to send it.

'There,' I said, 'your picture's gone to my mates together with your name and a shot of your tiny prick and that you live in Alton. If anything ever happens to me, they have instructions to cut if off with a rusty knife. That's a promise.'

Mumbled obscenities followed me as I walked away and then, bad move, a shout of defiance. His eyes lost their tiny sparkle as I picked up the rope end and threw it over a bough.

'You wouldn't dare,' he choked.

'Who's going to know, my very stupid friend? You had your chance to be sorry.'

I pulled the rope tight and raised him to tiptoe. He urinated and tried to speak. I slackened the rope a bit.

'Something you want to say before you go?'

'I'll tell you who dunnit,' he gasped.

'Done what, moron? You done, did, it. You were in my study.'

'Done them 'orses. You know, them 'orses that were ripped. I know 'er well enuf. She's my cousin. She's bad.'

I told him to tell me her name and he did. I stood looking at him for a few minutes. If Sid thought his cousin was a bad lot, she was probably not someone to upset on a dark night. I pushed a log by his feet, told him to stand on it and pulled the rope a little tighter and tied it off. On the card, I wrote: 'HORSE RIPPER' followed by the women's name and 'APPLY WITHIN.'

'Don't fall asleep,' I suggested. I put my *iwisa* and his clothes inside the car, shoved a rag down the petrol inlet, set it alight and walked home to clear up the mess. There was a big explosion before I had gone twenty yards. Sid started screaming. I think it must have been the heat.

Screaming sirens woke me from a deep sleep the next morning. Around lunchtime, two policewomen, little and large, called on door-to-door enquiries.

'Had I had a break-in?'

'Yes, five, all reported, but you are the first police I have seen that have asked me about them.'

'Sir, have you had one recently?'

'No.'

'Please check, sir.' I went for a quick check.

'No break in,' I reported.

'Sir, please show me your shotgun.'

'You'll have to turn your backs while I get the keys to the cabinet.'

I fetched the gun and handed it over.

'Not fired since last week,' I offered. 'The rabbits are on holiday.'

My security arrangements passed scrutiny.

'Sir, where were you last night?'

'At the pub, couple of pints, walked home alone, two miles took thirty minutes, had a sandwich, went to bed about ten thirty, got woken by sirens this morning, been working on my computer in my study ever since. I live alone. Why do you want to know?'

'This is a theft enquiry, sir. Several plastic bags of stolen goods have been found in a wood at Hawthorn. There's a burnt out car near by.'

The conversation rambled on, notes were taken and the officers left. I wondered if there would be any reason for them to come back. They never did.

This all happened in 1994. The early nineties were a bad time for some people who lived in Four Marks. The police had all but closed their station in Alresford, seventeen men with a sergeant at its peak, now down to one stressed individual working part-time. Alton station was 'under review'. It would take a murder or a hate crime to get an officer to visit a house in Four

Marks. Community police houses were closing everywhere. Residents, most well-meaning, but some with a need for power in their loins, started filling the gaps: volunteer watch groups, pompous speed checkers with yellow jackets, community police officers, telephone report lines and a 'bad news' website. Meanwhile, sleepy Four Marks was left unprotected and waiting to be violated. Organised yobs from Southampton and south London recognised the lack of real protection and toured the country lanes, watching for windows left open, cars parked outside isolated houses, farm machinery, garden sheds and the old and infirm living alone. Pictures were taken by locals of suspicious car number plates but nothing ever happened.

In early 1993, con artists, one male and one female, who clearly knew who to visit, paid calls on several old age pensioners. Using the pretext of trying to find a home for a cat, homes in Alton Lane and Hazel Road were targeted. While one low-life kept the occupant busy, another searched the house.[1] Two months later, another old gentleman was targeted by masked raiders who smashed a window with a piece of wood, forced the front door and took every last penny. Early the next year, the year I found Sid in my study, three masked men tried to break into the home of a retired couple. Their telephone line had been cut. They handed over their car keys to a hand thrust through a broken window. The gang left with the couple's lifeline – an aged Ford Fiesta. It was also the year when thieves left cars stolen to order in Weathermore Wood for handover.

In an extraordinary reaction, the great and the good of Alton and East Hampshire finally turned in 2020. The failure of Hampshire's police force to fight rural crime was denounced in an open letter signed by Alton's mayor, seventeen chairmen of local parishes and six East Hampshire councillors.[2]

The crime that caught the national attention, however, was the one attributed by Sid to his 'bad' cousin. Twenty-seven horse assaults, identified by *The Times*, took place in Hampshire between June 1991 and February 1993.[3] Four Marks was one of the epicentres, but became the focus of police investigations when a mare, Mountbatten, was found dead in her stable with cuts to her genitals. One account said that assaults started in Hampshire in 1966.[4]

Four Marks, indeed Hampshire, wasn't an isolated occurrence. Horse assaults were also reported from 1993 to February 1997 in Oxfordshire, Buckinghamshire, Cleveland, Hull, Dorset, Greater Manchester, Swindon, North Yorkshire and Wiltshire – 'over one hundred attacks in twelve months'.[5]

The Hampshire attacks were extensively reported. The *Daily Mail* added

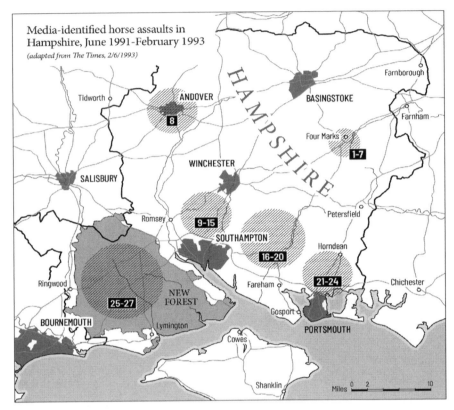

Media-identified horse assaults in
Hampshire, June 1991-February 1993
(adapted from The Times, 2/6/1993)

Hampshire horse assaults, January 1991 to February 1993.

a reward of £10,000 to the £8,000 already pledged by the International
League for the Protection of Horses, Naturewatch Trust and the *Horse & Hound*
and others.

Concerned Four Marks citizens set up the first 'Horsewatch' organisation
early in February 1993, the first of eighty-five such groups formed within
eighteen months. The police then established the 'Mountbatten Operation'
with twelve officers based in Alton.[6] At the first 'Horsewatch' meeting,
'hundreds of people crowded into Four Marks village hall, while others were
forced to stand outside straining to hear through open windows'.

Every so often a society becomes engrossed in a public frenzy directed at
a certain sort of crime. The sociologists call it 'moral panic'.[7] An outraged
citizenry tries to make sense of events that seem deviant, irrational and criminal.

'People who initially regard an event as senseless are liable, if it concerns them enough, to spend a great deal of energy and time trying to make sense of it.' Events are simultaneously both systematic and random: systematic because it seems that each assault was one act in a series, random because no one had any idea when or where the perpetrator would strike next.

There are patterns in the hunt for reason: social problems get identified that need fixing, vociferous leaders emerge, blame is distributed and controls sought over suspicious groups of people. The media and the police attempt to take the moral high ground and to direct the agenda.

If maiming a horse around the neck and genitalia is, in your view, the most awful crime, it might be best now to skip a page.

Horses and many other animals have been assaulted in England for centuries both systematically and routinely.[8] At times, animal maiming was undoubtedly a form of social rebellion. 'Maimers had grievances and the death of an animal in retaliation was, perhaps, preferable to the murder of a human being.' In studies where convictions were obtained, animal assaults often resulted from feuds between members of the same class or they involved individuals who frequently met each other: by horse carers on horse owners, on a competitor by harming their donkey that pulled craft goods, or by poisoning cats or dogs in a conflict between farmers and gamekeepers over the rearing of game birds. Cattle mutilation is primarily a US phenomenon. Not often, but regularly, horses sexually assaulted other horses. Pets also get hurt by otherwise loving owners in a flash of direct or referred anger. Dogs, cats and fluffy pets are continually mistreated and abandoned. Isolated incidents can be easily denied or declared relatively unimportant.

However, without a culprit to hand, the horse owners in this moral panic in Hampshire were consistently at pains to claim that the horse assaults were not isolated but a sequence carried out deliberately and sexually motivated. Strains of Equus lay close to the surface.[9] The term 'horse rippers' was used with hints of a bygone age of terror and a conviction that the perpetrator was male. The *Sunday Times* called them the 'most hated men in Britain' as if they were a group working in cohesion against horses as 'devil carriers'. The culprits were dreadfully sick with bizarre mental delusion.

No one tried to explain the assaults other than that they were reprehensible, aberrant and senseless.

One must ask why did the Hampshire assaults matter so much? That is not to say that they were not serious. Many people who were not directly involved thought them serious. The police declared them serious. But how serious were they compared to pensioners terrorised in their homes in the same year? Where was the comparable task force to protect older people?

Who were the victims? The horses that were generally passive in response? Or the owners who were active and vocal? Why, of all the problems facing the local society, were these episodes raised up?

In the previous chapter of this book, there is an episode of sheep killing and maiming in Colemore in 1922 where different attitudes and standards seem to apply.[10]

The police saw the horse assaults as constituting criminal damage so victimhood was legally ascribed to the property owners, people generally in the higher echelons of their communities with evident income, status and social influence. Although it is also illegal to cause horses unnecessary suffering, in this case the suffering became separate from the offence against property and secondary to it. Animals, like human slaves, are afforded in law the strange status of sentient property.

The police sought to broaden the matter. They looked to bond with local people who they declared as their 'eyes and ears' with the force claiming the sole right to do the detecting. 'If everyone is more vigilant, we can start to make a hole in the crime rates of Hampshire.' The public were to be on the look-out for shady characters, unfamiliar cars parked in the wrong place, as if this evil, identifiable, underclass was insinuating itself into the respectable world of Middle England. New age travellers, hunt saboteurs, eco-warriors, refugees, gypsies and asylum seekers, beware.

An attack on a horse might be a precursor to an assault on a human. From the beginning, police were predicting that 'horse rippers' might turn on children. Vulnerable, female young owners received strident warnings not to take risks by watching over their ponies during the night. A local girl was stabbed during this time leading a journalist to say that it was 'only a matter of time before these attacks turned from horses on to people'.

But what if the enemy was within?

What if the intended victims were not the horses, but the owners? What if the culprit did not have a pathological character? As a group, the owners rejected that they had done anything wrong in their animal care because they loved their horses. However, some began to suspect that their way of life was under attack and 'any' owner could be the real target. Animals and their bodies might be part of a struggle to protect the safety of the well-to-do and their national identity and cultural difference. Such anxieties are a manifestation of an endemic feature of middle and upper-class life in contemporary rural England. They are necessarily reinforced by claims of personal innocence.

'Common sense theory on deviance takes an act and then pursues assumptions about the actor's characteristics.' The ideological function of the process is to render highly suspicious those sections of the population that seem to have those characteristics. Victims develop the skill to establish that their suffering is unnecessary, serious, and caused by dangerous criminals.

'Bluntly, some victims are worthy while others are not. The worthier the victim, the more reprehensible the offender.'[11]

Below the surface, there are many traces of guilt, unease and defensiveness about the treatment of animals. There are a variety of institutionalised social practices in which horses are routinely and systematically assaulted which are not characterised as unlawful or socially unacceptable. In these locations, like laboratories, farms, racetracks and abattoirs, it is somehow much harder and less appropriate to criminalise the perpetrators of harms committed there.

Why is the nature of some horse assaults condemned while other behaviours are condoned? In the Hampshire moral panic about horse assaults, members of the public, the police, criminal psychologists, the media and animal welfare officials admitted only particular sorts of abused horses into their circle of concern. Their focus was not horse assaults in general, but individual animals or animals of wealthy people kept for recreation and sport.

Millions of animals are exploited in large-scale commercial processes. Annually 200 animals die on racetracks in Britain.[12] At Cheltenham, as many as ten horse deaths have occurred in one week, and now, commentators parrot the authority's concern for care whenever there is an incident. In 1993, twelve pregnant Welsh mountain ponies were injected with equine herpes, resulting in aborted pregnancies and paralysis. The ponies were killed to perform post-mortem experiments. Ex-racing horses are often sent to one of three British abattoirs licenced to slaughter horses. Annually, 25,000 horses are killed for meat in Britain.

Some six months later, I saw my housebreaker, Sid, in Alton High Street, or, to be more accurate, he saw me and darted down the alley by the *Baker's Arms*. Clearly he was disturbed for he ran full tilt into the back of a large woman carrying several bags of shopping. I picked him up by his collar from among the carrots and propelled him to the pub door.

'Don't worry, love,' I offered, 'I'll break his arms for you.'

I plonked Sid in a seat, but before I could say anything he spurted, 'I've given up on the thieving. Honest. I'm very sorry for what happened. I've turned a new leaf. I've gone straight. Got a job and all.'

'How did you get away, Sid?'

'Woman came along, toff, one of those horsey types. Came to see what the fire was. She read that sign you put around my neck and said she'd let me go if I told her the whole story.'

'And, then ...?'

'She came round my place the next day with two big blokes. Made me take them to my cousin's.'

I bought him a lager. 'And then ... ?'

'My cousin was dead scared. I was, too. We all sat round 'er kitchen table and 'ad a coffee. My cousin told 'em how she got 'er leg broke by an 'orse and 'ow she 'ad a limp. And 'ow the guy on the 'orse what did it didn't care and told 'er to piss off and she lost her job with being off sick, an' all.'

The long and short of it was that, after a couple of months' trial following the kitchen table revelations, the girl got a full-time job helping look after six horses.

'I go down and help out on Saturdays,' said Sid. 'It's good.'

He finished his glass.

'But, I tell you,' said Sid, 'she only did four 'orses and she never did no Mountbatten.'

ENDNOTES

[1] Mills, *Four Marks.*
[2] *Alton Herald*, 18/6/2020.
[3] *The Times*, 6/2/1993.
[4] *The Sunday Times*, 31/10/1993.
[5] *The Times*, 23/6/1997; *Daily Telegraph*, 19/9/1997; *Observer*, 12/10/1997.
[6] *Alton Herald*, 4/2/1993.
[7] Yates, 'Horse maiming'.
[8] Archer, 'Fiendish Outrage'.
[9] Play by Peter Schaffer, 1973. Also Shaffer, *Equus*, 2005.
[10] Chapter 16, 'The pub with no body.'

[11] Yates, 'Maiming'.
[12] 1995.

Reading list:

Archer, John E., 'A Fiendish Outrage'? A Study of Animal Maiming in East Anglia: 1830–1870 *The Agricultural History Review*, 1985, Vol. 33, No. 2, 1985, pp. 147–157

Shaffer, Peter, *Equus* (Simon and Schuster, New York 2005).

Yates, Roger, Powell, Chris and Beirne, Piers, 'Horse Maiming in the English Countryside: Moral Panic, Human Deviance, and the Social Construction of Victimhood', *Society & Animals*, Vol. 9, No. 1, 2001

18 BUNNY MAYHEM
Porton Down and myxomatosis

FOUR MARKS
1998   BODY COUNT: 1, PERHAPS MORE

Some people love rabbits. Some people eat them. Others loathe them.

Children have been trained to love rabbits. Until the 1850s, 'few books had been published which had animals as their central character,' but, since then, especially since the Great War, 'such books have been published in ever increasing numbers'.[1] Rabbits have featured in children's literature at least since 1865 when Alice followed Lewis Carroll's White Rabbit down the burrow to Wonderland. Characters include Brer Rabbit, Thumper, Bambi's playmates, Peter Rabbit, Winnie the Pooh's rabbit friend, Bugs Bunny and, latterly, Bigwig and Hazel on Hampshire's own *Watership Down*.[2] 'All these rabbits possess human characteristics and are portrayed sympathetically … It is not surprising that a public reared on such fare reacted with disgust to a viral disease that disfigured and killed such lovable creatures.

'Who could view with equanimity the prospect of Potter's Flopsy Bunnies riddled with myxomatosis?'[3]

There is a garage by the side of a house in Alton Lane where duck, goose and chicken eggs used to be sold on an honesty basis. To reach the eggs, one needed to dodge through, perhaps, thirty dead rabbits hanging from the ceiling. Whole rabbit is nowadays less frequently seen in local butchers reflecting the modern convention that pieces of meat are acceptable to display, but not skinned bodies.

Protein poisoning, also called rabbit starvation, is a rare form of acute malnutrition, first noted as a consequence of eating lean rabbit meat exclusively. The US military teaches that rabbit takes more vitamins to digest than it returns. In survival training, they recommend refraining from eating if rabbit is all that's available. Rabbit eaters, if they have no fat from another source, will develop diarrhoea in about a week alongside lowered blood pressure and a slowing heart rate. It is a condition akin to kwashiorkor, protein deficiency, which killed up to one million Biafran children in the Nigerian war of secession in the 1960s.4

Dr Paul-Félix Armand-Delille and Gordon Williams hated rabbits. In 1952, Delille, an elderly physician with an estate near Dreux, north of Chartres, in France, used his professional contacts to obtain a sample of the myxomatosis virus and released an infected rabbit with a view to eliminating the animal from his land. The disease quickly spread through much of France and neighbouring countries.[5]

Occupational health expert Peter Bartrip named Gordon Williams as the person who brought the virus to England, something Williams always denied, 'but his friends were not convinced'. Bartrip pointed out that Williams' farm was near the site of the first outbreak in Edenbridge, Kent. Williams had good contacts in Northern France from his war service and made a cross-channel visit shortly before the disease was discovered. 'Since importing the virus or infecting rabbits was not illegal in 1953, Williams had no need to deny responsibility for fear of prosecution. However, he had good reason to be coy about admitting involvement lest he incur the wrath of animal lovers, or those whose livelihood depended on rabbits, as others who welcomed the disease or spread it subsequently did.'[6]

The rapid and uneven spread of the disease was puzzling. The summer was 'dreadful' and not propitious for the insects that carried the infection. The pattern was highly erratic. There was an outbreak in mid-Wales before it reached Surrey. Myxomatosis passed quickly from Kent to Robertsbridge and Lewes, both in Sussex. Nine Scottish counties were next after an introduction by a tenant farmer from Durris, Kincardine, with a diseased carcase. All this happened before Middlesex, Cornwall and Devon had their first cases. Within a few more months, it was everywhere. Tens of millions of rabbits died. Within a short time, 'but only for a short time', rabbits disappeared from many parts of Great Britain.

Why the hatred?

'All British rabbits can trace their ancestry back to a warren.'[7] Rabbits were reportedly introduced onto the mainland from small islands on the Welsh and Bristol Channel coasts in the 1200s, happy with sandy soils for burrowing and the absence of large predators.[8] They were prized for their meat, their fur and for sport. Britain was covered in large warrens of pillow mounds, raised earthworks where valued rabbits were fed and which burrowed inwards. The surrounding walls were in place to keep away the poor people, not to keep the rabbits in. Watchtowers for warreners were a regular sight. Landowners extracted a heavy price, death or imprisonment, and later transportation, for their undernourished tenants who were caught poaching.

Many of the local hills that are now Forestry Commission plantations, Holt, Wardown, Butser and Oxenbourne, used to be kept as warrens, as was extensive land at Priors Dean.[9] Despite Chewton Bunny near Christchurch and Bunny Copse at Mottisfont, there is limited sign today of the felt hatter's 'coney', the old name for the rabbit.[10] Warrens, or 'coney garths' were often situated within manorial parks. In 1236, an attempt was made to stock Bishopstoke Park from a warren at Bitterne, probably unsuccessful for Henry III could only order rabbits from three bishopric warrens in Hampshire, forty each from Bitterne and Merdon and a hundred from the Isle of Wight.[11] During the fourteenth century, rabbits seem to have become a more significant part of the diet of the Bishop of Winchester; warrens were developed outside of parks, notably at Longwood and Overton.[12] A man and his horse made eighteen journeys in 1361 from Overton over the pass at Four Marks to the bishop's household at Farnham carrying 632 coneys; perhaps the same man took another 322 rabbits from Longwood to Wolvesey at the time of St Giles's Fair.[13]

The rabbits were driven from their burrows by ferrets and caught in nets. At Bishop's Sutton in 1405, one large net called a *haye and twelve purse nets were bought for this purpose.*[14] Four Marks was at the centre of a plethora of important warrens, from Farnham to Crondall and from Micheldever to Alresford.[15]

Winter crops were first introduced into Britain in the 1790s. Within a few years, once secure warrens proved porous as the rabbits dashed for the freely available food. There was good cover at the field edge from a decreasing number of predators, like the stoat, reduced as more land was taken for the new crops.

The rabbit's appearance when he is being followed, even when his foe is at a distance behind his trembling frame, little hopping movements and agonizing cries may be heard distinctly three of four hundred yards away, remind us of our own state in a bad dream, when some terrible enemy, or some nameless horror, is coming swiftly upon us ...'[16]

By the 1820s, William Cobbett extolled the rabbit as country food.

'Rabbits are really profitable. Three does and a buck will give you a rabbit to eat for every three days in the year, which is a much larger quantity of food than any man will get by spending half his time in the pursuit of wild animals, to say nothing of the toil, the tearing of clothes, and the danger of pursuing the latter.'[17]

A Select Committee in 1840 noted that rabbits were 'universally condemned as mischievous vermin' as they destroyed valuable crops.[18] By 1880, the Ground Game Act gave occupiers of land the inalienable right to destroy rabbits on their holding. In 1917, with the country 'nearly starved out' by the German submarine onslaught, control orders were introduced under the Defence of the Realm Act. By 1939, with a population estimated at fifty million, rabbits were branded 'horrid liver-fluked ravenous animals' that were 'an absolute menace to British agriculture'.[19] That year, Four Marks enjoyed its own rabbit catcher, John White of Dovecot in Hawthorn Lane.[20] On the eve of Britain's myxomatosis outbreak, rabbits were estimated at 100 million. Never had the rabbit threat been more serious; never had a solution been more urgently needed.'[21]

Myxomatosis is caused by a poxvirus. The natural hosts are tapeti, cotton-tail rabbits, in South and Central America, and brush rabbits in North America where it causes only a mild infection.

'Myxomatosis is an excellent example of what happens when a virus jumps from a species adapted to it to a naïve host.'[22] The disease causes a severe and usually fatal disease in unaccustomed rabbits. European rabbits were taken to Australia in 1788 by early settlers as a food. Escaped rabbits became feral and their numbers soared causing immense damage to crops and to the land through grass destruction from eating. In 1937, myxomatosis was intentionally introduced in Australia to eradicate the wild populations. The strategy failed, as it has everywhere. Bunnies bounced back bolstered by their high reproductive rate and the emergence of myxomatosis-resistant animals. Over time, the virus attenuates and milder variants win over its more deathly cousins.[23]

The disease is commonly transmitted via mosquito or flea bites, but can also occur by the bites of mites, flies and lice which move from one rabbit to another. It can also be transmitted by direct contact with runny eyes, noses and genitals and from open wounds. The virus prefers males to females, adults to juveniles and peaks in the British spring, February to April, and autumn, August to January.[24] Pets are at great risk. Poxviruses are stable and can be spread by contaminated water bottles, feeders, cages and people's hands.

> *Myxomatosis was a brilliant means of extermination. Almost overnight, the wrangles between the eradicators and preservationists became irrelevant. A natural rabbit clearance operation was underway, and the sight of the dead or dying rabbits in roads and lanes, fields and hedges, woods and gardens, showed its effectiveness. Because the rabbit population fell rapidly, there were fewer animals to cause damage and corn output broke many records. For the first time in many years, it was worthwhile fencing part of the downland and introducing piped-water because the stocking rates for sheep and cattle rose as the rabbit population fell. For the first time, many farmers appreciated the real extent and cost of rabbit damage. There was only one drawback – myxomatosis is a ghastly disease.[25]*

Richard Adams' rabbit characters called it 'the white blindness'. Death occurs ten to twelve days after infection. It begins with a swelling, then fever, then secondary skin lesions, discharges, respiratory distress, hypothermia and compete closure of the eyelids.[26]

Reaction in Four Marks and its surrounding villages to the arrival of myxomatosis was mixed, but not evenly divided. In 1954, the village was still very much a small farming community with chickens, pigs and smallholdings. The governments' Myxomatosis Advisory Committee (MAC) estimated that the animals caused £38–50 million damage nationally each year, possibly more. For every rabbit grazing on one hectare of winter wheat, a farmer loses one per cent of its annual yield.[27]

> *On the other hand, the Ministry of Agriculture and Food (MAF) was concerned, rightly as it turned out, that rabbits might acquire immunity so that any decline in their numbers might prove temporary. In this event, while continuing to be plagued, the animals would have acquired a new disease to no purpose. Wild rabbits would lose their economic value. Few people would eat the meat from a diseased rabbit, even though it was safe.[28]*

Bunny lovers took up arms against anyone thought guilty of spreading the disease and wanted the practice made illegal. It was not a matter of economics, but one of ethics and public opinion. The horror of the use of gas in the extermination camps of a war just won was widely quoted. Some actions were beyond the pale. The RSPCA announced that it wanted a prohibition order and took advertisements in newspaper personal columns,

Stop the deliberate spreading of MYXOMATOSIS!
Victims of this horrible disease – blind, misshapen, tormented – are being caught for sale as carriers, to be let free in infection-free areas ... Nothing can justify this callous encouragement of animal suffering, and the RSPCA appeals for your moral and material support in demanding an immediate legal ban.

In the midst of the increasingly emotional debate, it was noticed locally that the rabbit population of Weathermore Woods, by the side of the old road leading from Alton Lane to The Shrave, was unaffected. Here, instead of the usual mottled grey animals, there was a large warren of black rabbits.[29] Black rabbits were carefully reared in some medieval warrens; their fur was sought after by hat-makers and for ornamental trimmings on clothing so perhaps this colony was a throwback.[30] It was a game for local children to creep onto the pockmarked mound and then, as one, stamp their feet. The sound from below the ground as the rabbits stampeded deeper was 'like an express train'.

One evening in the spring of 1954, two civilian cars and a Bedford military truck from Devizes arrived at the woods. Five young soldiers from the Wiltshire Regiment, tanned from recent service in Hong Kong, were placed by their

Black rabbit in the woods.

sergeant on perimeter guard surrounding the warren. Men from the cars used their headlamps to release ferrets, which drove several dozen black rabbits into nets and from there into cages on the lorry. Within thirty minutes, all was quiet and normal except for the small group of boys standing near the mound discussing what they had seen.

The visitors were from the Microbiological Research Department of the Chemical Defence Experimental Establishment at Porton Down, some nine miles from Salisbury. The complex of laboratories was the UK's most secret, and soon to be most controversial, military research facility.

Any virus of the potency of myxomatosis was of interest to Porton Down's scientists who had already worked with early strains, first to check about potential danger to the public, then to assess whether the virus could be adapted to eradicate the rabbit population, and finally, as was the nature of work at Porton Down, to see whether the disease had any military value. Black rabbits that might have some genetic tolerance were of immediate interest.

Porton Down opened in 1916 in response to the German use of chemical weapons the year before against two French colonial divisions at Ypres. From a standing start, expertise was quickly developed in chlorine, mustard gas and phosgene.[31]

In 1942, Porton Down famously carried out tests of an anthrax bio-weapon at Gruinard Island in the Inner Hebrides. Eighty imported sheep died and the island was abandoned because of its toxicity. It took the deposit of a bag of polluted soil at Porton Down's gate and another of suspect material in Blackpool during the Tory Party's annual conference to prompt remedial action over forty years later.[32]

During World War II, research concentrated on chemical weapons like nitrogen mustard. In 1945, a startling discovery was made in occupied Germany. The Nazis had developed and produced thousands of tonnes of new chemical weapons which were far more toxic than the known poison gases. The Allies were keen to capitalise on the advanced state of German technology into organophosphorous nerve agents like tabun, sarin and soman. Within two weeks, Porton scientists had tested tabun on volunteers, even though they had very little idea of its effects on the human body. For the next four decades and more, Porton ran an extensive programme of testing nerve gases on humans in often painful and unpleasant experiments.[33]

The extent to which the men from Porton Down were prepared to make tests on ill-prepared soldiers, and on larger numbers of an unknowing public, lay hidden for many years. The facility was trapped in a half-world of secrecy that lay between righteous criticism if they were found later not to be on the top of their game and disgust at some of the methods used to protect the nation.

The years after the war were a dark period of great embarrassment to later governments as abused volunteers and investigative journalists fought to get at the truth.

Porton Down's scientists sent fifty-six men into their gas chambers in 1950 and exposed them to 'low concentrations' of sarin. The human 'guinea pigs' were given no protection as well as no treatment. The results of the tests on humans were compared with those on rabbits which had been put in the chamber at the same time as the men to see how little sarin vapour was needed to trigger a reaction in both animal types.

Army regular Lawrence McAndrew volunteered in the early 1950s after he spotted an appeal for subjects for common cold research on the noticeboard of his base. Instead, he was exposed to nerve gas.

In late 1952, Porton Down again exposed 105 men to sarin vapour which had been pumped into a gas chamber. The men sat outside the chamber and breathed in gas through a kind of siphon. A quarter of them inhaled more than the maximum to which volunteers could be safely exposed.[34]

Controversial open-air trials over large swaths of Britain, particularly Hampshire, began in 1953. Porton scientists wanted to investigate how easily a huge cloud of deadly germs could be dispersed over Britain from a ship or plane off the coast. 'There was a very real concern that Britain as a small, vulnerable island could be devastated by this kind of biological warfare attack.'[35] The scientists decided that a marker chemical, zinc cadmium sulphide, should be released to simulate the path of the cloud. There were at least seventy-six trials over most of England and Wales. In the first trial, the chemical was emitted in an arc from a disused RAF station near Beaulieu in Hampshire northwards towards Newbury, Berkshire. Next year, in July, further tests were measured around Basingstoke.

The tragic affair of Ronald Maddison in 1953 was 'Porton's darkest hour of all its human experiments ... in one of Britain's squalid secrets of the Cold War'.[36] Maddison died shortly after sarin was dripped onto his arm. It was not until 1999 that detectives from Wiltshire police force in *Operation Antler* investigated his death and also examined the more general allegations that unsuspecting servicemen had been duped into taking part in chemical warfare experiments. It was the first time that the long programme of human experimentation at Porton Down was subjected to a criminal investigation by a police force.[37]

Maddison's death was found to be unlawful. The government lost its appeal and settled in 2006. The same year, 500 veterans claimed they had suffered from experiments and three were awarded compensation in an out-of-court settlement. Two years later, the MoD paid 360 veterans £3 million without admitting liability.

Up to 20,000 people took part in various trials from 1949 to 1989, which included tests into LSD and CS Gas. A quarter of a million animals – mice, guinea pigs, rats, pigs, ferrets, sheep, marmosets and rhesus macaques – died. Rabbits were extensively used as they were 'very effective detectors' of poison gases, 'rather like canaries in the coalmines of old'.[38]

Late in 1954, the whole of Weathermore Wood was closed to the public for a week. The public were told that a large black cat had been seen and might be dangerous to children. It was thought to be an escaped puma. No cat was produced. When the soldiers left, no black rabbit was left at the warren. That is, not until next year when they suddenly returned.

The two years from that date were well known in Four Marks for the carnage among the village's rabbit population. One could scarcely walk in the fields without finding a grey rabbit dead or wheezing its last, blind, and with its skin covered in pustules and lesions.

In 1998, a young farmer from Four Marks died three days after contracting septicaemia from handling a rabbit infected by myxomatosis on his family farm. He became unwell, developed a rash, collapsed and was taken to hospital in Winchester. A cocktail of sedatives, antibiotics, adrenalin and platelets failed. The post-mortem showed that he was infected with a bacterium that causes pasteurellosis, know as 'snuffles', most commonly but rarely caught from an animal bite. It was thought that the illness entered his bloodstream through a scratch on his hand. His illness was complicated by an unrecognised virus thought to belong to the myxomatosis family; a virus that, we are told, cannot leap species. A blood sample was sent for analysis.

Local hares, although from the leporidae, the same family as rabbits, are from a different species. In the last ten years, several have been found dead locally with recognisable myxomatosis skin symptoms.

The farmer's family started to ask questions and openly discussed the need for an inquest. One evening, they had an unexpected unofficial visitor. The conversation was brief and the couple were given two days to consider a financial offer, which was only being made, they were told 'because you lived near Weathermore Woods'. They accepted and signed a confidentiality agreement.

The mother died last year. I went to see the father a few months ago. Long retired, he has terminal prostate cancer and is disgusted with what he signed away for gain. He feels remorse that he let his son down by waiving a full autopsy and an inquest although the money has paid for his grandchildren's passage through university. It's through university contacts that I first came to hear of the story.

The old farmer is still very bitter that, as he put it, 'Those bloody scientists killed my son. I've missed him all my life. Well, they can't reach me now. I'm dying and the money's all gone.' He readily agreed to read what I have written and offered two messages:

'Don't touch a rabbit corpse near Weathermore Woods where there is any sign of myxomatosis. Always wear gloves if you have any cuts to your hands and handle dead rabbits.'

Today, in the United Kingdom, an annual vectored virus called Nobivac Myxo-RHD is available to protect rabbits. Isolation is imperative, but once caught there is no real treatment.[39]

ENDNOTES

[1] HMSO, *Report of the Committee on Cruelty to Wild Animals*, 1951 reprint.
[2] Carroll, *Alice's Adventures*, 1865. Potter, *Peter Rabbit*, 1902. Salten, *Thumper*, 1923. Milne, *Winnie-the-Pooh*, 1926. Schlesinger, *Bugs Bunny*, 1938. Disney, *Bambi*, 1942. Disney, *Song of the South*, 1946. Adams, *Watership Down*, 1972.
[3] Bartrip, 'Myxomatosis'.
[4] Heal, *Disappearing*.
[5] Bartrip, *Myxomatosis*.
[6] *The Scotsman*, 21/7/1954; Aberdeen Press & Journal, 5/8/1954; *Farmers Weekly*, 29/10/1954.
[7] Sheail, *Rabbits*.
[8] Veale, 'Rabbit in England'.
[9] Harvey, *History of the United Parishes*.
[10] Coates, *Place-Names*.
[11] *Hampshire Record Office*, Eccl 159372, 159405.
[12] Roberts, 'Deer Parks'.
[13] *Hampshire Record Office*, Eccl 159278.

[14] *Hampshire Record Office*, Eccl 159409. Roberts, 'Deer Parks'.

[15] Sheail, *Rabbits*.

[16] Hudson, *Hampshire Days*.

[17] Cobbett, *Cottage Economy*.

[18] *Select Committee on Game Laws*, 1840.

[19] Sheail, *Rabbits*.

[20] This property was an important part of the murder discussed in Chapter 15: 'The pub with no body'.

[21] Bartrip, *Myxomatosis*.

[22] Wikipedia.

[23] Davis, 'Darwin's rabbit'.

[24] Ross, et al, 'Myxomatosis in farmland rabbit populations'.

[25] Sheail, *Rabbits*.

[26] Meredith, 'Diseases of the rabbit'.

[27] *Daily Express*, 17/6/2019.

[28] Bartrip, *Myxomatosis*.

[29] Mills, *Four Marks*.

[30] Sheail, *Rabbits*.

[31] Carter, *Porton Down*.

[32] Carter, *Porton Down*.

[33] Evans, *Gassed*.

[34] *TNA*, WO 195/12084/11264, 'Exposure of men to sarin vapour'.

[35] Evans, *Gassed*.

[36] Evans, *Gassed*.

[37] Carter, *Porton Down*.

[38] *TNA*, WO 195/10813, 'Exposures of unprotected men and rabbits to low concentrations of nerve gas vapour', Porton Technical Paper 143, 12.1949. 'Once again Porton has refused to publish this report.'

[39] *MSD Animal Health*, Milton Keynes.

Reading list:

Bartrip, P.W.J., 'Myxomatosis in 1950s Britain', *Twentieth Century British History*, Vol. 19, Issue 1, 2008, pp. 83–105; *Myxomatosis: A History of Pest Control and the Rabbit* (Bloomsbury Academic, London 2020)

Carter, G.B., *Chemical and Biological Defence at Porton Down, 1916–2000* (HMSO, Norwich 2000)

Davis, Josh, 'Darwin's rabbit is revealing how the animals became immune to myxomatosis', *Natural History Museum*, 2020.

Evans, Robert, *Gassed, British Chemical Warfare Experiments on Humans at Porton Down* (Lume Books, London 2019)

Meredith, Anna, 'Viral skin disease of the rabbit', *Veterinary Clinics of North America: Exotic Animal Practice*, Vol. 16, No. 3, pp. 705–714, 2013

Roberts, Edward, 'The Bishop of Winchester's Deer Parks in Hampshire, 1200–400', *Proceedings of the Hampshire Field Club Archaeological Society*, Vol. 44, 1968, pp. 67–86.

Ross, J., Tittensor, A.M., Fox, AP and Sanders, M.F., 'Myxomatosis in Farmland Rabbit Populations in England and Wales', *Epidemiology and Infection*, Vol. 103, No. 2, 10/1989, pp. 333–357

Sheail, John, *Rabbits and their History* (David & Charles, Newton Abbot 1971)

Veale, Elspeth M, 'The Rabbit in England', *The Agricultural History Review*, Vol. 5, No. 2, 1957, pp. 85–90

19 GRADWELL'S NURSERY TALE
Explosives, grenade launchers and a shovel

FOUR MARKS
1902   BODY COUNT: 1

In a village like Four Marks where incomers from outside Hampshire keep swelling its ranks, you do get some oddballs turning up. The place to look for these exotic individuals is in the various government censuses and registers. The latest complete list that is partly available to the public is the 1939 Register, one of the most important twentieth century genealogical resources for England and Wales. The 1921 census becomes available for scrutiny next year, 2021, after a hundred-year wait to protect the secrets of the lives of the nation's citizens of that time. The 1931 census for England and Wales was destroyed by a storeroom fire in Hayes in 1942. No census was taken in 1941 because of the war, so the 1939 Register is the only national census-like resource available from 1922 to 1951.

Once war became inevitable, the British Government planned to issue National Identity cards to enable wide-scale mobilisation and to prepare for the eventual introduction of rationing.[1] Up-to-date statistics were needed. Some preparations had already begun for a census in 1941, so the Government capitalised on this work to take a register of the civilian population. With the country on the brink of war, many Four Marks villagers had already signed up, thirteen in the army, five in the Observer Corps and seven in the merchant and royal navies. On the home front, there were three special constables and thirty-four ARP (Air Raid Precautions) wardens.

Identity cards were issued immediately and these continued in use until 1952. The Government constantly updated the 1939 Register to take account of changes of address or deaths. When rationing was introduced in 1941, they planned it with updated information from the 1939 Register. Designed before computerisation, the Register eventually formed the basis of the NHS registration system, which is why today the health system is so inflexible.

The year 1939, just on the edge of living memory, is therefore a good place to start to look for the unusual. There is one proviso. If someone was born less than one hundred years ago, the government assumes they could still be alive and their personal information on the Register is withheld from public view. In Four Marks today, this rule applies to 448 people from the 1939 population of 1,574. Their entries are literally blacked out. Year by year, however, more names are released. This tardiness does highlight the lack of interactivity of modern records. Does anyone believe that 448 people from Four Marks who were alive in 1939 are still alive today?

Among the 1939 'oddballs', Albert Jackson was in the 'Decontamination Squad'. He lived near three fishmongers. Other unsuspected occupations included a miner, a weaver, a threshing engine driver, a rabbit catcher, a china merchant, a repairer of fountain pens, a YMCA secretary, a wholesale bookbinder, a photographic operator, a ship's chandler, a country house chef and, retired, a valet, a butler and two tea planters.

The dominant occupation for all those looking for 'get rich quick' schemes was poultry farming on smallholdings. There were thirty-four owner-occupied farms with nineteen employed poultry hands, a workforce of over seventy. Betty Mills, in her village history, suggested there were just fifteen farms in 1935. Few had less than a thousand chickens, all free range, with long houses holding between 500 and a thousand birds.[2]

'Chickens provided a living for many of the speculators who came here … however, many a poultry farmer left the village less well off than when they arrived.' The purchase of a first car seems to have been a turning point. 'Arrive in a car and leave in a wheelbarrow.' Miles of wire was dug into the ground to deter foxes. The country-wise knew the easier method of bending the wire backwards on the surface all around the pen. Foxes never grasp that by retreating a few feet from the net wall, they could find a simpler way in.

There was only one 'egg merchant', Henry Head who lived at Woodside in Blackberry Lane.

Richard Court at Kings Drake, Lymington Bottom, was a cricketing all-rounder who played eighteen times for Hampshire before the war ended his professional sporting career. Nora Morris was a professional singer living at Holberry, Willis Lane; Alfred Sanerachis(?), a 'refugee writer' at Santar (possibly current day 'Green Acres'), Alton Lane; John A. De Walton, an artist illustrator of Woodchester, Telegraph Lane;[3] Henry E. Arrow, an artist at

Arrow's Stores; Stanley B. James, an author and journalist at Rosedale, Alton Lane;[4] and Jessie Rickard, poultry farmer and novelist, with Denis Gwynn, a journalist and publisher, lived at Brislands House, Brislands Lane.

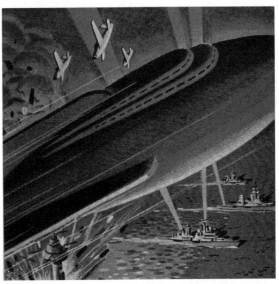

An illustration by John A. De Walton, Telegraph Lane,
from Percy F. Westerman's *The Flying Submarine*, 1912.

Rickard and Gwynn were important Irish literary and Roman Catholic figures of their day. Jessie Rickard, also Mrs Victor Rickard after her second husband who was killed at the Battle of Aubers Ridge in 1915, wrote over forty novels ranging from light comedy to detective stories, some of which found a large reading public. Together with Dorothy Sayers, G.K. Chesterton, Ronald Knox and others, she was a founder member of the *Detective Writers' Club*. It is possible that she penned *Murder by Night* while living in Four Marks.[5]

Gwynn, almost twenty years her junior, was steeped from birth in Irish patriotism. He was a journalist who wrote a dozen books on Irish

Bestselling author, Jessie Louisa Moore Rickard, 1876–1963 lived at Brislands House, Brislands Lane in 1939, pictured c. 1920.

political figures like Daniel O'Connell, Roger Casement, Éamon de Valera and William Smith O'Brien. *The Vatican and the War in Europe* (1940) was likely written in Four Marks. Rickard and Gwynn's lives were complicated. Rickard lived her final years at Gwynn's house in Montenotte, near Cork, where she was a close friend of Gwynn's wife, Alice, a Trudeau from north America. Alice's mother Hazel later became the wife of Irish artist John Lavery whose portrait of Hazel featured on Irish banknotes.[6]

However, both these writers missed a murder that had happened literally across the road.

I was sharing these and other stories with a group of old friends sitting around a long table at the *Castle of Comfort*. It was a relaxed evening with few egos on display. The guest beer was in good condition.

'You wouldn't have thought of Four Marks as a place where so many writers lived,' suggested Jim. 'Don't know why. Not dreamy enough, I suppose.'

'I've counted over fifty books that have been written by people there,' I offered. 'You can work anywhere as long as it's quiet. You just need to close the door to keep people away.'

'You still trying to put together a book of real-life murders?' asked Sam.

'Yup. I've got nineteen. I need one more. I wanted something a bit lighter to finish the book.'

'Hang on,' said Emily. 'I might have something for you.'

She got up and went to another table where a group of workmen were having a few lagers before going home to wash and change prior to going somewhere else for a few more lagers. After a couple of minutes of earnest conversation, she came back with a young lad with a shock of red hair and a struggling beard.

'This is Mr X,' she explained. 'He said he'll tell you his story as long as you don't identify him.'

'Deal, Mr X. Let me get some drinks in.'

Mr X took a long pull.

'Well, here it is,' he said. 'Some time ago, we were clearing ground at an old nursery in Brislands Lane. It used to be called Lymington Nursery. My job was to grub out the foundations of some of the glasshouses. The bricks they'd used were over a hundred years old and in good condition. The boss wanted them saved for another job. We were being pushed a bit because the owner'd got some heavy equipment booked.

Lymington Nursery in Brislands Lane, with greenhouses in the background, when owned by Henry Thomlinson, c. 1910.

'I was doing the shovel work. My mate had the small digger. Cut it short. We found a skull. Then we realised it was a whole body lying at the bottom of the old trench. It was covered in earth and a thin cement layer had been put on top to hold the bricks. We found some old coins, big pennies, and from the dates we worked out the bloke had probably been there from about 1900.

'We found something once before many years back and let people know. The police moved in and stopped worked for two weeks. The boss got really pissed. So we did a Plan B.'

'Plan B?' queried Charlie.

'Yeah, Plan B. We got the bones out quiet like and put them on the bonfire. Least said, soonest mended.'

'So, why's it a murder?' I asked.

'Well, maybe,' said Mr X. 'First off, the guy had a shovel underneath him, just like he's fallen on top of it. The rags he had left were real rough working clothes. Then, he was all covered over. My mate reckoned the guy who shovelled in the earth and poured the cement on top of him maybe didn't even know he was there.'

Mr X paused.

'Go on,' said Holly. 'You can't stop now.'

'Promise you won't tell who I am,' he said. 'I don't want no trouble with no law.'

There was a chorus of promises.

'Well, you see, his skull had a bloody great hole in it and there, right by his head, was this piece of jagged rock all blacked like it had been in a fire. It wasn't flint or anything like you might expect. It was a piece of hard rock, like from a larger boulder, like it had been in an explosion rather than a fire.'

'Have you got the rock?' asked Charlie. 'Might have been a meteorite?'

'Naw! Everything's gone. I kept the shovel, but the handle broke, rotted really, so I slung it. Could have been a space rock, I suppose.

'Bloody good shot it if was,' he offered. 'Thanks for the lager.'

That's where the story might have died except for two pieces of additional information.

The first I had known for some five years. I was out walking my dog Misty and was on my way home down Gradwell Lane when I fell to talking with an old chap who lived in one of the cottages. He was thinking about buying a flatcoat retriever and asked what I thought of them.

'Misty is typical,' I shared. 'They're called Peter Pan dogs. The day they grow up they die. Great with children. Not a bad bone in them. Part of the family.'

We got to discussing the cottages which sport a plaque high up with the build date of March 1902.

'Workers' cottages,' said my new friend as I accepted a cup of tea. 'Someone round here had a small farm, poultry and pigs and the like. This used to be Barn Lane then. It continues over Brislands Lane and down to the Winchester Road. The farmer wanted a couple of workmen on hand to look after the business and the animals so he put these up. Reasonable size, but we've put a garage on and added a glass extension on the back so we can get a view over to Kitwood and catch the evening sun.

'Funny thing was, when we put in the groundwork for the extension we found a large piece of granite, black it was, and cracked down the middle and split into smaller pieces. Looks like someone tried to shift it, maybe, when they built the cottages? My mate thought it was a meteorite. He'd seen one before.'

A few weeks after the pub conversation with Mr X, on a half-memory, I was checking through the census of Lymington Bottom around the turn of the nineteenth century. After a slow half an hour, I found what I was looking for. In 1901, Arnold Louis Chevallier, aged thirty-four, was 'living on his own means' with his wife Hannah, six years his senior, at Lymington House. Hannah was born in Barrow-in-Furness as were their three young children; Arnold was born in Geneva. There were three boarders: Marie Rough, a governess from Aberdeen; Frank Fairhead, an employed nurseryman from Leyton; and Arthur Weitzel, a farm manager born in London. Here was the connection with both a nursery and a farm that I remembered.

The Chevallier's basic history was easy to find. Ten years before, Arnold offered himself as a professor of languages while boarding with a bricklayer and his family in Camberwell, London. That same year, he married Hannah in Barrow. Hannah had a previous husband, George Banks Ashburner, who she married in Barrow in 1886. George, an iron ore merchant, had a previous wife. Perhaps, the older and widowed Hannah was an attractive financial match for Arnold, sufficient to raise him from a boarder to a man of means?

Arnold became a naturalised British citizen in 1896, interviewed in London, with documentation personally signed by the Home Secretary, Sir Matthew White Ridley. Arnold stated that he was a 'retired gentleman' of twenty-eight years, living at Moss-Side House in Barrow, a subject of Switzerland, with his wife Hannah where she gave birth to their three children, Aline Annie, Paul Etienne and Florence Renée. He gave his oath of allegiance in May before William Trimmer, solicitor, at his office in Alton High Street.[7]

In 1911, Arnold and Hannah still lived at Lymington House. Arnold's occupations had multiplied. He declared himself a mechanical engineer, a small arms and explosives manufacturing expert, also an inventor and a patentee. He was in the gun trade and also a farmer. It was quite a list. Most people, for instance, just recorded 'poultry farmer'. The children were almost grown up and the boarders had gone, perhaps to the new cottages?

How do I tie Arnold to the cottages? His wife, Hannah's, maiden name was Gradwell.

My theory was straightforward. Arnold, all gung-ho, built the cottages, naming them and the lane after his wife. The workmen hit a problem rather late in the day: an unexpected boulder right on the building line. Arnold was impatient. He put his supposed skills to work and blew the rock up. His measurements for his explosives were more enthusiastic than accurate. There was a shower of large debris. Nursery greenhouses were being built less than three hundred feet away across Brislands Lane. An unsuspecting workman was clearing a trench when a rock hit him on top of his head, caving in his skull and killing him instantly. He pitched forward on top of his shovel.

After the dust settled, there was no evidence to the casual eye. Early next morning, cement was poured into the waiting ditch.

It would be good for this story if Frank Fairhead, nurseryman, staying the year before with the Chevalliers, disappeared from the record after 1901. That would mean he could be the body in the ditch. However, it is not the case. Fairhead was brought to the trade by his father as a boy in Essex. He surfaces in a commercial list in 1924, at the wedding of a daughter in 1930 and in the 1939 Register in Staines. In 1911, the nursery was run by Henry and Louisa Thomlinson and his family from London, including daughter Louisa, aged ten. Their other daughter, Dorothy, age one, was the only one born locally which suggests the Thomlinsons might have moved in recently, perhaps because there was a vacancy.[8]

If all the facts were known at the time, I have to admit that Arnold Chevallier was probably not guilty of murder, but the unfortunate man was killed by Chevallier's actions. Perhaps manslaughter through carelessness or maybe an accidental death if heard by a friendly jury? Almost certainly, Chevallier never knew what happened.

We do know that Chevallier was still living at Lymington House in 1920.[9] His wife, Hannah, died in 1925 in Hampshire, aged sixty-nine. Here, sadly, her forgivable lie finally came out. She was not six years older than her husband, but twelve. Five months later, Arnold, aged fifty-seven, in this family of second marriages, wed again to Emma Farmer, twenty-three, of Alton. To move in a few months from a sexual partner of sixty-nine to another of twenty-three could be a shock to the system. Arnold died in Berkshire, aged eighty-two, in 1950, which might suggest an answer.

There it might end, but, like many good stories, there is a tailpiece.

I have to admit a serious miscalculation. I had written off Arnold Chevallier as a bombast; a young man who scratched a living teaching French and, perhaps German, while boarding with a bricklayer in London. A lucky marriage with an enthusiastic older widow provided him with capital, which eventually produced a ridiculously long tale of occupations for the 1911 census.

I was wrong. I ran a check with the US Patent Office for Arnold Chevallier and found a list of approved patents for serious weaponry filed in the US and the UK through to World War II. All were accompanied by detailed mechanical drawings and showed complex knowledge. One, filed first in 1915, explains improvements to small arms to make an automatic action more certain. At almost the same time, he posited an unusual shoulder-fired grenade launcher for use in the trenches of Flanders.[10] In 1926, in Great Britain, he sought to improve the workings of double barrel shotguns of the under-and-over type. Another invention, in 1932, on behalf of Chevallier Self Loading Fire Arms Limited of London, introduced reloading of rifles, shotgun and small arms by means of the power of the recoil. Each of these is interesting enough, but the third in 1926 adds another element for it was a joint application with Robert Churchill.

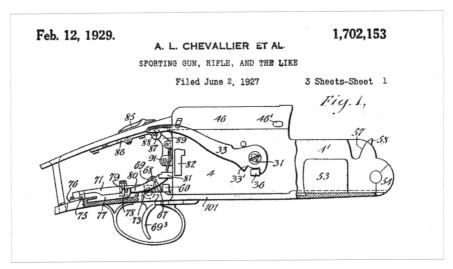

Part of a patent application for a sporting gun filed by Chevallier and Robert Churchill in the USA in June 1927. *US Patent Office*

Churchill was the most famous gunsmith in London between the two world wars. He was also the Metropolitan Police's gun expert and almost single-handedly responsible for dragging the science of ballistics into the twentieth century.[11] He was the prime witness in many of the most dramatic of the capital's murder cases.[12]

Churchill's biographer was MacDonald Hastings renowned war journalist, contributor to the *Eagle* boys' magazine and BBC TV personality of the 1960s. Hastings wrote, 'In the sensational cases in which he appeared, [Churchill's] arrival at the Assizes was a routine front-page picture for the evening papers … Churchill belonged to an age where, he said, "Counsel really prosecuted and juries glared at the prisoner in the dock throughout the trial. Now they are almost too shy even to look."'

There is no mention of Chevallier in Hastings' book.

ENDNOTES

1 www.findmy past.co.uk.

2 Mills, *Four Marks*.

3 *St Ives Times*: De Walton exhibited at the March 1923 Show Day while he lived at Abbey Cottage, St Ives. He worked in watercolours and drew the illustrations for Percy F. Westerman's *The Flying Submarine* (1912). Westerman was a prolific writer of children's literature, often centred on World War I.

4 James authored *The Men who Dared* (1917); 'Free Catholics', *The Month* (1923); *A Victorian Optimist* (1924); 'Dogma and Life', *The Month* (1925); *The Adventures of a Spiritual Tramp* (1925); *Christ and the Workers* (1938); 'Labour's Self Recovery', *Dublin Review* (1939) and *Becoming a Man* (1944), which will all cost you a pretty penny today.

5 *Cork Examiner and Irish Times*, 'Obituary', both 30/1/1963.

6 Gwynn, *Lost Ireland*.

7 *Certificate of Naturalization*, 8976, 8/5/1896. W Bradley Trimmer and Son, solicitors, are housed today in the same building.

8 1911 census.

9 *Kelly's Directory*, 1920.

10 Ferguson, 'Launcher'.

11 Churchill, 'Forensic Examination'.

12 Hastings, *Other Mr Churchill*.

Reading list:

Churchill, Robert, 'The Forensic Examination of Firearms and Projectiles', *The Police Journal*, Vol. 2, No. 3, 1929, pp. 367–379

Ferguson, Jonathan, 'The Blanch-Chevallier Discharger: A Shoulder-Fired Grenade Launcher for the Trenches', *Arms & Armour*, Vol. 11, Issue 2, 2014

Hastings, Macdonald, *The other Mr Churchill: A lifetime of shooting and murder* (Four Square, London 1963)

Official Gazette of the United States Patent Office, 1,454,039, 8/5/1923; 1,702153, 12/2/1929; 1,946,388, 6/2/1934

ONS, The 1939 Register

Reid, Colin, *The Lost Ireland of Stephen Gwynn* (Manchester University Press 2011)

Westerman, Percy F., *The Flying Submarine* (Musson, Toronto 1944)

20 THE MAD WOMAN AT BELFORD HOUSE

Hysteria and the younger female

FOUR MARKS

1908   BODY COUNT: 1

In the early 1900s, Alfred Harvey and his wife Eliza, both in their sixties, moved into Belford House, their recently-built, ten-room residence at the road bend near the middle of Lymington Bottom. Today, Belford House is a private residential home for elderly people. Alfred, christened Alphaeus, but evidently tiring of the unusual name, held many secrets for he knew intimately many of the richest people in England. In the loft of their new home, the couple installed their own dreadful embarrassment that they wanted desperately to keep to themselves.

Explaining why the Harveys did what they did needs an exploration of Alfred's career. I hope you think that his story is interesting enough in its own right. However, their legacy to Four Marks is much darker. In several ways, this is the most disturbing story in this book of murders.

In 2014, over a few months, I spread the word that I was looking for anecdotes about people who had been murdered in the village. I received several contacts

Belford House, c. 1920, with the old church opposite, now a ruin.

by email and telephone from individuals I didn't know with all sorts of mad-cap yarns. Most, I rejected out of hand. They were wind-ups that couldn't stand basic scrutiny. The post on one Tuesday brought a plain white envelope, locally franked, with my name and address typewritten. Inside was an alleged transcript, also typewritten, of a death notice from an unnamed newspaper.

Harvey, Eliza Eleanor: Born October 1887, St George, London; died December 1908, Ropley, Hampshire, aged twenty-one. May God forgive her.

Someone wasn't giving too much away. I sensed another made up story.

Eliza's death wasn't difficult to find.[1] She hanged herself over a hundred years ago from 'the stairs' at Belford House. The house has three floors. The upper stairs are not easy to hang yourself from. If you want to make a statement with your dangling body, the banister of the stairs to the left of the current main door would do the best job. The image would also be difficult to forget each time someone passed underneath. The death certificate put the 'May God forgive her' comment into perspective coming as it probably did from a man with a strongly religious background. Depending on your chosen church tradition, Alphaeus was the father of Joseph, the father of Jesus and of two of the apostles, Matthew and James the Less.

The identity of the newspaper was much harder to find. In fact, I failed. I checked the *Hampshire Chronicle, Hampshire Advertiser*, the *Portsmouth Evening News*, the newly formed *Farnham Herald* and *The Times* of London, the latter for reasons which will become apparent.

I decided to use the genealogical internet to go back to Eliza Eleanor's grandparents, perhaps the beginning, and hope the story unfolded.

Alphaeus was the last of four children born in Exminster, near Exeter in Devon, in 1839, to John and Jane Harvey. John was the village tailor and Jane helped in the business; their workshop home recorded as just a 'house in the village'. As soon as they could, the children scattered for employment; by 1861 all had left.

I guess you could say that Alphaeus, now Alfred, landed on his feet. He moved well over a hundred miles to Ramsbury in Wiltshire, a country home of Angela Burdett-Coutts, one of the wealthiest women in England. The house was called Littlecote and twenty-three-year-old Alfred was placed for training under the butler, Thomas Danford. Altogether, there were fifteen servants.

Burdett-Coutts was the daughter of Sir Francis, 5th Baronet, and Sophia, daughter of the banker, Thomas Coutts. In 1837, when she was twenty-three, Angela unexpectedly inherited £1.8 million (today equivalent to some £160 billion) from her step-grandmother. It is worth spending some time understanding Angela's lifestyle as it presented itself to a young Alfred fresh from a poor Devon village.

Lady Angela Burdett-Coutts, c. 1840. Unidentified painter, *National Portrait Gallery: NPG 6181*

After her enrichment, Angela Burdett-Coutts became the subject of great public curiosity receiving numerous offers of marriage. She spent much of her time at Holly Lodge Estate in Highgate, just outside London, famous for her receptions, and also lived part of each year at Ehrenberg Hall near Torquay. Perhaps, Alfred's very first employment in the household was here near to his own home.

Burdett-Coutts was a great friend of Charles Dickens (who dedicated *Martin Chuzzlewhit* to her) and prime ministers William Gladstone, Benjamin Disraeli and the Duke of Wellington. Angela proposed marriage to the duke despite the great disparity in their ages. When Angela was sixty-seven, she shocked polite society by marrying her twenty-nine-year-old secretary, American William Bartlett. Through a clause in her step-grandmother's will concerning marriage to foreign nationals, she had to give up three-fifths of her income to her sister.

Burdett-Coutts will best be remembered as a philanthropist. She founded, with Dickens, a home for young women 'turned to a life of immorality'. She was a benefactor to indigenous Africans, and to the Church of England, building two churches and endowing church schools and the bishoprics of Cape Town and Adelaide. She erected the Greyfriars Bobby Fountain in Edinburgh, was a co-founder of the London Society for the Prevention of Cruelty to Children (RSPCC) and sponsored the Royal Society for the Prevention of Cruelty to Animals (RSPCA), the search for drinking water in Jerusalem, explorations to the Holy Land and Africa (David Livingstone and H.M. Stanley), built the Columbia Market in Bethnal Green, London, and pioneered social housing and, with Florence Nightingale, nursing missions.

Delightfully, she was president of the British Goat Society; her surname became Cockney rhyming slang for 'boots', and, in 1878, in a service at Westminster Abbey attended by Edward VII, she was buried standing up because there was so little room for new coffins.

She appeared in George Macdonald Fraser's *Flashman's Lady*, James Brooke's *The White Rajah* and Terry Pratchett's *Dodger*. George Meredith wrote a poem in her memory.

The Littlecote servants must have held their breath each time Burdett-Coutts arrived to stay.

At thirty-two, Alfred Harvey arrived in Curzon Street, Mayfair, London, where he was in second position among the twelve servants attending Charles and Olivia, the Earl and Countess of Tankerville. Charles Bennet, the 6th earl, was styled Lord Ossulton before handing the title to his eldest son. Bennet, a landowner and Conservative politician, was Captain of the Gentlemen-at-Arms assigned to the personal protection of Victoria at the beginning of her reign. The Queen then appointed him personally to Lord Steward of the Royal Household. Bearing a white staff as the emblem and warrant of his authority, he was the first dignitary of the court. His family seat was at Britain's 'most haunted' Chillingham Castle in Northumberland.

Charles's wife, Olivia, was the eldest daughter of George Montagu, 6th Duke of Manchester, at Kimbolton Castle, Huntingdonshire, the final home of King Henry VIII's first wife, Catherine of Aragon.

Unkind, perhaps, but while Alfred Harvey may have moved downmarket with regard to the wealth of his new employer, he could not have moved closer in the circle intimately surrounding the British sovereign. Who knows whom he met and where he went as he conducted his duties? Certainly, Alfred's professional and presentational skills in pandering to the requirements and smoothing the daily paths of his social betters were now finely honed.

To put it another way, anything which upset his standing and acceptability to the aristocracy might well be taken as a personal attack on his integrity.

To understand what happens later, it is important to have some feel for Victorian Curzon Street. In 1871, on census night in April, living cheek by jowl were, for example, William Cowper-Temple, 1st Baron Mount Temple, Liberal member of Parliament, and for some years private secretary to his uncle, the Prime Minister Lord Melbourne, who so decisively put down the Hampshire Swing Rioters;[2] William Wentworth FitzWilliam Dick, one of the Conservative members for Wicklow, Ireland; General Sir George Bowles, one-time colonel of the 1st West India Regiment, and lieutenant of the Tower of London, and for those of you who enjoyed Sean Bean as 'Sharpe', fought with the Coldstream Guards at the battles of Talavera, Salamanca and Vittoria,

the capture of Madrid, the sieges of Ciudad Rodrigo, Badajos, Burgos and San Sebastian, the passages of the Nive, Nivelle and Adour, the investment of Bayonne, the battles of Quatre Bras and Waterloo, and the occupation of Paris.

A few doors away were the Earl and Countess of Dartrey in the county of Monaghan, Ireland; Lord Cremorne, Lieutenant Colonel in the Coldstream Guards; Edward Dawson, a commander in the Royal Navy, and Lady Mary Dawson, his sister; Sir G.E. Nugent, baronet and Jean Nestor Tirard, the Queen's hairdresser.

deputy lieutenant for Buckinghamshire; and much more of the same until, at number 39, Monsieur Jean Nestor Tirard from Calvados, France, hairdresser to the Queen.

In the twenty-two houses between the residence of the Earl of Tankerville and Curzon Chapel there were forty-three couples and their children cossetted by 111 servants: butlers, under butlers and valets; coachmen and grooms; footmen and boys; maids for the ladies and the house, kitchen and parlour; housekeepers and cooks; governesses and nurses and general servants.

Alfred moved during the 1870s to become house steward at Harewood House in Yorkshire, one of England's premier buildings and home to the Lascelles, since married into the royal family through Mary, Princess Royal, the only daughter of George V. The Lascelles confirmed their wealth by buying West Indian plantations and slaves in the late seventeenth century, much to their current embarrassment. Alfred, in effect, ran the house for Henry Thynne Lascelles, 4th Earl of Harewood, who had fourteen children through two wives. Lascelles was a great benefactor to local hospitals in Leeds. Some of the employment records of Harewood survive; Alfred earned £80 a year.[3]

Harewood House. *Gunnar Larsson, commons.wikimedia.org/w/index.php?curid=435429*

The money was sufficient to support a wife and family. Alfred, aged forty-one, married Eliza Dearsley, aged thirty-three, in her home town of Hilgay in Norfolk, a long way from Harewood. Her father, James, was a master bricklayer, who with Mary had eight children. Eliza's parents never left Hilgay and Eliza was seemingly put out to service as soon as was practicable. There is a probable brief sighting of her, age thirteen, in 1861, in domestic service to a mechanic's family in West Bromwich.

Who knows at this time and distance but, given the disparity in age, location and, above all, situation, one hopes that it was a love match between Alfred and Eliza? The change in circumstance for the bride must have been bewildering. The couple 'lived out' at Harewood in 'The Stank', a run of superior estate workers' cottages built a hundred years before by Edwin Lascelles, the 1st Lord Harewood.

For those interested in popular culture, Elton John and Westlife have performed concerts in Harewood's grounds, the house was used as a location for *Victoria*, *Downton Abbey*, *Mary Berry's Country House at Christmas*, the comedy film *King Ralph* and, since 1996, part of the estate was developed into a permanent village for the ITV soap opera *Emmerdale*.

Between 1882 and 1884, there was a significant turn of fortune for the Harveys. Alfred was installed as 'proprietor' of the Hotel Curzon. This was no mean establishment, but a plush meeting place and overflow house, as contemporary photographs show, for the guests of the inhabitants of Curzon Street. I place 'proprietor' in quotes because it suggests ownership. Buying a place in Mayfair would cost more than could be saved on an £80 annual salary at Harewood.

Yet, in 1891, Alfred and Eliza were resident at numbers 59–60: five floors, a basement and an attic, and including, around the corner, 23–24 Bolton Street, with three young children and six staff. The three children were Alfred John, born in Harewood, and Percy Daniel and Eliza Eleanor, both born at the hotel.

The Harveys had come into money and, of course, one looks to one of Angela Burdett-Coutts, Charles Bennet, the 6th earl of Tankerville, or Henry Lascelles, 4th Earl of Harewood as the provider on unknown terms: an investment, a loan, a gift for exceptional service, perhaps. Whatever the source, the money stuck, not disappearing in interest repayments or extravagances.

Then there is a conundrum. In 1901, a twenty-six-year-old bookkeeper, Myrza Greenfield is the 'head' of the Hotel Curzon household with twenty-one

Hotel Curzon, exterior and lounge, 59-60 Curzon Street, (and 23-24 Bolton Street), Mayfair, 1907. © *Historic England, BL19939, BL19940/002*

servants, perhaps some of them personal to the ten hotel guests from England, the USA, Ceylon and Ireland.

And the whereabouts of the Harveys, not yet installed in Four Marks? Eliza is living in Herewood House, Enfield, north of London with two of her children, Alfred John and Eliza Eleanor. Herewood House had no connection with Harewood House. Next door is Charles Dearsley, Eliza's brother, with his family, a brick manufacturer, their father's trade. Alfred Harvey spent the night in a boarding house down in Deptford near the river.

I was puzzling over what might be going on – selling of the hotel, waiting for completion of the new Four Marks property, marital problems, a distancing by the third child Percy, now seventeen – when I received a second letter from my 'informant': the same plain white envelope with typewritten name and address. The contents were more peremptory:

Eliza Eleanor was a wayward young lady. There was trouble in the family. Have you found this out yet? Let me know what you have discovered. Leave your notes in an enveloped marked 'Box 27' pinned to the noticeboard in the Four Marks Post Office.

I thought the cloak and dagger a bit silly. I had no wish to become involved in the private affairs of some obsessed person especially when they knew my address. However, I was intrigued by the Harveys' story. I had been told of the suicide and found it to be true. The implication was that there was far more to it. I decided to go one step further. My notes were typed up anyway so I did what I was told and pinned them to the board.

'Details of owners of box numbers are confidential,' I was told sharply.

So, Eliza Eleanor was thought 'wayward'. The choice of word suggested a female's delicacy rather than male bluntness. Did Eliza have an eye for an unsuitable partner? Or many partners? Had the money of Curzon Street provided too many unearned graces and too much of an allure?

While I waited for more hints, I decided to see whether I could track down any more of the Harveys after the move to Enfield. There was a jumble of information.

In 1907, Percy turned up at Herewood House in an apartment of five rooms over two floors for which he was paying £26 a year. His mother and two siblings had gone, but his father was there also, at least, I assumed that was the identity of 'A.A. Harvey'.

It was the following year that Eliza Eleanor died. The census for 1911 was a sad affair if you knew the background. Alfred and Eliza were together again but in their new home at Belford House. Alfred, aged seventy-one, had bought himself a farm and was employing labour; one suspects a poultry farm as that was the current Four Marks fashion.[4] Their son, Alfred John, aged twenty-eight was sticking close, of 'no occupation'; not 'unemployed', but not needing to work. There was no sign of Percy.

It seems like Alfred soon took ill, perhaps the shock of finding his daughter, perhaps not wanting to live walking under the banisters several times a day, perhaps a broken heart. His Devon family, parents and three brothers, were all long dead. Alfred and Eliza bought a property called Avington in Crabton Close Road in Boscombe, maybe for the sea air.[5]

When Alfred died in 1914, this son of a poor village tailor left almost £8,000, nudging close to £1 million at today's values. There was no indication of where the money had gone. I assumed to Eliza. Probate was granted to two presumed friends from the Alton area, not to rich friends in London or acquaintances from Curzon Street, and not to either or both of his sons.[6] John Albert Hayden was a grocer and a baker in East Worldham and James Biggs Longman, one-time butcher and then a farmer at Theddon Grange, lived in one of the premier local country houses at Wivelrod.

Eliza, eight years younger than her husband, died in 1928 in Alton, at some time probably moving back to the area to be near one or both of her sons.[7]

Alfred John, unmarried, was at Rawdon House, 78 High Street, Alton, next door to the current *Ivy House*.[8] He lived there at least from 1927 through to 1939, still 'independent'. Minnie Withers lived in and did the domestic work.

When his parents moved to the South Coast, Percy joined them and married Edith Harding who was already carrying the first of three daughters. This family moved into Belford House while Percy had set up his own motor engineering business, Foster & Harvey in Station Road in Alton.[9]

At some time in this saga, one or more of the children moved into Lymington Farm, the old *Lymington Arms*, later bought from the Harveys by the Read family, local farmers and butchers. 'The place was a tip with many roof leaks and rooms full of rot and rubbish. My father was told that there had been a big family fight after which everything had been burned. The children were a classic case of not knowing how to handle money and ended with nothing.'[10]

I was mulling Percy's probate when I received my third envelope. Percy, then of Seafield Road, Southbourne, Hampshire, died in 1935 in a local hospital, a little over fifty years old. He left all his estate to his wife: £114 0s 3d.

I thought you would be better than this. Eliza Eleanor lost a baby in childbirth. She went mad. Her parents locked her in the attic for over a year. Everyone pretended she was dead.

Several things fell loosely into place. Eliza Eleanor had lived at a time when lunacy law amendments had failed to win time in a crowded Parliamentary agenda. The leader of the Conservative opposition, Lord Sainsbury, told peers that 'something had to change in order to prevent the inconvenient being falsely imprisoned by their relatives or spouses.[11] 'Motives of that kind were familiar in fiction,' he said, but he feared that 'they were not altogether strange in real life'. Literary and non-fiction melodramas both played their part in bringing home to the legislature the mechanics of malicious incarceration.

I asked a friend of a friend for a private tour of the Belford House attic. There were just two rooms up a narrow staircase, one more of a storeroom with a water tank, but the other quite a large and well-appointed bedroom. What upset me was that there had evidently once been bars on the windows. Why put bars upstairs and not on the two floors underneath? The bedroom door had once held a clasp lock for a padlock. There were two holes in the door jamb for long-disappeared bolts.

I remember making a poor joke about keeping the maids under control. My friend said she thought the room too well decorated for servant's quarters.

'A lot of this furniture is good Victorian oak,' she offered. 'It's always been here.'

If I took my bossy informant's letters at face value, it looked like Eliza Eleanor had 'got into trouble'. Could it be that her mother had taken her to Enfield away from a threat at the Hotel Curzon? Had the inherent disgrace been such that Alfred or Eliza felt forced to sell up and leave? Surely, Alfred, with his rags to riches experiences and his intimate knowledge of all those country houses, would have been more resilient? But, then, we were talking about the turn of the century. Perhaps, the loss of the baby – stillborn or killed at birth, mangled in a bungled abortion or slipped away to be handed to who knows who – had made Eliza temporarily unstable? Was the locking up the result of a desperate desire to keep Eliza out of a harsh institution? Was it punishment? Or was it because of her parents' shame?

Eliza may have been pining for her lost child, but, equally, she might have been longing for her lover? She might well have been seriously mentally ill?

When Alfred placed his supposed advert, what was he asking God to forgive? I had thought the suicide, but perhaps he meant that a baby outside of wedlock was the greater crime? A lot might depend on who the father was, whether he had been named, and whether there was great disgrace in that knowledge? Had money changed hands? Was he rich and famous, low and unacceptable or, perhaps, too close to home?

If the letter was correct, Eliza had been locked in a room for over a year, with barred windows, seeing no prospect of release. That might be enough to drive anyone mad. Then, one night with everyone asleep, she found her bedroom unbolted. After trying the locked outside doors, she decided there was no hope. Standing alone in the almost black hallway, rather than return to her room, she made her final decision, assuming, of course, that it was her decision.

I left my latest set of notes fixed to the Post Office noticeboard marked for the attention of 'Box 27'.

I decided to read up on insanity among women in Victorian times, not for clues so much, but because I thought a great wrong had most certainly been done. I needed some context. My instinct was that it most probably was suicide, but it was also as close to murder as one could get.

What I found when the books arrived horrified me. These days, postnatal depression and anxiety are addressed with some compassion. In Eliza's time, women who suffered from these conditions, or alcoholism, senile dementia or social transgressions such as infidelity, moral insanity as they called it, were often confined at home or in an asylum.[12] Women were thought to be at particular risk of mental illness caused by supposed disorders of the reproductive system. Male doctors saw hysteria everywhere and women's sexuality was a prime focus.

Some believed that mental conditions could be identified through the new science of photography and worked to capture 'the exact point that had been reached in their scale of unhappiness'.[13] Treatments were often as bizarre as they were dangerous: electroconvulsive therapy, long periods of solitary incarceration, chained and shackled; experimental drugs; calomel[14]; antimony, now used in fire retardants; leeches placed on the pubis and lengthy, freezing baths or showers to cool fevered brains and sexual organs.

Many of the private homes that offered 'services', often run by non-medical men, did little more than lock people away. Anyone able to persuade two doctors to sign certificates of insanity could cause inconvenient or embarrassing female relatives to disappear, especially if that gave them access to the 'patient's' private wealth. Self-harm was frequent; death unremarked. There was little incentive for the asylum, living on the profit from fees, to discharge anyone.[15]

The fourth letter arrived as I was reading a mental health charity website. 'Mind' recognised that, today, almost twenty per cent of women in the UK have a mental health disorder, compared to thirteen per cent of men.[16]

My informant's mood and tone had shifted. I felt a cold breath pass over me. In my conceit, I had thought of myself as the hound off the leash chasing information in a spirit of righteousness. That wasn't the case at all. I had been the hare, guided down paths overhung with thick branches that kept out the sunlight. I had become the prey, gullible and duped. These letters had little to do with the sad death of an unfortunate young women.

© Bethlem Royal Hospital Archives

You really are stupid. You care more for some Godless whore than for a real woman in distress. I may have to punish you. Can't you see what is staring you in the face? I give you all this help and you let me down. What happened to Alfred's money? My money. This is your last chance.

Photographic proof: Emma Riches: Insanity caused by childbirth, mid-nineteenth century. *Henry Hering, Bethlem Royal Hospital Archives*

I sat down with a drink and had a long think. Broadcasting across Four Marks that I was looking for stories with evidence of murder may not have been the brightest idea. People who live with murder in the family may themselves not be balanced. This avaricious woman, who had played me, sounded as if she needed rapid medical attention.

I thought it time to call a halt. I wrote my last note to 'Box 27'. I said I knew nothing about the whereabouts of any money, nor was I going to search for it. The police had been informed. Post Office staff had been instructed to photograph the person who collected this note. If my informant wanted to stay out of prison, she should go quietly into the night.

It's been some time now and nothing has happened to me. There have been no more letters. The Harveys are often in my thoughts. I did check on the Ancestry website about six months ago with a morbid curiosity about some fact I thought I had missed. I noticed that against the entries for Alfred and Eliza and their family, that someone new was researching. Errors of fact that I had let pass by had been corrected. Some of my discovered information had been added. There was a contact facility, but I left well alone.

I still double lock my door at night. I have a new friend, an Alsatian called Max. I've decided to stop writing this book.

ENDNOTES

1 Alresford (the old registration district) 2c 93, 4Q 1908, covering Ropley, the old parish, before the establishment of Four Marks in 1932.
2 Chapter 6: 'Knowing one's place'.
3 harewood.org.
4 Chapter 20, 'Gradwell's nursery tale'.
5 By 1928, this property was a small private school.
6 Probate record, ancestry.
7 This is a best guess from limited records.
8 Kelly's Directory, 1927. 1939 Register.
9 Kelly's Directory, 1920.
10 Norman Read, 2020.
11 Wise, Inconvenient People.
12 Wallace, Painted Bridge.
13 Dr Hugh Diamond of photographic portraits, Henry Hering, 1850s, Bethlem Hospital archive.
14 A mercury chloride compound, beautiful black, a miracle drug used to cure almost any disease.
15 Daily Mail, Wallace, 12/5/2012.
16 mind.org.uk, accessed 2018.

Reading list:

Reade, Charles, *Hard Cash* (London 1868)

Stevens, Mark, *Life in the Victorian Asylum, The World of Nineteenth Century Mental Health Care* (Pen & Sword, Barnsley 2015)

Wallace, Wendy, *The Painted Bridge* (Simon & Schuster, London 2012)

Wise, Sarah, *Inconvenient People: Lunacy, Liberty and the Mad-Doctors in Victorian England* (Vintage, London 2013)

FOUR MARKS TIMELINE:

From the perspective of this book

BC	Prehistoric pathway on upper southern slope of Four Marks ridge
	Possible meteorite in Gradwell Lane
200–300	Roman road through Chawton Park Wood
407	Saxon raid on Roman villa at Old Down Wood
1189	Bishop de Lucy constructs dam to hold a great fish pond in Alresford
1237	Servant of merchant Hector Arras robbed in the Pass of Alton
1248	Murdered stranger found by Richard Squirrel in the Pass of Alton
	Theft of £100,000 from two Brabant merchants in the Pass of Alton
1249	Trial in Winchester of robbers at the Pass of Alton and of corrupt local jurors
	Half of defendants are freemen of Alton and district
	Richard Kitcombe of Kitwood hanged for providing food to outlaws
	Walter Bloweberme defeats Hamo Stare in trial by combat
	Hamo Stare left to rot at Gibbet Copse at head of the Pass of Alton
1261	Henry ll's baggage train robbed in the Pass of Alton
1267	Henry ll defeats Adam de Gourdon in face-to-face combat.
1272	Adam de Gourdon attacked and loses prisoners in the Pass of Alton
1273	King's Highway (Henry II) broadened by clearing trees 200 feet either side
1280	Suspect charter found claiming improvements to Itchen Navigation
1318	Silver and a horse belonging to William Micklepayn stolen in the Pass of Alton
1400s	The Dark Ages
1559	John Knight of Chawton bequeaths ten shillings to mend The King's Highway
1605	John Knight of Chawton contributes to the upkeep of the The King's Highway
1644	Battle of Cheriton
	Murder of Royalist musketeer Rupert Pinchin and two men in Blackberry Lane
	Hanging of Richard Kiddle in Farnham
1652	All lands of John Pinchin of Shalden confiscated

1665   Act to improve the Itchen Navigation

1709   'Violent petition' against enclosure of Ropley Commons

1710   Completion of Itchen Navigation from Southampton to Winchester

Enclosure of Ropley Commons

1740   Enclosure of Chawton Common

1749   Enclosure of Farringdon Common

1753   Act to widen and make good the Winchester turnpike (to become the A31)

1798   Proposal to build a canal tunnel between Alresford and Alton rejected

Death of a pauper boy on the Alton to Winchester turnpike

1807   Proposal to build a canal from Ropley to Rotherfield Park using a barge railway

1809   Proposal to build a second canal tunnel between Alresford and Alton rejected

1810s   Lavender cousins run smuggling network from Ropley and Portsea

1822   Thomas Goddard surveys sites for a semaphore line from London to Plymouth

1825   William Cobbett rides through Chawton Park Wood

Attempt on life of Vicar of Ropley by smugglers

1828   William Howley appointed Archbishop of Canterbury

1829   George Ogbourn takes over Farringdon Semaphore Station

1830   Sam Claythorne, naval handyman, hanged by Ropley residents

George Ogbourn's *Court of Inquiry* at Portsmouth

Food price and wage riots in Alton, Bighton, Headley, Holybourne and Selborne

Robert Maggs arrested at Lymington Arms

1831   Trial in Winchester of the Hampshire 'Swing' rioters

1833   Robert Maggs hanged in Melbourne, Australia

1847   All semaphore crews made redundant

1849   Enclosure in Newton Valance

1861   Alphaeus Harvey is butler to Angela Burdett-Coutts, the UK's richest woman

1863   Murder of Irish workmen at the *Shant*

1867   Murder of Fanny Adams

Murder of Frederick Baker

1868   Medstead station opened

1869   Last barge travels the Itchen Navigation from Southampton to Winchester

1871	Alphaeus Harvey is butler to the Earl and Countess of Tankerville
1880	Alphaeus Harvey manages Harewood House for the 4th Earl of Harewood
1882	Alphaeus Harvey takes over the Hotel Curzon, Curzon Street, London
1891	House building using local materials opposite the *Windmill Inn*
1894	Homesteads Limited buys site of Carterton, Oxfordshire
1895	Purchase of Four Marks land by William Carter
1896	Double auction of Lymington Farm Estate
1897	Sale of Carter's Herbert Park estate in Four Marks
1900s	Bungalow building in Blackberry, Alton and Willis Lanes
	Eliza Eleanor Harvey locked in the attic of Belford House
1902	Arnold Chevallier builds Gradwell Lane cottages; blows up 'meteorite'
	Nursery worker accidentally killed in Brislands Lane
	Marianna Hagen buys land, J.J. Tomlinson donates price, for first school
	Religious services held in school
1908	Eliza Eleanor Harvey hangs herself from stair balcony at Belford House
	Mariana Hagen establishes 'iron' church mission opposite Belford House
1909	James Worthington agrees there is life on Mars
	Hilaire Belloc seeks the Pilgrims' Way in Blackberry Lane
1910	Social and multi-purpose Institute formed, meets in borrowed premises
1912	Large Four Marks and Medstead land sale by Winchester College
1913	Opening of observatory in Blackberry Lane
	Edward Thomas cycles through Four Marks
	Opening of Institute building on site of today's village hall
1914	Edward Thomas discovers the 'Wild Girl' and writes 'Up in the Wind'
	Alphaeus Harvey dies leaving almost £8,000
1914–30	Arnold Chevallier submits armament patents
1919	Death of Walter Schmitz, U-boat commander
	Closure of observatory in Blackberry Lane
1920s	Clement Vavasor Durell writes mathematical books reaching world record sales
1930s	John A. De Walton producing illustrations for best-selling authors
1932	Four Marks civil parish formed
	Flyers Amy Johnson and Mildred Bruce use field off Alton Lane as landing strip

1935	Old *Windmill Inn* demolished
1937	Re-naming of railway station to 'Medstead & Four Marks'
1939	Prominent Irish writers Jessie Rickard and Denis Gwynn live in Brislands Lane
1940	Rickard, *Murder by Night*, and Gwynn, *The Vatican & the War in Europe*, written
1940s	Development of scrap yard at Dovecot, Hawthorn Lane
	Significant war debris fell on Four Marks
1942	Death of Henry Oggier, valet and refractor telescope owner
1953	Church of the Good Shepherd built, later extended
1954	Myxomatosis arrives in Four Marks
	Black rabbits taken from Weathermore Wood
1960	Multiple deaths of elderly Four Marks residents
1962	Death of visitor at the *Pub with No Name*
1978	Bulgarian writer Georgi Markov dies from poisoned umbrella tip in London
1980	Death of James Worthington, astronomer, in Florida
1991–93	Horse mutilations in Four Marks
1993	Four Marks targeted by out-of-county con artists
1998	Young farmer from Four Marks dies after handling a rabbit with myxomatosis
2000s	Human bones burned in Brislands Lane
2014	Four Marks residents asked to contribute murder stories for book
2017	Sri Lankan mother and child disappear
2018	Four Marks troll commits suicide
2019	Young drug seller dies under interrogation by local parents
	Suspected people smuggler killed after several overnight stops in Four Marks
2020	*The Four Marks Murders* published

CONCLUSION

The murder capital of Southern England

A BRIGHT SUNSHINY DAY

Shortly after eleven on Wednesday, 10 June 1896, a steam locomotive eased to a halt at Medstead Station. It brought the last train that morning on a unique, non-stop service from Waterloo. Those who bought an early newspaper for the journey could have believed that the only important event in the capital that day had already happened: the hanging at Newgate two hours before of sixty-year-old Amelia Dyer, one of the most prolific serial killers in history.[1] Over thirty years, she was later estimated to have murdered almost 400 infants in her care.

Dyer's drop would not have been the only topic on the train. All the 2s 6d single seats were taken. At Medstead, every passenger disembarked to form an almost orderly line. A representative of the Land Company, of Cheapside in London, led the crocodile just over half a mile to a large marquee pitched near the junction of Lymington Bottom and Blackberry Lane. May had been the driest month for many years, not beaten by a worse record until 2020.[2] The June sun sent temperatures climbing to over twenty-eight degrees.

In the stuffy tent, the travellers inspected plans of 145 'small villa farm sites' ranging from 50 x 500 feet to two, three and five acres, part of the 'Lymington Park Estate near Medstead'.[3] There was no mention of 'Four Marks'. The intending buyers gazed at models of cottages they could order, £100 for brick and £80 for wood, supplied by Messrs Allen & Co of Charing Cross. The more adventurous might have showed interest in a 'bold hotel corner plot'. There were also twenty-five 'shop and cottage' opportunities.

Adverts for the sale had been placed exclusively for the last month in *The East London Advertiser,* the *Westminster Gazette,* the *Essex Guardian* and *The Tower Hamlets Independent and East End Local Advertiser.*[4]

More than half of the 'very choice' freehold sites, the 'cheapest and highest on the market', had been bought at the first auction in April.[5] This day was to be the last chance to own a piece of this 'lovely rural rustic part of sunny

Hampshire, within easy drive of Winchester City and Cathedral, and near the celebrated Sir Roger Tichborne's Rich Estates'.[6]

With favoured plots selected, the substantial luncheon, free to buyers, began at noon: cold beef, ham, pies, cheese, salad and beer with juices for the ladies. At 1.30, directly the plates were cleared, the auctioneer mounted a platform and began his work.[7]

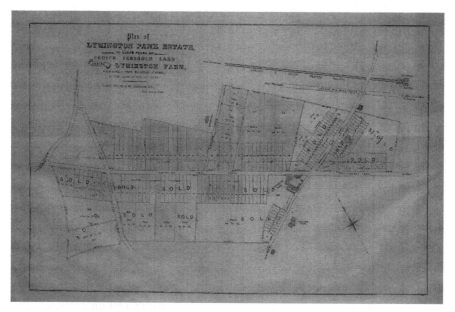

Photograph by Michael Huggan

After some two hours, the community of Four Marks was born. Within five years, the population of this small area to the south and east of the London to Winchester road had almost trebled to close to 250 people with over thirty new homes.[8] Those whose bids were successful received free return train tickets, free deeds, abstracts and plans, suffered no tithe or land taxes and heard the happy news that legal costs were kept to a minimum by being shared across all buyers. There was also a choice between outright purchase or a ten per cent deposit followed by sixteen quarterly payments.[9]

These people who visited this unknown and unremarkable empty quarter of Hampshire came from all parts of London. Policemen were reported good purchasers at a similar contemporary sale in Essex along with 'licensed victuallers, pawnbrokers, housekeepers, caretakers, chemists, small tradesmen, engravers, fish porters, ivory turners, tennis-bat makers and others'.[10]

The census of 1901 for Ropley, five years later, does not give previous addresses but, in the streets of the 'Lymington Park Estate' and close by, many new inhabitants had some unusual birthplaces for north Hampshire: some just 'London', but also Battersea, Bloomsbury, Bow, Bowes Park, Camberwell, Chiswick, Ealing, Holborn, Hornsey, Islington, Kilburn, Kingston-upon-Thames, Leyton, Old Bailey, Paddington, St Pancras, Stamford Hill, Tooting, Tottenham, Tower Hamlets, Walworth, Westminster and Windsor.[11]

At the sale in Essex, buyers gave their reasons: 'Healthy place to live', 'A fine place for a Sunday outing', 'The cheapest railway in the kingdom', 'A place to retire and keep poultry', 'It's for my wife and children', 'An investment', 'To build on', 'For resale', 'Buying and retailing at 4d a week to workmen'.

Who knows if the sale went to plan? There was no third offering, so presumably sufficient plots were taken. Did the developers care for what purpose? From today's house distribution, many plots were bought together to provide large gardens or smallholdings. Few of the shops materialised. The hotel, a standard suggestion in all Land Company's estate offerings, was never built, but then, its presence already having given authority to the plan, was it ever likely to be?

What the Land Company's exciting auctions established was the legitimacy of local development. Not all the new housing came from their sales. As the company kick-started growth, they popularised the idea of a local community. Other estate owners and local people with land to spare tried their hand at selling the rural dream. Speculators were hard at work seeking to buy, to wait and to resell.

The Land Company bought their estate from the Hemming family. Lymington Park Estate surrounded Lymington Farm, a substantial set of buildings on the corner of Brislands Lane, grandly renamed Lymington Park Road for the auction, and Lymington Bottom, called Medstead Main Road.

In 1889, Lymington Farm was occupied by Charles Frederick Hemming, landowner and farmer.[12] Two years later, the census shows the farmer and his family still there: Charles F Hemming, 60, his wife Caroline, 60, and their daughter, Dorothea, 17. Charles and Caroline were naturalised Germans while Dorothea was born in London. 'Carl' Frederick, born in Saxony, was a shipping butcher; Caroline was likely born in Hanover. A shipping butcher provided a complementary service to a family butcher, shipping meat in bulk, for instance to vessels, institutions or establishments with a high demand. It was a lucrative trade. Charles had lived and worked in Tower Hamlets for perhaps thirty years, one of the principal areas targeted by advertisements of the auction. Tower Hamlets, the second largest parliamentary constituency in the country, was also a radical centre for electoral reform through the sale of forty shilling plots of freehold land to artisans and the working class. This advocacy is shown, later, to be an important background to the development of Four Marks.[13]

Charles, Caroline and four children, including Dorothea, the youngest, were naturalised in London in April 1878.[14] Charles died in 1894. By 1896, his Lymington Park Estate was sold by Caroline. In the first quarter of 1900, Caroline died in Kensington, west London, a suitable retirement area for a widow with means. A few months later, on 25 June, her daughter, Dorothea, applied for a British passport. The next year, in August, Lymington Farm, almost forty acres, was on the market, freehold, for £700.[15] About the same time, Dorothea travelled by steamer to Buenos Aires followed by several voyages to New York where the trail, for now, peters out.

The 'mother' of Four Marks was a German widow from Hanover who sold her acres to the Land Company. This company was still recorded as the owner in 1898, presumably waiting for the new freeholders to complete their quarterly payments.[16]

Civic Four Marks is less than ninety years old. It was deemed worthy of its own identity in 1932. The major development that first turned Four Marks from a few houses on the Winchester Road opposite the *Windmill Inn* began about 125 years ago when a substantial number of 'foreigners' arrived from London. Before 1896, 'natives' were born in Ropley or a surrounding parish, like Chawton or Medstead. Early Four Marks, other than as a spot on a map, is not very old.

AN EMPTY, BUT BUSY, PLACE

One purpose of this book is to put the neighbourhood's past into a new perspective, to give it the long-term history it has never really had. If you have read the twenty chapters, my hope is that, deaths apart, you know far more now about what has happened in this little place. This conclusion, hopefully, will put even more skin on the bones. I admit to limited conjecture; counter-arguments are welcome. Somewhere in the story of this new settlement may hide clues as to why so many murders occurred here. There is no way to know for sure, but the number of untimely departures do seem excessive for such a small area. Is it all just coincidence or are there more concrete or sinister reasons?

Origins of a place name may have nothing to do with its beginnings as a community. There is only one 'Four Marks' in Bartholomew's Gazetteer, but there is a 'Foremark' a few miles to the east of Burton upon Trent. The toponym is Old Norse from *forn*, 'old', and *verk*, 'fortification', and is possibly associated with the winter camp of the 'Great Heathen Army' at Repton in 874.

No one has argued for Vikings founding Four Marks and yet the Norwegians and the Danes met the local Saxon inhabitants in two bloody battles near Alton, Aethelinga-dene. After victory in 1100, Olaf of Norway, and Swein, the Dane, went to Whitchurch, then to the Worthys and arrived at the gates of Winchester.[17] The Saxon Chronicle records a second 'sanguinary' battle the following year after Danish pirates landed on the south coast from where they 'plundered and laid waste'. The Saxons of Hampshire met them again at Alton. Sixty-one local men fell, but the Danes held the field although a 'much greater' number of invaders were killed.[18]

It matters little, although some might still seek an argument. I like the idea of some of the Vikings retreating to the high ground at Four Marks, building a defensive foundation at, say, Medstead or Kitwood and melding into society. In passing, another story attributes the founding of Alresford to the Danes.[19]

The name 'Four Marks' was chosen because of a long-time quadripoint, meeting place, of the four parish boundaries of Medstead, Ropley, Chawton and Farringdon near the current Boundaries surgery.[20] These boundaries had their origins in the Saxon territories of Neatham, Bishop's Sutton, Selborne and Fawley mentioned in Saxon chronicles and charters. Another claim is made for the name used in a suspect document of 1548 on a page headed 'Perambulations of the Manor of Alresford' of a 'certain vacant piece of land called *Fowrem'kes because of four adjoining tithings …*'.[21] I say 'claimed' because no one since has re-found the document. A 'large white stone' marking the joining point existed in 1759 and might originally have been a natural feature. It was reportedly destroyed by workmen during road construction in the 1960s.[22]

Apart from the accident of boundaries, 'Four Marks' for almost all of its pre-history and most of its modern times was an empty, but busy, place. People passed through without great notice. It was a chalk ridge, capped with clay and flints, covered either by trees or furze scrub, that separated the towns of

The Boundaries, undated, on Winchester Road before the road was straightened.

Alton and Alresford or, perhaps better, the south coast and the future capital at Winchester from the Thames and London. The ridge reaches its high point of about 215 metres on a line between Telegraph Lane and the centre of Medstead. It is no mountain, but it was a simple, tiring climb. The ridge was an inconvenience, a barrier to travel, to commerce and to community. People who gained the foothill on either side wanted to get to the bottom on the other side. For the walkers and riders of years ago, it made little sense to seek a route around.

Four Marks has no rivers, only memories of an ancient stream along Lymington Bottom where some ten gravel pits indicative of a watercourse have been found. The old river likely connected the ponds at Medstead and Five Ash to the road lake at the primary school crossroads and to the run of marling pits leading to Plain Farm pond.[23] Saxon meres, ponds, dotted the high ground as at the top of Blackberry Lane and the current Four Marks fishing haunt.[24] Local gravels have been found to include Early Stone Age implements and contemporary shells and fossils of red deer and of a famous elephant, *elephas primigenius,* the woolly mammoth.[25]

Chalk downland has few surface streams.[26] Under the skin of loam, there are two layers of chalk, the first coarse and impregnated with yellow stones, the second altogether finer and stone free.[27] The lower layer rests on a bed of

294 THE FOUR MARKS MURDERS

impervious clay. Rain falling on the downs percolates through the chalk to the bed and then builds upwards saturating as it goes. When the chalk can take no more, the water flows over the clay until the chalk above is thin enough for it to push through the surface as springs. In the 1930s, these springs could be seen rising on the grass verges opposite the *Anchor Inn*.[28] Water is now extracted across the road from the *Shant*.

The two local rivers, the Wey and the Alre, are significant because their watersheds meet at the high point of Four Marks: the seepage on one side falls to the source of the northern branch of the Wey near Flood Meadows in Alton (among the newest large housing development) and travels through the town to Weybridge and the Thames; move a few feet south on the crest and rainwater drains to a spring in Bishop's Sutton, the source of the Alre. The Itchen comes from Cheriton and joins the Alre south of Alresford to flow through Winchester, past Southampton Football Club's stadium at St Mary's, and into the Solent.

USING THE RIDGE

The Four Marks ridge had two principal geographic and historic effects: to provide a home for those who sought a benefit from high ground and, a much larger affair, the founding of routes across the barrier.

The high homes and work places span the centuries. Follow the line from Medstead to Four Marks Golf Club. North-west of Medstead Manor, there is a strong, sub-rectangular defensive enclosure, or ringfort, now part of a copse.[29] It has one entrance on its south east side. It is possibly Iron Age, about 500 BC, but could be medieval. Nearby, to the north, there are two tumuli, burial mounds, overlooking the countryside which are believed to date from 1000 BC. Medstead village is a hill settlement noted in 1086 in the Domesday Book. A pre-Roman ridgeway from the Old Sarum area, the Lunway, crosses through Four Marks from the north following the drier southern side of the hill and is itself crossed near the *Windmill* by a summerway, probably Belloc's 'Old Road', from today's Alresford following the quickest, driest, 'up-and-over' route to the Wey.[30]

The land around the *Windmill* is dotted with clay and chalk pits and kilns to provide road and building materials.

Mike Sanders chose a house, originally a colonial shack, in Telegraph Lane in 1985 for his ham radio and television activity, the roof now covered in multiple antennas.[31] Higher frequencies require a line of sight path and this spot is best for Bournemouth and Southampton. Further along, after the last house and away from the trees, the signal to the north is considerably improved.

Mike transmits and receives digital television using radio for talkback. He also has a satellite transponder, the dish pointing south east, provided by the Qatar government (the prime minister is a radio ham) which allows him to exchange TV pictures all over Europe, South Africa and South America.

Just down Blackberry Lane, the old celestial observatory operated during World War I, the site chosen for the pollution-free sky.[32] Back on Telegraph Lane, the Royal Navy Semaphore Station was erected in 1829, the same building used as a Fever Isolation Hospital at the turn of the century.[33] Close by is one of some 6,500 trig points, 'triangulation pillars', built in the 1930s to hold a theodolite and used by the Ordnance Survey to map the country. Ceremonial beacons to commemorate the anniversaries of the Armada and of the Queen's silver and diamond jubilees were lit nearby.

CROSSING THE RIDGE BEFORE 1700

To explore the ridge crossings, I have taken a leaf out of Rathbone's map in his *Chronicle of Medstead* of 1966. Some thought this to be a copy of a sixteenth century map, but Rathbone admitted that it was a map 'of what I know'. My modern attempts can be found later on two pages which address, first, routes before 1700 and, second, the more sophisticated infrastructure helped by the coming of new travel technologies.

The earlier map begins with the pre-Roman ridgeway, notes the Saxon land boundaries and their gates and ends with the King's Highway.[34] I make no claim for great accuracy, especially given the clustered nature of the crossings. In some cases, there is ongoing debate and excavation, especially with the Roman roads and the King's Highway and its variants. I have not done enough work to take sides.[35]

What I hope these two maps show well is how busy this little bit of hillside was through all of English history. I suspect every king and queen, indeed everyone of importance travelling from London to Winchester, passed through Four Marks or Medstead. Every army, from marauding pre-historic bands to the Romans and Saxons, possibly the Vikings, certainly the civil war soldiers of Stephen and Matilda and the Roundheads and Cavaliers to the Tommies and

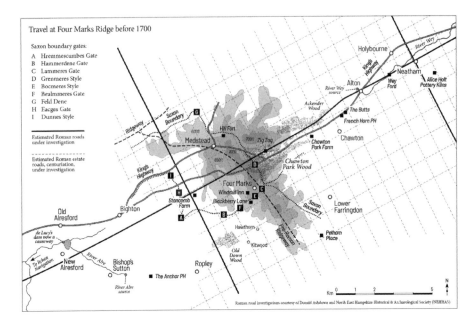

ABOVE AND OPPOSITE: Maps before and after 1700 of the ridge and its many crossings.
Roman and centuriation content, Donald Ashdown and NEHHAS

Canadians on their way to Flanders trenches and the Yanks with their tanks in
World War II.

My advice is to try to forget the A31, today's Winchester Road, and to take
a time traveller's vantage point somewhere near Boyneswood and sit in your
notional deckchair as yesterday goes by.

> *As the early people spread and explored, established their camps and traded, so the
> first Celtic network of 'roads' evolved. The earliest of these are known, generally, as
> Ridgeways. This is because the first settlements were on the higher ground and the
> 'ways' which joined them ran along or just below the ridges; as far as was possible
> they avoided rivers and low ground. The main highways ran west and east across the
> southern downs from Cornwall to Kent; the most southerly of these came from the west,
> crossing the river Candover at Totford, and then going along the south side of Wield
> Wood and on to Burkham. At Barton's Copse, a branch ridgeway broke off and went
> south past Heathgreen to Hattingley and then to the present centre of Medstead, where
> it continued south past Roe Downs to leave the parish somewhere near the Windmill
> Inn. These were foot-paths made only by man and beast walking along the same track
> for countless generations.[36]*

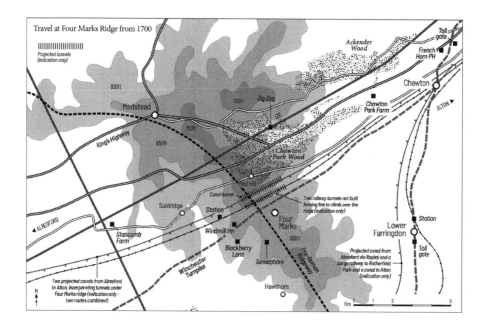

The earliest known archaeological find in Four Marks is a Neolithic polished flint axe, pre-1100 BC, from near the junction of Uplands Lane with Brislands Lane in 1957.[37] A gold wrist torque, dug up by a plough in Lyeway, was assigned to the Bronze Age, about 1000–800 BC. A Bronze Age barrow stands in an open field on the western side of Old Down Wood.

After these early herders had driven their sheep and cattle along the ridgeway, the Romans forged their main and, partly lost, route from Neatham up a designed zigzag in Chawton Park Wood to Winchester, possibly a three-lane highway.[38] This way is under intense scrutiny at the moment, but there is good evidence for the lines on the map caused by centuriation. If events in Rome had taken a different path in the early 400s, this area might have been a massive vineyard. Some of today's squarish plots in Four Marks may have more to do with Roman centuriation as with the modern straight line field boundaries of the auctioned plots of the Lymington Farm Estate. What I will predict is that, once all the excavations have completed and old records been fully correlated, the Roman road of Four Marks and Medstead will be seen as a major national thoroughfare alive with contemporary habitation and cultivation.

The later Saxon field boundaries are a firmer bet. King Ina granted charters to the Church of Winchester, the most ancient of which concerning Alresford and remains in the records. The grant of Alresford by Ina's son, Cenwealth, who became king in 642, was confirmed by Egbert about 826; by Edward the Elder in 956; and after that by Edgar. This charter also has its detractors, but its Saxon description of the local boundaries and their gates and stiles has been confirmed by subsequent Anglo-Saxon documents. These boundaries can be closely traced today and have been added to my pre-1700 map. *Lammeres Gate*, 'Claypond Gate', is a good candidate for an early site of the Four Marks boundary stone, but as the other eight gates show on the map, Four Marks was at the centre of important Saxon husbandry.

> ... *Swa be Mearce to Grenmeres Stigele Thonan to Lammeres Geate Of tham Geate to Bocmeres Stigele Thonan to Bealmmeres Geate Of tham to Hammerdene Gate Thonne to Hremmescumbes Geate* ...[39]

> ... *so by the bounds to the Stile of the Green Pond, thence to Claypond Gate, from that gate to the Stile at the Pond of the Beech tree, thence to the Gate at the pond where vetches (?) grow, from that Gate to Hammerdean Gate, thence to Hremmescumbes Gate* ...[40]

In each case, the main gates are compounded with *mere* suggesting the 'internal division of wood pasture and the controlling of access to watering holes'.[41] These early ponds give added significance to the age of those in and around Four Marks. Hammerdon Bottom is identified as Ropley Stoke in a Winchester College terrier of 1786.[42] Ravenscombe Gate is 'clearly determined' today in Ranscombe Farm a half mile from North Street.[43] The combe is the wide hollow which runs up by Bighton and the Gate was at the two heads of the hollow. Hammerdean Gate was 'almost certainly' where the Soldridge road runs about a hundred yards north of the railway. The Saxon word *straet*, which signified a way through a hamlet, is common with, for example, North and South Street in Ropley.

The Old English word for a 'ridge' is *llinc*.[44] Perhaps an earlier name for Four Marks might be *Lammerslink?*

There is a long-term debate about the path that pilgrims travelled from Winchester via Alresford across the Four Marks ridge to Canterbury after 1170.[45] This pilgrimage was the great adventure of the Middle Ages. Five suggested routes, not shown on the map, are probably equally correct as travellers adapted to the weather, threats from robbers and varied advices given. Fearon advocated a northern route via Medstead and Wield before dropping down to

Chawton.[46] A second road went through Bighton and missed Medstead. The third route followed close by the valley floor to Ropley where it briefly parted company with a fourth way, Belloc's discovery up Blackberry Lane.[47] The final option was to cut across country from Ropley to West Tisted and Pelham Place, *pèlerin* being French for pilgrim.[48]

The King's Highway travels from Bighton past Medstead and down through Chawton Park Wood from about 1285. There is a later branch to Odiham.[49] The English roads were originally tracks struck out by travellers or by the drivers of pack-horses, making their way as best they could from place to place. They made long circuits to reach fords where they could cross streams; they chose the high ground to escape the bogs, and they deviated from the straight course at all obstructions.[50] A number of conjectured routes are shown on the map.

A system of quite passable bridleways existed across the kingdom. There was comparatively little wheeled traffic and only of the most primitive kind. Every one travelled on foot or on horseback, and nearly all goods were carried on the back of animals. Heavy materials were taken by water, 'going by small boats far up the most insignificant streams'.

The Webbs, renowned husband and wife early historians, saw from *Piers Plowman* and Chaucer, from municipal and manorial records, and from the drawings of the period, a vision of a 'really enormous amount of wayfaring life' in the fourteen and fifteenth centuries.[51]

The more important landowners usually held estates in different parts of England so that there was a perpetual coming and going between them. The practice of appeals to Rome involved an astonishing amount of journeying of ecclesiastic and legal agents of one kind or another. The common people seem always to have been on the road, on pilgrimages, seeking employment, or visiting the towns. The innumerable local markets, and still more, the periodical great fairs, must have required huge concourses of travellers from longer or shorter distances.

The later main road from Alton to Winchester followed the King's Highway, which in turn was close to the Roman road.[52] Turning right at the Butts, the way went past the *French Horn* and the Sports Centre up through the wood to Red Hill and near Medstead where it continued to Bighton and Old Alresford, Abbotstone and along the Itchen valley to Kings Worthy.[53] Soon after the formation of de Lucy's dam, a causeway was carried across it forming the accustomed communication between New Alresford and Alton.[54] This was the road of commerce, connecting the villages as a requirement and providing a route between the big towns. It was in heavy use well into the early twentieth century.

SQUARING THE CIRCLE

The notorious bungalows and shacks of early Four Marks arrived around 1900. Why did so many speculators rush to this unoccupied spot and present it to aspirant Londoners as paradise in Hampshire? I say 'spot' because the whole of the about-to-be-developed area was scarcely a mile across in any direction and tucked for the large part in the extreme north west corner of old Ropley reaching no further south than Kitwood and part way down Brislands Lane.

To find an answer, I am going to pause early in the 1700s and pass into the realm of part speculation.

In 1709, three yeomen applied to the crown for the enclosure of Ropley Commons 'at present of small annual value, but capable of improvement, in case the tenants of the same manors might have the liberty of enclosing, ploughing, and sowing the same, and many poor people would be employed in making such improvements, which will tend to the public good'.[55] This was the first private bill of enclosure ever passed in the United Kingdom; it is of national importance and became the country's template.[56] The bill included a claim by Jonathan, Lord Bishop of Winchester, to enclose a park in Farnham, an influential friend to have in passing a new Act through a parliament run by the landed aristocracy. William Godwin, late of Ovington, Richard Seward of Bishop's Sutton and Henry Whitear of Old Alresford, sought an estimated 500 acres (at 640 acres to a square mile), an area which can be visualised as a circle of one mile diameter.

The bill acknowledged that apart from long-term tenants' homes, the commons were available for 'cattle levant and couchant'.[57] No mention was made of other vital uses like self-feeding pigs turning the land or the gathering of wild fruit, berries and kindling for cooking and winter fuel.

My conjecture is that this 'circle', of whatever shape and discontinuity, was the home of Four Marks and its bungalows. The land, which had been waste or common, was taken into select private ownership, sold on, re-parcelled and the least profitable eventually arrived in the hands of developers. There is no known map, but there are four mentions which place the old commons as the home of the speculators of 1900: first, Lymington Park Farm was once known as Common Farm, and, second, Hagen in her *Annals of Old Ropley*, claims that 'one of the earliest of the modern enclosures was that of the common land near Kitfield, Ropley'. Kitfield Farm is that place of many changing uses on the corner of Gradwell Lane and the road up to Kitwood. The last two mentions are conclusive statements from the Winchester College terrier of 1786. William Budd held a four acre piece of the 'Common inclosed adjoining to the north side of the road by Farringdon Common'.[58] In other words, apart from the freak of a boundary, the upper commons of Farringdon and Ropley were one. In 1797, a minute entered into the terrier noted a dispute over the value of land between Budd and the College. The surveyor, Tredgold, wrote that 'the lands of Ropley differ greatly in value: those of the North side [the waste and Commons] are by no means as good as those of the South'.

Crucially, the 'Ropley' yeomen claimed they were 'indifferently elected and chosen by the [existing] tenants to divide and allot the [land] according to the tenants' several interests and rights'. Yet, after the bill was passed by the Lords to the Commons, 'a violent petition [was received] against it'. The petition was brushed aside and the Ropley Commons bill was rushed through in four days by the landowners and received the Royal Assent on 5 April.[59]

Before 1774, it was not even incumbent on a landowner to let his neighbours know that he was asking parliament for leave to redistribute their property. Facts set out by dismayed petitioners and their reception showed the disdain with which these complaints were held. 'The proprietors ... generally agree upon the measure, adjust the principal points among themselves and fix upon their attorney before they appoint any general meeting.'[60]

Almost immediately, another petition arrived in parliament asking for the bill for enclosing Ropley Commons to be repealed on the grounds of the partiality of the three yeoman, now appointed commissioners. The commissioners counter-petitioned, 'claiming their allotments were just' and, unsurprisingly, carried the day.[61]

The Hammonds drove their fighting standard into the soil of enclosure; their pages bubble with denunciations.[62] 'What stand could the small proprietor make against such forces?' they asked, especially when they could neither read nor write and barely knew which direction led to London. 'The only prospect of successful opposition to the lord of the manor, the magistrate, the impropriator of the tithes, the powers that enveloped his life, the powers that appointed the commissioner who would make the ultimate award, lay in [an] ability to move a dim and distant parliament of great landlords to come to his rescue.'

Almost alone, Tate saw the Hammonds' criticism as 'one of the most brilliant works of historical fiction in the English tongue'.[63] Later historians joined the Hammonds in their contempt: Neeson thought the pro-enclosure lobby wished to change the social structure of rural England; Thompson saw it all as 'a plain enough case of class robbery'; our own Cobbett thought the 'poor were sacrificed and needlessly sacrificed'.[64]

Once the encroachers and smallholders had been allocated their squats, they needed to hold onto them. The first invoice from the Hampshire yeomen demanded a contribution to legal costs, the second covered the cost of hedging and new roads, always set to a high and unaffordable level. Although, the cottagers had not requested enclosure, the land owners in parliament had decided that they would be made to contribute to its wider cost.

'To meet the expenses ... the small man was ever tempted, and sometimes forced by financial distress, to sell his holding to a richer neighbour, or to some capitalist who was seeking land. Thus, the indirect result of enclosure was consolidation. The poorer sold and the rich bought.'[65]

In the Ropley Commons bill, it was all sweetly put: Each tenant, in 'manner directed, should fence and hedge in ... and keep the fences in good repair'. In effect, doing what Godwin, Seward and Whitear instructed.

The last word to the Hammonds,

> *Even if the small farmer received strict justice in the division of the common fields, his share in the legal costs and the additional expense of fencing his own allotments often overwhelmed him and he was obliged to sell his property. The expenses were always heavy ... The Lords of the Manor could afford to bear their share because they were enriched by enclosure : the classes that were impoverished by enclosure were ruined when they had to pay for the very proceeding that had made them the poorer.*[66]

It seems like Four Marks now has some 'grandfathers', Godwin, Seward and Whitear, but more in the sense meant by the *Mafiosi*. Their approach to prising ownership from the cottager became standard fare in many hundreds of enclosures for the next hundred and fifty years. Ropley Commons may have been the first and provided the model, but within a few years the two other great commons, Chawton, 1741, and Farringdon, 1749, that swept up to the northern side of the Four Marks ridge were also privatised.[67] The difference was that this land was not waste suitable for housing; it was more valuable for pasture.

AFTER 1700: TRAINS AND BOATS AND STAGECOACHES

As wheeled transport became more common, the road through the Chawton wood deteriorated. A turnpike road was deemed the answer to the muddy, potholed mayhem with its travellers forced to contribute at tollhouses to the upkeep of a safe and fast path. There were, however, several cherished local ways over the ridge: up Swelling Hill from Ropley Soke; tracks from Farringdon past the Woodside Farms (which extended to Alton) and by the current St Swithun's Way; along Brightstone, Kitcombe and Mary lanes; and other routes from Colemore, Monkwood and West Tisted.

The early route of the present A31, chosen in 1753, was an existing path through largely open terrain. The road is the beginning of activity on my second 'after 1700' map.[68] There was no habitation in the way and no easy chance for long-distance travellers to dodge sideways and miss the tolls. The turnpike passed through Chawton, parted with the Gosport turnpike, and

LEFT: The turnpike milestone at Four Marks on the A31 by the junction with Lapwing Way: 52 miles from London and twelve to Winton, an old name for Winchester. Its posher cousin, the 48 milestone, is in the truncated Winchester Road, Alton, on the corner from the new roundabout slip road by the Butts railway bridge. Both positions tally with Paterson's Itinerary of 1785. The plates that were attached to the stones on this section of turnpike were made by Taskers foundry of Andover. *Diane Heal*

entered Four Marks along The Shrave. It had little effect on an empty area: there were five dwellings in 1697 which grew to fifteen in 1839. The likely most disturbing effect was the free use made of the local pits to provide road-building materials. Those responsible for maintenance had a legal *carte blanche* to raid local properties for what they needed.

This was the time of the stagecoaches from the capital to Winchester and which dashed through Four Marks, mostly leaving London in the morning, but carrying the Royal Mail in the evening. The route was competitive: Collyer's coach took ten hours, but the 'Independent', the 'Eclipse' and 'The Age' claimed eight hours. Ogilby's map in 1675 mentions a place where the road 'passes through water' at Alresford, likely the Itchen ford at Seward's Bridge.[69] *Paterson's Itinerary* of 1785 ignores the turnpike and passes through Chawton Wood to close by a marked South Town, by Medstead, again without mention of Four Marks.[70] Paterson also shows the milestones from London: the '48' and '52' exist, among others, today.

Canal mania in the 1790s stirred the newspapers, but nothing happened on the ground. Three projected routes are included on the map: two proposed long tunnels under Four Marks, the other a barge-carrying railway near Ropley.[71]

There was little domestic activity in Four Marks before the late nineteenth century. A 1759 map of Hampshire shows two windmills: one behind the site of the *Windmill Inn*, now the Co-operative food store, and a second, all traces gone, where the once important Barn Lane joins the A31. The 1817 and 1870 Ordnance Survey maps note only a couple of dwellings near the small green at the Windmill Inn. It was not even a favoured stopping point on the turnpike, but rather a place to pass through at best speed. Medstead's old Windmill Inn and the Lymington Arms have limited claims to be coaching inns, probably concentrating on attracting lesser traffic. The Anchor at Ropley Dene is the stop most mentioned in contemporary timetables, eight miles being sufficient for tiring horses facing or just finished with a major climb.

William Cobbett described riding in 1825 from Alton to Alresford via Medstead 'in order to have fine turf to ride on and to see, on this lofty land that which is, perhaps, the finest beech-wood in all England'.[72] Beside the wood, on the Alton side of the hill, the pasture lands of the Chawton Estate stretched down to the villages of Chawton and Lower Farringdon in the valley. Farringdon Common reached over the ridge to the old Ropley boundary. The open land on the hill's south side was uninhabited gorse and bracken. An early name for Blackberry Lane was Furse Bush Lane.[73]

Alton opened its station in 1852 connecting the town to London. An extension from this new terminus to Winchester had been a gleam in the eye since the 1840s. Two tunnels were considered (making four with the two canal tunnels), but rejected as too expensive. A great gouge was instead cut at the highest point at the bridge in Boyneswood Road. The line was finally built in 1865, but was of little immediate benefit to the villages centres it avoided. It followed closely the route of the turnpike, but always sought the best gradient for the steep climb over the ridge to aid early steam locomotives.[74] The crews called it 'going over the 'Alps'. Alresford was the only town of note along its seventeen-mile route; Medstead got its station in 1868, although almost two miles away from the village. If one of the railway tunnels had been built, there would have been no Medstead station.

Till almost 1900, the history of Four Marks was one of passage. The Saxon boundary stone was circled at some distance by long established traditional villages, Medstead, Chawton, Farringdon, Newton Valence, West Tisted and Ropley, with their medieval churches, clear centres, village greens where fairs or markets were once held, alehouses, general and food shops, a heritage of agriculture with busy forges, road and path connections to neighbouring places, carriers for transport, and traditional functioning social infrastructure. These villages contained all of the land of a hardly-existent Four Marks on the outskirts of their parish boundaries.

COUNTING THE BODIES

The difficulty with making counts about what went on in Four Marks is that the place only became an official parish after all current available censuses were completed.[75] Census information was taken every ten years from 1841; the latest data fully released is for 1911. Next year, 2021, will see personal data from 1921 made available. In none of them were people or homes in the village separately counted.

When the boundary of the new civil parish of Four Marks was drawn, lands from six parishes were included. The civic boundary can be seen on the murder map at the beginning of this book.

Parts of Chawton (1 per cent of the new parish), Farringdon (17 per cent) and Newton Valence (13 per cent) were acquired so that a straight line above of the whole of Telegraph Lane – effectively the ridge line – could mark the new northern boundary. Medstead (4 per cent) lost a sliver to make the railway the new divider to the west. A small parcel of land just the other side of the railway bridge (including Norman Read's, butchers) was placed in Four Marks until 1981 when it reverted to Medstead. The rest of the new parish, other than a small piece from East Tisted (2 per cent), came from Ropley (64 per cent) with an ugly dogleg divider to make sure the village pond and Kitwood were part of Four Marks while Old Down Wood was not. The new civil parish lines were almost everywhere well within the ecclesiastical boundary. The exception was along part of Telegraph Lane and near the pond.

To recognise Four Marks' new status, the railway station's name was changed to 'Medstead and Four Marks' in 1937.

However, there is plenty of information to be found about inhabitants of the area before its establishment. The numbers are wrapped in the parishes which previously oversaw local government. The numbers need to be unpacked.

The method used to gain 'Four Marks' information from each census was to follow the paths walked by the enumerators as they travelled house to house to compile their lists. Those dwellings, which would have been in Four Marks in, say, 1851, if the parish had existed, can mostly be identified. This approach is not perfect. It is not always possible to know whether a house, pulled down over a hundred years ago, was one side or the other of the new parish line. Some street and house names have changed. However, this is not a serious

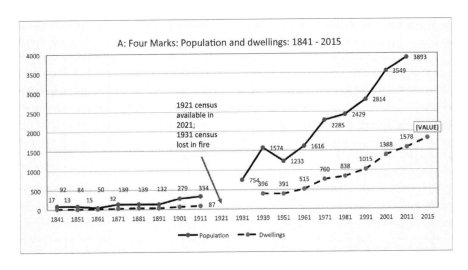

A: Four Marks: Population and dwellings: 1841 - 2015

concern when looking at the total count and long-term trends. Data added to the population study from 1931 onwards came from a number of official sources and is specific to the newly-formed Four Marks.[76]

In the years 1841–1861, comfortably under a hundred people lived in, perhaps, twenty dwellings in the parish-to-be.[77] The great majority of them were far from the ridge and the fledgling main road and were instead clustered around the long-established farms, mainly at Hawthorn and Kitwood. Today's housing centres were empty country.

The Windmill Inn near the turn of the century with its horse pasture. © *Alresford Heritage*

In the ten years to 1871, the population doubled to 139, the dwellings likewise to thirty-two. At first thought, this would suit the claim in Wikipedia and elsewhere that the area was first settled by veterans of the Crimean War, 1853–56. The idea that a grateful government would give out land for a selection of returning veterans is dubious. If the doubling had been the result of the war, one might expect the increase to have happened before 1861 and not ten years later. A close examination of the occupants in 1861 suggests no war-weary from Sevastopol, but a less exciting handful of fertile local families who worked the land, agricultural labourers, farmers, carters and a shepherd. The influence of Hawthorn and Kitwood remained strong. No independent verification has been found thus branding the attractive Crimean story a myth.

The period from 1871–1891 was static: under 140 people living in less than

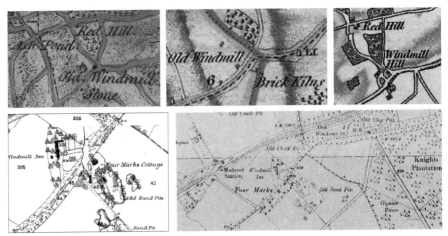

Windmill Hill in 1759, with its boundary stone and 'old windmill'; 1791, with brick kilns;
1810, with probable Windmill Inn and front green; 1879, with a solitary Four Marks
Cottage; and 1897, named as 'Four Marks' with the first cluster of, perhaps, nine dwellings
surrounded by chalk, sand and clay pits. With plentiful wood nearby, and brick and lime
kilns, building materials were readily available. © *Crown Copyright (1810, 1879, 1897)*

forty dwellings. *Black's Guide* of 1879 had no room for Four Marks on its map
of Hampshire, but it did recognise North Street in Ropley.

By this time, a converted farmhouse, *The Windmill Inn*, for some ten years
from 1875 called the *Four Marks Inn*, was well established, set back at an angle
from the road with a large paddock in front for resting horses.[78] One census
night, the building might be almost empty, but ten years later holding thirteen
people: the publican and family, servants and travellers.

In 1875, there is a 'Four Marks Cottage', later Four Marks House.[79] The
sequence of five maps shows the late, small scale establishment of this area
after 1759. For the first time, in 1897, there are identifiable concentrated
dwellings. They occur across the turnpike from *The Windmill Inn* with, perhaps,
nine spaced houses in an area called 'Four Marks'. Here, we have four Saxon
boundaries meeting at a stone, then, at that spot, a cottage, later a house called
'Four Marks', and a few yards away, on an 1839 map, a Four Marks Lane, now
called Weathermore Lane.[80]

The use of local pits before 1900 would repay some serious investigation.
Maps around 1900 show the immediate area studded with chalk, sand, gravel
and clay diggings with beech woods to east and west. There were brick kilns
near The Windmill in 1791 and the 1891 census shows several brick kilns

down The Shrave, especially at Brick Kiln Lane. The building development of William Ivey's land required significant brickmaking for which he probably built a kiln on an adjoining twelve acres.[81] Evidence has been found of lime kilns opposite the Shant, behind the *Lymington Arms*, and on the corner of Hussell Lane and Foul Lane in Medstead. This latter was discovered when digging the foundations for an extension. The kiln was made of brick with a five-foot internal diameter.

WELCOME TO PARADISE

At least five major developers descended on Four Marks in the years between 1896 and World War I bringing with them different motives varying from social improvement to the plain venal. In the ten years to 1901, there was a second doubling in the size of the settlement: inhabitants to 279 and dwellings to sixty-seven, and by 1911 a further increase to 334 and to eighty-seven.

We now know that the 1901 growth was attributable in part to the auctions in 1896 of the Lymington Park Estate. The auctions were seemingly seen as a success. Perhaps Medstead and Four Marks, especially those parts near to the railway, but mostly away from the main road where plots of old common land were available, were seen as some sort of 'promised land'. Copycat developers followed. William Carter, owner of Herbert Park, of whom more shortly, was probably the next. Then a local man, Frank Gotelee, who bought most of the former land of William Ivey in Medstead in 1901, and who tried to sell freehold plots for development although with less success.[82] Winchester College Estate conducted a major sale in May 1912.[83] There were likely many individual transactions.

Land Company provided a map for their Lymington Park Farm auctions. Also recently found, are two further maps, one covering Carter's Herbert Park offering and the other from Winchester College.[84] Together, the three maps contain 242 plots comprising an estimated 251 acres, about half the total acreage enclosed in 1709. The three maps also cover almost every nook and cranny of the early Four Marks developments with the exception, a big one, of those early bungalows on the southern side of Blackberry Lane remarked on by Belloc in 1909; about twenty-three according to the 1912 map of Winchester College. It follows that, in order to complete the picture, at least one major developer is missing from the years before World War I. It also follows that, while some bungalow constructions may have been haphazard and built upon sub-divided plots, there were no significant independent land grabs. All these first buildings originated from land provided by a handful of speculative developers.

The College's brochure promised 'Valuable Freehold Small Holdings, Accommodation Fields, Splendid Building Sites and Bungalow Plots'. One catalogue has pencil notations of the sale prices from a disappointed bidder. Lots 1 and 2 (both at £140) offered over fourteen acres in land east from Lymington Bottom between the railway and the Winchester Road. One half was seen as a splendid building site with 'Southern Slope and Grand Views' and the second an important corner building plot for use as a 'fine site for a residence' or 'exceptionally adapted for profitable development by sub-division'. Lots 3 and 4 (together £190) promoted almost ten acres for building, with a combined 730 feet of frontage, to the north of the middle of Blackberry Lane. Both were occupied by A & C Wyeth. Lot 5 was an isolated four acres in country south of Telegraph Lane ideal for an 'Accommodation Plot'. Lot 6 was two 'valuable fields' (£190) of a combined twelve acres north of the railway between Lymington Bottom and Stoney Lane, also suitable for sub-division. There were further lots in Soldridge.

William Carter was an early entrant to the list of developers interested in Four Marks. Carter was born in Dorset in 1852, the son of a master builder.[85] In America, he made a fortune in property. In the 1880s, he returned to Poole and acquired Kinson Pottery from which, much later, would come the decorative Poole Pottery. At the end of the nineteenth century, Carter bought vacant sites in the south of England with the idea of encouraging people back to the land by offering one-acre smallholdings at a reasonable price. His company, initially William Carter Estates, later became Homesteads Limited. Some of his purchases were local: Ropley Common Farm (presumably some of the auction plots from Lymington Park Farm); Beech Place Estate[86] and Goatacre Estate, both in Medstead; Down House Estate, Andover; and at East Oakley and Kempshott Village Estate, near Basingstoke.

At least part of Carter's land in Four Marks, originally part of Bailey's Farm, was renamed Herbert Park. This area included the whole of the south of Alton Lane to the Farringdon parish boundary, including the current Jocks Lodge (1916) and Pooks Hill (1917) and all the land on the south of the road from Hawthorn Road past the school-to-be to Kitwood and, there, at the crossroads, the land on the north to touch a then much larger Old Down Wood.

The Homestead Movement had defining characteristics: cheap, rural or semi-rural land suitable for market gardening or self-sufficiency, and a basic house, usually single-storey 'colonial' style bungalows in a 'do-it-yourself' community. Homestead's influence extended to the United States, Australia and New Zealand.

Initial pride-of-place in England went to Carter's development at Kempshott, advertised widely as a 'well located freehold property on high ground above Winchester'. The land was 'very good, having grown as much as forty-two bushels of wheat to one acre and specially adapted for cutting into poultry'. Several standard 'colonial bungalow' designs were available for submitting to Basingstoke Borough Council. Homestead's developments were sold without utilities: no clean water (use of a water tank or a well), no electricity (generator, sold fuel stoves and fireplaces, kerosene or gas lamps) and no sewerage (outside earth closet toilet).

This will all seem very familiar to older residents of Four Marks. Perhaps the village should twin with Kempshott?

If you are ever in West Oxfordshire you might try a further slice of Four Marks nostalgia in the town of Carterton, another William Carter development. Homesteads bought local land in 1894 which was divided into plots of six acres. Each sold for £20 with bungalows costing £120. It was a colony of smallholders and became renowned for black grapes and tomatoes, sold at Covent Garden. Many of the settlers were 'retired soldiers and people moving from the towns'. Perhaps it was from Carterton that the myth of Four Marks' military roots was formed?

However, to put all these developments in perspective, as late as 1920, Kelly's Directory felt able to say that Ropley parish contained several small scattered hamlets of which Lyeway, The Soke, Charlwood, Kitwood and Monkwood were the principals, with no mention of Four Marks.

ROLL UP, ROLL UP! FREEHOLDS FOR SALE

There may be a tendency to dismiss Four Marks' initial growth spurt over the turn into the twentieth century as nothing more than speculators on the make with a ready market of dreamy, hopeful smallholders with more money than sense. To do so, would be a big mistake.

The move to Four Marks was towards the end of an important radical movement that is little remembered today and was founded in the aspirations of the skilled working and trading lower middle classes. The Four Marks phenomena was closely tied to the wresting of the parliamentary vote away from the aristocracy and the landowners and provided a watershed to the development of friendly and mutual building societies.

'A key part of the explanation is to be found in the freehold land movement, a loose confederation which emerged in the late 1840s, causing a short-lived but illuminating flurry in political circles ... It came close to dominating popular politics.'[87] The fight, over many decades, is not a subject to condense or digest easily, but it is one on which the modern-day universal franchise – your right to vote – was dependent.[88] Electorally, at that time, the ruling Conservative Party was a morally corrupt organisation. What followed helped the Liberal Party rise to power on a broad programme based on the supremacy of parliament, expansion of the franchise, free trade, the abolition of slavery and, eventually, the completion of equal rights for Catholics.

Freehold land societies, of which there were many hundreds across England and Wales from London northwards, with tens of thousands of members within five years, provided their members with freehold properties at cost together with the associated advantage of a parliamentary vote.[89] Democrats and Liberal activists thought there was an imperative need to extend the franchise to develop 'working-class self respect and improvement'.

'The wish to improve their condition is taking root in the universal heart of the working classes,' observed Thomas Cooper in 1850.[90] That same year, one of the five newspapers founded exclusively to serve the freehold movement asserted, 'A new era has commenced.'[91] The 'discovery' ... in practical politics was the facility to create forty-shilling votes in the counties:

Why should an Englishman henceforward supplicate parliament, in vain, to grant him a vote, when he may owe to his virtuous prudence and economy his own enfranchisement. The cost of a single pint of beer a day [over several years] amounts to more money than would buy a country qualification.[92]

The Freeholders' Union are engaged in the two-fold labour of extending the franchise and multiplying the number of landed proprietors. We hardly know which of these two is the more important and needful. The monopoly of political power and the monopoly of the land are the two parent evils in this country, from which a multitude of lesser ones grow; and it is not possible to attack the one but through the other, or to effect any

great or beneficial change in the condition of the mass of the people, until both these
monopolies are abolished.[93]

The purchase of the county forty-shilling franchise was a relatively simple exercise made possible by a miscalculation by the ruling landowners when they moved to thwart attempts to extend the vote and to retain their own undue influence. The retention of an old clause in the 1832 Reform Act meant all owners of freehold property worth forty shillings or more, £2 (at a notional annual rental of five per cent), or who owned a £10 house, were eligible to vote.[94] The legality of the clause was fought through the courts by the landowners, but they lost handsomely. It was observed that 'it did not take much more than a paddock and a pigsty to qualify'.[95]

Freehold land societies offered plots of land grouped on estates using them as allotments and, in some cases, developed houses on them. Building and legal costs were shared and, thereby, kept to a minimum since the cost of conveyancing was a major disincentive to working-class purchases.

Those workers and artisans who joined the movement, or took advantage of the friendly and mutual building societies which resulted, were generally examples of probity, self-help and thrift. A source in Birmingham reckoned that 'out of £50,000 paid into one freehold-land society, one-third was rescued from the public-house'.[96] It was not surprising, therefore, that the societies' ranks contained considerable numbers of radical thinkers, non-conformists and teetotallers. One might expect that the migrants' arrival in bulk in, say, Four Marks brought with them respect, order and sobriety. It is also possible to 'discern vestigial agrarian sentiments in the largely urban membership'.[97]

Such a man will infuse fresh blood into the constituency. He will not give a vote like a
browbeaten tradesman or a dependent tenant-farmer. His landlord will not be able to
drive him to the polling-booth like a sheep. On the contrary, he will go there erect and
free – a man not a slave.[98]

These incomers were roundly supported by Liberal parliamentarians, a few of whom had their seats saved, or returned, by an influx of new voters targeted at their constituencies.[99] Chief among them were the statesmen Richard Cobden and John Bright, leading free traders, famous for battling the scourge of the Corn Laws, and who, in my opinion, really should have streets in Four Marks named after them.[100] Cobden saw the freehold land movement as 'the only stepping stone to material change' and meant it to clothe an attack on the landed interest. In a speech in London, Cobden took the example of Hampshire in 1841 where there were 93,909 male adults over twenty years, but only 9,223, less than ten per cent, registered electors (no female having the vote).[101]

Over time, the political and altruistic elements of the movement dwindled. Building Societies became more hard-headed. The National Freehold Land Society, set up in 1849 to extend the franchise through property ownership, transformed in 1856 into The British Land Company which, in one of its early iterations, may have been called the Land Company.[102] British Land today has about £15 billion of assets under management with past developments including London's iconic 'Cheesegrater' (the Leadenhall Building), the Corn Exchange, Broadgate, Plantation House and Regent's Place, Meadowhall and, in Dublin, St Stephen's Green.

For at least twenty years, the marketing tactics of the Land Company changed very little: extensive newspaper advertising; country sites near railway stations; large, 'choice' community developments, frequently in Essex, for like-minded people from close-knit urban areas, often the East End of London, always suitable for allotments, bungalows and poultry farms; the offer of cheap home construction; the suggestion of hotels and shops; a surface affinity with the Freehold Land Movement; a free, or cheap, train ride to view the site and, later, to enjoy 'family' visits; a free lunch followed by an auction in a tent; and easy terms made palatable by centralised, legal services and costs.[103]

If Caroline Hemming was the 'mother' of Four Marks, then the Land Company was its 'father'. This association between the village and a possible progenitor or close competitor of one of the UK's great corporations of the twentieth century provides a new perspective.

SETTLING IN: AN INOPPORTUNE TIME

The great depression in British agriculture to the mid-1890s had many complex causes, but its effect at the farm gate was devastating. While the fall in farm prices by forty per cent benefitted the factory worker, it ruined many a smallholder. Over half a million people left the land.[104] Ropley and district saw a spate of suicides around the turn of the century. Much of the local countryside was neglected. Hedges were left untrimmed, pastures were weed-ridden and buildings dilapidated. 'Farmers who owned their own land were obliged to sell their property at give-away prices.'[105] Land was divided, sold, re-divided and built on and some sharp speculators, legal and illegal, made good money.

Nonetheless, the effect of the auctions and direct sales on the landscape of Four Marks was dramatic. Within a few years, Hilaire Belloc described a recent and 'extraordinary little town of bungalows and wooden cottages' in Blackberry Lane as he walked the area in 1909.[106]

Isolated bungalows sprang up along other side lanes like Alton and Willis. As the working man's wage grew, the demand for wheat fell and was replaced by calls for a 'good chop'. Husbandry was more profitable than tilling the fields. Pigeon and rabbit became staples.

The years before World War I were not a good time for a move to a rural idyll, especially for those half of the incomers who depended on working the land for a living. The weather was harsher in Four Marks than in the surrounding countryside and this was an exceptionally cold period. Today, one result of the village's elevation remains a particular micro-climate. In winter, the approach roads can be snow-blocked while Alton enjoys rain. In summer, Four Marks may be covered in cloud, especially in the morning, while Alton is in sunshine. It was a hard life with no electricity, running water or sewerage and no telephones to call for help.

In those early years, a few people were reported found frozen in their homes.

However, the most needed infrastructure was established before the war. Four Marks school was largely a gift of two benefactors. Marianna Hagen of Ropley was the driving force.[107] She bought the plot of land in 1902 from Mr J.J. Tomlinson, a retired haberdasher, who in turn gave the purchase price towards the cost of construction. At first, church services were held in the school. In 1908, Miss Hagen moved the 'Iron Room', a corrugated iron and timber hut from Ropley Soke to opposite Belford House where it became the mission.[108] It is now, sadly, a derelict eyesore. Around 1910, a social and multi-purpose Institute was formed which met in borrowed premises. A permanent building arrived in 1913 and this has since been incorporated into today's Village Hall in Lymington Bottom.

AFTER WORLD WAR I

The 'plot mania' following 1896 may be described as the second phase of the development of Four Marks. The third phase which followed the end of World War I meshed with a Government promoting the development of smallholdings in the hope of reducing unemployment. Land was cheap as the 'rural elite had suffered many casualties and could no longer manage their estates'.[109] Between 1918 and 1922, twenty-five per cent of the area of England was bought and sold. Parcels of land were acquired from hard-pressed landowners by those looking for the romanticised life of the countryside.

Buyers were encouraged by an unlikely consortium of politicians, like Stanley Baldwin, by the Board of Agriculture looking to dispose of surplus army huts, by the Arts and Crafts movement,[110] and by books from the travel writer H.V. Morton and the romantic novelist Mary Webb.[111] Companies were formed, many unscrupulous, to facilitate the sales of 'plots of heaven'. There were ready buyers and, with minimal building guidelines for the country and little enforcement, temporary buildings were constructed on plots of one to two acres, selling in 1932 for £200.[112]

The shacks that went up alongside Carter's 'colonial bungalows', a few ordered by near-penniless owners, were sometimes worse than those from the last invasion. These new homes were often sorry affairs of wood, sheets of asbestos without cavity insulation and corrugated iron roofs.[113] Even chicken houses were given a new lease of life. There were similar developments, especially in the Monkwood area. Newcomers turned their hands to pig breeding or to chicken farming on the poor chalk and clay soil. There were soon at least fifteen poultry businesses and these were to more than treble.[114] The isolated properties led to occasional closer relationships than was, perhaps, appropriate.[115]

There is a gap in population numbers in the 1920s until the 1921 census becomes available next year after its one hundred year quarantine. However, we do know that the population growth continued to 754 in 1931, an increase over 1911 of 470 per cent, and to 1,574 in 1939, living in just under 400 dwellings, an increase over 1931 of 455 per cent.[116]

During the Great Depression of the late 1920s, economic output fell by over twenty-five per cent and did not recover until late in the 1930s.[117] Smallholders again felt the pinch with falling gate prices. People rushed to sell and land prices plummeted. Another wave of migrants followed as even poorer aspirants found they could now afford to move from town to country.

This was the mostly up, but sometimes down, population growth that led to

Four Marks' birth as a parish and wiping away any current need, other than as a curiosity, for the Four Marks boundary marker.

Until 1911, those in paid employment in Four Marks numbered less than one hundred, four times that in 1841. Between 1911 and 1939, the number leapt to over 400. The traditional occupations in agriculture saw steady growth as more land came into cultivation. To be expected, the number of transport and construction workers grew to support the building boom.

Two new employment categories entered the list by 1939. The first, a professional and clerical class of about seventy people, catered for the needs of the new population of over 1,500. The second was a Four Marks peculiarity: the growth of poultry farming, the dominant occupation for all those looking for low-skill, low-labour, 'get rich quick' schemes on smallholdings. Just before the war, there were thirty-four owner-occupied egg farms with nineteen employed poultry hands, a workforce of over seventy.[118] The local countryside at the outbreak of war still provided over half of all employment.

In 1939, most 'unemployed' in the sense of unpaid were, unfairly, housewives. Of the much-discussed invasion by the retired military there are only occasional signs. What one does see, forcefully from 1891, is the arrival of people 'living on own means'. In their ranks, were several who make significant appearances in the preceding chapters.[119] After World War I, Four Marks provided, for an increasing number, an attractive, and perhaps cheap, retirement home.

FOUR MARKS FOR FUN

The fourth phase, which began slowly shortly after the turn of the century, was an entirely different example of social change.

The invention of two new popular forms of transport, bicycles and motor vehicles, transformed Winchester Road along its length.[120] This single-carriage-way was eventually dotted with flowering cherry and ornamental apple trees. In a steady growth from between the wars and into the 1950s, businesses catered for a 'mobile, fine evening and weekend pleasure pursuing population' heading for the country. Premises 'sprouted like mushrooms' providing fuel and mechanical assistance for motorists and cyclists and, with the townies who came by railway, for sustenance with general stores, road houses, wholesome refreshment rooms, small shops made of rickety ex-Canadian Army huts, cafés, the *Windmill Inn* and, even, *The Blinking Owl*, a good class restaurant with a dance floor. Those shops, which might otherwise have spread around the side streets with the bungalows, instead congregated prominently on Winchester Road taking best advantage of the needs of both visitors and locals.

One hesitates to describe Four Marks as a tourist attraction. However, the railway station and a good road helped provide a destination for the energetic or a family trip from either side of the hill.

There is a seedy side to this good life along the A31. Two contrasting aspects of Four Marks operated side-by-side and happily enough. Some of the buildings, dangerous to health and limb, were erected by local characters who might politely be called 'wide boys'. Loans were always available, but slipped repayments were vigorously pursued. Scrap businesses, stolen property and, later, war surplus, some of dubious origin, abounded. Village drinking houses were places of assignation for those preferring not to be seen together in their home towns. There were at least two brothels, repeatedly named in verbal reminiscences, and a night club where 'loose' women attracted visitors.

THE CASE OF THE MISSING GRANDPARENTS

By 1951, dwellings had stabilised at just under 400 while the population had declined by 300 to 1,233 whether lost in the war, not yet returned or moved away. It is noteworthy that throughout the period from 1841–2011, the male to female ratio in the village area remained steady, 48:52, reflecting no more variation than a national average which contained more longer-living women. This is the period of happy childhood recalled by today's oldest living village generation.

In its final and ongoing phase from 1961, Four Marks began to change forever: the population more than tripling in the next fifty years, the number of dwellings quadrupling. There were 3,893 inhabitants in 2011. There has been an explosion in piecemeal and large estate development in the last ten years. I would hazard now well over 6,000 souls. From what the planners are admitting, there is much more to come.

The village population study is able to provide an insight into the rate at which people from outside Four Marks came to live here. The census of 1841 is of limited use in identifying birth places as the enumerators were instructed to ask only whether residents were born in or out of Hampshire. It was also taken in June when most of the country population were at work in the fields. From then until 1911, less than fifty people, each decennial, survived birth in Four

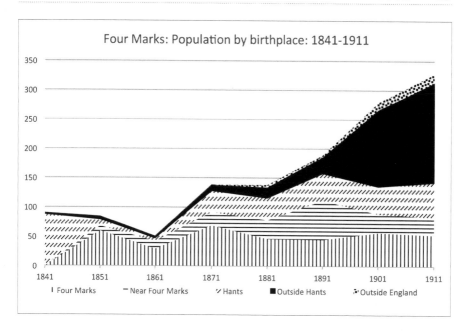

Four Marks: Population by birthplace: 1841-1911

Marks, about five a year. Initially, from about 1861, incomers were mainly from nearby parishes or wider Hampshire. The rush of people from outside the county began in 1896 so that, by 1911, more than half of all inhabitants were 'foreigners' without Hampshire birth links. This trend is shown dramatically by the burgeoning black wedge in the second chart (*see opposite*).

With recent and continuing spurts in new housing, this ratio will have increased. Four Marks today is more cosmopolitan than some large cities with the great majority having no local roots and few who can take you to local grandparents.

DISPROPORTIONATE MURDER

Four Marks has grown a great deal in the last 150 years from almost nothing, a few isolated farms and a windmill. It stuttered into life in 1896 and became a legal construct in 1932, lines drawn on an administrator's chart, without a beating heart. Homes lacked basic utilities and the settlement was without much of the infrastructure that traditional parishes accumulate in religion, education, commerce and entertainment. The period after World War I saw a consistent growth in inhabitants, faltering only immediately after World War II, in which the new village roughly doubled its population every twenty years. This dramatic rise continues to today and, one suspects, beyond.

So, in all the information in this Conclusion, are there are any clues to explain local depravity, the cloud of disproportionate murder?

First, few people have long-term ties to the village. When work calls, whole families may well be gone tomorrow. If they don't gel with ever-changing neighbours, they may find less community to fall back on compared to that which is available in surrounding 'old' villages. Looser relationships can lead to a decline in the social glue that provides inter-personal support and, even, respect. There is limited 'popping in next door'. Individuals, especially the fun-seeking young with access to ready transport, are likely to identify more strongly with Alton, Winchester or Basingstoke than with streets a walk away from their home.

Second, undoubtedly, the Four Marks ridge, the watershed, has played its part. At least ten of the twenty murders described in this book stem from the need to get over the hill.[121] As travellers use the main road, they may not recognise a place of character. Its immediate worth to them today is an opportunity to buy petrol and fast food.

Third, much of the old village is a disparate place, even before the arrival of the new estates. Independence is characterised by four walls and a high hedge. This separation has led, for some, to individual sets of standards with most care given to privacy and personal 'rights'. Half of these twenty murders can, by one degree or another, be recognised in this isolation. For those of a retiring character, heartache and discontent may follow.[122] It can be lonely in Four Marks.

Finally, as with the rest of the country, but exacerbated by heavy growth and low local planning demands, there is a steady decline in infrastructure. A new town with its eventual new main road is coming, I believe, in five, ten or twenty years, which will have the effect of combining Four Marks with Medstead and, yet, splitting it in two with a four-lane carriageway. There is a constant dichotomy between changing, yet again, the Lymington Bottom junction by introducing traffic lights, slowing traffic and creating jams, or taking a national view that the A31 is a major road that needs completing.

Village facilities have not kept pace: mains drainage, potholes, BT's copper wiring, an under-powered water supply, the 'in and out' Post Office, parking at the two shopping centres, the loss of seven public houses (including the soulless, modern *Windmill Inn*, but with due deference to the fff brewery's little gem and the Golf Club), a tired village hall, the bursting primary school, no secondary school, stretched doctors' surgeries hidden behind Covid-19 triage barriers, no police patrols ...

There are, of course, exceptions and many benefits. Four Marks is not a bad place, far from it as early readers of this book have told me. The countryside around, with its many footpaths, is excellent. The village has a sufficient selection of good shops, small eating places and take-aways. Communications are good to large towns, airports and motorways in all directions.

However, more and more people will arrive well before there is any major improvement in social facilities, basic infrastructure and protection from out-of-area criminals. Increasingly, residents will think of taking security, if not the law, into their own hands.

I think more murders are a certainty.

(ENDNOTES)

[1]   *St James's Gazette*, et al, 10/6/1896.

[2]   *The Sun*, 27/5/2020, and several 'weather' websites.

[3]   Sale map, 10/6/1896, courtesy of Norman Read.

[4]   16, 23, 30/5/1896, 6, 8, 13/6/1896.

[5]   23/4/1896 at 1 pm, *St James's Gazette*, 18/4/1896.

[6]   The decision to flaunt the Tichborne Estates, centred near Alresford, is curious as the Tichborne Ropley estates were only advertised as the seller in one journal (Jane Hurst: *Alton Gazette*, 24/4/1896) and giving an auction date of 27/4/1896 to include 'Medstead farmhouse plus two cottages, 10 acres'. If the mention of Tichborne was to impress, why not prefer Rotherfield Park or Jane Austen of Chawton whose penny novels were for sale at 'all good railways stations'. The answer may lie in another legal cause célèbre and long-running court case of Victorian times, avidly followed by newspaper readers, that of the 'Tichborne Claimant'. An imposter presented as Sir Roger, heir to the family fortune, thought dead in a shipwreck off Brazil in 1853. Arthur Orton, the claimant, after conviction and many years' hard labour, finally confessed to the crime in 1895, the year before the auction. The Tichborne name and the 'richness' of its estates would have been well known to many of the passengers. A further complication is that the Lymington Park Estate had been common land until 1709 (8 Ann, Private Acts, No. 20). How then did the near-bankrupt Tichborne family gain ownership? They were not part of the buying cartel of three yeomen.

[7]   *The Pall Mall Gazette*, 9/7/1891, reporting a similar sale in Benfleet, near Southend-on-Sea.

[8]   Discounting the inhabitants of the much older farms at Kitwood and Hawthorn which later became part of Four Marks parish (Fletcher, *Population study, Four Marks*, 2020) and see following.

[9]   *The Tower Hamlets Independent and East End Local Advertiser*, 13/6/1896.

[10]   *The Pall Mall Gazette*, 9/7/1891.

[11]   Fletcher, *Population study.*

[12]   *Kelly's Directory*, 1889.

[13]   Gillespie, *Labour and Politics.*

[14]   *Ancestry.co.uk*, accessed 2020.

[15]   *The Builder*, 3/8/1901.

[16]   *Kelly's Directory*, 1898.

[17] Kitchen, *Winchester*.

[18] Lewis, *Topographical Dictionary*.

[19] Marsh, *Taste of Alresford*.

[20] Old English *mearc* or boundary. Coates, *Place-Names*, from earlier Gover, *Place-names*.

[21] *Hampshire Record Office*, in a document seen by Gover and part-confirmed by Coates. See discussion in 'Myths and Mysteries' in Mills, Four Marks. Fowrem'kes was also used by Rathbone in a map drawn in 1966.

[22] Mills, *Four Marks*. Cornick, *Early Memories*.

[23] *Hampshire Record Office*, 38M48/5. Shore, 'Hampshire Valleys'. Five Ash Pond is recorded in Taylor's map of 1796. Also Box, 'Hampshire in Early Maps'. Overy, personal, 2020.

[24] Chapter 11, *Honey and blackberries*.

[25] To be seen in the Curtis Museum. Curtis, *Alton*. Shore, 'Hampshire Valleys'.

[26] Shore, 'Springs and Streams'.

[27] Cobbett, *Rural Rides*, 'deep loam bordering on clay, rich in colour and full of yellow-looking stones, which still rise up on ploughing'.

[28] Mason, *Ropley*.

[29] Williams-Freeman, *Field Archaeology*.

[30] These routes are discussed in Hawkes, 'Old Roads'.

[31] Video4Business, The Studios, 39 Telegraph Lane, *email*, 2020.

[32] Chapter 3: *Pathways to heaven*.

[33] Chapter 7: *Sending a message*.

[34] Chapter 13: *Murder on the Highway*.

[35] Hampshire Field Club Proceedings: Calow, 'Investigation', Weston, 'Roman Roads' and Whaley, 'Roman Roads'.

[36] Rathbone, *Chronicle*.

[37] Mills, *Four Marks*. The axe is in the Curtis Museum.

[38] Chapter 5: *Roman Remains*.

[39] Grundy, 'Saxon Land Charters'.

[40] Adapted from Duthy, *Sketches*.

[41] Langlands, *Ancient Ways*.

[42] A terrier is a private survey of land owned by an institution, in this case those parts of Ropley Manor belonging to Winchester College, and conducted by Morley Copeland in 1786–88 (21412, No. 15).

[43] Grundy, 'Saxon Land Charters'.

[44] Gray, 'Walking'.

[45] Chapter 3: *Pathways to heaven*.

[46] Fearon, *Pilgrimage*.

[47] Cartwright, *Pilgrims' Way*. Belloc, *Old Road*.

[48] Curtis, *Alton*.

[49] Rathbone, *Chronicle*.

[50] Jackman, *Transportation*.

[51] Webbs, *King's Highway*.

[52] Powell, 'Neatham'.

[53] Wood, *Historical Britain*. Ogilby, *Britannia*. Box, 'Hampshire in Early Maps'.

[54] Chapter 13, *Murder on the King's Highway*.

[55] Private Act, 8 Anne, c. 16 (*Parliamentary archive*, HL/PO/PB/1/1709/8&9An41).

[56] Young, *Annals of Agriculture*. Burke, *Annual Register*. *The Spectator*, 19/2/1876.

[57] A French phrase, taken into English law, which signifies the rising and lying down of cattle. Here, it accepts that cattle have been using the land for a long time.

[58] 21412, No. 40.

59   Hammonds, *Village Labourer. Commons' Journal*, Vol. xvi, pp. 374, 376, 381, 384, 386.

60   Chapman and Seeliger, Guide to Enclosure in Hampshire. The base record is in the *Commons' Journal*, 16, pp. 476 and 509 (delivery awaited).

61   Young, *Six Months' Tour.*

62   Hammonds, *Village Labourer.*

63   Tate, *Village Community.*

64   Neeson, *Commoners.* Thompson, *Working Class.* Cobbett, *Rural Rides.* Also, well worthwhile for acerbity, Johnson, *The Disappearance of the Small Landowner,* and Curtler, *Enclosure and Redistribution.*

65   Johnson, *Disappearance.* Hill, *Social History.*

66   Hammonds, *Village Labourer.*

67   Other enclosures followed: Chawton, 1741; Farringdon, 1749; Medstead and Bentworth, 1798; New Alresford, 1805; Greatham, 1848; Headley, 1849; Newton Valence, 1849; Steep, 1856.

68   Mills, *Four Marks.*

69   Ogilby, *Britannia.* Calow, 'Investigation'.

70   Paterson, *Direct and Principal Cross Roads*

71   Chapter 15: *The phaeton, the boy and fake and dream canals.*

72   Cobbett, *Rural Rides.*

73   See in this book, Chapter 11: *Honey and blackberries.*

74   Chapter 1: *Battle of the Shant.*

75   The Local Government Act 1929 dealt with, first, management of the country's poor and, second, redrawing local government footprints to provide greater efficiency. All boards of guardians for poor law unions were abolished and their responsibilities transferred to county authorities. Separately, some urban and rural areas had diminished populations unable to provide the resources needed to deliver modern local government services. As a part of this review, Four Marks was seen as a new parish capable of standing on its own two feet as a part of Alton Rural District.

76   The 1939 Register (explained in Chapter 19: *Gradwell's nursery tale); dated maps; the local Neighbourhood Plan, 2016; and the Office for National Statistics (ONS).*

77   Fletcher, *Population study, 2020.*

78   The old *Windmill Inn* was demolished about 1935. Part of its fabric was incorporated into buildings at Lymington Barns.

79   See Chapter 16: *The pub with no body.*

80   *Four Marks Village Design Statement,* 2001.

81   Keith Brown: The estate contained 'valuable brick earth, gravel and chalk'. The site was offered for let, including a pug mill for clay mixing, in 1865. Ivey claimed 'considerable loss' in a legal claim the following year, and offered the whole for auction in 1871 (*Hampshire Telegraph,* 12/5/1865; *Hampshire Chronicle,* 8/7/1865; William Ivey v Mid-Hants Railway Co, 26/11/1866; *Hampshire Chronicle,* 26/8/1871).

82   Keith Brown, email, 2020. For William Ivey, see Chapter 1, 'Battle of the Shant'. Also a map of an unsuccessful auction of extensive land in Medstead in 1871 by Ivey (Hampshire Record Office).

83   Winchester College archive, L14/49/9, 'Copy and draft deeds and other papers relating to property in Medstead, 1864–1912'. The College held another auction of about 350 acres in the Swan Hotel in Alton, 4/9/1894. This concerned lands in Medstead and Soldridge.

84   Herbert Park: *Hampshire Record Office,* 38M48/5.

85   Jane Hurst, kempshotthistorygroup.org.uk.

86   *Hampshire Record Office,* 79M78/P4.

87   Chase, 'Out of Radicalism'.

88   Gillespie, *Labor and Politics.* Hamer, *Politics of Electoral Pressure.* Prest, *Politics in the Age of Cobden.*

89   Ewing, 'Freehold Land Societies'.

90   *Cooper's Journal,* 17/1/1850.

91   *Freeholder,* 1/1/1850.

[92] 'The Freehold Franchise', *Reformer's Almanac*, 1849.

[93] *Freeholder*, 1/6/1850.

[94] Prest, *Politics in the Age of Cobden*.

[95] Nossiter, *Influence*.

[96] Beggs, 'Freehold Land Societies'.

[97] Chase, 'Out of Radicalism'.

[98] Ewing, 'Freehold Land Societies'.

[99] Beggs, 'Freehold Land Societies'. Ewing, 'Freehold Land Societies'. Chase, 'Out of Radicalism'.

[100] Beggs, 'Freehold Land Societies'.

[101] Cobden, public meeting, the London Tavern, 26/11/1849, in *The Times*, 27/11/1849.

[102] Smith, *No Stone Unturned. Marsh, Centenary of British Land*. 'The British Land Company' have no record of 'The Land Company' believing the full company name was always used. Unfortunately, records of this time were almost all destroyed following bombing in the Blitz. As a result, there are no records of sales in Hampshire or of a company office in Cheapside, only in Moorgate Street, London (private email, 2020).

[103] For example: *Southend Standard and Essex Weekly Advertiser*, 22/2/1894. *Barking, East Ham & Ilford Advertiser, Upton Park and Dagenham Gazette*, 10/8/1895. *Daily Telegraph & Courier*, 2/6/1896. *London Evening Standard*, 2/6/1896. *Westminster Gazette*, 10/7/1901. *London Daily News*, 13/7/1901. *Daily Mirror*, 17/5/1907, 4/11/1907. *East London Observer*, 3/8/1907. *Tower Hamlets Independent and East End Local Advertiser*, 17/8/1907. *West London Observer*, 18/10/1907.

[104] Collins, *Agrarian History*. Hunt and Pam, 'Responding to Agricultural Depression'. Perry, *British Agriculture*.

[105] Mills, *Four Marks*.

[106] Chapter 11: *Honey and blackberries*.

[107] Chapter 4: *Smugglers and the Vicar*.

[108] The mission was reported to have been first built to save the souls of the Irish navvies working on the railway (Chapter 1: *Battle of the Shant*, Mason, *Ropley*. The mission's replacement, the Church of the Good Shepherd, opposite the village hall, was built in 1953 and later enlarged.

[109] Mills, *Four Marks*.

[110] A descendant of the movement can be found at the Edward Barnsley Workshop in Froxfield.

[111] Morton, *In Search of England*: 'I have gone round England like a magpie picking up the bright things that please me' (1927).

[112] Cornick, *Early Memories*.

[113] Cornick, *Early Memories*.

[114] Fletcher, *Population study*.

[115] Chapter 14: *Care of the innocents*.

[116] ONS. The unique Register of 1939 is discussed in Chapter 19: *Gradwell's nursery tale*.

[117] Cole and Ohanian, *Great UK Depressions*.

[118] Chapter 15: *Gradwell's nursery tale*.

[119] Chapter 20: *The mad woman at Belford House*.

[120] Betty, *Four Marks*. Cornick, *Early Memories*.

[121] Chapter 6: *Debris*.

[122] Chapters 2: *The elf and the archbishop*; 4: *Smugglers and the Vicar*; 8: *Fanny and the wolf*; 9: *Knowing one's place*; 12: *Trolls are bad people*; 16: *The pub with no body*; 17: *First catch your low-life*; 18: *Bunny mayhem*.

Reading list:

Beggs, Thomas, 'Freehold Land Societies', *Journal of the Statistical Society of London*, Vol. 16, No. 4, 1853

Box, E.G., 'Hampshire in Early Maps and Early Road-Books', *Hampshire Field Club*, Papers and Proceedings, 1934

Burke, Edmund, *Annual Register*, Vol. 39 (London 1800)

Chapman, John, and Seeliger, Sylvia, *A Guide to Enclosure in Hampshire, 1700-1900, Hampshire Record Series, 15, 1997*; 'Formal and Informal Enclosures in Hampshire, 1700–1900', Hampshire Papers 12, 1997; 'Charities, Rents, and Enclosure: A Comment on Clark', *The Journal of Economic History*, Vol. 59, No. 2, June, 1999

Chase, Malcom, 'Out of Radicalism: the mid-Victorian Freehold Land Movement', *English Historical Review*, April 1991

Cobbett, William, *Rural Rides in the Counties*, Vol. ii (1831; CUP 2009)

Collins, E.J.T., edited, *The Agrarian History of England and Wales*, Vol. VII, 1850–1914 (CUP 2000)

Curtler, W.H.R., *The Enclosure and Redistribution of Our Land* (OUP 1920)

Gillespie, Frances Elma, *Labor and Politics in England: 1850-1867* (1927; Frank Cass, London 1966)

Gray, Stephen, 'Walking Through Anglo-Saxon England', *Proceedings of the Hampshire Field Club and Archaeological Society*, New Series, No. 12, 1989

Grundy, G.B., 'The Saxon Land Charters of Hampshire with Notes on Place and Field Names', *The Archaeological Journal*, Vol. 83, 1921

Hamer, D.A., *Politics of Electoral Pressure: Study in the History of Victorian Reform Agitations* (Harvester Press Limited, Hassocks, Sussex 1977)

Hammond, J.L. and Barbara, *The Village Labourer, 1760–1832: A Study of the Government of England before the Reform Bill* (1911; reprint London, Longmans, Green 1995)

Hampshire, Guide Books for Tourists (Adam and Charles Black, Edinburgh 1879)

Hawkes, C.F.C., 'Old Roads of Central Hants', *Proceedings of the Hampshire Field Club and Archaeological Society*, Vol. 9, No. 3, 1925

Hill, Christopher P., *British Economic and Social History, 1700–1982*, 5th edition (London, Hodder Arnold 1985)

Hunt, E.H., and Pam, S.J., 'Responding to Agricultural Depression, 1873–1896: Managerial Success, Entrepreneurial Failure?', *The Agricultural History Review*, Vol. 50, No. 2, 2002

Hunter, Robert, 'The Movements of the Inclosure and Preservation of Open Lands', *Journal of the Royal Statistical Society*, Vol. 60, No. 2, June 1897

Johnson, Arthur H., *The Disappearance of the Small Landowner* (1909; reprint London, Merlin Press 1979)

Kehoe, Timothy J., and Prescott, Edward C., *Great Depressions of the Twentieth Century* (Federal Reserve Bank of Minneapolis 2007)

Kempshott History Group, 'Homesteads Ltd and the Homestead Movement', www.kempshotthistory.org.uk, accessed 2020

Kirby, T.F., *The Charters of the Manor of Ropley, Hants* (The Society of Antiquaries, London 1902)

Kitchin, G.W., edited by Freeman, F.A. and Hunt W., *Winchester, Historic Town*, (Longmans, Green, London 1903)

Langlands, Alexander, *The Ancient Ways of Wessex, Travel and Communication in an Early Medieval Landscape* (Windgather, Oxford 2019)

Marsh, Sally, *A Taste of Alresford* (Oxfam, Alresford 1985)

Marsh, William C., *The Centenary of the British Land Company Ltd, 1856–1956* (British Land Company, London 1956)

Mills, Betty, *Four Marks, its Life and Origins* (Repton Publishing, Four Marks 1995)

Neeson, J.M., *Commoners: Common Right, Enclosure and Social Change in England, 1700–1820* (CUP 1993)

Nossiter, T.J., *Influence, Opinion and Political Idioms in Reformed England, Case Studies from the North East, 1832–1874* (Branch Line, Brighton 1975)

Perry, P.J., edited, *British Agriculture 1875–1914* (London, Methuen 1973)

Prest, John, *Politics In The Age Of Cobden* (Macmillan, Basingstoke 1977)

Ritchie, J. Ewing, 'Freehold Land Societies: Their History, Present Position, and Claims' (Project Gutenberg, transcribed from a William Tweedie pamphlet, 1853, Birmingham City Library)

Smith, John Weston, *No Stone Unturned: A History of the British Land Company 1856–2006* (The British Land Company, London 2006)

Tate, W.E., 'A New Domesday of (Georgian) Enclosures, Hampshire Section', Vol. 15, Part 3, 1943; 'Field Systems and Enclosures In Hampshire', Vol. 16, Part 3, 1947, *Proceedings of the Hampshire Field Club and Archaeological Society; The English Village Community and The Enclosure Movements* (London, Gollancz 1967)

Thompson, E.P., *The Making of the English Working Class* (1963, reprint London, Penguin 1980)

White, Rev Gilbert, *Natural History of Selborne* (1860; Gresham Books, Old Woking 1979)

Whitehead, Jack, 'The Origin of British Land', www.locallocalhistory.co.uk, accessed 2020

Williams-Freeman, John Peere, *Field Archaeology as Illustrated in Hampshire* (Macmillan, Basingstoke 1915)

Young, Arthur, *Six Weeks' Tour Through the Southern Counties of England and Wales* (London, 1768); *Annals of Agriculture and other Useful Arts*, Vol. 37 (Bury St Edmunds, 1796)

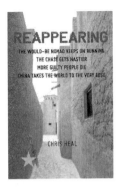

978-1-9161944-1-0 • Paperback • 306 pages
234 x 156 mm • 40 B&W illustrations, 8 maps • July 2020

When an elderly couple save you from a bad death in the Sahara, there's an honest debt to be paid. But this couple have unexpected plans: one leads to the bedroom, the other an impossible trip back to Europe where the author is wanted in Brussels for the murder of the president of the European Union. In both cases, determined killers lie in wait.

Friends turn out to be, well, unfriendly. *Reappearing* is Chris Heal's sequel to his semi-autobiographical *Disappearing*.
All he ever wanted to do was to shrug off his identity, throw off the claws and trappings of government, big business and petty bureaucracy. He wanted to become free of other people trying to run his life.

But the authorities weren't happy with the idea. A senior policeman in National Counter Terrorism said Heal's first book was 'subversive' and 'should not receive the breath of publicity'. Another, attached to the European Commission, called him an amoral, calculating, mass murderer. 'Whether alive or not, he should be brought to book.' Heal's last journey takes him through the decline of the French empire, the terror of Islamic insurgency and the modern African slave trade. His nomadic life leads him to places he really shouldn't visit; meeting people it's best not to know. All the time, he follows clues that might lead him to his unknown father, fearful of what he might find and might have to relive. For a man in his seventies, Heal manages quite well until the Chinese decide to take a hand.

This is an intelligent detective story, wrapped up in a global travel adventure and set against the background of twentieth century history. What kind of worthwhile freedom is possible in a technology-driven planet run by control freaks? Reappearing is also a scary prophesy of everyone's near future in a world increasingly dominated by Chinese political, military and commercial power.

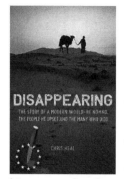

978-1-9161944 -0-3. Paperback • 324 pages • 210 x 147 mm
55 B&W illustrations, 4 maps • June 2019

Chris Heal, one of many adopted names, wrote *Disappearing*, an almost-always-true autobiography, to try to save his life. On the run, north of Timbuktu, it looks like it didn't work. The book responds to the columnist Juliet Samuel who called for the 'corrective of a modern Don Quixote, a bolshy pensioner with a mission' and to T S Eliot, 'Old men ought to be explorers'.

Set in today's world, the protagonist, a man in later years, is so upset by his life experiences, the casual death which follows him, his constant brushes with bureaucracy, predatory business, the political establishment and the surveillance culture, that he decides on a great experiment: through careful and sometimes illegal planning, can he rid himself of his identity? When the times comes can he just get up and go, travel and not be found?

Anger at *Disappearing*

This a subversive book that should not receive the breath of publicity. Among other crimes, one can learn how to kill silently, dispose of bodies, hotwire a car, make a Molotov cocktail, fraudulently extract a pension without tax, and evade mechanical and electronic surveillance. These are skills best kept within the purview of government agencies.

Detective Chief Inspector, National Counter Terrorism Security Office

The author is taunting us with his knowledge of the unsolved murders of Juncker and Selmayr. This was a wicked crime; we are dealing with an amoral, calculating mass murderer. Whether alive or not, he should be investigated and brought to book in name or in person.

Secretariat, European Commission

Heal views the European Union as a wicked organisation, but there is no doubt that he is a celebrant of European culture. Squaring the circle that he inhabits is fundamental to the success of the federal project.

Assistant Secretary, Foreign & Commonwealth Office

I assumed that most of this book was fantasy, but the facts check out. I sensed that the author had been there, from rock climbing to Van Gogh, from flamenco to the Biafran war, from begging in Winchester to travelling through the Sahara. I now think much of the story may be true. It could even mostly be true.

Surveillance officer, The Security Service, charged with finding the author

The book explains how an individual can divest themselves of identity, go off grid and use terrorist-supporting Hawala to move money. Heal's success is a direct threat to our banking system and a danger to Western civilisation.

Senior Executive Officer, International Monetary Fund, Informal Funds Transfers

978-1-911604-41-19. Hardback • 768 pages • 234 x 155 mm
100 B&W illustrations, 12 colour maps • June 2018

Just before throwing off his identity and embracing a nomadic life, Chris Heal published in 2018 an applauded social history of two brothers, u-boat commanders in WWI. He examined their lives and careers against the politics and culture of their day. Applauded that is, until the BBC encouraged him in a radio book programme to explain his views on the European Union and Germany's modern-day role in running the continent. Then the roof fell in.

Plaudits for *Sound of Hunger*

The depth and breadth of this book is staggering. You would have to read a dozen others to get anywhere close to what's given you. The author wants you to know that WW1 was not won by the titanic slaughters, but by the slow starvation of the civilian populations of Germany and Austria. This is mature erudition from a man of three score and five who has produced a magnum opus to which I say, 'Bravo, Sir.' This is the kind of book I love because as soon as you finish it you start reading it again to see what you missed and enjoy it all over again.

Jack V Sturiano

This handsomely produced volume will be recognised as a distinctive and valuable contribution to the history of the First World War. Its author has been very careful in his research and shows both commendable levels of objectivity combined with real imaginative sympathy for his subjects. This is gripping stuff and should not disappoint its audiences. Four years into the publishing jamboree that is the War's centenary, here is a title that stands out and deserves its place on (and one hopes frequently off) the shelf.

Dr Richard Sheldon

Chris Heal's writing is densely packed with a wide variety of subject matter that flows thick and fast, but it rewards the reader with a deeper understanding of this critical period in German and European history. It covers events that are usually recounted at the national and international geopolitical level. It is much rarer to have a social, family and personal viewpoint and that is why Sound of Hunger *makes a valuable contribution to the current literature.*

Dr John Greenacre

A major contribution to WWI military history ... excellent work ... the author writes extremely well and his style is both lucid and engaging ... such a scholarly source book is a welcome addition to my bookshelf ... an objective, dispassionate foreigner's view of German history.

Col John Hughes-Wilson

Avon Local History & Archaeology. Pamphlets • Both parts
42 pages • 147 x 210 mm
Part 1: the Rise (ALHA 13): 10 illustrations, 3 maps, 1 figure;
Part 2: the Fall (ALHA 14): 3 illustrations, 6 maps, 6 figures •
June 2013, reprints: 2015, 2020

These books are a pair, both of which are best sellers in the ALH&A series and available through Amazon. The first tells of the beginnings of the felt hat industry in the mid-16th century to its heyday around the end of the 18th century. The second traces and explains the industry's rapid decline in the 19th century. Both books are based on Chris Heal's doctoral thesis, 'The Felt Hat Industry of Bristol and South Gloucestershire, 1530-1909', completed in 2012, aged sixty-five, at the University of Bristol. Copies of the thesis are available for download from the British Library's EThOS web site (ID THESIS00618690). There is a supporting booklet describing a Hatters' Trail, which is available from the Watley's End Residents' Society; over 5,000 have been printed.

Plaudits for *Felt-Hatting*

Chris Heal's immensely impressive scholarship has identified more than 6,000 hatters and their businesses scattered throughout the region's towns and villages ... reminding us of the importance hats once held in English daily life and the considerable contribution the industry once made to the national economy ... Heal traces not only the rise and fall of the industry over three centuries but its culture of association, traced through the development of benefit clubs and unions ... and considers wider social issues in the hatting community; its drinking and recreational customs, its connection to Methodism, and the effect of the manufacturing process upon the health of its workers. 'Stubborn, well-organised, drunk, illiterate, poor, diseased and disposed to violence as they may be,' he concludes, 'the feltmakers of South Gloucestershire supplied work of high quality' ... The real value of these booklets lies not only in what they reveal about the organisation of the hatting trade, but in their strength as a case study of the response of a well-organised craft industry to economic and social change from its early modern origins to the industrial age. They are well written and very thoroughly researched.

Professor Steve Poole

Until well into the 20th century no man, rich or poor, would be about his business without a hat, and although millions of felt hats were made each year for the home market and millions more for export, today it is a largely forgotten industry. Also forgotten is the important role that felt hatmaking played in this part of the West Country for over 300 years, employing many thousands of men in the second largest manufacturing industry in south Gloucestershire after the cloth industry. Being always a 'cottage' industry, dominated by local families who left no substantial industrial or technological remains, it has consequently been overlooked by later researchers. This has now been thoroughly rectified by Chris Heal's study.

Mike Chapman